# STARGÅTE
## SG·1™

## INSURRECTION
### Book three of the Apocalypse series

## Sally Malcolm & Laura Harper

# FANDEMONIUM BOOKS

An original publication of Fandemonium Ltd, produced under license from MGM Consumer Products.

Fandemonium Books
United Kingdom
Visit our website: www.stargatenovels.com

# STARGÅTE

## SG·1

METRO-GOLDWYN-MAYER Presents
RICHARD DEAN ANDERSON
in
STARGATE SG-1™
MICHAEL SHANKS  AMANDA TAPPING  CHRISTOPHER JUDGE  DON S. DAVIS
Executive Producers JONATHAN GLASSNER  BRAD WRIGHT
MICHAEL GREENBURG  RICHARD DEAN ANDERSON
Developed for Television by BRAD WRIGHT & JONATHAN GLASSNER



WWW.MGM.COM

Print ISBN: 978-1-905586-78-3   Ebook ISBN: 978-1-80070-037-6

To my brother, Colin. Thanks for everything, wee man.
L.H.

To all our loyal and patient readers — thank you.
S.M.


Acknowledgements
Huge thanks to James O'Kane, who loaned his name to one
of our characters in exchange for a generous charity dona-
tion. We hope you like what we did with him, James.

Historical note:
This story is set in season three of STARGATE SG-1,
between the episodes *One Hundred
Days* and *Shades of Gray.*


"Insurrection is the most sacred of rights and
the most indispensable of duties."
— Marquis de Lafayette

# Previously,
# in the Apocalypse series...

## Stargate SG-1: Hostile Ground

When SG-1 is attacked on a routine off-world mission, and Daniel is seriously injured, SG-1 flees back through the Stargate. But instead of finding themselves in the SGC they arrive on a desolate world—one with no DHD.

Meanwhile, on Earth, General Hammond launches a desperate search and rescue mission to find the team. If he fails, and O'Neill doesn't return to investigate recent thefts of technology from their allies, there's a very real chance that the Protected Planets Treaty will collapse. If this happens, Earth will be open to attack from Apophis.

Radiation in the soil near the gate is very high so SG-1 decides to move on, despite Daniel's grave injuries. But the team are soon captured by a group of humans who tell them about the Amam, a monstrous race who came through the Stargate many years ago and feed on the people's life force.

SG-1 dismisses this story as myth until they come across a downed fighter ship and find its alien pilot. After saving him from a mob of angry people, the creature repays them by saving Daniel's life—he puts his clawed hand on Daniel's chest and restores him to full health. But, moments later, another alien ship appears and sweeps SG-1 up in its transporter beam.

Waking up cocooned inside an alien ship, SG-1 witness one of the aliens feeding on another human and realize the stories of the Amam are real. With the help of a local man, Hunter, who bears the mark of the Goa'uld Hecate, SG-1 escapes. Hunter promises to take them to a man called Dix, who can help them escape the planet.

Back on Earth, the Protected Planets Treaty has fallen and

Apophis's attack is imminent. While Colonel Maybourne leads Earth's refugees to a new world, General Hammond sends out a final SOS to their friends in the moments before the SGC is destroyed. No one comes to Earth's aid.

Meanwhile, Hunter leads SG-1 through the Shacks, an enormous shanty town, and then underground to Dix's base. It's only when SG-1 meets Dix and recognizes him as Teal'c's son, Rya'c — now a grown man — that they realize the ruins in which they're standing are the remains of the SGC…

They're already on Earth, but it's not the Earth they left behind.

## Stargate SG-1: Exile

Rya'c tells SG-1 that they are one hundred years in the future and that he is First Prime to the Goa'uld Hecate. They discover that, a century earlier, SG-1 disappeared on an off-world mission and, shortly afterward, Colonel Maybourne's plotting brought about the collapse of the Protected Planets Treaty. As a result, Apophis was free to attack Earth. Forty years after Apophis's invasion, the Amam (who Rya'c calls Wraith) arrived from another galaxy in a ship built by the Ancients.

Until recently, Hecate has been helping refugees escape Earth and flee to the human colony known as Arbella. However the people of Arbella have recently shut their gate. Their new leadership is suspicious of outsiders and wants their world to remain hidden and safe.

Looking for help, SG-1 travels to Arbella. Carter and Teal'c hope to find a way to travel back in time and change the past; O'Neill and Daniel are more concerned with helping people in the here and now.

They are greeted as heroes by some on Arbella, and as defectors by others. It's clear that Arbella is a divided society. The Combined Military Force (CMF) supports SG-1 and wants to return to Earth and fight the Wraith, but another faction, led by the head of the security service, Agent Karin Yuma, wants to cut off ties with the galaxy and stay hidden.

The president is caught in the middle. Several years ago, his wife, Lana Jones, disappeared in an off-world mission and he's been opposed to exploration ever since. SG-1 offers to help find Lana, in the hope that this will persuade the president to help Earth. Eventually, they're allowed to leave Arbella to embark on the mission.

SG-1 returns via the Stargate on Earth, which they now know was moved from Area 51 and hidden in Scotland during the Goa'uld invasion. There, they start searching for the president's wife and encounter the Wraith who saved Daniel. His name is Sting. He helps them find the place where Lana is being held: a laboratory owned by a Wraith queen called Shadow, where Goa'uld symbiotes are being implanted into Wraith hosts to create a deadly hybrid army.

Sting's own queen, Earthborn, is opposed to Shadow. Believing that Earth has corrupted them, Earthborn wants to take the Wraith back to Pegasus where they belong. In return for Sting's help in finding Lana, O'Neill promises to help Earthborn pilot Atlantis home. Together, SG-1 and Sting raid the laboratory, where they find Harry Maybourne working for the Wraith. His life has been artificially extended by frequent use of a sarcophagus and he is now insane.

Maybourne betrays SG-1 to a Wraith/Goa'uld hybrid called Boneshard-Sobek. They manage to fight their way free, but Boneshard and Maybourne escape even though the lab is destroyed. Before they leave, SG-1 finds Lana, although she is very weak and confused. With Sting's help they take Lana back to the Stargate and from there to Hecate's ha'tak in orbit around Earth and prepare to return her to Arbella.

But before they leave, Hecate, who they haven't yet met, requests an audience with SG-1. They are taken to her throne room and are horrified when they see her.

Because her host is none other than their old friend Dr. Janet Fraiser…

# CHAPTER ONE

**Hecate's Ha'tak — 2098:** "This must be disconcerting for you."

Struggling to get breath past the knot in her throat, Sam could only stare at the woman — the *Goa'uld* — walking toward them. Dressed in a simple white gown, like something a Greek statue might wear, with her hair curled and piled high on her head, it was nonetheless Janet Fraiser. Her face, her kind eyes, her expression — they were all as Sam remembered from the last time she'd seen her friend just a few weeks ago.

Give or take a century.

"Disconcerting?" the colonel snarled. "I can think of another word for it, you b —"

"I understand," Janet — Hecate — said. Her tone was sharp, but to Sam's ears it sounded more like Janet's doctor voice than the overbearing insolence of a Goa'uld. "But I would ask that you listen to me, Colonel O'Neill. All is not as it first appears."

"Yeah? Because it *appears* like you're wearing a friend of mine."

Hecate glanced down at herself, smoothed her hands over her diminutive form. "Janet Fraiser…" She glanced back up, her gaze finding and holding Sam's. "Janet was dying when she was brought to me. She'd been shot and left for dead by one of your people. A traitor called Major Newman."

Sam tried to swallow but that knot was still tight in her throat and her mouth was dry. Even so, she managed to scratch out, "Janet would have rather died than become a host."

Daniel huffed his agreement, his silent anger blistering.

"I won't lie to you," Hecate said, moving closer to Sam. Her eyes were so like Janet's, the same warm shade of brown, filled with the same bright intelligence, that Sam had to grit her teeth against a wave of grief. She struggled against the conflicting desire to put a bullet through this creature's head and to pull Janet into her arms and beg her forgiveness for allowing this twisted future to unfold. "I won't lie to you," Hecate repeated. "And I won't pretend that I gave Janet a choice. I'm not *Tok'ra*." Her lips twisted on the name, disdain showing through her pleasant tone. "But I didn't choose this host at random. Janet Fraiser possessed a great deal of knowledge that I valued, and many insights into the healing arts." She glanced toward Daniel. "You know that I'm well regarded for my knowledge of medicines?"

"Of poisons," Daniel corrected, jaw clenching around the words. "If I remember my mythology correctly — which I always do."

A faint smile touched Hecate's lips. "History has been unkind to me," she said. "But so it often is to those of our sex, is it not, Sam?"

Sam didn't answer; she wasn't about to debate feminist interpretations of history with a Goa'uld. Instead she said, "What do you want with us?"

Hecate lifted her chin, folded her hands in another gesture painfully reminiscent of Janet. "I'll come to that in a moment," she said, "but first I need you all to understand something. Although it was not my intention when taking this host, Janet Fraiser has changed me. That is, she has changed my perspective of many things. I sought her medical insight, but, in opening myself to the mind of the host, a…" She hesitated, a flicker of distaste crossing her face. "…a blending, of sorts, took place. I have been changed. I feel…" Again, another frown. "I feel a loyalty to this world, and for many decades now I have been working to free it from the invaders. From the Wraith."

"Huh," the colonel snorted. "Well, congratulations on your spectacular lack of success with that."

Hecate snapped her head around to look at him, her eyes narrowing. "Colonel O'Neill," she said, "I am familiar with your insolence. Janet has many memories of it. But you should know this: it was I and my First Prime who kept the Stargate open for refugees to flee Apophis's rule on Earth. And after the Wraith came, we continued to do what we could to provide safe passage to those humans who wished to serve us and fight the invaders."

"Your First Prime?" Teal'c said from where he stood at Sam's shoulder, his voice flat with disapproval. "You mean my *son*."

Sam glanced at Rya'c, who was standing beneath the shadowed colonnade of Hecate's throne room. He wore an expression of studied neutrality, but his shoulders were tense and his back stiffened when Teal'c spoke.

"Rya'c was a child when the Goa'uld invaded this world," Teal'c said. "Why would you make him First Prime?"

Hecate smiled. It was a sad, almost wistful expression. "Rya'c serves me well, and has done so for many years. But before him there was another." Again, her attention switched back to Sam, and Sam braced herself. In truth, talking to Hecate through Janet's face was harder than a lot of fire fights she'd experienced; there was no way to fight back, nowhere to take cover, she just had to endure. "Perhaps it will convince you that I'm being honest," Hecate said, "when I tell you that the first to serve me as First Prime was not Jaffa. He was a man called Dixon."

The colonel's frown was dubious, cutting right between his eyebrows. "*Dave* Dixon?"

"Yes," Hecate said with another wistful smile. "Colonel Dixon was extremely loyal to Janet Fraiser. He blamed himself for her apparent death, but when he discovered that she still lived — within me — he dedicated himself to our service."

"Bullshit," the colonel said, although Sam could hear the uncertainty beneath the expletive and saw the way he glanced at Daniel as if to confirm his opinion. "Dixon wouldn't serve a snakehead."

Hecate's expression flattened. "You're wrong, Colonel. He served for many years, helping those humans who wished to escape Earth." Her expression shut down, eyes dipping toward the floor. After a moment, and in a very human voice, she said, "He died during the Wraith invasion. Even my skill could not save him. But his name — the name of 'Dix' — had become legend among your people, Colonel, and it lives on still." She lifted her head, once more defiant in a way Sam recognized all too clearly as Janet. "A fitting epitaph for a brave man, don't you think?"

Sam's gaze travelled back to Rya'c, the man everyone now called 'Dix'. As much as it was difficult to believe Hecate, it would certainly be an elaborate lie.

The colonel didn't answer Hecate's question, his expression cool and shuttered although his fingers curled and uncurled at his side; like her, he was missing the weight of a weapon in his hands. "You still haven't answered Carter's question," he said. "What do you want with us?"

Hecate paused for a moment, as if changing tack. "Very well," she said. "To put it simply, I need your help."

The colonel barked a laugh. "And why the hell would we help a Goa'uld?"

"Because we share a mutual objective."

"Oh, I doubt that."

Frowning slightly, Hecate tipped her head. "Wrong again, Colonel. We both want to free this world — this galaxy — from the Wraith, and to destroy the abominations that their queen is creating."

"You know about that?" Daniel said. He sounded cautious, interested despite his better judgment. "About the Goa'uld-Wraith hybrid?"

"I know a great deal, Daniel. Including how to destroy them — all of them."

"All the hybrids? You mean there's more than one?"

"There will be." Hecate swept her imperious gaze across them as if measuring each in turn. "There will be *thousands*."

Sam's stomach clenched at the prospect, but she couldn't

contradict Hecate's assertion; they'd seen the tank of symbiotes in the Wraith lab on Earth, they'd seen the Wraith being bred as hosts. Queen Shadow was building an army.

"Janet Fraiser always believed that one day the great SG-1 would return to save Earth," Hecate continued. "Many doubted her. Many called her faith foolish and condemned her as a traitor. But now you have the chance to prove that she was right, that her faith in you was justified." Hecate's smile was suddenly very much like Janet's, full of quiet conviction and stoicism. "Your world needs you," she said. "How could you possibly turn your backs?"

**Arbella — 2098:** Salem sat bright on a rust colored horizon when General Roz Bailey left the Combined Military Force headquarters that morning. The sight of Arbella's smaller moon so early in the day reminded her how rapidly the weeks were passing and how soon winter would be upon them. The dirt crunched, brittle beneath her boots, and the air had lost its humidity, having the familiar bite that she always found refreshing after months of cloying heat. In a few weeks, they might even have snow. If Roz had been one who believed in omens, she'd perhaps have thought how the change of season could herald a shift on a much larger scale for all the people of Arbella. But she was more pragmatic than that. The snow would fall no matter how things turned out with SG-1.

But as she made her way through Laketown, she decided that rational thinking might be an uncommon commodity these days. The atmosphere rang with a tension that some might call anticipation or even excitement. Roz knew it was neither of those things.

Conflict wasn't a new thing on Arbella. Ever since the First Gens had broken ground here, there had been philosophical and political differences so complex and ingrained that one hundred years of history had done nothing to erase them. Some would say that there were two factions that could be traced back to those loyal to the SGC and those who believed that Stargate Command had been responsible for all the ills that had befallen humanity. On the face of things, she supposed that was essentially true.

But Roz knew it could never be as simple as that. She'd read the history books, and then read them again, the second time around trying to find what wasn't said in typeface — those elusive truths that hid between the lines. The story of Arbella was a troubled and twisted thing.

The most obvious quarrels made themselves known in the Fu-Bar. After too many pitchers of Steiner's Original, the CMF hotheads would clash with those from the security force, resulting in a few broken chairs.

But there were other, uglier, conflicts. The ones that took place in the dark, where whispers were more damaging than shouts.

In the past few weeks, both battlegrounds had witnessed an escalation of hostilities.

Roz supposed it had been inevitable from the moment Rya'c had contacted her. After all, four legendary (or notorious, depending on your position) figures from humanity's past couldn't suddenly rise from the dead without creating a stir. First of all, it was to be expected that the very reality of their existence would be questioned. She herself still found it hard to believe that they were back after all this time. But she'd become something of an expert on SG-1 — and Jack O'Neill was most definitely Jack O'Neill.

From the buzz around Laketown, it was clear that some were more willing to accept the team's existence than others. She'd heard that the likes of Lieutenant Jefferson were spreading word that the CMF was getting ready to storm Earth; that was a rumor she'd have to stifle soon enough, never mind the fact she hoped it might be true. The last thing she needed was some ill-conceived attempt at a coup if the plan to find Lana Jones didn't pan out.

Which brought her to the reason for her morning excursion. Roz was on her way to the Stargate base to meet with President Jones and propose a strategy that she hoped would ease tensions while achieving what she believed would be best for all the people of Arbella.

By the time she reached the end of the cliff's path, the sweat on her skin from the exertion was counteracted by the cold of the summit. She supposed it was a good tactic for gaining the upper hand in negotiations, to have the person out of breath and sweating by the time they met with you.

Roz nodded in greeting to the guards who let her pass without question. Despite being on the opposing team, as it were, she liked to keep good relations all around and so was never averse to buying a drink or two for members of the security force when she saw them in town.

Those good relations, however, were not always mutual.

"Jed," she said to the man who met her inside. Officer Jed Hayden quirked his lips in an expression that was almost a sneer, before turning on his heel and walking down the corridor without a word. She'd been through this routine on more than one occasion and knew that she was expected to follow.

"Wait here," he said, when they reached the anteroom outside the president's office. Fifteen minutes later, he appeared again with the instruction that Jones was ready to see her.

The first thing that struck her when she entered the office was how tired Gunnison Jones looked. Reddish stubble was starting to show on his normally clean-shaven face and shadows had appeared beneath his eyes, making him look more gaunt than usual. The next thing she noticed was that they weren't alone. Agent Karin Yuma sat in a chair against the far wall, straight-backed and cross-legged in neatly pressed slacks and a smart button down. Even in the rough, workaday environment of Arbella, Roz couldn't think of a time when the woman looked anything but completely put together.

"Thank you for joining us, General," said Jones. "I only wish it were under better circumstances."

That set her off balance. She wasn't aware that there were 'circumstances'. She'd been planning the opening lines of her proposal since she'd secured the meeting, but now all she could manage was an uncertain "Sir?"

He leaned forward on his desk, eyes scanning across some papers that lay scattered on its surface. "SG-1. I'm sorry your faith in them didn't pay off."

Roz glanced from Jones to Yuma; the woman's face remained impassive. "I don't think we can say whether it has or hasn't paid off as of yet, sir. It's only been —"

"It's been a week, Roz." Jones' tone was brittle and, for the first time since she entered his office, he met her gaze directly. There was something raw and fractured there. She wondered if it had perhaps been dangerous to play with stakes that were so high for him. He had a lot invested in this plan with SG-1, and if it didn't pay off…

"Mr. President," she said, trying to keep her voice as measured as possible, "a week isn't nearly enough time. We don't know what progress they've made in the search. I appreciate that it's your —"

"I don't believe you appreciate anything, General Bailey. You don't know the damage you've done in bringing them here. You brought a *Jaffa* to Arbella, for God's sake!"

"Sir, with all respect, I think the damage already existed. But I was hoping to speak to you about the way we can use this… opportunity to build on relations with Dix and… and perhaps revisit an open door policy…" She trailed off, cursing herself for allowing them to put her on the defensive. She was better than that. This was her best opportunity to persuade the president that keeping the gate closed wasn't necessarily in Arbella's best interests — and she was blowing it.

"With all *due* respect, General Bailey," he said, and Roz didn't miss the emphasis, "the damage was done as soon as they began spreading their dissent among the CMF — *your* people, might I remind you."

"Dissent? That's not even remotely true. Where are you getting this intel?" As if she even had to ask. Yuma was vocal in her silence.

"Eye-witness accounts from Laketown. I hear they started a fight in that dive your people call a bar."

"Sir, that means nothing if it's not substantiated."

Jones clasped his hands together. "You think it's unsubstantiated, Bailey? Are you honestly telling me that there's been no seditious talk since they came here?"

Roz looked away, thinking of Jefferson and the tattoos she wasn't supposed to know existed, and the meaningful glances she'd seen exchanged by the men and women under her command ever since SG-1 had made their presence known in town.

Jones leaned forward, fixing Bailey with a sober look, one that spoke to their years of friendship. "I'm giving you the benefit of the doubt here, Roz, and assuming you don't have any part in this plot to destroy what we've built here. But you are treading a dangerous line."

She met his gaze, taking a breath to steady her composure. This was too important to let Yuma be the only one who had his ear. Roz knew she had to make him listen to what she had to say.

"Mr. President, I understand your reservations, and I know how much is personally at stake for you. But I trust SG-1. They've convinced me that the history we believe to be true is all wrong. I'm convinced they *will* help us. I'm just asking you to give them a chance to prove the same to you… What's this?" Her last remark was directed at the piece of paper that Jones held out to her. She took it from him and scanned its contents. It showed rows and rows of data and formulas, none of which made any sense to her.

Instead of answering her, he glanced sidelong at Yuma. The agent rose and approached them, gathering more of the papers from the desk. "They're print-outs, General Bailey," she said. "From the data center. The one to which you so kindly granted SG-1 access." Yuma favored Roz with a cold smile. "Apparently Samantha Carter — excuse me, *Major* Samantha Carter — had a very specific search criteria."

A sour taste had crept into Roz's mouth. "I don't understand."

"Solar flares, General. Do you know why solar flares are useful?"

Bailey stared at lines of type, unable to answer.

"Time travel. Your SG-1 is trying to travel back to where they came from. So you tell me, General, how exactly can they help us when they plan to erase us from existence entirely?"

Teal'c was finding it difficult to comprehend all that they had discovered. Bad enough that his son was First Prime to Hecate, but to now learn that the Goa'uld he served had taken his friend, Janet Fraiser, as host was almost too much to bear. And Rya'c had said nothing of it. He had hidden the truth from them as long as possible, no doubt knowing how they would react. It spoke a great deal of his guilt.

And yet the story Hecate had told of Colonel Dixon, of their joint role in the deliverance of Earth's refugees, told a more complex story — if one chose to believe it. But the Goa'uld were creatures of deception, their empires were built upon lies, and Teal'c could trust nothing that left Hecate's mouth. Yet now Rya'c strode before him at her shoulder, and Teal'c had seen the reverence with which the name 'Dix' had been held by the Tau'ri left on the world below, had heard it spoken across continents as a byword for freedom... In truth, he did not know what to think, save that this future must be cut off before it began.

He cast a sideways glance at O'Neill as he walked, satisfied by the tight-lipped skepticism he could see on his friend's face. They had been at odds over the past weeks, but surely now O'Neill and Daniel Jackson would be convinced that nothing but ending this corrupted reality would suffice. Permitting the abomination that walked ahead of them to exist was unthinkable; they owed it to the woman who had been Janet Fraiser to keep this future from unfolding.

Sensing his gaze, O'Neill looked over at him. His expression was grim, but he said nothing and Teal'c could not read the colonel's intention in his guarded eyes.

"This," Hecate said, coming to a halt before a nondescript door, "is the heart of my work." Her attention was fixed on Major Carter, and Teal'c did not think that was accidental. The major and Dr. Fraiser had been close friends and no doubt Hecate planned to trade on the fact. "I think you'll be interested, Sam," the Goa'uld said with a smile. "We have made great progress, not least because of the knowledge I have gleaned from Janet Fraiser."

"Stolen," Major Carter corrected, her voice clipped and angry. "You mean the knowledge you've *stolen* from Janet."

Hecate's face softened into an expression eerily close to that of her host. "It is more complex than you understand, Sam," she said. "Come, let me show you."

With that, Rya'c stepped forward and the doors slid open. When he moved to one side, to let Hecate pass, Rya'c's gaze came to rest for a moment on Teal'c and their eyes met. Teal'c saw defiance in his son, as well as resignation. Rya'c was not ashamed of his decision, Teal'c realized, but neither did he expect his father to understand or approve of his choice to serve Hecate.

Teal'c was not sure that his son was wrong in his assumption. Yet, for the first time since they had met, Teal'c felt something soften toward the man before him. He refused to call it understanding, but he found himself forced to acknowledge that Rya'c's decision may have been more nuanced than he had at first imagined.

It was an uncomfortable realization, one on which he did not wish to dwell. Instead, he chose to focus on the room that lay beyond the doors. It was a laboratory and Hecate swept into the room with a pride that was rather more Goa'uld than Dr. Fraiser.

With few exceptions, the Goa'uld preferred to steal their technology rather than create it and so Teal'c found himself astonished by the extent of Hecate's laboratory. It was a large room, white and clinical, reminiscent of the laboratories he had seen at Stargate Command. A quick look at Major Carter confirmed that it was indeed extraordinary; her eyes were round, as if impressed against her will.

"Where did you get all of this?" she asked, taking a couple of steps into the room. "This is — I'm no biochemist, but this looks like state of the art equipment. Or it was, a hundred years ago."

Hecate's smile broadened. "As I explained, Janet Fraiser's knowledge of medicine and medical research has been invaluable. Much of this equipment was salvaged from research laboratories in the aftermath of Apophis's invasion." She made a dismissive gesture. "Apophis cared little for the advancement of science; he wanted only to take what he deemed valuable." Her gaze drifted over to Daniel Jackson. "As you learned to your cost."

Daniel made no reply, simply folded his arms across his chest.

"Whereas you," the colonel said, "are what? Some kind of Renaissance Goa'uld?"

Hecate spread her hands, a strangely self-deprecating gesture. "I have always been interested in medicine," she said. "An interest only heightened by my blending with Janet Fraiser."

Teal'c noticed Major Carter stiffen at the Tok'ra word 'blending', her gaze darting to the colonel's. Something unspoken passed between them, but Teal'c did not catch its meaning.

"So let me guess," Daniel Jackson said, studying Hecate over the rims of his glasses. "You're going to poison the Wraith. That's your *modus operandi*, right?"

The look Hecate returned him was cool, and Teal'c thought he saw a glimpse of frustration shimmer beneath the surface. "When faced with an infestation," she said, "extermination is the only option."

"Extermination?" Daniel Jackson's eyebrows climbed toward his hair. "The Wraith are sentient creatures. You can't treat them like cockroaches."

Silence followed, awkward in its intensity.

After several heartbeats, and sounding discomforted, O'Neill said, "And we're their *soylent green*, Daniel. You saw the camps, what they do there."

"They will strip this galaxy bare," Hecate added, "as they have done their own galaxy. Sentient or not, the Wraith are a plague. They must be destroyed."

Daniel Jackson made no answer, although he appeared unsatisfied. Instead, Major Carter spoke, "If it's a poison," she said, "what's your delivery mechanism? The Wraith are all over the planet, right? Are we talking a virus or —"

Raising her hand for silence, Hecate said, "Faster and cleverer than that, Sam. We'll use the Wraith against themselves."

"How — ?"

"The hybrid," Hecate continued, walking further into the laboratory to where a number of vials sat in a glass case. "I have a source inside the court of Queen Shadow, which is how I come to know of the hybrid."

"A source among the Wraith?" Colonel O'Neill sounded unconvinced. "They don't seem the sort to be bought off with a couple of Goa'uld trinkets."

Hecate smiled, but it was a flat expression. "Nevertheless, it is true. I know of Shadow's plan to create an army of Goa'uld-Wraith hybrids, to use them to conquer this galaxy and then to return to Pegasus and wipe out all Wraith who will not bend their knee to her."

Had they not heard something similar from the Wraith, Sting, Teal'c might have considered such an elaborate plan to be implausible. However it mirrored Sting's warning too closely to be coincidental. O'Neill ran a hand through his hair, lips pressed tight, and Teal'c suspected his mind was tracking a similar path. However, all the colonel said was, "Go on."

"It is a simple plan," Hecate said, "and yet brilliant."

Daniel Jackson huffed, low in his throat. "Modest."

Hecate ignored him. "The Wraith are naturally intolerant of naquadah," she said. "It is poison to them. They cannot feed on a Goa'uld host or," her gaze slipped toward Major Carter, "a former Goa'uld host. Therefore, in order for a Wraith to host a Goa'uld, their intolerance must be overcome."

"Some kind of immunosuppressant?" Major Carter guessed.

"Yes. " Hecate gestured to the vials. "Shadow plans to vaccinate all Wraith so that they may be implanted with a Goa'uld. I have gained a sample of the immunosuppressant and developed a countermeasure. When deployed, it will negate the effect of the immunosuppressant and the hybrids will be poisoned by the very Goa'uld they carry. An elegant solution, don't you think?"

O'Neill remained unimpressed. "If it's so elegant, what do you need us for?"

"To provide a test subject."

A bristling tension ran through them all. O'Neill took a step back, his hand reflexively reaching for a weapon that was not there. "I don't think so," he said.

"No." Hecate lifted a reassuring hand. "You misunderstand me, Colonel. I need you to *bring* me a test subject, not become one." She gestured toward the glass cabinet containing the vials of liquid. "Sam will tell you that, without a live trial, we have no proof that my countermeasure will work in the field." She fixed her eyes on O'Neill. "I need the prototype hybrid, Colonel. And I need SG-1 to retrieve it from Shadow's hive."

A beat of silence followed, each of SG-1 glancing at the other, uncertain. Eventually O'Neill said, "Let me get this straight.

You want us to go pick up this hybrid from the middle of a Wraith 'hive' — I'm guessing that's a ship and nothing to do with bees — and bring it back here so you can see if your poison works?"

"Exactly."

"And why can't you send 'Dix' here?" His gaze flickered back to Rya'c. "Or some of his buddies down in the Shacks? They're pretty good in a fight, and they know the Wraith."

"Because, first, we don't know where it is," she said. "The hive is cloaked. But your friend, the Wraith…? He knows. And, more importantly, I need your genes, Colonel. Shadow's hive —"

"Was built by the Ancients," Major Carter said, more to O'Neill than Hecate. "She needs your Ancient genes to get inside, sir."

"Not to mention his skill," Hecate said with an ingratiating smile. "And you, of course, Sam, as a former host, are immune to Wraith feeding. Together, you make a formidable team."

Teal'c was amused to see O'Neill roll his eyes at the flattery; vain creatures that they were, the Goa'uld would never understand a man like O'Neill, whose pride lay in his team and not himself.

"So, let's say we do this," the colonel said, "which, by the way, I'm *not* saying. But let's say we get the hybrid and your poison works. You're gonna use it to kill all the Wraith who've been implanted with a snake?"

Hecate inclined her head, "Yes."

"And their Goa'ulds too? Because that's a lot of dead snakes…"

Her expression changed, face sobering. "For every victory," she said, "there is a price to be paid. I'm willing to sacrifice my own kind to rid the galaxy of the Wraith." Chin lifted, she somehow managed to look down at O'Neill despite her diminutive stature. "Are you willing to do the same, Colonel O'Neill?"

"Well, that's not really the question, is it?" he countered. "The question is whether I'm prepared to trust the word of a snake-head. And I gotta tell you, Heck, the odds aren't looking great."

From behind them, at the door, there came an irritable grunt. Teal'c turned to see Rya'c staring at O'Neill, his brow contracted. "Did I not warn you, my Lady, that their prejudices would stand in the way of their cooperation?"

Teal'c lifted an eyebrow; no First Prime he had ever known would be permitted to speak in such a way to their mistress.

Hecate, however, appeared unperturbed. "Perhaps you have less faith in your friends than I do, Dix."

"Perhaps that is because I know them better, my Lady," he said, and offered a stiff bow.

Hecate gave no answer. "I will give you time to consider my offer, Colonel O'Neill, although I cannot give you long. Shadow is moving to implant all her Wraith and once her hybrid army is created, she will leave this world and begin her conquest of our galaxy. And who will stand against her then?"

No one replied and her gaze swept over them all until it caught and lingered on Major Carter. The major shifted under that gaze, so much like Dr. Fraiser's and so profoundly different, but did not speak.

"The Asgard are long gone," Hecate continued, "the System Lords do nothing but squabble, and the Tau'ri… " She let out a breath, a sigh of frustration. "You have seen for yourself what they have become, cowering on Arbella and afraid to lift a finger to reclaim their home world." She took a step closer to O'Neill, fixing him with her gaze. "No, Colonel. I am your only hope. I am humanity's only hope. You may not like it, but just as Janet Fraiser, Dave Dixon and Rya'c have done before you, so you will come to accept that it is the truth. Only together can we free Earth from the Wraith. There is no other choice."

# CHAPTER TWO

**Earth — 2098:** Sting watched with disturbed feelings as the last of the humans they had brought back from Shadow's facility made their way through the trees toward the vast sprawl of the encampment below. Most of them had survived, their bodies repaired by the gift of life, though their minds would be forever damaged.

Curious. Not long ago, he would have thought nothing of their minds. What need had kine for rational thought when their purpose was only to nourish their masters? But his encounter with O'Neill had altered his perspective, given him pause. It was uncomfortable to consider how many like O'Neill he had fed upon, more uncomfortable still to consider how many he must feed upon in the years to come. He was what he was, after all, and nothing could change that.

"Something occupies your mind," Earthborn said, stepping out from the hive to stand with him. "You are troubled."

He turned to look at her, her face concealed in the shadows cast by the ruin of their hive and her thoughts clouded, less tranquil than her words. "There is much to be troubled about, my queen."

Her inner smile brushed against his mind. "A diplomat's answer," she said, and put a hand on his arm, just above his wrist, as she turned her eyes toward him. *You do not like being beholden to the humans.*

"I do not trust the humans," he replied aloud. "And yet in that we have no choice."

"O'Neill is trustworthy," Earthborn said, lowering her hand from his arm. "He will return, and, when he does, Stormfire will track him and we will find him once more."

"Stormfire…" Sting allowed the word to hang between them, the rest of his thought unfinished.

After a pause, Earthborn said, "His mind grows more disturbed, it is true, but he is still able to do what we require. And he has the human to assist him."

Sting permitted himself a slight baring of his teeth. "The human cannot—" But he stopped and thought again of O'Neill, of what he had recently learned of humans. He let out a breath. "Perhaps," he conceded. "Perhaps the human may be of more use than I had previously believed."

"He understands a great deal about Lantean technology," Earthborn reminded him, mildly. And Sting remembered that she, born of this world, had always been more curious about the humans that surrounded them than he. It was a dangerous fascination, however, given who and what they were. Humans could not be friends; at most they could be expedient allies. He was certain that O'Neill felt the same way.

"We must be cautious," he reminded Earthborn. "We cannot trust humans to act in anything but their own interest."

He felt rather than saw Earthborn's wry smile. "In that, then, we are the same. But it does not follow that an alliance of convenience is weak; both parties are invested in the mission's success."

"Yes," he agreed, "until the mission is over. And then…"

Earthborn sighed in agreement. "And then we must all watch our backs."

They stood in silence for some time longer, watching the humans they had saved slip into the camp below unchallenged. Far away, on the other side of the valley, sat the mountain on which the ship of the enemy had once rested. Sting remembered it still; the ostentatious impracticality of the thing perched up there. The parasite-gods had fallen easily to the ruthless efficiency of the Wraith. Their enslaved Jaffa had fought only for the honor of their imposter gods, but the Wraith had fought to live, to feed, and for the survival of their race. Their victory had been assured from the start.

He allowed his eyes to drift down to the sprawling camp,

humans crushed inside ready to be plucked at the whim of Shadow's blades. It left a sour taste in his throat, made his feeding hand ache. There was no pleasure in feeding on such wretched creatures without the thrill of the hunt to stir his blood to life. Shadow's corruption surely stemmed from this weakness — from the way the Wraith had fallen into sloth and gluttony.

*Shadow has always been corrupt,* Earthborn said into his mind, her inner voice cool against his heated thoughts. *I feel that about her.*

*You have never met her, my queen.* Yet Sting was aware there were connections between queens, especially those of the same family, which he could never fully understand. *But you are not mistaken. She was always the shadow to your mother's light.*

He felt Earthborn's pleasure at the compliment, but when she spoke again it was to say, "This monster she has created — a hybrid of Wraith and Goa'uld — it cannot be the product of a sound mind. No Wraith of honor would concede to such a blending. It is unthinkable."

"And yet she proposes to create an army of such creatures." He turned his eyes on her, weighing how much to say. "Such a hybrid race would have an advantage over other Wraith. Were they to return to our own galaxy the consequences would be catastrophic."

Earthborn bared her teeth, a hiss of anger. "It cannot be allowed to happen."

"It will not," Sting said, although he felt less certain than his words and hoped Earthborn could not sense the doubt in his mind. Too much of their plan rested on O'Neill, on the survival and honor of a man he might have fed upon only days ago.

"He will return," Earthborn said, proving that he could hide nothing from his queen. Once more her hand touched his, an intimate gesture. *I trust him.* Her thought was a balm to his troubled mind, it soothed but did not eliminate his concerns. *For now,* she allowed. *I trust him for now.*

Behind them, the hive groaned — a strained settling of its decaying body. Soon it would be dead and they would have to leave.

Earthborn looked behind her, reached out a hand to touch the skin of her mother's ship. "We must make Stormfire ready to depart," she said. "He must travel with us to the Lantean city when O'Neill returns."

"With us?" Sting echoed. "No." Stepping away from her he strove to keep his tone respectful. "My queen, we cannot take Stormfire with us — he is too unpredictable. He could endanger us all. And," he hesitated briefly, but suspected she had already taken the thought from his mind, "you cannot travel there. It is too dangerous."

He felt her irritation bristle, saw it in the ripple of her shoulder blades down her back. "It is not for you to determine —"

"I am your consort," he replied, imbuing his voice with as much authority as he dared.

She turned on him, chin lifted high and lips pulled back from her teeth. "And I am your queen."

Sting offered a bow, but did not break contact with her eyes. "A queen I will not risk on a mission so uncertain. If I die, it is no loss."

"If you —"

Despite the breach of protocol, he talked on. "If we take the Lantean city from Shadow — if we defeat her — we will need a queen to lead our people home. There is no one who can do that but you."

He felt her anger and, beneath it, her fear — a silver thread of it, well hidden, but startling nonetheless. Fear for him, for the loss of him. *I will return,* he told her, rising and daring to reach for her hand. In other times and places, it would not be permitted, but here, where all that they once were teetered on the edge of destruction, he deemed it possible. *I will return to you, my queen,* he said and touched his brow to hers. *I swear it.*

"Look, I'm not saying we have to trust her," Jack said. "I'm saying what other choice do we have?"

Daniel ran a hand through his hair and tugged off his glasses. He was tired, his eyes itched, and there was something heavy lodged in the center of his chest making it difficult to think straight. Of all the people he'd known at the SGC, why did it have to be Janet?

He sighed, squeezed the bridge of his nose, and said, "The dubious morality of 'exterminating' the Wraith aside, you know it's impossible for a host to influence a Goa'uld, right? Not while the Goa'uld is conscious. Even Sha're…" He trailed off, letting the rest speak for itself.

They were back in the quarters Rya'c had provided for them, perched tense and uncomfortable on the ugly furniture of the living area. Hecate had given them an hour to decide; they didn't seem to be any closer to a decision than they had been twenty minutes earlier.

From where she stood by the window, her gaze fixed on the stars outside, Sam said, "Actually, Daniel, I'm not so sure."

He blinked at her, surprised to hear Sam, of all people, take that line. "What do you mean?"

With a slight head shake, she turned to face him, almost as if she was dismissing her words before they were spoken. "It's just something Hecate said…" She glanced at Jack. "She talked about 'blending' with… with Janet." She clamped her jaw shut for a moment, as if getting a grip on herself, and then said, "You heard that too, right, sir?"

"Yeah," Jack sighed, slumping back into his chair. "I heard it."

"It sounds like something a Tok'ra would say," Sam carried on, in case Daniel hadn't got it.

He had, of course. "She's not Tok'ra," he pointed out. "And, Sam, we have to assume that's exactly what she wants us to think. She wants us to look at her and see Janet." He rubbed a hand across his mouth, but it did nothing to scrub away the bitter memory of seeing his friend like this, or any of the memories it triggered of his wife. "We can't let her play us."

"I'm not," Sam insisted, although the way her eyes darted off and back to the window made Daniel wonder how much she believed it. How could any of them say they weren't affected by hearing a Goa'uld's words falling from Janet Fraiser's lips?

"Look, the questions is," Jack said, "do we go along with her plan or not?"

From the far side of the room, Teal'c said, "Her plan will not serve to end this timeline, O'Neill."

Daniel resisted the urge to groan; they'd been over and over this. "Teal'c —"

"There's no way to end this timeline," Jack said, pushing to his feet and turning to face Teal'c. "Not soon, anyway. And maybe never. Teal'c, it's a moot point. We're here and we have to deal with what's right in front of us."

"He's right," Sam said quietly. "Teal'c, as much as I *hate* seeing Janet like this, and Rya'c, and *Earth*... we're out of options. At least for now." Her attention shifted from Teal'c back to Jack. "Sir, I think we should agree to the plan. For one thing, it could get us onto this Ancient hive ship." She shot a quick look back at Teal'c. "Who knows what we might find there? Maybe their computers are powerful enough to predict a solar flare that can take us home? There's nothing here or on Arbella that can help us."

Jack acknowledged the point with a nod, and then turned his eyes on Daniel. "Thoughts?"

He sighed and slipped his glasses back on, blinking up at Jack. "We can't trust Hecate," he said. "But..." His thoughts skittered off for a moment, chasing down a new idea.

"But?" Jack prompted, impatient as ever.

"But maybe we can mitigate the risk."

"How?"

Daniel frowned down at the floor between his feet, thinking it through. "If Hecate's serious about freeing Earth from the Wraith — and about leaving, once it's done — then Earth's gonna need some help, right? In the aftermath."

"I guess. What do you have in mind?"

"Arbella," he said, looking up to meet Jack's skeptical eye. "I'm serious, Jack. We have President Jones' wife — we can take her home, like we promised. What better way to get him on our side? To get Arbella to come through the gate and take the fight to the Wraith? We know we already have friends there — they *want* to fight for Earth, Jack. They want to reclaim it."

"Some of them," Jack conceded. "But we have enemies there too."

Which was true, but that didn't mean it wasn't worth the risk. "I'll go," Daniel said. "I'll talk to Gunnison Jones, tell him what happened to his wife — explain how we're going to drive the Wraith out. I'll be more use there than on the hive ship, and if we can bring the Arbellan CMF through the gate to back us up, then that might just be our ace in the hole. At the very least, it's an insurance policy against Hecate reneging on her deal." He spread his hands. "And if she won't let us go, if she refuses to let us gate back to Arbella? Well, then we have to ask why she doesn't want a human army on Earth once the Wraith are gone."

Jack frowned, his mouth a tight line.

"It's a good point, sir," Sam said. "It tests Hecate's intentions and it means we're not just relying on her Jaffa against the Wraith. Strategically, it's a good plan."

"It's a dangerous plan."

Daniel laughed. "Jack, we're trapped in a screwed up future, caught between the Wraith and the Goa'uld. *Everything* is dangerous."

Jack's mouth twitched — what served as a smile for

him—and he said, "Someone tell me we've been in worse situations than this and gotten out of it?"

Daniel exchanged a helpless look with Sam, but she just shrugged. Teal'c said nothing, only straightened his shoulders.

"Yeah," Jack sighed. "That's what I thought." Head bowed, he stood in silence for a moment. Sam watched him carefully, as though she was about to say something, and Daniel couldn't catch her eye. But she didn't speak and eventually Jack looked up, encompassing them all in a single glance. "I told you before that I wasn't gonna give orders anymore," he said. "Where we are now… There's no Air Force, no chain of command. No United States. Those old rules, they don't apply anymore. They can't."

"Sir—"

"Carter, zip it," he said. "My point is that if we go into the field, then we go in as SG-1. And we go in with me as your CO and with the usual chain of command in the unit; otherwise we'll die out there. But if we do that, it's because you *choose* to follow me. The only authority I have out here is what you give me. I'm not ordering any of you to take this mission. But me? I'm in. I'm gonna find Sting and have him take me out to the hive ship."

"I'm coming with you, sir," Sam said immediately.

Jack held her gaze for a moment and then nodded. "Okay."

Daniel looked at Teal'c, stoic on the other side of the room. "I'll go to Arbella," he said, "rally some backup among the CMF." He tipped his head, studying Teal'c. "I could use someone to watch my back."

For a moment, he thought Teal'c might refuse, that his insistence on undoing this reality would be too inflexible. But then his shoulders relaxed and he gave his customary nod. "Then I shall travel with you, Daniel Jackson."

He felt a wash of relief and smiled his thanks, not just because he'd have Teal'c with him but because Teal'c was still part of this. SG-1 was still working together, despite what Jack thought about his right to command them, despite their conflict over how to resolve the mess they'd found themselves in. SG-1 was still a team. "Then that's it," he said, pushing himself to his feet. "That's the reply you give to Hecate, Jack. You and Sam go to the hive and bring back her test subject; Teal'c and I go to Arbella and bring back an army. And then we fight for Earth."

For a moment, they all just looked at each other. It felt as if they were right at the top of a rollercoaster, waiting to tip over the edge with gravity taking hold and no way back.

Into the tense silence, Jack said, "Well gang, looks like we're splitting up to search the creepy haunted mansion. What could possibly go wrong?"

**Arbella — 2098:** It was with a practiced eye that Karin Yuma spooned leaves into the earthenware pot. She plucked the kettle from the stove at just the right moment before the water boiled, to avoid scalding the leaves, and added the precise amount to the teapot. She would let it infuse for two minutes exactly before pouring the brew into her cup. Then she would empty it down the drain and repeat the process.

She never drank the tea she made — the leaves that were grown in the peaty soil to the south of Laketown had a harsh and bitter taste — but the routine focused her mind, sharpening her thoughts. She would need a keen edge to maintain effective control of the current situation.

The morning had gone well. Or rather, it had gone as she'd anticipated. Careful planning, vigilance and analysis of all eventualities were the key to a satisfactory outcome. The knock at her office door was yet another expected eventuality.

"Come in, Jed."

There was a pause before the door opened to reveal Jed Hayden. "How did you — ?"

"Sit down."

The young officer was hesitant as he entered the room and

sat in the chair opposite. Yuma had gotten rid of her office desk long ago, finding it more effective to note a person's body language without any visual hindrance — and for them to note hers. She crossed her legs and waited for Hayden to stop fidgeting. Then she smiled and inclined her head, the indication that he should speak, though she knew why he was here.

He took a breath, as if readying himself to talk, but then noticed the steaming teapot on the table. "Oh, may I have some?"

Yuma's patience began to wear thin. "No."

Hayden frowned and cleared his throat. "Alright. What about the president?"

"I'm sure he has his own tea."

"That's not… You know that's not what I mean."

"Speak your mind, Officer. I'm busy and you didn't make an appointment."

"What did Bailey have to say?"

"First of all, that was classified and pertaining to planetary security. Secondly, I'm sure you know as well as I did what she had to say from where you were listening by the door."

Hayden tugged at his collar and sat forward in his chair. "Okay, if we're cutting the crap, Yuma, then I'll spell it out. What are you going to do about SG-1?"

"You're awfully quick to believe it's actually them."

"Well, you believe it's them, so that's good enough for me. So what are you going to do about them? They're dangerous."

Yuma almost smiled. Jed Hayden had a lot to learn about keeping his composure, but he could read a situation well. It was one of the reasons she had him working for her. "Not so dangerous as you might think."

His eyebrows shot up. "Are you kidding me? Most of the CMF think they're returned messiahs. You've got more eyes than me in town, Yuma. You must know the buzz. You've got the likes of Stan Jefferson ready to lead a charge on Earth if Jack O'Neill gave the word. With Roz Bailey on their side, that sort of dissent could blow up quickly. Bailey and Jones have been friends for a long time, and if she has the ear of the president… Well, if that's not dangerous then I don't know what is."

Yuma waited for him to finish, then stared at him until he fell back in his seat and looked away. "Jed, I'm going to ask you a question and I want you to answer me as honestly as possible. That ok?" Hayden shrugged his agreement. "Alright then… Do you think I came through the gate yesterday?"

"What? I don't —"

"It's quite simple. I asked you if you thought I came through the gate yesterday. Because you clearly assume I have no understanding of how things work on my planet."

"I didn't —"

"I'm well aware of the talk in Laketown and I have a full understanding of how volatile the situation could be if not controlled. But this thing will only blow if there's a spark to light the fuse. Do you know what that spark would be?"

"Of course. SG-1."

"That's right, Jed. SG-1. And they're not here anymore. Do you honestly think I'd have allowed Bailey's mission to rescue Lana Jones to go ahead if I'd thought there was any possibility of success?" She didn't have to explain her plan, of course, but Hayden was antsy, and nervous people often made mistakes. He needed to know that all that was required was a cool head here. "SG-1 will fail, they won't come back, and Jefferson, Kiowa and the rest of their crew will finally see firsthand what the history books said all along — SG-1 are cowards who run."

Hayden scratched the back of his neck and shook his head. "But it's Jones's wife. It's personal for him. Won't he be willing to risk more?"

It wasn't that Hayden made a bad point. Indeed, if Gunnison Jones did find that his wife was alive and well, and that Jack O'Neill's people were the ones who'd rescued her, then much of what Yuma had worked for would be disrupted. She wasn't an idealist by any means, but the Arbellan way of life was one that had afforded her many opportunities, and she would not allow external factors to destroy it. Lucky then, that this was a consideration she'd already taken into account.

"Exactly. It's his wife. And when he realizes that the hope Bailey offered him was worthless, what do you think will happen to his opinion of the good general?"

Hayden nodded, but then said, "What if they succeed?"

"Jed, Earth is occupied by the Wraith. SG-1 is going up against an enemy that made even the Goa'uld turn tail. Do you honestly think they'll win?"

He returned her gaze. "They said they did before." There was silence in which Yuma was almost certain she betrayed nothing of that small doubt inside that had already said the same thing.

The radio at Hayden's hip crackled into life suddenly and he jumped, pulling it free and toggling it on. "This is Hayden, go ahead." A burst of static was the only reply. "Say again?" This time something that sounded like words could be heard through the noise. With a sigh, Hayden said, "I'll have to go outside. Nothing ever gets through these walls."

"Don't let me detain you," replied Yuma as he left the room. She walked to the small stove to boil more water, but just as she was emptying the old tea from the pot, footsteps pounded up the stairs and the Hayden burst back into the office, his expression stricken.

"It's the gate room. They've had contact from Hecate's ship. It's SG-1 and they've found Lana Jones."

# CHAPTER THREE

**Earth — 2098:** Hecate's ring transporter deposited them in the ruins of the SGC. Jack caught the uneasy look Carter gave him as they stepped away from the rings, her eyes darting around the gloomy walls before landing on Rya'c — or 'Dix' as he was known here.

He'd accompanied them to ensure safe passage back to the surface, but it was the first time they'd been alone with the man since they'd found out the truth about Hecate, and Rya'c was one big knot of tension. "This way," he said, without preamble, and led them in silence through Stargate Command's shattered corridors.

All around, there were people at work clearing rubble from what had been the gate room — men and women with Hecate's mark on their forehead: a mark of resistance here, not slavery. It was difficult for Jack to adjust to the difference and to accept that Rya'c may have made the best choice after all. Maybe Dave Dixon had too, all those years ago. Trapped between the devil and the deep blue sea, what else could you do but build a raft?

"These are the people you will need," Rya'c said, breaking the silence that had fallen between them. "When Daniel and my father return from Arbella, these are the people who are already at war with the Wraith."

Keeping a watchful eye on the people around him, Jack couldn't disagree. He remembered Hunter, up in the Shacks, and the other humans who fought for 'Dix', and wondered what made the difference between those who cowered and those who took up arms and fought back. "You've trained them?" he said.

"Yes, although in insurgency rather than outright battle. But they are eager to fight."

Jack didn't doubt that, but it was another question that

came to mind as they picked their way past the rubble. "Why did you come here?" he said. "After Earth fell, why did you come here?"

Rya'c walked half a pace ahead of him, his back straight, and turned to look at Jack over his shoulder. "Where else would I go?" he said simply. "Apophis was my enemy and the Tau'ri were my friends — my father's friends."

"Janet was your friend too," Carter said on a low breath.

Rya'c looked at her and a flinch twitched his face. "Yes she was. I knew it would be difficult for you to understand, but Hecate... She is different to the other Goa'uld. And perhaps that is because of Dr. Fraiser."

"The Goa'uld say that nothing of the host remains," Carter reminded him. Jack didn't miss the bitter flavor to her words.

"I do not believe that is always so," Rya'c said. "Neither did Colonel Dixon, or he would not have served her as he did." He stopped, turning fully to face them, chin lifted. "You were not here when Apophis came, when the Wraith came. Do not judge us for what we have done to fight for your world — and for the future of this galaxy."

After a beat, Carter ducked her head. "I'm sorry," she said. "You're right. We can't judge you for what you did then."

Although, the unspoken implication went, we *can* judge you for what you do now.

Another uncomfortable silence fell. Jack cleared his throat. "You should get these people ready," he said. "If you tell them to rise up against the Wraith, they will."

"And I will do it," he said, turning his eyes on Jack, "if I think you have a chance of winning."

"If?" Jack lifted an eyebrow. "You don't think Hecate's plan will work?"

Rya'c's expression flattened. "Ask me that question again, O'Neill, when you have returned with the hybrid, and when my father and Daniel have returned with the Arbellan army."

"Oh. So it's *us* you don't trust?"

Walking on, Rya'c only said, "I will not argue with you, O'Neill. There is a long climb to the surface and you should save your breath."

At his side, Jack saw Carter swallow a smile at that, but he let it slide. Who was he to demand her respect now? In this screwed up future, she wasn't his subordinate anymore; she was with him here out of choice. He tried not to think too closely about all the implications of that...

They walked on in a silence broken only by the muted nods and words of greeting from Rya'c's people. Jack felt their eyes tracking him and Carter, but didn't feel threatened. They were suspicious, perhaps, but they trusted 'Dix'. That said a lot about the man as a leader, not that Jack was surprised; Rya'c was a chip off the old block and there was no one more worthy of trust and respect than Teal'c.

It wasn't much longer before Jack started to recognize the rubble-filled corridors through which they were walking, the scratch of red paint on the floor painfully familiar, and eventually Rya'c stopped at the base of the ladder that would take them to the surface. It was a long climb indeed and he gave a preemptive wince on behalf of his knees as he squinted up past the rusting rungs. He couldn't even see a glimpse of light at the top. "They know we're coming, right?"

"They will be waiting," Rya'c said.

When Jack pulled his head back from inside the access hatch, he found Rya'c watching him with a steady gaze that reminded him too much of the boy's father. "So I guess this is it," Jack said.

"For now. I am certain you will return."

"You betcha," Jack said. Then, more seriously, "And so will Teal'c."

Rya'c shifted. "The people of Arbella can be...difficult."

"Well, if anyone can sweet talk them it's Daniel."

Rya'c simply bowed his head. "I have every confidence in them." After a pause, he added, "And in you. I hope —" He glanced at Carter. "I hope you feel the same about me. Though I serve Hecate, I am still the boy you once knew, O'Neill."

Jack had to swallow hard because suddenly there was something knotty in his throat. "I know," he said, and pressed a hand to Rya'c's shoulder. "And so does Teal'c, okay? This just — This isn't the life he wanted for you when he rebelled."

"I understand," Rya'c said. "But it is the life I have lived. I cannot regret it."

Jack just nodded, gave Rya'c's shoulder one last squeeze, and said, "Carter? Let's get climbing."

"Master," the human said, his head ducked as he stepped outside of the hive. "Stormfire would speak with you."

Quelling his irritation at the interruption, Sting turned away from Earthborn. "On what matter?"

"There is something he wishes you to see," the human said. "I believe it is — I believe it involves the Lantean."

Sting exchanged a look with his queen, hope and triumph bright in her mind.

*I told you he would return!*

Sting urged a note of caution. *Let us see what we shall see.* To the human, he said, "Take me to him. Is he… How is he, today?"

The human met his eye, briefly. "It's one of his better days."

In that brief exchange, Sting was started to see intelligence in the creature's face that he had not noticed — had not thought to notice — before. The human, he realized with something akin to shame, was not so different to O'Neill. And, like O'Neill, he must have a name. It had never occurred to him to ask, or to care, what that name might be; the human was food, he was a slave. The notion was discomforting.

Lost in his thoughts, Sting followed in silence as they made their way through the dying corridors to what remained of Stormfire's laboratory. Already, much of the cleverman's work had been put away, ready to be transported who knew where — somewhere away from the hive, although his half-formed plan of moving to the laboratories Shadow had created on Earth was no longer possible. They had nowhere to go, yet it would be more dangerous still to remain within the hive once it had died; the decomposition process would infect them all.

Stormfire himself stood swaying against one of the benches, head bent over something in his hands. Tentative, Sting reached out with his mind, but the whorls of red fire and chaos that met him forced him back. He would not willingly touch such a mind, afraid of what it might do to his own. So, instead, he spoke aloud. "Stormfire, what is it you have found?"

He turned with a grin stretching his thin lips. "Blood," he said. "I can smell it."

Sting spared a glance for the human, who had retreated to the far side of the laboratory. He was packing away the Lantean objects Stormfire had collected, taking careful inventory and making notes as he did so. Clever, Sting thought. It occurred to him now, in a way it never had before, that this human who Stormfire had recruited may know more than Sting would like about the Lantean technology that was Stormfire's obsession.

It would behoove him to keep an eye on the human.

"He is back," Stormfire said, pressing something into Sting's hands.

Glancing down, he saw that the device was the same disk Stormfire shown him weeks before — when O'Neill had first escaped. Dark, with the gray-white lines favored by the Ancestors, it showed a map of the vicinity of the hive. And, within that map, blinked a single light. Sting raised his eyes to Stormfire. "This is him?"

"He is below the mountain," Stormfire said, "but moves closer." He scraped a claw across the surface of the device. "Here, he has moved so far already." He bared his teeth. "He is coming back to us."

Sting did not respond, though from the trajectory Stormfire indicated it seemed likely that O'Neill was indeed fulfilling his part of the bargain, as he had promised.

"I told you we could trust him," Earthborn said as she stepped into the laboratory.

"You did," Sting replied; he did not comment on whether or not he agreed. He had no doubt that O'Neill worked to his own agenda. He looked back down at the Ancestors' device. "O'Neill will approach through the human encampment," he said. "I will meet him and bring him here."

Earthborn lifted her head. "That place is not safe. Shadow's blades patrol there."

"And we cannot risk O'Neill falling into their hands."

Her concern was palpable, beating between them like heat. Sting was aware that he should not feel it so readily — that it was, somehow, improper for him to intrude. Yet it could not be helped. Shadow had brought them to a place where all propriety had been abandoned, a place where she would pollute Wraith with the parasite-gods. There were many rules that did not apply here.

"Take a dart," Earthborn said. "Use the culling beam to —"

"Shadow will see it immediately," he countered, "and she will deploy her darts in response." Then, between themselves alone, he said, *Do not fear for me, my queen. I shall be safe.*

"It is not safe to go on foot, alone," she said aloud. "The humans are restive in that place."

From behind him, Sting heard a noise and turned to see the human approach. Diffident as ever, he ducked his head and said, "Master, allow me to go in your place and meet O'Neill. I can travel unnoticed in the Shacks and I know the place well."

Sting bared his teeth. "And how likely is it that you will return to us?"

The human — the man; he was a man — looked up at him and perhaps because of his new-found familiarity with human expressions Sting saw something sharp and determined in his face. "You wish to leave this world," he said and, though there was a tremor in his voice, he did not look afraid. "I wish to see you go. It's in my interest to help you find a way to fly the Ancestors' city and to leave us in peace."

Although he did not show it to the human, Sting was taken aback by the statement.

Stormfire just laughed, his manic cackle loud in the laboratory. "Clever, clever creature," he said and snatched the Lantean tracking device away from Sting and gave it to the human.

At his side, he felt Earthborn draw closer. Her mind was amused, a frisson of delight that was unexpected as her gaze travelled over the man. "Those are brave words," she said, "to speak before a queen."

The man said nothing, but neither did he cringe back. He simply watched them and waited for Earthborn's verdict: death or trust. They were the only possible responses to such a speech.

*We have already trusted O'Neill,* Earthborn said into his mind. *And this human speaks the truth; our objectives coincide.*

*There are many ways he could betray us.*

*Yes. But Shadow is enemy to us both.*

She spoke wisdom and Sting could not deny it. Instead, he turned to the human. "How will you know O'Neill when you see him?"

An expression Sting could not fully interpret crossed the man's face — something deep-seated that lit his eyes bright. "I can use this to locate him in the camp," he said, holding up the tracking device. "But when I find him, I will know his face. There are those who always believed Colonel Jack O'Neill would come back. And I was one of them."

Sting narrowed his eyes, as if by closer inspection he could ascertain what the man was thinking. But of course he could not; human minds were closed to him. "You will bring him to the edge of the encampment," he said. "And no further. I will meet you there."

The man gave a bow of respect, as was proper. "Very well."

As he straightened, Sting stepped forward and curled his fingers into the man's clothing, lifting him onto his toes. He flexed his feeding hand and made sure the human could see it. "You will not betray us."

The man licked his lips, glanced at the hand-mouth Sting knew was gaping — he was still hungry — and nodded. "I won't. I won't betray you."

For a moment longer Sting held him there, felt his life pulsing under his skin, then he let him go. "I will know if you have," he warned. "Now leave."

With a nod, the man straightened his clothes and headed for the door, but at the last moment Earthborn spoke. "What is your name?" she said.

He stopped, turned back with evident surprise. "My name?"

"You have a name?" Earthborn asked. "A given name?"

"Of course."

"Then I would know it."

He paused for a moment, as if considering her request, before he said, "James. My name is James O'Kane."

Earthborn tilted her head. "Very well, James O'Kane. Go, with my thanks, and bring O'Neill to us."

Sting said nothing. But for a queen to ask a human its name? Truly, their kind was on its knees.

The Shacks were much as Jack remembered them, crammed with human misery and desperation. But everything was different now, knowing where they were — knowing that this place had once been his home.

As he stepped out of the makeshift hut that hid the entrance to the ruins of Stargate Command, the sun glowed bright through the ashy cloud blanketing Earth. He pulled out his sunglasses to fend off the glare. Carter did the same. But he couldn't help feeling they were hiding from more than the sun; they were hiding from the reality of what surrounded them.

Behind them the mountain — Cheyenne Mountain — rose up black against the bright sky and for a moment he just looked at it and tried to figure out why he hadn't recognized it before. Was something different?

Carter must have guessed what he was thinking, like she so often did, because she said, "The peak's changed. It was probably damaged when Apophis used it as a landing platform."

He gave a grunt of assent and pushed the thought of a ha'tak crushing the landscape of his home out of his mind. There were enough crappy images floating around in his head — things he'd actually witnessed — without adding imagined horrors to his photo album.

"I guess this was Colorado Springs once," he said by way of reply, turning to look out over the sprawling camp. "You think there'd be more left."

Carter cocked her head. "Would you?"

She was right, of course. He'd seen his fair share of war zones on Earth. It was astonishing how fast war destroyed what it had taken hundreds, even thousands, of years to build — that thin veneer of civilization they all pretended was infinite. "Come on," he said, scanning the ridge above the camp until his eyes found what he was looking for. "We should head for Sting's ship — he'll be waiting for us."

"Sir?" Carter nodded to her right and when Jack glanced over he saw a familiar face watching them from beneath the shadow of one of the surrounding shacks.

"Hunter," he said, and found a smile.

"Didn't 'spect to see you back here," Hunter said, pushing himself to his feet. "Thought you was headed home."

"Long story." That was a can of worms Jack really didn't want to open. "We decided to hang around a little longer," he said. "See if we can't help."

Hunter tipped his head, his hair falling to one side over Hecate's mark. "Then you're serving the goddess now?" He sounded doubtful. "You don't bear her mark."

"We don't serve anyone," Jack said, keeping it light. "But Dix sent us here — we're allies of his."

"And where you headed?" Hunter said. "I can take you. Shacks ain't safe if you don't know the right path."

There was something wary in the man's face, a look of distrust that sent warning sparks along the length of Jack's spine. Hunter may be a friend, but given Aedan Trask's dislike of working with Sting, Jack was pretty certain that Hunter wouldn't like their plan. He'd risked his life helping them bust out of Sting's hive, after all. It would be difficult to explain why they were walking back in.

At his side, Carter shifted. Her unease was as palpable as his.

"We could use a guide to take us back to your place," Jack decided. "We can find the way from there."

Hunter's eyes narrowed. "The way where?"

"Out," Jack said, glad for the sunglasses hiding his eyes; they made it easier to keep his expression neutral. "Can't say more than that."

After a hesitant beat, Hunter shrugged. "Then I ain't gonna ask," he said. "I trust Dix, an' if you're on his business I guess I gotta trust you too."

It was close enough to the truth not to feel like a lie and Jack gave a nod. "Keep your eyes open," he said as they started to walk. "And keep your family close. Things might get interesting in the next few days."

Hunter squinted at him over his shoulder and then turned back around to watch where he was going. "Always keep my eyes open," he said. "That's how come I lived so long."

It took the best part of half a day to work their way through the labyrinth of the Shacks to the scrap of wood and tarpaulin Hunter called home, and by then they were losing the light. Carter walked next to Jack in silence the whole way, her thoughts clearly elsewhere. He didn't have to guess where; she and Fraiser had been good friends. There weren't a lot of women in Stargate Command, and Carter and the doc had been close. No surprise she was taking this hard. Bad enough that they'd thought Janet — all their friends — were dead, but to know that Fraiser had been suffering all those lost years…? It twisted hard and tight in the pit of his stomach.

And it had to end. One way or another, they had to end this. If they couldn't unmake this crappy future then they'd sure as hell fix it.

"You should stay with us tonight," Hunter offered, his gaze darting from one to the other where they stood outside his home. "There's been Snatchers everywhere these last weeks."

Jack didn't doubt it after the damage they'd inflicted on Shadow's operation, but that was exactly why they didn't have time to waste. "We'll take our chances," he said, throwing a glance at Carter to confirm.

"But thanks for the offer," she added and gave Hunter a smile. It didn't reach her eyes, though; it was just a facsimile. "And for your help."

Hunter grunted his acknowledgment. "I gonna see you again?"

Jack exchanged a look with Carter, but her face was inscrutable. "Sure," Jack said. "We'll be back." He hoped that wasn't tempting fate.

They didn't linger long after that, heading out into the camp in silence. All around were the hushed sounds of fear, of humans huddling against the things that moved in the night. It was difficult not to picture how this camp must have begun — all those terrified people in Colorado Springs who hadn't even known there was an enemy, let alone that it was at the gate, until Apophis had broken down the damn doors.

He couldn't imagine their shock; couldn't help feeling that, somehow, it was his fault. If he'd only gotten them home on time… If Daniel hadn't been injured and they'd gotten through the gate just a couple minutes sooner then everything would be different.

"Colonel?" Carter's voice was pitched low, a perfect patrol whisper.

He glanced over at her, but couldn't see much more than her profile and a glint of her eyes in the almost total darkness of the Shacks. No open fires here; everyone was hiding in the dark. "Carter?"

"I've been thinking."

"Uh-oh," he said, but smiled to take the bite out of it.

She gave a soft huff of amusement. "It's, uh," she lowered her voice further, "about the plan."

"It sucks. I know."

"It's just — We'll be lying to Sting," she said. "I mean I know he's one of them, but if Hecate's plan works then all of Shadow's Wraith will die."

"But *he* won't," the colonel countered. "Earthborn won't."

"No, but think about it. With no Wraith to lead — no hive — would they even survive in their own galaxy?" She shook her head. "I doubt they could ever go home, sir. Even with Atlantis."

The *just like us* remained unspoken, but was no less weighty for being silent.

Jack scrubbed a hand through his hair, resettled his cap afterward and tugged the bill low over his eyes. It's not like he hadn't thought of that already, he'd just chosen not to dwell. "It's the only plan we got," he said, which, all things considered, was both a crappy argument and an unanswerable one. "We get rid of the Wraith, then we get rid of the snake," he said. "My enemy's enemy and all that."

"Yes, but —" She cut herself off with a small noise of frustration, head shaking.

He waited for a couple moments to see if she'd carry on, but she gave him only silence. "But what?" he was forced to prompt.

Another shake of her head. "Nothing. It doesn't matter."

"Carter…"

"It's nothing."

"C'mon," he said. "But *what*?"

She let out a sigh, almost hissed it through her teeth. "It's just — What about Janet, sir?"

And, yeah, that was the root of the problem, the intractable horror of this whole stinking situation. It was one thing to do a deal with the devil, but when the devil's wearing your friend's face…? Watching Carter, he said, "You think there's anything of her left?"

"Yes," she said immediately. "Look at what happened with Skaara and Klorel."

And he'd known she was gonna say that. "But it's been a hundred years."

"I know." She was silent for a beat. "But we've got no evidence that time makes any difference. And, sir, if there's a chance that Janet is in there…?" She turned her face to him, those wide eyes bright in the dark. "We can't just let Hecate leave and take Janet with her. We can't leave her —" Carter's voice cracked and she broke off, turning her face away.

"We're not gonna leave her like this," Jack said, just to make it clear. "Once the Wraith are out of the picture we'll deal with it."

"How?"

"I don't know. But we will, I swear. We are not gonna leave Janet like this, okay?"

She nodded. "Yes sir."

"And we've got time to figure out a plan, right?"

Another nod. "Maybe the Tollan? Maybe, in this reality, they can help like they did with Skaara…?"

"Maybe." Although he was doubtful. If the Tollan had let the Protected Planets treaty fail, if they'd sat back and watched Earth fall to Apophis, and then to the Wraith, without lifting a hand to intervene…? Well, he didn't rate their chances of getting the sanctimonious bastards to save Janet Fraiser from a literal fate worse than death. Not that he was going to say any of that out loud. Not that he needed to; he was pretty certain Carter was thinking the exact same thing. "We'll find a way," he said instead. "You got that, Carter?"

"Yes sir," she said, and it sounded like she was convincing herself as much as him. But he let it slide; at this point, faith and hope were pretty much all they had left.

The camp was eerily quiet in these dead hours of the night and Jack couldn't shake an uneasy prickle along the length of his spine. He felt eyes watching them from the shadows. People here didn't sleep; they were always on watch.

The sooner they were out of there, the happier he'd be, although the sight of Sting's ship, crouching low on the skirt of a rocky ridge that he now recognized as The Horns, didn't exactly fill him with joy. He wasn't sure what made him feel worse — the fact that they were going to trust these Wraith or the fact that they were going to betray them.

"Sir," Carter said, drawing to a halt. "Did we take a wrong turn?"

"Is there a *right* turn?" The whole place was a maze, constantly shifting.

"We need to be east of that escarpment," she said, gesturing to the mountains. "And I don't think—"

"Jack O'Neill." The unfamiliar voice came from his left, pitched low.

Zat raised, Jack peered into the darkness. He couldn't see anyone. "Who's asking?"

"I'm here to help you," the voice said — a man. "Don't shoot."

Jack shifted his grip on the weapon, but didn't lower it. "Come out where I can see you."

There was a scuffing of footsteps and a flare of gray light — not a flashlight, but something technological — before it was hidden. A man emerged from the darkness, tall with close-cropped sandy hair. His well-worn jacket looked military — something handed down from before the invasion, perhaps. Both his hands were in the air. "Sting sent me," he said. "I'm to bring you to him."

"And you are?"

"My name's James O'Kane, Colonel."

"And you *work* for Sting?"

A slight smile touched the man's face. "Better that than feed him."

"You're what they call a 'feeder', aren't you?" Carter said from where she stood at Jack's side. "Humans who serve the Wraith."

James glanced at her and Jack didn't miss the way his eyes widened. "Major Carter," he said. "I didn't expect—" He cleared his throat. "It's an honor to meet you."

She exchanged a glance with Jack. "You know me?"

"Of course. You're SG-1. You're—" He stopped, cocking his head toward the sky. "We have to go."

Jack peered up and a moment later he heard it too: a high pitched whine. "Wraith?"

"Shadow. Her darts are patrolling. We should leave the Shacks as soon as we can."

"You got no argument from me," Jack said, holstering his weapon.

Carter did the same, although she still looked wary. "How far is it?"

"Not far," James said. "Sting is waiting for us just beyond the perimeter."

"Sweet. Lead the way, Jamie."

With a nod he turned away, but then stopped and looked over his shoulder. "Stay in the shadows," he said quietly. "And it's James, by the way, not Jamie."

"Fine, whatever," Jack said, shooing him forward. "Just get us the hell out of here, Jim."

Carter shook her head, moving past him to follow O'Kane, but Jack didn't miss the smile she tried to hide. He counted it as a win.

# CHAPTER FOUR

BY THE time they'd reached the edge of the camp, dawn was graying the horizon. They'd stopped a couple times when Shadow's darts had passed too low overhead, hunkering down under scraps of tarp amid the silent, dead-eyed residents of the Shacks.

Once, Jack had heard the word 'feeder' hissed in the dark and O'Kane had stiffened at the implicit threat. But nothing had happened, no one had stirred.

These people had given up. But maybe — if this crazy-assed plan worked — SG-1 would be able to give them hope and that would be enough to get them on their feet and fighting.

Eventually they slipped past the watch towers in the indistinct light of pre-dawn, O'Kane leading them into the tree line where he stopped dead.

Jack almost ran into the back of him. "What are we — ?"

And then Sting was there. Gray as the morning, he simply emerged from the shadows. Startled, Jack's hand was on his weapon before he could stop himself.

Sting glanced down at the zat, unimpressed. "You have come to assist my queen?"

So much for small talk. "Nice to see you too, buddy. How've you been?"

Sting blinked his alien eyes and said, "Shadow's blades are in the skies above us. Every moment I am here I am in danger of discovery. I repeat my question: have you come to assist my queen pilot Shadow's hive?"

"Let's just say we have a proposal."

Sting's gaze travelled to Carter and back. "Then tell me —"

"I'd rather talk to your boss."

Sting hissed out a breath through his teeth, glanced up at the sky, and then turned with a swirl of his long coat and stalked through the trees. With a shrug in Carter's direction, Jack fell in behind him, Carter at his side, and O'Kane — presumably — keeping an eye on them from behind.

It was a short, steep climb to the shattered remains of Sting's ship. The air this high was cold and Jack ducked into the scant warmth of his jacket. He wondered if it ever got warm here in this sun-deprived world. Carter peered up at the hulk of the ship, something between pride and regret on her face as she took in the damage she'd caused. Not that the thing had been space-worthy anyway, but it was a total wreck now.

Sting stopped beneath the shadow of its hull and glanced at James. "Tell Stormfire we have returned. Prepare him."

With a nod and a wordless look at Jack and Carter, O'Kane slipped inside the ship and was gone.

"Pet monkey?" Jack said to Sting. "Thought you guys didn't go in for the whole 'worshiper' thing?"

"We do not give him the Gift of Life," Sting said. "He is here to —" He paused, and for a moment it looked like he was confused by his own answer. "He assists Stormfire." The expressions on his face were subtle, not easy to decipher, but when he spoke there was genuine distress in his voice. "You have seen what has become of Stormfire."

And he had. The Wraith was more than a couple of fries short of a Happy Meal — unpredictable and dangerous. "What's he got to do with this? We're not bringing Crazy along for the ride."

"That," Sting said, "is for Earthborn to decide. But there is no one who understands the devices of the Ancestors better than Stormfire." He paused, his attention shifting someplace else, and then he said, "Come. Earthborn awaits you."

The only other time he'd been aboard the ship, Jack had been too preoccupied with staying alive to do a whole lot of sightseeing. Now, however, even in the weak light, he could see how decrepit the whole thing was — the damn ship was *oozing*.

"It's dying," Carter said. She was one step ahead, almost

side-by-side with Sting. "Your ship is dying."

Sting's shoulders stiffened. "Yes."

After a beat, Carter said, "Is all Wraith technology like this — part biological?"

"Much of it is," he said. "To our great advantage. A skilled hive master can heal a damaged hive quicker than even the Ancestors could repair their ships. And a queen..." A soft hiss escaped. "There is no bond stronger than that between a queen and her hive, or a blade and his dart. Especially when in battle. They act as one."

And Jack could certainly see the advantage of that.

"Fascinating," Carter said, scanning the corridor as they walked. He could almost see her filing data away, trying to figure out how she could use this technology when they got home... If they got home. He shoved the doubts aside: one impossible situation at a time.

Sting slowed his pace and then turned into a small chamber that branched off from the corridor. Inside, the light was better but only by a small margin. It was enough, however, to reveal Earthborn rising to her feet from within a curved pod that may have been a bed or some kind of freaky cocoon. He let his attention linger on it for a moment before turning to the Wraith queen.

She was as imperious as ever, elegant and alien. Maybe, to Wraith eyes, she was even beautiful. From the way Sting watched her, Jack guessed she must be — either that or he was simply smitten.

Jack chanced a slight glance at Carter, then turned a smile on Earthborn. "See?" he said. "Told you I'd be back."

Earthborn inclined her head. "Teal'c and Daniel are not with you."

"No." He flattened his expression, giving nothing away. "They had other things to do. But you don't need them, do you? You just need me and my funky genes."

She didn't answer, her gaze sliding over to Sting. He could

almost hear their silent conversation: Sting urging caution, Earthborn throwing it to the wind.

When her attention returned to Jack, she said, "What is the proposal you bring?"

He spread his hands, striving for honesty. He wasn't lying, exactly. He was just selecting the truths he told with care. Hopefully her mind-reading powers only worked on other Wraith. "We'll help you," he said. "You get Carter and me to Shadow's hive, and we'll help you fly it."

Earthborn tilted her head. "Why Major Carter?"

"Because Carter's the best shot we got of figuring out how to fly the damn thing." And that was no lie — if she happened to stumble across one of the hybrids they needed to bring to Hecate then so much the better. "No offence to your crazy scientist."

"You refer to Stormfire?" Earthborn said. She didn't sound pleased. "His mind has been damaged, it is true — by war and by loss and grief — but he will be respected."

"Just so long as he doesn't throw me in jail again."

Earthborn didn't answer that, her attention once more on Sting. "My consort is incorrect," she said after a moment, as if she thought Jack could hear them. "Stormfire has great knowledge of the Ancestors' technology. He will be an asset on this mission."

"Uh, no." This was a line he wasn't prepared to cross for anyone. "He'll be a liability. I don't care how he got broken, but he's not coming with us. He could jeopardize the whole mission." He narrowed his eyes, trying to read her like he would a human. "I think you know that."

Averting her gaze, she said, "You will come with me now and we will talk with him. He has schematics of the ship, devices that may be of use to us when —"

"Us?" Sting said.

Earthborn's attention snapped to him, teeth bared in obvious irritation.

Sting took half a step backward — maybe he hadn't intended to say that out loud — but he didn't look contrite. "My queen, you cannot travel to Shadow's hive."

"And who are you to say what your queen can and cannot do?"

Sting's face hardened and there were a couple of long, uncomfortable beats of silence while they argued it out between them. Carter cleared her throat and lifted a curious eyebrow. Jack met her look with a shrug. Her guess was as good as his regarding who was going to come out on top, but his money was on Earthborn.

But then Sting said, "Shadow will sense you the moment you step aboard." He turned to Jack with a look that demanded backup.

Not that he wanted to get in the middle of this particular domestic dispute, but his ass was on the line too — and, more importantly, so was Carter's. And Earth's. "If that's true," he said, "then Sting's right. This has to be a covert op, or it'll fail. And then none of us will come back."

Earthborn's eyes flicked back to Sting — an obvious tell. Jack knew where her priorities lay.

"Once we have control of her hive," Carter added, "then you can confront Shadow. Which I guess is what you want?"

Earthborn narrowed her eyes. She looked like she was picking through Carter's thoughts — an uncomfortable image, given what they were hiding. "Very well," she said at last. "But know this: Shadow is mine to destroy and I will have her."

Jack shrugged his agreement, despite the way his stomach clenched with unease. Young though Earthborn appeared, she was not a woman — Wraith — to be crossed. Which was, of course, exactly what they were planning on doing.

Peachy.

From space, it was easy to detach oneself, Daniel thought. Standing by the window in the coolness of the ha'tak's viewing chamber, a certain objectivity established itself. He could be anywhere in the galaxy and the murk of brown spinning against the crisp blackness of space could be any planet. They would simply do what they always did in these situations: whatever it took to save the day.

But hard reality came in the knowledge that somewhere on this ship was his friend, Janet Fraiser. And somewhere inside her was a Goa'uld controlling her every word and movement. He'd gone through too much pain believing that Amaunet had not destroyed all that once was Sha're, clinging to the hope that his wife could be saved. He wouldn't return to that fantasy this time. But the fact that it was *Janet*, of all people, who was now playing host to the very thing he detested most... It was a twisted cruelty and once again Daniel couldn't help but envisage ways they might still save her.

But logic and experience told him that any hope of snatching a victory from this bleak situation lay in their plans to take down the Wraith. Which was why his mission to Arbella was so important. The planet below wasn't just anywhere; it was Earth, and the stakes were higher than they'd ever been.

The door behind him hissed open and Daniel pushed himself away from the window to see Rya'c enter. It was somewhat comforting to note that he'd changed out of the armor of Hecate's Jaffa.

"Has there been a reply?" asked Daniel.

Rya'c shook his head.

Daniel threw his hands up. "What the hell is keeping them?" Rya'c had sent word through to Arbella some time ago that SG-1 had succeeded in their mission and Daniel had thought the response would have been immediate. He found it more than surprising that a man like Jones, who'd seemed so desperate to get his wife back, would allow any delay in her return.

"You should not concern yourself, Dr. Jackson. In my experience with Arbella, I've often found their politics to be... thorny. It makes dealing with them problematical. They are a very closed off people."

"But, Rya'c, this is the man's wife we're talking about here. He's the leader of their world. Surely he has some sway in getting her back home as soon as possible?"

Rya'c rubbed a hand across his chin and frowned. "I admit I had hoped for a quicker resolution. But we must be patient."

Daniel took a breath and paced over to the window again. "I'm sorry. I guess you know a lot about patience."

"The Jaffa lifespan is all relative, Dr. Jackson. Our years don't seem as long to us as they might to you." He paused before adding, "Though it has been a long century."

"So do you think this is the end game?"

"I think..." Rya'c pursed his lips, considering. "I *hope* it is the beginning of a new chapter." Daniel tilted his head in question and Rya'c continued. "I spent many years resenting my father. I realize now it was unfair to him — indeed, I probably always knew it. But sometimes anger at the hand of fate asserts itself in irrational ways, and I blamed the Tau'ri for taking him from us. The boy I was back then would not have fought for the people of Earth. But then I met a person who reminded me of why my father chose to fight for you, of why he'd made his choices. And I honor that person to this day."

Daniel thought of the name Rya'c had chosen to be known by. "You mean Dave Dixon?"

Rya'c smiled and shook his head. "No, though Colonel Dixon was indeed a noble warrior and my choice of name is inspired by him. No, Dr. Jackson, it was Cassandra Fraiser who reminded me of the goodness inherent in the human race, and the worthiness of their fight. She was a soldier of noteworthy strength."

Daniel's eyebrows rose, thinking of the kid he'd last seen wearing braids and doing her math homework at Janet's kitchen table. "Cassandra? Cassandra was a soldier?"

Rya'c's face lit up with something almost like awe. "She was more than that. She was a leader. Colonel Dixon taught her to have compassion, but to be passionate about doing what was right."

Daniel smiled and looked away, lost for a second in the past. "I think maybe her mom had a lot to do with that first."

Rya'c inclined his head. "Perhaps. The Lady Hecate exhibits many traits that would indicate Janet Fraiser was a compassionate person."

The statement cut through Daniel's warm memories and he swallowed down the bitter taste. "You say Colonel Dixon taught Cassandra. You mean he raised her?"

"As I understand it."

"So when did he become Hecate's First Prime? And more importantly, why?" Daniel hadn't really known Dave Dixon, but Jack had respected him and that spoke to the man's character. He couldn't understand why someone like that, a military officer, would make the choice to become the right hand man to a System Lord. Unless… "You said that Colonel Dixon was loyal to Janet. Were they, um…?"

Rya'c held out his hands. "I can only surmise what Colonel Dixon's reasons were for choosing allegiance to my mistress. Though I do know that, without the Lady Hecate's intervention, Cassandra Fraiser would have died when she was sixteen."

"How?"

"The goddess was able to counter the effects of a retrovirus implanted inside Cassandra by the System Lord, Niirti. I believe this may have convinced Dixon that Janet Fraiser had indeed blended with the Lady Hecate."

Daniel squeezed his eyes shut. It was a lot to process and he wondered how Cassie had dealt with it all; losing her mother, only to see her again in the form of a Goa'uld. He was glad Dave Dixon had been there for her, when the rest of them weren't. He wondered if she'd ever blamed them for Janet's death — because, irrational though he knew it was, he couldn't help but blame himself. "Thank you," he said to Rya'c. "It's some comfort to know she had a friend in you."

"She had many friends, Dr. Jackson. And many followers. Cassandra Fraiser dedicated herself to defeating the Wraith. It will be fitting if SG-1 sees her legacy fulfilled."

With a frown, Daniel cast a glance back at the planet below, thinking of Sting and Earthborn and how the legacy Rya'c spoke of would see their people wiped out. It was necessary, he knew, to rid Earth of the Wraith, but the method they'd chosen did not sit well with him. But if what Hecate had told them was true, allowing Shadow's plan to come to fruition would be much worse.

He was saved from having to respond by the door opening once more. "Master Dix," said the young Jaffa who entered. "Arbella has made contact. They wish for Dr. Jackson and Teal'c to return with the president's wife."

It was with some anxiety that Daniel donned his BDUs in readiness for the return to Arbella. He shared a glance with Teal'c and thought he saw the same unease in the grim set of his jaw. The delay in Arbella's response was unsettling, made more so by the fact that apparently it wasn't Roz Bailey who had made contact, but the inscrutable Agent Yuma.

They made their way to the gateroom where, moments later, Rya'c entered with Lana Jones by his side, empty-eyed and shuffling. Rya'c's arm was around the woman and it looked as if he was holding her up. Daniel grimaced, thinking of what she had gone through — and how Jones would feel seeing the woman he loved reduced to such a shell.

"I worry that the return of his wife in such a condition will do more harm than good to our cause," said Teal'c in a low voice. It seemed harsh to think of their own agenda at such a time, but Daniel knew it was an important consideration; they needed Gunnison Jones on their side.

He walked over to Rya'c, taking Lana's arm and gripping her round the waist as gently as possible, while still holding her upright. The woman sagged against him, but didn't seem to register his presence. "Good luck, Dr. Jackson," said Rya'c, before turning to Teal'c. "*Tal'ma'te*, father. *Chel nok.*"

Teal'c bowed his head in acknowledgement and then stepped through the event horizon, with Daniel and Lana following seconds later. On the other side, they found themselves greeted by the cold eyes of Agent Yuma — and the wrong end of at least a half dozen automatic weapons.

"Well, this all seems familiar," he muttered, turning to Teal'c, only to witness him falling to the ground. Daniel barely had time to register the blow to the back of his own head, before the cold floor of the gateroom came up to meet him and blackness descended.

Despite the circumstances, Sam couldn't suppress a jolt of excitement when she stepped into the Wraith laboratory. They knew so little about the Ancients — the Gate Builders — and this place was brimming with artifacts and technologies the Wraith claimed were Ancient in origin. While the colonel talked with Earthborn, Sam let her eyes wander. The first thing she noticed was James O'Kane standing unobtrusively in the shadows. She nodded to him and he gave a sober nod in return.

Letting her eyes rove further she took in dozens of devices — some in pieces, some complete — all with the same consistency of design: sleek lines, muted colors, gentle organic structures. It was different, in almost every way, from the raw power of the Stargate. But then, she supposed, the gate network was probably one of the Ancient's earliest creations and their race had endured for millennia. It was no surprise their aesthetic taste had matured.

"Hey, Carter." The colonel jerked his head to beckon her over. "We need your smarts over here."

'Over here' was a long work bench where Sting and Earthborn stood with another Wraith, one Sam hadn't seen before. Unless…? She glanced at O'Neill, who gave a subtle roll of his eyes. "Carter this is 'Stormfire'," he said, putting air-quotes around the name. "He was the one trying to kill us last time we were here."

Right. She remembered: Stormfire was Jack's friend 'Crazy'. Getting a close look at the creature now, with his matted hair and off-kilter gait, Sam could see where the colonel was coming from with the name. Stormfire had nothing of the deadly poise possessed by Earthborn and Sting. He cocked his head and hissed a breath through his bared teeth, eyes somehow too wide. "This is your cleverman?"

"Less man, more clever," the colonel said. "And, yeah, Carter's a scientist. Also, she's coming with us. That's non-negotiable, by the way."

"And what do you know?" Stormfire said to Sam. "What do you know, cleverman?"

"What do I know?" She wasn't sure how to answer that. "Um, in general or specifically?"

"About the Ancestors." Stormfire took a shuffling step forward, his clawed fingers flexing like he was contemplating breakfast.

Sam willed herself not to take a step backward, pushed the memory of clawed fingers on her chest to the back of her mind. He couldn't hurt her, even if he tried. "Probably not as much as you," she conceded, "but I'm a quick study. Why don't you show me what you've got?"

"What I've *got*?" He barked a laugh and twisted around with his arms spread wide. "Everything and nothing. And eyes. Yes, yes. I have eyes and ears, but not hands to touch." He glanced at her over his shoulder. "Do you understand? Not hands to touch."

Beside her the colonel shifted, clearly made uncomfortable by Stormfire's erratic behavior. Given that he'd held the colonel prisoner for a couple days, Sam couldn't really blame him. But she thought she understood what Stormfire meant, why he was frustrated. "You can't access most of their technology," she said. "Because you don't have the Ancestors' gene."

Stormfire just hissed and, into the silence that followed,

Earthborn said, "None of my kind possesses the gene; the Ancestors designed it to be so."

"Because they didn't want you to use their stuff?" the colonel said.

"They created us," Earthborn said with a hint of old anger. "They abandoned us. And then they learned to fear us." She looked at Sting and something passed between them before she turned back to Sam. "I understand that in our own galaxy there are those who venerate the Ancestors as deities. But I cannot do so. If they were gods, then they were capricious and cruel."

The colonel grunted in agreement. "There's a lot of that going around."

Earthborn cut him a curious look — a little too curious. O'Neill shifted beneath it, as if he was afraid she might pluck Hecate's plan right out of his head — and, who knew, maybe she could? He should never have alluded to the Goa'uld and the colonel knew it.

Attempting to divert her attention, Sam said, "How much do you know about Shadow's hive? You said it was created by the Ancestors."

After another beat, Earthborn's gaze left the colonel and she gestured to Stormfire. "Show us the schematics." To Sam she said, "These were taken from Atlantis by Stormfire some years ago, however I believe they remain accurate."

But Stormfire wasn't cooperating. Instead, he shook his head, setting his ratty hair swaying. "What use are maps," he said, "if you can't open the door?"

"Never mind that," Earthborn snapped, "I would see —"

"Never *mind*?" Stormfire growled, sweeping one arm out as if to knock everything on the bench to the floor. But before he could, his hand was caught by O'Kane.

"Master," he said. "Take care."

Stormfire glared at him, teeth bared. But O'Kane didn't seem frightened. He just returned the glare until Stormfire's arm relaxed and he snatched his hand out of the man's grip. "There is too much to mind," Stormfire muttered under his breath and turned away from the bench.

O'Kane watched him go, and then said, "I can show you the schematics."

Moving to a console, O'Kane touched the interface. Sam recognized the alien script that spilled across the screen from her own attempt to penetrate the Wraith's computer system. But, unlike her, O'Kane clearly knew what he was doing.

"James," she said, moving to stand at his shoulder, "you can read that?"

"Some of it, yes. Enough to be of use, at least." He touched something and the screen filled with schematics rendered in three dimensions, turning slowly to illustrate all aspects.

"Wow." Sam sucked in a breath and glanced over at the colonel. "It's huge, sir."

He cocked an eyebrow. "So I've been told."

Really, that did *not* warrant the smile that twitched at the corner of her mouth, so she bit down on it and fixed her eyes on the screen. "Does it show the labs where the hybrids are being created?"

"Until I saw it for myself," Sting said, "I would never have believed such a monstrosity possible."

"This development," Earthborn said, "is new. It is likely that these plans predate it."

Which was unlucky; it meant they'd need to access Atlantis's computers to track the lab down first. There was no way they could simply search a ship of this size. "What's that?" Sam said, pointing to a thin line that ran along the edge of the plan. She thought she knew, but hoped she was wrong.

Behind her, she could feel O'Neill come to stand at her shoulder. "Looks like a shield," he said.

O'Kane nodded. "Yes, Colonel. That's exactly what it is."

"Which is why you will need to enter the city in a dart," Sting said from the other side of the bench. "I will pilot and communicate with the hive."

It also meant that, to leave with the hybrid, they'd need to get out the same way. Sam looked at the colonel and, from his somber expression, she knew he was thinking the same thing. Sting would get them in, but getting out with the hybrid was going to be a problem.

"You know," the colonel said, with that lazy charm he occasionally deployed, "I'm a pretty good pilot myself. Think I could fly one of your darts?"

Sting's eyes narrowed. "That will not be necessary."

"Yeah, but if it was? I mean — is it like the Ancient gizmos? Do I need Wraith DNA to operate a dart?" He gave a slight shudder — Sam probably only noticed it because she was standing so close. "Would I need to plug myself in, or something?"

After a beat of silence, Sting said, "It would not be as efficient, but it would be possible for a human to pilot a dart. If necessary." He showed his teeth and added, "Do you foresee it becoming necessary, O'Neill?"

"Always need a Plan B," the colonel said with an easy smile. "And usually a plan C, D and E."

Sting didn't reply to that, just stared at O'Neill. He obviously didn't trust them and it made Sam squirm because he had good reason. Their deal with Hecate didn't sit right with her, but what choice did they have? Let Shadow develop an army of hybrids? Besides, they had no reason to trust the Wraith any more than Hecate — less so, perhaps, given their nature. Better the devil you know… And yet it still felt wrong. It just did.

Into the silence, O'Kane said, "Actually, I think there might be some kind of short-range ships on the hive. I've been studying the schematic and think I've identified docking bays." He touched the screen. "Here. And also here. It's possible the ships are still aboard Atlantis; the Wraith wouldn't be able to fly them and you could use one of them to leave the hive if it wasn't possible to return to the dart."

Sam gave the colonel a sharp look. If O'Kane was right, then O'Neill with his Ancient gene should be able fly one of those ships.

He caught her eye and smiled. "Plan B, then." Turning to Sting, he said, "So I guess we should talk tactics..."

But they knew so little about Ancient technology, about this alien environment they were heading into, that Sam couldn't help feeling like they were going in blind. She threw a glance at Stormfire, but he was murmuring to himself, engrossed by one of the Ancient devices, and she knew the colonel was right. Bringing him would be impossible.

While the colonel and Sting talked, Sam turned to O'Kane. "Is there any way you can download the schematic so we can take a copy with us? It'll be pretty difficult to orient ourselves when we arrive."

He shook his head. "But I have made some sketches in my files," he said, turning to a shadowed area at the back of the laboratory. "Would you like to see?"

Catching the colonel's eye — he was half watching her while he discussed infiltration and exfiltration with Sting — he gave a slight nod. Not that she needed his permission in this strange new world, but it was habit and oddly comforting to maintain the illusion of chain of command.

Following O'Kane further into the lab, she let her eyes drift over the myriad devices scattered across the benches. Stormfire had quite the collection. In the furthest corner, James kept his research. A series of bound paper volumes of notes, quaintly old fashioned even by her standards — positively ancient by his.

"I prefer not to keep my research in the hive's database," he explained as he offered her one of the thick books. "In case we ever need to move on at short notice." For an instant, he met her eyes and then looked away; she knew what he meant. With his research so portable, if he ever wanted to escape he could take it all with him.

"Understandable," she said, keeping her voice neutral as she began to flip through. It was all very well ordered, although most of the writing was in a language Sam didn't understand. "Is this Ancient?"

"Quite old, yes."

"No—" She smiled. "No, sorry. I mean, is it the language of the Ancestors?"

"Oh! Yes. Most of it is Lantean." He pointed to a couple of other sketches. "That's Wraith."

Sam nodded and continued looking through the book. There were schematics and diagrams meticulously copied out and labeled, but none of it was in English. "This is a Stargate," she said, looking up from one sketch.

"*Astria Porta*, yes. There is one in Atlantis."

And that provoked a whole slew of questions Sam didn't have time to ask. She kept looking through the book, page after page of detailed drawings and notes. "This is very impressive," she said, looking up with a smile. "But I—" She stopped, her eye caught by something. It was an odd boxy shaped ship labeled *navis temporis*. "What's this?"

O'Kane crooked his head to see. "Ah, yes, that's one of the short-range ships I was talking about." He took the book from her hand and flipped forward a couple more pages. "Here," he said, "this is where they're kept—directly above the *Astria Porta*. Given their dimensions, I think they're designed to descend through this shaft and actually fly through the *Astria Porta*—the 'Stargate'."

"Wow," Sam said. "They're little gate-ships."

"I suppose you could call them that…"

Sam nodded, but her mind was caught on something else and she flipped back to the previous picture. "*Navis temporis*," she said. "That's what the Ancestors called them?"

Scratching a hand through his short hair, O'Kane said, "I don't think so. That just refers to this one—it means something like 'ship of time.'"

Sam stared at him. "Ship of time?"

"Something *like* that." He gave an awkward shrug. "I found the image in an encrypted file belonging to someone called Janus. I think he was an inventor; he'd filed details of all sorts of projects."

Running her finger over the drawing, Sam tried not to get her hopes up. "Did it say what the project's objective was?"

"No. Only that it was terminated."

"Terminated why?"

"That's all it says on the file."

In all likelihood, *navis temporis* didn't mean what Sam hoped it might. What were the odds of finding an actual time machine just sitting there waiting for them? And yet... "It's still on Atlantis?"

"There's no mention of it being destroyed," O'Kane said. "Unless that's what 'terminated' means." He pointed to some other words, none of which Sam could read. "It says it was held in the docking bay with the other, um, 'gate-ships'."

Sam gave a thoughtful hum and looked over to where the colonel and Sting were talking. If anyone could invent time travel technology, it would be the Ancients. But there was no way to know if that's even what this was or if it had ever worked. It certainly wasn't enough to warrant changing their plans and so there was no point in taking it to the colonel. Yet. And, anyway, who knew how he'd respond to the idea of going back and fixing things? He seemed pretty wedded to this messed up version of the future.

So Sam filed the possibility away in the back of her mind and handed the book to O'Kane. "You read Lantean?"

"Stormfire has allowed me to study it, yes. But it's limited to what's available on documents such as these." He frowned down at his book. "I hadn't considered that someone other than I would need to interpret these notes."

"It's okay," she said, although really it wasn't. They needed more than just blind luck if they were going to find the hybrids and — "Wait." She turned back to the colonel. "Sir?"

O'Neill looked over. "Carter?"

"Colonel, what if we bring James with us?" She put a hand on his shoulder. "If you're willing, that is?"

His eyes widened and fixed on Earthborn as he said, "Of course. If my service is required."

"Sir, we'll need to access Atlantis's computer systems to locate the hybrid lab. And James can read Lantean — that could really come in handy."

But the misgiving on the colonel's face was obvious: James O'Kane was an unknown quantity and therefore the last person the colonel wanted with them on a covert mission. "Carter, you can figure out —"

"Yes sir." She cut him off before he went too far down the 'Carter can do anything' route. "Given time, I could probably figure it out. But we won't have that kind of time. And if James is already familiar with the language and the technology we'll be dealing with, then why reinvent the wheel?"

The colonel's lips tightened. She could see him turning the idea over in his head, looking at all the angles. "Sting, what do you think?"

Sting was silent, but from the way he was watching Earthborn it was clear that they were having a private discussion. After a moment, he looked away and said, "It is testament to the disorder of this world that I should consider embarking on a mission of such importance in the company of none but three humans. However, I am instructed to do so." His gaze flicked to Earthborn and back. "I serve at my queen's pleasure."

The colonel's lips curled at the corner. "I'll take that as a yes."

Sting inclined his head, but didn't comment.

"This task you undertake," Earthborn said, "is of the utmost importance. You must destroy the abominations Shadow is creating before they are hatched. It is the only chance we have to free my people from Shadow's hold and to return to our home and the life for which we were born."

*Hunting humans*, Sam reminded herself when her stomach gave a guilty twist. *Eating people.*

"This mission will save us all," Earthborn continued. "It is worth making bargains with the enemy to achieve it, is it not, O'Neill?"

Sam found herself gazing at the floor, uncomfortable with how close that got to their hidden truth.

"Sometimes," the colonel said, "you just gotta do what you gotta do to survive."

# CHAPTER FIVE

**Arbella — 2098:** Consciousness returned in a slow bloom of pain and dizziness. Daniel waited a few moments for the dull ache to ease, before sitting up, rubbing the back of his head. "Ow… What the hell happened?"

"We have been imprisoned," said Teal'c. He sat cross legged on the bunk opposite, staring at the door.

Daniel squinted around the small room, patting his pockets. "Hey, did they take — ? Oh. Thanks," he said, when Teal'c proffered his glasses. "Are we still in the Stargate facility?" he said once he could see properly again. The bare walls gave nothing away.

"We are. Agent Yuma had us escorted here. Or rather I was escorted. You were carried."

Ignoring what he suspected was straight-faced Jaffa sass, Daniel stood and walked over to the door, trying the handle. It didn't budge. He sensed Teal'c watching him and gave him a sideways glance. "Already tried that, huh?"

Teal'c merely inclined his head.

Returning to the bunk, Daniel climbed up on it to peer out of the tiny window. In the near distance, the lights of Laketown sparkled in the approaching night. Twilight cast shades of violet across the landscape, mingling with the ochre of the Arbellan rocks to create a picture that was quite beautiful. He'd seen enough of this society's inner workings, however, to understand that not all here was as shiny as it seemed. Their current accommodation was proof enough of that, though he'd thought that the success of their mission would have engendered a little more warm feeling towards them. "Do you know where they took Lana?"

"I only saw her being led out of the gateroom. I assume they have taken her to President Jones."

"I guess he's not big on gratitude, huh?" It was a glib comment, but Daniel kept returning to what Teal'c had said before they'd come through the gate. He could imagine how Jones might feel, having his wife finally returned to him, only to find her so broken, her mind perhaps irreparably damaged. Of course SG-1 weren't to blame for her condition, but it was possible that wouldn't matter to Jones. Daniel knew too well how irrational one's thoughts could be when it came to the wellbeing of the woman you loved. "So any ideas on how we get out of here?"

"There is a guard on the other side of that door. I could easily disarm him if we can find a way to open the door. I know the route back to the gateroom, however..."

"However it's full of security force officers," finished Daniel. "Not that I'm doubting your skills, Teal'c, but I don't like the odds of us against a room full of armed men and women."

"I agree," said Teal'c. "Their officers are poorly trained and lack any battle readiness; however their numbers would compensate for that. We would never make it to the Stargate."

"Let's think about how we'd get the door open first. Has anyone been in?"

"Not since they brought us here."

For an alarming moment, Daniel wondered if they just planned to leave them here until they starved to death, but he dismissed the idea. The Arbellans might be bull-headed and insular, but he'd not sensed that they were cruel. Yuma was likely just making them sweat it out. As if in response to his thoughts, there was the sound of the door being unlocked and Daniel jumped back just as it opened. From the corner of his eye, he saw Teal'c stand in one fluid motion, tense and ready for action if necessary.

A guard whose face he didn't recognize held the door open for Agent Yuma to enter. She was trailed by two other guards who took up positions inside the room. The door guard left, locking the door behind him.

"Sit please," she said, gesturing to the bunk behind Teal'c.

"Uh, I think I'd rather stand," said Daniel.

Yuma's expression didn't change as she turned to one of her guards and said, "Have them sit."

Teal'c stepped forward at the same time the guard did, hands balling into fists, but Daniel stayed him with a hand on his arm. "Alright," he said to Yuma. He knew it for a power play; he also knew that she'd just established the upper hand. He felt some of the tension leave Teal'c's arm, but he knew the Jaffa would be ready to move if danger presented itself. He only hoped he could keep up if the time came. "I'm not sure why we're being held here," Daniel said to Yuma. "We had an agreement with President Jones. You know that."

"No, Dr. Jackson, *SG-1* had an agreement with the president."

Daniel gave a puzzled laugh and glanced at Teal'c, before pulling at his own sleeve so that Yuma could see the patch there. He raised his eyebrows expectantly, knowing he was being facetious, but feeling a dangerous urge to provoke the woman.

With a brief glance at the SG-1 patch, she gave him a cold smile and said, "You are one half of SG-1. Where are Colonel O'Neill and Major Carter?"

"On Earth," he replied.

"Doing what?"

"Uh, not much. All their favorite hang-outs are pretty much dust these days."

"What are they planning?"

The agent's attitude was beginning to rile. Daniel was hungry, thirsty and the base of his skull was still really resenting the blow from the butt of a gun. "They're doing what Arbella won't and trying to save Earth from the Wraith."

Yuma laughed — the only real human gesture she'd shown since entering the room. "Alone?" she said, incredulous.

Daniel hesitated, angry with himself for saying too much. Now he could either lie, making Jack and Sam look reckless and stupid, and risk being called on it, or he could tell the truth about their temporary truce with Hecate — a Goa'uld who had been involved in the first invasion of Earth.

Teal'c saved him from the choice. "Agent Yuma, I do not believe the movements of Colonel O'Neill and Major Carter need concern you."

"Is that so?" she said, and Daniel didn't like the assurance of her tone. This wasn't going anywhere good. "Perhaps I should be more concerned with their — and your — movements in Laketown. Or even the datacenter?"

Unease clawed at Daniel's stomach. "I don't —"

Yuma's raised hand cut him off. "Sedition is a serious offence on Arbella, Dr. Jackson. Especially when those accused conspire to destroy everyone who has ever lived here and everything we have ever created."

It was useless to deny Yuma's accusations; he doubted very much that she would have plucked the idea out of thin air, and so Sam's research must have left a trail. "That's not what we wanted to do," said Daniel, though he knew the truth of his words was very much open to interpretation. Wasn't that what the four of them had argued over? Even now the idea of changing the past and erasing the Arbellan people from history was very much on the table — it was only the lack of means that had stopped them. So far.

"That's exactly what you were planning. Even the Jaffa doesn't deny it." Teal'c's silence was indeed damning, but Daniel couldn't blame him for refusing to lie about his stance on the matter; he doubted it would make a difference anyway. "So I ask again," continued Yuma, "where are O'Neill and Carter? And how are they planning to strike against Arbella?"

"What? They're not!" It was one thing acknowledging the plan to rectify the timeline, but Yuma surely couldn't believe that SG-1 would strike directly against what were, in effect, their own people. She gestured to one of the guards, who grabbed Daniel from the bunk and shoved him up against the wall.

When Teal'c made a move, the other guard had a weapon in his face in less than a second. Daniel held out a hand to tell him he was okay.

"Tell me where they are," said Yuma again, her voice stony.

"They're on Earth trying to defeat the Wraith."

"You're lying."

"I'm not."

"Where are they?"

"On Earth," he ground out. "Trying to defeat the Wraith. Which maybe they wouldn't have to do, if you people would just accept responsibility and do something to help."

"Where are they?"

It was clear nothing he said would convince her, but he wasn't confident they'd get out of the room in one piece if he revealed the full extent of the plan to Yuma. However, there was an alternative. "Let me speak to General Bailey."

Yuma stepped closer to him and narrowed her eyes. "And what does Bailey have to do with this?"

"Nothing. But whatever we have to say, I want to say it to her." Over Yuma's shoulder, he could see Teal'c, tension in his stance, the guard's weapon still pointed at his temple.

"You should understand, Dr. Jackson. Roz Bailey is not your ally. And any association with you does not reflect well on her. Are you telling me that she's aware of whatever plan you and your teammates have concocted?"

"There is no plan."

After another moment of scrutiny, Yuma stepped back and gestured for her guards to stand down. "Alright, Jackson. If this is how you want to play it. But trust me, I'm a resourceful woman. You have information. I want it. And one way or another, I will get it." She turned and walked toward the door, but just before she knocked to attract the door guard's attention she said, "Bring the Jaffa."

"No!" Daniel ran forward, but a backhand across his face sent him crashing to the ground.

Teal'c lunged for Yuma, but before he could lay a hand on her a gunshot echoed loud in the room.

At first, Daniel thought it was a warning shot — until he saw the bloom of red, barely visible on Teal'c dark BDUs. "Teal'c!"

The Jaffa sagged, caught by the two guards before he could hit the ground, and then was dragged from the room.

The slam of the door was hardly audible above the ringing in Daniel's ears. And then he was alone in the room with only the spatter of blood on the tiles to show that Teal'c had been there at all.

**Earth — 2098:** Sting had not visited Shadow's hive since before Brightstar's death, yet he remembered the discordant sense of wrong that permeated the Ancestor's city. He began to feel it even as he approached, skimming his dart low across the planet's choppy southern ocean toward the fracturing light where Atlantis crouched beneath its shield. To his eye, the city was a dead thing. There was no life in the technology of the Ancestors, unlike the living hives of the Wraith, and for Shadow to make her home there was as obscene as anything else she had imposed upon her people.

His people too, he reminded himself. Many of those who now bent the knee to Shadow had once served Brightstar. She too, though it pained him to doubt the wisdom of his long-dead queen, had once been seduced by Shadow's dream of venturing beyond their galaxy and into these plentiful, corrupting feeding grounds.

But Brightstar could not have known the consequence of that choice — the degrading effect of a human population so abundant that there was no need to sleep, no need to hunt. Wraith were more than creatures of pleasure. They must feed to live, but they should not live only to feed and grow fat and lazy in their indolence.

It would end soon, however, if all went to plan. Those who had deserted Brightstar would bend their knee to her daughter, and Earthborn would lead their people — whole once more — back to the hunting grounds of his youth. There, they would be Wraith once more.

He glanced down at his controls, the indicators showing him three lives held safe within the dart's buffer. O'Neill, Carter, O'Kane: allies of convenience and he knew he could trust none of them to further his interests. O'Neill least of all. The humans had their own agenda and no matter how strongly Earthborn believed it coincided with their own objectives, Sting knew the humans would serve their own welfare first — as would he. And, although O'Neill and Carter had once saved his life, he would not hesitate to drink them dry if they sought to betray his queen.

As alliances went, it was uneasy.

Beneath him, the gray ocean bucked and swelled and the dart jolted through the turbulent air currents. Ahead, loomed Atlantis. Sting braced his mind for the contact that would soon come from Queen Shadow's blades — those charged with sweeping the area for incoming assault. The parasite-god, on occasion, still sent her fighters to harry the Wraith, though it had been many years since a concerted attack had been launched.

Sting had assumed it was because the enemy had been cowed by Shadow's power, yet, having seen the hybrid creature she had bred, he began to suspect that something more sinister was at play.

*Identify yourself.* The sharp demand snapped into his mind, shattering his thoughts.

Here was the most dangerous part of the deception. *I am Keenedge, summoned by Queen Shadow to report upon the disaster at the laboratory,* Sting said, projecting his memory of the young blade's mind: sharp and slick, youthful and arrogant. If the Wraith who spoke to him had known Keenedge, or if he had once known Sting, the ruse would fail. Sting kept his mind focused and let his unease play into the deception. *I fear our queen is displeased.*

He sensed discomfort from the Wraith, some fear, and a desire to break the contact. *Proceed to dock,* he said, layering his thoughts with something like condolence. *It will go worse for you if you keep her waiting.*

*My thanks,* Sting said. It took great effort to suppress the wave of relief that followed until he was certain his connection with the other's mind was severed. Even then, he permitted himself little more than a smile as the energy shield shivered out of existence long enough for his dart to pass through.

The light on his console blinked at him and he tried not to feel like a traitor to his own kind, bringing these humans here to overturn the power of a queen. But Earthborn had made her decision and it was his duty to obey. He served only one queen, after all.

Atlantis, as inhabited by the Ancestors, had been a city of harsh light, spindly spires and barren outdoor platforms. Much of that was now softened by a thick layer of hive-flesh, although it could not disguise the alien structure of the city. But rather than comforting, Sting found the sight disconcerting; the hive-flesh grew in clumps and tendrils, hanging heavy between towers and sagging in pouches from the balconies that dotted the city. It only added to the grotesque deformity of the hive, and Sting would have averted his eyes had he not been searching for a suitable place to empty his passengers from the buffers. Outside, in the glare of daylight, would be best; Wraith eyes worked less well in such conditions. He could leave the dart on one of the platforms, where no Wraith would willingly venture. And it would be easier to escape from there than from the middle of a heavily guarded dart bay.

It took a couple of passes over the city to identify what he wanted: an empty platform at the far end of one of the city's piers. He came in low and slow, engaged the culling beam in reverse as he swept the dart over the platform and hoped his aim was true. Only a small error would see the humans floundering in the ocean and he suspected the cold water would kill them before he could snatch them out again.

But his third pass over the platform showed him O'Neill and the other two dropping into a low crouch on the pier. O'Neill lifted an arm to wave and Sting brought his dart around to land, kicking up grit and making the humans turn their backs, covering their faces against the swirl of dust as he touched down.

Wasting no time, he opened the cockpit before the engine had started to cool, leaving the dart to take care of herself as Sting climbed out and down. The first thing he heard in the cold Atlantis air was Carter saying,

"...incredible. Daniel would love this."

"Daniel can tag along next time," O'Neill said, squinting up at Sting. "So here we are, safe and sound," he said, in a tone that betrayed as much mistrust as Sting felt. In that, at least, they were in agreement: neither trusted the other.

Sting jumped down onto the landing platform. "Did you imagine I would drop you in the water?"

"It crossed my mind."

"There would be more rewarding ways to kill you," Sting replied and flexed his feeding hand to emphasize the point.

O'Neill's response was an unreadable smile. "Jamie," he said. "Which way now?"

Stormfire's assistant — it was difficult to associate him with the name 'James O'Kane' — looked up from the file he carried, frowning. "I think this is the *Pila Orientalis*," he said. "And it's James, not Jamie, please."

"Right," O'Neill said. "You want to try that in English this time, Jimmy?"

O'Kane blinked in irritation and said, "Roughly, that would translate as the 'east walkway'." He tapped his book and said, "The control room where the *Astria Porta* is located is housed in the central tower. We should be able to access their computer system from there and locate the hybrid laboratory."

"The central tower," Carter said, shading her eyes as she looked up at the imposing structures looming above them.

"That thing's huge."

"It's a city," O'Kane said. "What did you expect?"

Neither O'Neill nor Carter answered that, so Sting said, "We must hurry. Our arrival will soon be detected."

O'Neill nodded. "Then lead the way, Jimmy."

"It's — never mind," O'Kane said, and headed out along the length of the pier.

O'Neill and Carter exchanged a brief, smiling look, and then followed side by side, both wary and alert. Sting threw a regretful glance at the dart — too exposed in the open, but there was no more he could do to hide her — and followed. If their mission was successful he would not need the dart to return to Earthborn.

He tried not to think about the enormity of that small word 'if'.

# CHAPTER SIX

WHATEVER Jack had been expecting when they started their little jaunt to the Emerald City, it wasn't this: sweeping spires and arches filling the sky, an elegance of architecture unlike anything he'd seen off-world. Nothing like the ostentation of the Goa'uld or the sleek, impersonal lines of the Asgard, this city was beautiful. Or it would have been if it hadn't been for the ugly termite nests growing all over the damn place, strung in bulging sacks between the towers and giving him the urge to poke them with a stick and run like hell.

Inside, it was worse. What once must have been wide, well-proportioned corridors were overgrown with Wraith crud, making them dark and oppressive. Hot, too. He could feel sweat on his neck, running slow down his spine.

"Hive-flesh," Sting murmured as they passed a wall scarred and slimy with the stuff. Sting was careful not to touch, though, and Jack remembered that this 'hive-flesh' was alive — that it might be able to recognize that Sting played for the wrong team. "Even here," the Wraith mused, eyes gleaming in the low light, "it tries to bring life."

Whatever. To Jack it just looked gross, as parasitic as the Goa'uld and even more alien. It reminded him way too much of those cocoons his team had woken up in after Sting — and he hadn't forgotten that it was *Sting* — had ordered them swept up in a snatcher beam and Saran-wrapped as snacks for his queen.

"O'Kane," Jack said, pitching his voice low as he drew level with the man. "How far up the tower do we need to go?"

"Almost to the top," he said, consulting his book. "But I believe... There may be a transportation method to take us there."

"Like an elevator?" Jack glanced back at Carter and couldn't keep the incredulous amusement off his face. "The Ancients built elevators? Do you think they play Ancient Muzak?"

Carter cracked a smile as she crowded closer and squinted over O'Kane's shoulder. "I doubt it's an elevator, sir," she said, spoiling his fun. "But perhaps it's some kind of internal transporter, like Goa'uld transport rings?"

That sounded more credible. He pushed his ball cap up away from his eyes and peered at the scribbles in O'Kane's book; none of it made much sense. "We don't want to just beam into the middle of Wraith Central," he said, pointing out the obvious.

Carter hummed her agreement. "There," she said, touching something on the drawing. "What's that? It has a transporter terminus and it's on the same level as the gate room, but it's separate."

"Could be anything," Jack said, and, damn, but he hated not having up-to-date intel. "Could be a Wraith bathroom for all we know."

Behind them, Sting bristled. "That is unlikely."

"Sir, it has to be better than transporting direct to the gate room," Carter countered. "And we'll have the element of surprise."

"And nothing but a couple of zats to fight with."

"I also am armed," Sting reminded him. "And, in addition to my stunner, I have a number of explosives."

"Okay." Jack rubbed at the back of his neck, settled his cap back in place. It was better than nothing. "That's our best plan?" he said to Carter.

She gave a slight shrug. "Yes sir."

"Sting?" Jack said. "What do you think? You've been here before, right?"

"Many years ago, although I was not permitted entry to the command areas." He glanced at O'Kane's book. "It is impossible to tell what the room is for — possibly, it is a retiring room for Queen Shadow. Or a place where she meets with her zenana.

It is likely she would have private quarters close to the heart of her hive's command."

None of which sounded encouraging and Jack shared a wary glance with Carter.

"However," Sting said, "I do not know how — or even if — Shadow can communicate with this hive. It is… malformed, mere hive-flesh grafted onto the Ancestors' city. It may be that she does not command her hive as other queens do. It certainly does not fly at her command." His odd, reptilian eyes came to rest on Jack. "And Carter is correct about one thing: we will have the element of surprise."

"I say we go for it, sir," Carter said, settling on the balls of her feet, ready to go.

And that was enough for Jack; what choice did they really have, anyway? "Okay," he said. "Let's go find the elevator."

As it turned out, the transporter did kinda look like an elevator. Or a closet. Jack eyed it suspiciously as they crowded inside — talk about sitting ducks. "Are we sure this is a good idea, Carter?"

She was studying a control panel on the back wall of the tiny chamber, all of which had lit up as they'd stepped inside. In answer to his question she only said, "Sir, it looks like this can take us anywhere on the transportation network." She touched her fingers to the screen. "Ready?"

Not really, but what the heck? "Beam us up, Carter."

He heard her huff a laugh, there was a moment of dislocation, and then… Nothing changed. Jack blinked. "Did it work?"

"I think so." Carter was still staring at the controls. "At least, the schematic is showing us on the command level of the central tower." She came to stand with him before the doors, her zat unholstered and ready. "I guess all these elevators look the same on the inside, sir."

Which meant there could be anything on the other side of that door. "Here goes nothing," he said, and hit the door control.

It slid open onto a dark room — well, more like a glorified alcove — with an archway on the far side opening onto a shadowy corridor. In silence, Jack gestured for the others to follow as he crept toward the arch and peered into the corridor beyond. It was swathed with Wraith gunk, the light too dim to make out details.

After trading a swift look with Carter he stepped out, weapon raised, Carter moving to cover his back.

"Clear," she said, keeping her voice low as she scanned her half of the hallway.

"Clear," Jack confirmed. "Any idea where we are?"

"We should be just outside the gate room, sir."

Sting glanced further down the corridor. "There — that door," he said, stalking towards it with his long coat flapping. He held a hand close to, but not touching, the hive-flesh clinging to the door. Head cocked, it was clear that he was listening.

"There are Wraith inside," he murmured. "Several. They are...bored."

"Well," Jack said, "why don't we make their day more interesting?" He leveled a finger at O'Kane. "*You* stay out here."

"But I —"

"Uh!" He was brooking no argument on this; O'Kane was an unknown quantity and he didn't want him getting under his feet in a firefight. "Stay put until we call you." To Carter he said, "You're with me. Sting — take point."

Sting turned a narrow gaze on him and said, "I would rather not have your weapon at my back, O'Neill."

"Oh for —" He bit off the curse. "You think I'm gonna shoot you in the back *now*?"

A slow blink, a baring of teeth. "We will move together," he said, and drew his stunner.

Gritting his teeth against the argument, Jack said, "Fine. On three. One, two —"

Sting hit the door controls and they were out into a large room. A half dozen Wraith lounged at their posts on a mezzanine level at the top of a sweeping staircase. In Jack's peripheral vision, a Stargate loomed.

Caught unaware, the Wraith were slow to respond when Jack opened fire. His zat didn't make much of an impact, but Sting's blaster took out two of the bastards before they could even draw their weapons.

But it wasn't enough to suppress their fire completely, and a bolt of blue energy hit the floor at Jack's feet, sending him dancing backward. Sting kept advancing, though, and Jack ducked in behind him, Carter on his heels.

They made it to the foot of the stairs as another Wraith went down at the top, convulsing under Sting's stunner fire.

"Cover me!" Jack barked, dashing up the stairs and diving full-length onto the floor as Sting's weapons-fire spat overhead.

Crunching into an inert body, Jack pulled the stunner from its lifeless fingers and opened fire.

Carter was right behind him, sheltering at the top of the stairs as she took out another Wraith just as it reared up from behind a console at the back of the room.

"Sir!" she yelled. "Behind you!"

He spun in time to see two of the faceless Wraith — Sting had called them drones — charging up the stairs from the level below. He took out the closest one and Carter took the second with her MP5 — must have been saving the last of her ammo. Jack followed up with a shot from his stolen stunner to finish the job.

Sudden silence rang in his ears, punctuated only by his harsh breathing as he climbed to his feet. Eight Wraith were down, but he, Carter, and Sting were unscathed. Something of a miracle.

Carter was already at one of the consoles on the mezzanine, practically standing on a sprawled Wraith body. "Sir, we need to secure the doors. I think you have to do it."

"Me? Carter, I can barely work my TV remote."

"James!" she called. "Get up here." She gave Jack a worried look. "Reinforcements must be on their way."

"They are," Sting confirmed, shifting uneasily. "You must secure this room now."

O'Kane came barreling up the stairs into the control area, and to his credit he didn't even look frightened. If anything, he looked fascinated. Kind of like Daniel. "This is incredible," he said, glancing around with round eyes.

"I know." But Carter didn't spare a glance from the console. "How does the colonel take control?"

O'Kane looked at him. "Ah — you just have to tell it to do it, Colonel."

"What?"

He gestured around. "Lantean technology was designed to interface with the minds of the Ancestors. If your Lantean gene is powerful enough, the city should respond to your commands."

"Carter?" There had to be a button or something to press.

Eyes wide, she could only shrug. "Sir, there are a dozen Wraith components grafted onto the Ancient technology. Even if I had time to get through it —"

Doors opened from some kind of balcony at the back of the room and two Wraith drones appeared, weapons raised.

"O'Neill!" Sting barked, opening fire on the newcomers. "Take control. Now!"

Ducking a bolt of stunner fire, Jack slammed a hand down onto the console. It was ridiculous, but he'd seen plenty of insanity in the three years he'd been leading SG-1 so what was one more piece of crazy?

Closing his eyes, he tried to concentrate on the city — on this room. On doors closing, shields rising. Locking everything down. Something shivered, just beyond his perception. Almost an echo bouncing back to him. Then something *moved* and it was darker. He could hear himself breathe, Carter too, sharp and quick. And then Sting, O'Kane. And others — a dozen others — and then everyone until it was all pressing in and he gasped himself upright, eyes flashing open.

Carter was staring at him. "Sir," she said, somewhere between awed and astonished, "you did it."

Carefully climbing to his feet, he saw that enormous doors had closed over all the windows and that the room now stood in twilight.

Sting bared his teeth, hissing out a breath. From outside came the dull thud of weapons fire against the blast doors and Jack had a feeling that he'd only succeeded in trapping them here.

For the first time since they arrived, he took a good look around the place. It was cavernous, proportioned like a cathedral, with a grand set of stairs sweeping down to the Stargate. He frowned and took a step closer to the railing of the mezzanine. The gate looked...different. For starters, there was no ramp and the chevrons were all wrong.

"They're different constellations," Carter said from behind him. "If we needed further proof that this thing came from another galaxy, that's it."

Snatching his cap from his head, Jack scrubbed a hand through his sweaty hair. "Could we dial the Earth gate from here?"

There was a pause. "I don't know, sir. I don't know how that would work exactly."

Which ruled out the gate as an escape route. Peachy. "Sting — any idea how we get out of here in one piece?"

The Wraith bared his teeth. "We fight."

"I don't like those odds," he said, although he wasn't sure they had an option. Biting down on his anxiety he said, "Carter, O'Kane — figure out where Shadow's keeping her Frankenstein lab."

"We're on it, sir."

Turning back to the strange Stargate, Jack considered their options. After a moment, he felt a presence at his side and looked over to find Sting standing near him, his attention also fixed on the gate. "Had Earthborn a hive to return to," he said, "we could step through the *Astria Porta* and leave this galaxy behind." He slid Jack a sideways glance. "Then we would not require you to pilot this abomination."

There was an undertow of melancholy in the Wraith's voice that tugged at Jack's guilty conscience. "Homesick, huh?"

"If you mean that I yearn to return, then yes. I am 'home sick'."

Daniel would have probably offered reassurance — 'Don't worry, you'll see your home again' — but Jack couldn't. Not with Hecate's scheme weighing on his shoulders. If they saw her plan through to the end, it was pretty unlikely that Sting or any of the Wraith would ever go home; most of them would die right here.

*Just like the billions of humans they've killed*, he reminded himself. They were fighting for the survival of their species after all; there was no room for sentimentality.

"Sir?" Carter said. "I think we've found it. But there's a problem."

"Color me surprised," he said as he turned around.

Carter was frowning at the screen, O'Kane next to her, bent over and scribbling something in his notebook. "The lab's here, in the central tower. But it's protected by a force shield."

"Can't I just…" Jack tapped his head, "use the Force?"

"Not this time, sir. It's a Wraith shield and access to its controls is protected by an encrypted code." She made a face. "Shadow obviously takes the security of her hybrids seriously."

Sting made a noise in the back of his throat. "It is possible that there are Wraith among Shadow's hive who feel as I do about the abominations she creates."

"Right," Carter said. "So she's got to protect it from her own kind too."

Sting lifted his head, straightening his broad shoulders. "This news is good," he said. "It speaks to the potential for revolt once Earthborn has staked her claim to lead our people. I cannot believe that even half of Shadow's blades support what she has done here."

Jack just gave a nod to that, his guilty conscience making it difficult to meet Carter's eye as he said, "So how do we take out the shield?"

"There is a way," she said, shifting her feet in the way she did when delivering bad news.

He let out a sigh. "But?"

"But you won't like it."

"Try me."

"The shield is powered by a generator located directly above the lab. If we take that out, the shield will fall. But the snag is, there's a back-up generator located directly below the lab. It's designed to kick in if the first one goes off-line. It's a built in system redundancy that will—"

"How long do we have?" Jack said, getting straight to the point.

Carter blinked as she changed tack. "Uh, thirty seconds, sir."

"Thirty *seconds*?"

"Yes sir — and that's only because the system is routing through Wraith technology rather than Atlantis's own. It's less efficient in this environment. Thirty seconds is how long it would take the second generator to register that the shield is down and to power itself up."

"It's not long enough."

She nodded. "No sir. Not if we all go in. But if O'Kane and I took the generator off-line while you and Sting waited at the shield, you could get inside during that thirty-second window."

"Can we drop the shield from inside to get out?"

"Not without the code."

Jack chanced a look at Sting. "Any way you can mind-read that from one of your buddies?"

"If their minds were weak, possibly. But it is likely that such an important code is known only to blades or clevermen with superior intellects. I would not be able to take it from them without their permission."

"Sir," Carter said, "O'Kane and I can go down and take out the second generator once we've finished the first. It'll take a few minutes to get there, and you'll have no way out until we take it off-line, but I think it's our best shot."

As plans went, being trapped in a lab with a bunch of Goa'uld-Wraith hybrids pretty much sucked. But it was what they had. "How heavily are the generators guarded?"

"I think we can do it, sir."

And that was no answer at all, but he'd known Carter long enough to trust her judgment. She was brave, but not stupid; if she said she could do it, she could do it. O'Kane on the other hand… "You ever fired a weapon, Jimmy?"

He looked up, blinked back a flash of irritation at the name, and said, "Yes, Colonel. I've had some training." He made a face. "Years ago now."

"From who? Dix — the Resistance?"

O'Kane's gaze darted to Sting, whose head had tipped to the side in that listening-carefully gesture of his. Jack got the feeling that Sting didn't know a great deal about O'Kane, a stupid consequence of treating all the humans around him as glorified cattle.

Standing up a little taller, O'Kane said, "I come from a place called Arbella, Colonel. I was trained to use a weapon before being sent on a mission to find new resources and allies… Unfortunately, the mission failed. We were attacked." He paused, his throat working as he swallowed. "I'm the only survivor."

Carter's eyes went wide. "The mission with President Jones' wife?"

"How do you — ?" O'Kane looked stunned. "Have you been to Arbella?"

"Yeah," she said, turning to Jack in mute appeal. "We've, uh, visited."

And this was all shades of interesting, but now wasn't exactly the time to catch-up on Arbellan politics. "Point is," Jack said, "you know how to handle a weapon."

Still reeling, O'Kane managed to pull it together enough to nod. "Yes."

Taking his zat from its holster, Jack handed it over. "One shot stuns, two kills." O'Kane took the weapon, but Jack didn't it let go right away. "You watch Carter's back," he said. "That's what you do. Understand?"

"I understand," O'Kane said and Jack let go of the weapon.

Carter was watching him with an indecipherable expression and Jack met her look and held it without backing down; he wasn't ashamed of where his priorities lay. Not now, when everything was upside down and there was so little left to lose.

After a beat, Carter's attention switched to Sting. "First thing we need to do is get to that transporter."

"The way out will be guarded," Sting said, confirming Jack's suspicion. "I sense several Wraith in the corridor beyond the door — four drones and their blade."

"The drones," Carter said, "can you control them?"

Sting shook his head. "Not with their blade so close."

"But can you fool them?" Jack said.

"Fool them?"

He threw Carter a look. "I'm thinking we make like a Wookiee."

It took her a moment, and then she smiled. "Sting, could you convince them that we're your prisoners?"

He gave it some thought, and then inclined his head. "Perhaps, although not for long."

"But long enough for us to get the jump on them?" Jack felt a flare of adrenaline, hot in the center of his chest. He took a breath. "Sounds like a plan to me."

"I am learning that you use the term 'plan' lightly," Sting

observed. "I am uncertain whether that is strength or weakness."

Jack twitched half a smile. "I like to call it 'desperation.'"

**Arbella — 2098**: Roz Bailey had never believed in hunches. Her personnel were trained to rely on good judgment and keen observation. In her experience, gut instinct was too often fed by the primal need for a fight and that was what got people hurt. She'd never been a soldier who hungered for battle, but she knew it was often necessary. The Combined Military Force was primarily a peacekeeping corps, but just because the people of Arbella were living in a time of peace didn't mean that everything was rosy.

The closed door directive meant that the CMF had never seen off-world conflict, and, despite her own stance on the matter, the security of her homeworld had always been her priority. But if it was really was as bad on Earth as Jack O'Neill had said, then surely it was Arbella's responsibility to take action? Those people left on Earth were still *their* people. After the meeting with President Jones, however, Roz doubted that any political sway she might have had remained intact. As far as Jones was concerned, SG-1 had betrayed them — and Roz found it hard to argue the point.

The idea that they had lied to her stung, and though she had tried to tell herself that Yuma was fabricating the evidence from the datacenter, looking back, she realized that the clues were likely there all along; she just hadn't wanted to believe them. She'd thought that she and Jack O'Neill were on the same page and, in truth, she guessed they were. From what she'd read of SG-1 over the years, there was nothing they wouldn't do to look out for each other.

But Roz Bailey had never been one to accept a situation at face value; there were always other stories and she wanted to hear this one told from the horse's mouth. There was only one other person close to the matter that she trusted. Locking the door, she retrieved the communication device from its hiding place in the chest of drawers. After a few minutes, Dix's face appeared in the small globe.

"General Bailey, all is well I hope."

"That's what I'd like to ask you, Dix. Questions have been raised about SG-1's movements while on Arbella and I don't have the answers to give. Would you care to enlighten me about what they were really looking for in our datacenter?"

Dix's eyebrows drew down and she wasn't sure if it was concern or confusion. "I had no knowledge that they had accessed your datacenter, General. Was this without permission?"

"No, they asked for permission, but lied about their reasons. Apparently they were looking for records of solar flares. What does that tell you?"

Dix looked to the side and she saw he was genuinely puzzled. There was no hidden agenda or double-cross here — he had no more idea what O'Neill and his team had been up to than she. "Solar flares," he said. "I remember my father telling of such a phenomena. It resulted in —"

"Time travel," finished Roz. "Yes, the archives that the Founders brought from Earth gave a full account of the gate transporting SG-1 to the past. President Jones suspects that this was their plan all along. To rewrite history — to change the timeline."

Dix nodded slowly, processing her words. "He believes they wish to erase all that has happened from existence."

She shrugged, her brain recoiling from the implications.

"And what do you think, General?"

She sighed against the heaviness in her chest. It was a question she had asked herself often, even before this latest news, ever since SG-1 had walked through the gate. To her and to most of Arbella, those four people were ghosts from a strange and painful past. They were the stuff of both legend and infamy, and they had found themselves in a future they must have thought impossible. Could she honestly say, if faced with the same predicament, that she'd have been content not to challenge the hand she'd been dealt? "I think that's exactly what I would do if I were Jack O'Neill," she said.

Regardless of their actions or their motives, however, Roz couldn't deny that she was still dependent on SG-1 succeeding in their mission if she had any hope of getting the president to listen to her. Their absence was more worrying than anything they might have done in the datacenter.

"General," said Dix. "I would urge you not to make judgements on SG-1." He took a breath as if considering his words. "I too have found myself these past weeks having to face many old and lingering resentments."

Roz cursed inwardly. She knew, of course, the relationship between Teal'c and Dix—or rather Rya'c as he was once known—and yet she'd been so caught up with her own concerns that she hadn't given any thought as to how Dix might be handling the startling revelation that his father was still alive. As First Prime of Hecate, Dix was always so stoic and resilient; it was easy to forget that he must be dealing with his own troubled emotions. "I'm sorry, Dix. I'm being thoughtless. I didn't mean—"

Dix shook his head. "I understand your concerns, General. But all I ask is that you have faith in SG-1 and allow them to explain their motives. Despite the feelings I have harbored for the past hundred years, my father is still a man of honor. I know that his actions will have been for a sound cause. Speak to him and he will assure you of their just intentions."

"Dix, I'll be more than happy to hear your father and the rest of SG-1 out. But we're running out of time here and Yuma has the president's ear. If we wait any longer then I've a feeling that Jones is going to order the gate closed for good. Have you had any word from them at all?"

The image on the communication globe flickered as Dix drew back, his brows drawn down. "I don't understand, General. Neither Daniel Jackson nor my father have contacted me since travelling through the gate."

An icy dread wormed its way into the pit of Roz's stomach. "Travelled through the gate to where, Dix?"

"To Arbella of course. They found Lana Jones and left from the Lady Hecate's ship yesterday."

It was then that Roz knew the true extent of the game being played here — and who was currently on the winning side. Because Karin Yuma had just made her move and there wasn't a damn thing Roz could do about it without losing completely.

# CHAPTER SEVEN

SAM HELD her breath, chin tipped down, trying to look defeated as the colonel opened the door leading out to the corridor beyond the gate room.

Ahead of them, Sting said, "Hold your fire!" His stunner was aimed at the drones who were crowding in through the open door, their blade behind them.

The drones hesitated, but the blade didn't. "Who are you?" he said, pushing through his men to face Sting. As far as Sam could tell, the blade looked younger than Sting and there was an arrogance about him that she recognized; she'd seen a dozen cocky young officers with the same swagger.

"I am Keenedge," Sting said. Sam felt his hand grip her shoulder and propel her forward, toward the door. She flinched, involuntarily, from his touch, his claws biting into her shoulder. Her response, at least, would look natural. "I must bring the prisoners to Queen Shadow."

Ahead of them, the drones moved away, although their weapons didn't drop and their faceless heads turned toward the blade. Sam could feel the suspicion arcing between them; they weren't buying it.

But Sting wasn't stopping. He pushed her forward, O'Kane keeping close to her side and the colonel up front. "I must —"

"Keenedge fell," the blade said, words hissing through his teeth. "He died in the breeding facility."

Sam glanced behind her, behind Sting, and saw the blade's weapon raised.

"You're mistaken," Sting said. "I —"

"He was my nest-mate," the blade said. "I am not mistaken — *Sting*. Did you think I would not know Earthborn's consort when he is standing right before me?"

For a long moment, nothing happened. Sting stared at the

young blade, one hand still braced on Sam's shoulder, and the blade stared right back. There was fury in his reptilian eyes.

And then Sting pushed Sam forward, hard, and opened fire on the drones.

Stumbling, Sam got her feet under her and yanked her zat out from under her jacket a moment after she heard the colonel open fire with his stolen stunner.

"Carter," he barked. "O'Kane, go!"

One of the drones was down and the colonel was half crouched behind its massive body, using it as cover while he fired on the remaining three.

Sting and the blade were fighting hand-to-hand, throwing each other against the wall with enough force to break bones. Human bones, at least.

"Sir!" she protested.

"I said go!"

Damn it, but he was right. Grabbing O'Kane's arm, she hauled him toward the transporter. "Find the generator room," she barked as he darted inside. Crouching just inside the door to the transporter, she laid down covering fire for the colonel. Another drone was down, a third gone to help its blade with Sting.

"I've got it!" O'Kane called from inside the transporter.

Sam hesitated for a beat and then pulled back to let the door slide shut. "Hit it," she said. A moment later, the sounds of fighting stopped and all was silence. Pushing herself to her feet, she paused to catch her breath and glanced over at O'Kane. "Okay?"

He nodded. "I hope they'll be alright."

"Yeah." She swallowed a sudden surge of unease. "Me too." Shaking it off — there was work to do — she said, "We have to give them time to get to the hybrid lab. That means, once we take the generator room, we're gonna have to hold it. We can't let anyone raise the alarm."

"I understand."

"Okay." She turned to face the door. "Then let's do it."

The transporter opened onto an empty corridor, wide and free of hive-flesh. Walking silently, Sam made her way out, hugging the wall as she led O'Kane toward a junction at the far end. She gestured for him to stop as she approached the transecting corridor, and peered cautiously around it. At one end, a large picture window filled the wall and spilled milky light onto the floor. At the other end, the corridor finished in a set of double doors and another corridor disappearing off to the right. Beyond which, according to O'Kane's schematic, lay the generator room.

So far, so good; there were no guards outside. Of course, that probably meant there were Wraith inside.

Pulling back around the corridor, she turned to O'Kane. He looked shaken but in control. Giving his arm a reassuring touch she said, in a low voice, "Can we open the doors without the colonel's genetic key?"

"The Wraith must be able to," he pointed out.

"Do you know how?"

"There should be a touch pad," he said. "Next to the door."

"That easy?"

He shrugged. "Unless they've disabled it. They might —"

Footsteps.

Sam held up her hand for silence, flattened herself against the wall. It was difficult to tell the direction, but it sounded like it was coming from the corridor leading away from the lab. She dropped into a crouch and peeked out from around the corridor. It was a risk, but she needed intelligence enough that it was a risk worth taking.

There were two Wraith — neither were drones — approaching from the right of the generator room doors. Their white hair was luminous in the sunlight, black leather coats flaring out as they strode toward the doors. One of them touched something on the wall and Sam watched as the doors slid open. Inside, she saw a glimpse of what could have been computer consoles before the open doorway was filled with another Wraith. Taller than the first two, he wore his hair in an elaborate braid and, from his bearing, it was clear that he was the superior.

None of them spoke. Sam imagined their conversation was happening inside their heads. Then the two Wraith bowed, long hair dropping to hide their faces, and turned to leave. As they did so, the Wraith inside the room glanced both ways along the corridor — he looked uneasy — and the doors slid shut.

A warning had been given. Damnit. So much for the element of surprise.

On the other hand, if there was only one Wraith inside the room, perhaps their odds weren't so bad?

Pulling back around the corridor, she glanced at O'Kane. "When we get in there, you need to get into the system and identify the generator controls. I'll take care of the Wraith."

O'Kane swallowed hard, but nodded.

"Okay," she said, pushing back to her feet. "Follow my lead."

And then she was moving, O'Kane at her shoulder.

The hours before nightfall passed excruciatingly slow, and shadows moved across the Arbellan plains like creeping fingers. Roz Bailey waited until Salem was almost at its zenith before leaving her quarters. This was a mission that needed the cover of darkness, but as she made her way through Laketown's alleys, her hair tied back and hat pulled low over her brow, she felt as though she couldn't be more conspicuous had she tied a bell around her neck. There was, of course, no reason she shouldn't be outside at this time, no reason she shouldn't walk the streets she'd known her whole life. But intent heightened her guilt, even though she knew there was a wrong to be righted here. She wasn't sure what had happened to Daniel Jackson and Teal'c since they'd left Dix and walked through the Stargate, but whatever the hell had happened, she was convinced they hadn't made it down from the Stargate base. And that was the reason for her night-time excursion.

Eventually, she reached her destination. The door to the Fu-Bar was open, as it always was, and she hovered in the entrance, scouting the crowd for the face she sought. Lieutenant Jefferson sat at a table in the center of the room, his broad personality filling the space as he laughed with other members of the CMF. She recognized every face of course, but it was Stan she was here to see — though she wondered how many of those around the table would need to step up when the time came.

Jefferson spotted her as she approached the table and his laughter died as he made to stand. A small shake of her head stopped him and he froze with his hands on the table. Roz nodded at the bar and Jefferson dipped his head in acknowledgement. Roz took a stool and waited. A few moments later the lieutenant elbowed in beside her, holding up two fingers to the barman.

"You'll let me buy you a drink, ma'am?"

"Ditch the ma'am, Jefferson," said Roz, staring forward. "In case you haven't noticed, I'm here in an unofficial capacity."

Jefferson glanced at her with a smile, his eyes taking in the hat and civilian clothes. "I see that, ma… um, Gen — ?"

"Roz will do."

He coughed and shifted at the departure from protocol, as the barman sat two mugs of frothy beer in front of them, glancing at Roz with curiosity. She fought not to roll her eyes; so much for keeping this on the down low.

"So, Roz, what can I do for you?" said Jefferson, clearly uncomfortable with the informality.

"Why don't you tell me about the tattoos first?"

Jefferson froze with his mug partway to his mouth. He stared ahead and after a moment took a sip, wiping the foam from his top lip. "What can I say? Some of us like ink. I guess it's a military thing."

"Cut the crap, Stan."

He sat his mug down on the bar and looked around. The place was rowdy, as it tended to be at this time of night. No one seemed to be paying them any attention, but Roz knew there were eyes and ears everywhere. "I'm not sure what it is you're asking, General."

Roz didn't bothering correcting him this time, realizing that any attempt to remain below the radar was futile in a place as small as Laketown. "I'm not asking anything, Lieutenant. I'm saying I know what the deal is with you and your network. I'm saying I know who they are and what you've been preparing for all these years. I'm saying I know what you've been planning ever since SG-1 returned."

Apparently understanding that there was no further point in avoidance, Jefferson looked her straight in the eye. In contrast to the bullish, slightly dense façade that he projected to the world, she saw shrewdness in that look. It gave her confidence that she had made the right call.

"So much for plausible deniability, huh?" he said with a shrug. "What's going on, General?"

"How easily can you get up into the base?"

At that, he looked cagey. "Depends what you'd call easy. And what it's for. Wouldn't it be easier for you to just walk through the front door?"

She took a sip of her beer. Steiner's Original, they called it, a brew going back to the time of the First Gens. She wondered if it tasted like it could dissolve stomach lining even back then.

Just weeks ago, she would have had no hesitation in walking through the front door. Since his landslide election, President Jones had been a man she respected and trusted—but even the most astute of leaders could be misguided in choosing the people to whom they listened. And Gunnison Jones had chosen Karin Yuma. When Lana had disappeared, Yuma had preyed on Jones' vulnerability. Roz's fatal error had been thinking she could do the same thing, with the justification that it was all for a noble cause. In reality, she wondered if she was just as guilty as Yuma of targeting a man's weakness. Now, it seemed, she was the paying the price. She just hoped that both Earth and

Arbella wouldn't suffer also. "The front door has been closed to me for a while," was all she said to Jefferson.

He nodded, looking thoughtful. "I guess I could reach out to a few friends. It would depend on a couple things." His tone was level, all previous unease at the absence of chain of command apparently forgotten; Roz was on his turf now.

"Like what?"

"Like whether the risk was worth it? We have a valuable hand here, General. We play it too early...?"

"Yeah I get it, soldier. What if I said this was the big stake you've been waiting for?"

Jefferson raised his eyebrows. "And what would that stake be, ma'am?"

"It's SG-1," she said, seeing no need for further preamble. "They need our help."

Jefferson straightened, his expression all intent and determination. "What do we need to do?"

Sam opened fire as soon as the doors slid back. She saw one Wraith dive for cover behind a bank of computer equipment, but out the corner of her eye she saw another rise to its feet.

She swung toward it, fired twice.

It was the one she'd seen before, braided hair running down each side of its head. It staggered under the assault, but didn't go down. Teeth bared, the Wraith lifted its feeding hand and lunged toward her. Sam twisted away, but not fast enough, and it grabbed her hair with its other hand. Kicking out, she missed its legs and went down, the force of its grip dragging her to her knees.

The Wraith leered at her, head cocked. "I will enjoy this," it said. "It has been some time since I have had something so fresh."

Behind her, O'Kane cried out in horror and the Wraith plunged its hand into Sam's chest.

For a moment, she was back on Sting's hive with the Wraith's claws in her chest and her life beginning to ebb. But, this time she knew something the Wraith didn't; it couldn't feed on her. A small advantage of the legacy Jolinar had left in her blood. And it gave her an opening.

As a startled look crossed the Wraith's face, Sam yanked at its wrists with both hands, dislodging its feeding hand. Rolling away, she snatched her dive knife from her leg-holster as she jumped to her feet and slashed out across the Wraith's palm. Right into its feeding gland.

With a scream, it reared back, clutching its wounded hand to its chest. Sam pressed her advantage. Moving in dangerously close, she jammed the knife up under the Wraith's chin and into its throat. With a yell, she yanked the knife back and kicked the creature back, sending it stumbling.

Gurgling, scrabbling at its throat, it collapsed to its knees. Sam let it fall, stepping back breathless.

"Sam!"

She spun in time to see the other Wraith lurching toward her, and threw herself to one side, rolling over and back up to her feet. She still had the bloody knife in her hand, but this Wraith had its stunner drawn.

Its gaze locked with hers, lips pulled back.

Sam retreated, looking for options. There was nothing behind her, and the Wraith stood between her and the door. Not that leaving was an option. And then something caught her eye: O'Kane, behind and to the left of the Wraith. He only had the colonel's zat, which wouldn't do much good, but the dead Wraith's stunner lay discarded on the floor close to where it had fallen. If O'Kane could reach it…

"It will be an honor," the Wraith hissed, "to bring you before my queen."

Stepping left, Sam said, "I think I can live without the honor."

As she'd hoped, the Wraith moved with her, keeping her in the sights of its stunner and beginning to open up a route for

O'Kane to reach the weapon.

"Besides," she added, taking another small step, "Shadow's not going to thank you for letting the rest of my team escape."

The Wraith shifted its grip on the weapon, but didn't lower it. "They are not my concern."

"Really?" Another step. "They should be."

O'Kane, after a bemused moment, seemed to catch up with what Sam was doing and started to move as she moved — keeping hidden behind the Wraith. He was almost at the stunner.

"You should be very concerned," Sam said with another step. The door was to her left now, the Wraith no longer between it and herself. She paused for a moment to consider her next move, then took a gamble and glanced over at the door — letting the Wraith see her doing it, letting it think it knew her game plan.

Its head turned toward the door. Just for an instant, but long enough.

O'Kane grabbed for the stunner, fumbled it into his hands and fired. His first shot only clipped the Wraith on the shoulder, sending it spinning, but O'Kane fired again and this time the shot was true, right in the center of the Wraith's back. It went down convulsing.

For good measure, Sam sent two shots from her zat into the thing and it stopped moving.

"Get the door," she barked, and O'Kane ran for it, hitting the panel on the wall. The doors slid shut with a soft hiss and they were alone in the silent room. Now, they had work to do. "Help get me into the systems," she said, heading for one of the consoles. "We need to secure the doors."

At least the Wraith shield wasn't subtle.

It stretched over the lab doors with a sickly green hue, shimmering and distorting everything behind it.

Jack crouched behind a turn in the corridor, using a clump of 'hive-flesh' as cover and trying not to breathe its faintly acrid smell. He could see figures moving behind the shield — ordinary Wraith, by the look of them. But maybe hybrids…

Retreating back to where Sting was waiting, he said, "I see six in there." Three-to-one: he didn't like their odds.

"Yes, I can sense them. But we will have the element of surprise."

Jack raised an eyebrow. "They're gonna need to be *really* surprised."

"Our objective must be the destruction of the facility and of any hybrids in incubation. Our survival is secondary to that objective."

"Speak for yourself."

"If we fail here —"

"I'm not planning to fail. And I'm not planning to die." He threw a glance at Sting, taking in his long colorless hair with the slender braid down one side. The Goa'uld were ostentatious bastards — everything about them was designed to intimidate and impress — but the Wraith looked like they prided themselves on their appearance for different reasons. More human reasons, if that was the right word. "I'm gonna guess that Earthborn wouldn't consider your survival as secondary to the mission."

Sting's eyes flared wide in outrage, his chin lifting. "My queen —"

"Cut the crap, Sting," Jack sighed. "I saw her when she thought you were dying. So don't go all smoking martyr on me, okay? We both have reasons to get out of this alive."

After a long, silent pause Sting said, "And your reason is Major Carter?"

He allowed a half smile, a slight shake of his head. *Touché.* "My team," he said. "My friends." He glanced up, fixing him with a steady look. "My *planet.*"

"I do not *intend* to die," Sting said. "However, if it is necessary…"

"How about we make sure it isn't?" Jack blew out a breath.

"That explosive you're packing? Does it have a timer?"

"It does. And it should allow sufficient time for Carter and… O'Kane to reach the second generator." Sting hesitated before saying the name, as if it was strange to think of his slave as someone with a name — and all that a name implied. "But they must be swift."

"Otherwise we'll be strawberry jelly along with the hybrids. I get it."

Sting blinked at him. "If by that you mean dead, then yes. The explosive is powerful enough to leave little behind at close proximity."

"Nice." Jack shifted, easing the pressure on his bad knee. "So we get in there, set the charge, and then hold them off until Carter gets the shield back down. And hope no one sends backup."

Sting nodded. "As you might say, it 'sounds like a plan'."

Sounds like a *crappy* plan. Not to mention an incomplete one; there was the little matter of getting hold of a hybrid to take back to Hecate… Fact was, there was no way he could do that without Sting's help. And that meant he needed to explain a few things.

Jack took a breath, tugged at the bill of his cap. "Listen," he said, glancing over at Sting. "There's something else."

He sensed, rather than saw, Sting stiffen. It was more like a shift in the air between them, a cooling of comradeship into unease. "What do you mean?"

"I — There's something else I need to do in there."

Sting narrowed his eyes. "We are here to destroy the hybrids," he said. "What else would you need to do?"

"I need to take one," he said. "I need to take one of the hybrids."

"Why?" Sting's lip curled over his sharp teeth in a breathy snarl. "They are abominations. They must be destroyed."

"They are," he agreed. "And they must, I agree. But…" And, crap, but he felt guilty. "Look, what if there were other hybrids, someplace else? We've already seen one lab on Earth. Who's to say there aren't others?"

"Then we destroy them too — once we have control of the Ancestor's city."

Jack rubbed at the back of his neck. "But what if there was another way?"

Sting's fingers flexed and Jack swallowed the memories of the dead dropping, shriveled, to the floor. "I do not like deception, O'Neill. You made a deal with Earthborn. This was not part of it."

"You're right," he said. "I did make a deal with Earthborn. But I also made a deal with Hecate."

Sting snarled, jumping to his feet. "You have betrayed us!" His stunner was already in his hand, rising.

"No!" Jack help up both hands. "Keep your voice down, will you?"

"You are spies of the parasite-god! You —"

"Okay, this is why I didn't tell you in the first place!" Jack hissed. "I'm not her spy. I hate the Goa'uld. Trust me. But she has a way to kill *all* the hybrids — all the Wraith waiting to become hybrids."

Sting surged forward, grabbed Jack by his jacket and slammed him up against the wall. "You fool. She lies, she does nothing but lie. Her kind is without honor."

"Hey!" Jack shoved Sting's hands away. "I know, okay? I *know*. But — Maybe she's not like the others? She's —" It was difficult to explain; he wasn't convinced of it himself, not wholly. "The woman whose body she's possessing was a good friend of mine. Of all of us. And she's… Look, I don't trust Hecate, but she's been fighting for Earth for decades. And she has every reason to want the hybrids dead."

"She wants us *all* dead," Sting spat. "Still, years after the war ended, her forces harry us." He tipped his head, studying Jack with cold eyes. "Who do you think shot me down that day you first found me?"

"Like I said, she's been fighting for Earth."

"The parasite-gods fight only for themselves."

But not Janet. "Look, I hate freakin' snake-heads. Hate 'em. But I have to believe that Hecate is different — that Fraiser has influenced her somehow."

"Fraiser is the human she possesses?"

"Yeah, and she would never —" She would never want to be a Goa'uld. Jack pushed that thought aside. "Look, you both want the same thing; Hecate wants the Wraith gone from this galaxy and you want to go."

"Hecate wants the Wraith *dead*."

"Not if she has a faster option!" His voice echoed along the corridor and he winced at the sound. Jamming a lid on his anger, he tried to channel Daniel's diplomatic mojo instead. It didn't exactly come naturally. "Earthborn," he said, quietly, "is someone Hecate can work with once the hybrids are dead. Hecate wants to leave Earth, you want to leave the galaxy… And, frankly, we want you both gone. Everyone's a happy camper."

Sting bared his teeth in irritation. "I did not take you for a fool, O'Neill."

"Good. Because I'm not." He leaned against the wall, and tried not to cringe at the give of the hive-flesh at his back. "Look, Sting, this is the only way. Help me bag one of the hybrids, then come with me when I take it to Hecate. We all want the same damned thing here and the only way to get it is to work together."

But Sting just shook his head, hissing in a breath. "It is one thing," he said, "to ally myself with humans. But to ally myself with an avowed enemy of my species? That is too far."

Jack lifted an eyebrow. "I know plenty of people who'd say the same about an alliance with the Wraith. But here we are."

"Wraith and humans are not enemies; we do not seek the extermination of your species."

Jack barked a laugh. "Looks kinda different from where I'm standing, buddy."

Turning his head away, drawing back a step, Sting said, "You did not tell Earthborn of your agreement with Hecate."

"No." There was no way around that one. "Would she have agreed if I had?"

There was a long pause before Sting answered. "These are uneasy alliances, O'Neill, and dangerous times. I cannot answer for her."

"Then answer for yourself: will you help me?"

Sting's gaze swung back to Jack, and despite his alien features his disquiet was evident. "I cannot trust Hecate. But…I find that I do trust you."

Jack swallowed; that was a weight of responsibility and he was pretty certain he didn't deserve Sting's trust. But he'd asked for it and had no damned choice but to shoulder the load. Standing up straighter he said, "We have an expression where I'm from: my enemy's enemy is my friend." He clapped a hand on Sting's shoulder. "So I guess that makes us friends."

Sting glanced down at Jack's hand on his arm, then copied the gesture. Jack tried not to wince at the feel of claws digging through his jacket sleeve into his muscle. "At least until our mutual enemy is defeated."

Jack raised an eyebrow, but didn't comment; there were a lot of bridges to cross before they got to that point. Instead, he reached for his radio and toggled it on.

"Carter, O'Neill. Sit rep."

After a hiss of static, her voice came back. "We're in the generator room, sir. Working on getting the shield down. What's your position?"

"Outside the lab. I've got eyes on the shield. What's the ETA on getting it down?"

A longer pause, then, "Couple minutes, sir?"

"I counted six Wraith inside the lab," he said. "Appreciate it if you could get that second generator down ASAP. We won't be able to hold them long." He didn't tell her about the timer on the grenade; she'd work as fast as she could and the added pressure wouldn't help.

His radio cracked again. "Understood, sir. Stand by. Carter out."

He released the radio and fixed his eyes on Sting. "We get outa this," he said. "I'm gonna owe you a beer."

"If we get out of this," Sting corrected, "you're going to owe me your *life*."

Jack wasn't sure, but he thought that might have been a joke. For some reason, it made him hopeful.

"Okay," Sam said. "I've got the generator ready to crash."

Next to her, O'Kane nodded. "I've almost — Okay, found it. There are stairs we can take that bypass the laboratory and take us right to the second generator room. It'll be faster than using the transporter. It's —" He paused, looking more closely. "Actually, it's next to the launch bay for the gate-ships." He looked over at her. "If necessary, that might be another way out?"

Or more than a way out. Sam blinked, turned back to the console where she was holding fire on crashing the generator. "The *navis temporis* is in there?"

"Among the other ships," he said. "Yes."

"Right." And she really shouldn't be thinking about what a 'time ship' might be, except that, if it was what she hoped it was, it could change everything. It could undo this whole screwed-up future. It could save Janet. She cleared her throat, tried to focus on the task at hand. *Time and place, Carter.* "Thanks, James," she said. "You're right, we might not be able to get back to the dart and one of those gate-ships would be a good alternative."

"So long as Colonel O'Neill is with us; he's the only one who could fly it."

She flung him a quick smile. "Better make sure we save his bacon, then." She reached for the radio. "Ready?" O'Kane nodded and Sam toggled the radio on. "O'Neill, Carter. We're ready on your order."

After a beat, his voice came back thin and full of static. "Copy that, Carter. We're moving into position. Stand by."

She blew out a breath, keeping her fingers steady. The colonel and Sting would need to be close enough that they could use the thirty-second window, but not so close that they lost the element of surprise. Not that it would take the Wraith long to react, but every second counted.

"How long will it take us to get down to the other generator?" she said

"Maybe ten minutes?"

"Let's make it five."

Her radio squawked. "Carter. Now."

She hit the controls, watched as Wraith script cascaded down the yellow screen — codes and processes she couldn't read — and then began to fragment, to stutter. Part of the screen froze, then another. Then the whole thing stopped dead. It was well and truly crashed. "Blue screen of death."

O'Kane gave her a puzzled look. Then, behind her, the noise of the generator began a slow descent from its modest hum to a low, sinking whine. And then it stopped too.

"Sir, shield is down."

A hiss of static. "I see it. We're going in."

Then nothing more.

"Okay, move it." Sam vaulted over the console and ran for the door, O'Kane on her heels.

The clock was literally ticking.

# CHAPTER EIGHT

IT WAS difficult to measure the passage of time in a room with no windows, but to Teal'c it felt like hours since he'd been dragged bleeding from the cell in which he and Daniel had been held. This time, a guard had been left in the room with him, and Teal'c thought he recognized him as one of the civilian officers who had met SG-1 when they'd first arrived on Arbella. The man had remained silent, looking vaguely uncomfortable, since Yuma had left him here alone with Teal'c. If O'Neill had been here he might have goaded the young man, his offhand humor disguising a unique style of intimidation. Teal'c preferred to settle for silent staring.

At any other time, he could easily have overpowered the slightly built officer, but the bullet wound to his side still bled, his symbiote taking more time to heal it than he would have liked. He'd remained conscious though, which counted in his favor, and from what he could tell the bullet itself was no longer in his body. Despite his weakened state, he would bide his time until the moment to escape presented itself.

The door opened with a creak that echoed loudly in the empty room and the officer jumped as Agent Yuma and another guard — the burly one who had shot him — entered. Her eyes flicked to his side and the blood-soaked shirt, but her face betrayed no emotion. He watched her as she crossed the room, but refused to speak. Yuma picked up a metal chair from where it stood against the wall and placed it in the center of the room, facing Teal'c where he sat on the low bench. She sat down, crossed her legs and folded her hands in her lap. Teal'c had witnessed the same body language from certain Tau'ri politicians and those military personnel whom O'Neill liked to refer to as 'desk-jockeys'. If Yuma hadn't just had him shot, her manner alone would have set Teal'c on edge.

"You know, there really was no need for all of this," she said, her tone entirely reasonable. "We only want your co-operation. Arbella bears you and Dr. Jackson no ill will."

Somehow Teal'c doubted that she spoke for the whole of the planet, or even the whole of Laketown. And if she did speak only for herself, it was clear she did not speak true; ill will flowed from this woman in waves. "Where is Daniel Jackson?" was all he said.

"Your friend is safe for now," she replied, and the meaning of those last two words was not lost on him. "All we want is information from you."

"I have no information to give."

Yuma smiled. "I appreciate there is an established pattern to these things, Teal'c — believe me, I'm no stranger to quelling dissent amongst those who seek to challenge the established order on Arbella — but I'd hoped that we could dispense with it on this occasion. You must know how desperate your situation is." She sat forward, pressing her palms together as if to reinforce her point. "You have no allies here." Teal'c only stared ahead, refusing to speak. He knew that there were those among the CMF, like Lieutenant Jefferson, who would stand behind SG-1 if the call to action was made. He also knew that it could cost them their lives, given the harsh price to pay for sedition. He would not be the one to hand them that death sentence.

Nevertheless, Yuma apparently took his silence as answer enough. Her eyes narrowed and she tilted her head. "Ah, I see. You believe you do have allies. Or one at least. Give me their names and I'll arrange safe passage for you and Jackson back through the Stargate."

"I have no information to give," repeated Teal'c.

A gesture from Yuma and the larger guard strode forward. Seconds later, Teal'c was doubled over, a well-aimed punch to his wound sending sparks of pain throughout his body. "Teal'c, you must understand, I already have my suspicions about those who plot against our government. You would only be providing us with intel we already have."

"Then why, I wonder, do you seem so determined to extract it from me?" he said, gritting his teeth through the pain. His comment, it seemed, did not please her, and at her command, another blow was inflicted, this time to Teal'c's jaw. In the corner, he saw the younger man, whose name he now remembered as Hayden, flinch.

"What are your plans and who are you working with on Arbella?"

Teal'c spat blood on the floor and said, "Where is Lana Jones?" For the first time, he saw Yuma's composed exterior flicker. Hayden flashed her a glance that spoke volumes. The last he'd seen of the president's wife, she was being led down a corridor, supported by two guards. Teal'c had seen Yuma exchange what looked like heated words with Hayden, which left the young officer visibly perturbed. Teal'c was sure that not all was as it seemed.

"Lana Jones is none of your concern."

"I merely wish to know why we are being held here when we succeeded in the mission President Jones set us."

Yuma stared at him for a long moment, and then stood, brushing imaginary lint from her pressed slacks. "I see that you aren't in a frame of mind to talk to me right now. That will change." Teal'c was wondering if it was worth pointing out that, as First Prime to Apophis, he had been trained to withstand more than a few well placed punches, when she added, "We'll see if Dr. Jackson is perhaps more open to persuasion."

Teal'c clenched his jaw. It was one thing for him to endure such interrogation, but the thought of his friend suffering the same was almost intolerable. Still, though, he could not break. He would not give the names of Jefferson and his men, and he knew that Daniel Jackson would tell him the same.

Yuma waited for a moment and then, with a brief nod, said "Very well," and had the guard open the door. "We'll have someone come and tend to your wounds," she said, sounding almost magnanimous. "We aren't savages after all."

A short time after they'd left Teal'c alone, the door opened once more and a young woman in the uniform of the security forces entered. She knelt by Teal'c's bunk and opened the case she carried. Inside were bandages and other medical supplies. She lifted his shirt and began to clean and dress the wound with skilled efficiency.

Teal'c closed his eyes and let her work, his thoughts going to Daniel Jackson. He knew that he would withstand a beating—his friend was stronger than he appeared—but Teal'c just wished there was something he could do about it.

"Okay, we don't have much time, so listen carefully."

Opening his eyes, Teal'c looked down at the woman whose eyes were still focused on her task. He wondered if he'd heard correctly or if loss of blood was affecting his mental state. "I am listening," he said.

"They monitor this room with video, but there's no audio so they can't hear us," she continued. "If I take too long, though, they'll get suspicious. Don't react—just listen to what I have to say."

Teal'c closed his eyes once more and let his head rest against the wall.

"We'll come tonight," she said, applying what felt like a bandage to the wound. Teal'c tried not to react to the pain. "The guard changes at 1800 hours and we'll have one of our people in place. We'll get you out."

A knot of suspicion formed in Teal'c's gut; how did he know that this woman wasn't a plant by Yuma to get him to share the intel she needed? He glanced at the woman out of the side of his eye. "You don't trust me," she said with a smile, not meeting his glance. "That's good. But know that you can." She turned slightly so that her back was fully to the small, black eye fixed to the far corner and pulled aside the collar of her shirt. There, etched in the skin just beneath her collar bone, was a symbol that had come to mean much to Teal'c these past three years — the glyph for Earth. "My name is Hanna," she said. "I think you know some of my friends from Laketown."

So apparently the divide they'd witnessed between military and civilian on Arbella wasn't so clear cut as they had believed. And apparently they had more allies than either he or Yuma had supposed. Nevertheless, it made no difference if he had an entire platoon sent to rescue him; there was only one way he was leaving this base. "I will not go without Daniel Jackson."

She gave a terse nod and continued dressing his wound. "Of course. We're making arrangements to free him too."

"And Lana Jones?"

Hanna's hands paused in taping the bandage to his side. "What are you talking about?"

"We brought her from Earth. I had assumed that she was being taken to her husband, but I am uncertain now if that is the case. I believe she may also be held somewhere on the base."

Hanna frowned. "This complicates matters."

"Lana Jones is in need of medical care. I cannot allow her to be used as a pawn in Yuma's plans."

For the first time, Hanna looked at him directly. "She won't be the first. But this is certainly the first time she's played with such high stakes." She stood and began packing away the empty packets and surplus bandages. "Don't worry, Teal'c. We'll need Lana Jones too. 1800 hours. Be ready."

And with a bang on the door, she was gone, leaving Teal'c with nothing to do but wait.

The shield disintegrated, a falling away of its bright haze, and Sting was moving.

O'Neill kept pace, shadowing him with the practiced ease of a blade with years of service. Wherever O'Neill came from, he had honed his skills in battle. It was something Sting could respect.

Gesturing to his left, O'Neill moved right so that they came in through either side of the doorway. There was no time for subtlety.

As soon as they crossed the shield's threshold, Sting felt it — a disturbing presence in his mind, corrupted and wrong. The whole of the city stank of it, but here, in this place of monstrous creation, the sensation clawed at his skull.

It was the hybrids. Their twisted minds cried out to him from where they writhed in what looked like adapted hibernation pods. There were times, Sting knew, when an injured Wraith would restore itself to health through a period of protracted hibernation. It was possible that these things required such measures to adapt to the presence of the parasite within. The thought disgusted him and he turned away from the sight in horror.

*What are you doing here?* The sharp question came from a subtle mind of ambitious talent. Sting knew it well.

Slowly, he turned. *Adroit,* he said to the cleverman who stood, hands poised on his instruments, at one of the laboratory benches. Once, Sting had called Adroit friend — long ago, when he and Boneshard had both served Brightstar. *It sickens me to find you here.*

*Sickens you?* Adroit peeled back his lips in disdain. *You always did lack imagination.*

"Hey," O'Neill's voice snapped in his ear. "If you're done with the staring contest, can we focus here?"

Behind them, the force shield snapped back into place. Its static hum almost danced across his skin. They were trapped.

Inside the room, all was tension — a held breath before the first blow. Six Wraith watched him, clevermen all. No blades among them. Adroit, he sensed, was their leader.

Pulling the explosive from his pocket, Sting slid his thumb to arm it and held it aloft. "The abominations you create here must be destroyed," he said out loud. "You face a choice, clevermen of Shadow." He jerked his head behind him, toward the force shield. "Open the shield, retreat with us and live, or refuse and burn with the monsters you have created."

At his side, O'Neill shifted his stance. He held his stolen

stunner in both hands, steady, and although O'Neill's mind was closed to Sting he could feel tension radiate from him like heat.

From the clevermen, he felt fear, anger, and confusion. They did not know who he was or how he dared challenge the will of their queen.

"I am Sting," he said. "I am consort to Queen Earthborn, who would have your allegiance and take you from this toxic world. She would take you home and restore the pride of the Wraith — a race who hunt and cull. We were not created to be farmers of men." He flung a hand toward the hibernation pods. "And we were not created for *that*."

He could sense O'Neill's gaze on him, but the man kept silent. In Sting's hand, the explosive pulsed as the timer counted down. "Who will join me?"

No answer came. And then Adroit stepped forward. "Queen Earthborn? Queen of a dying hive, with no more than fools and old men to serve her." His gaze switched to O'Neill. "And what is this? You consort with kine now?"

"I will be happy to watch you die," Sting snarled. "Traitor."

*I fear,* Adroit said, mind-to-mind, *that our fates will be reversed.* Then he made a swift gesture and one of the clevermen on the other side of the room moved toward the hibernation pods.

"Hey!" O'Neill snapped. "Stay where you are."

The cleverman — his mind a shimmer of disdain — ignored him and reached for the pod.

O'Neill fired, his blast catching the Wraith's shoulder.

But O'Neill was too late; Scorn had already begun the deactivation process. He slumped to one knee, clutching his shoulder, teeth bared. "Now you will understand," he hissed.

Behind him, the fluid drained from the hibernation pod as the Wraith — the abomination — inside began to stir to wakefulness.

Sting felt its mind stir too, thick with an alien presence; it was a cold and foreign hatred that had nothing to do with the purity of Wraith hunger. It spoke of violence for the sake of domination, conquest for the sake of terror. He recoiled from the sensation, even as he recognized it.

Sting bared his teeth as the pod opened and the hybrid opened eyes that flared gold.

"Ah, crap," O'Neill said. "It's Bonehead."

Boneshard, Sting had known; both he and Adroit had served with him in Brightstar's zenana. But he refused to see this creature as the Wraith he had once claimed as kin.

"O'Neill," Boneshard said, though he spoke in the resonant voice of Sobek, the parasite within.

"Here we are again." O'Neill levelled his weapon, though Sting doubted it would be effective against this creature. He suspected that O'Neill knew the same. "How's the hand?" O'Neill said.

Boneshard flexed his feeding hand, injured in their previous confrontation. Of course, it was healed. On his other hand, he wore a jeweled device of the parasites. "And where is the rest of the great SG-1?" said Sobek. "Do you fight alone?"

"Oh, they're off kicking ass elsewhere."

Boneshard's eyes shifted from O'Neill, skated over Sting, and landed on Adroit. "You do not kneel before your god?"

Sting felt Adroit's flare of indignation, masked quickly by fear-stench as he hurried to bow low. "Sobek," he said. "This Wraith has come to destroy us. He carries an armed grenade."

The hybrid's gaze swung toward Sting. Then he bared his teeth and Sting felt Boneshard's mind slam into his. *I will take you apart bone by bone,* he hissed. *I will consume you, Sting of Earthborn's hive. And then I will consume your girl-queen.*

Sting adjusted his hold on the grenade, the pressure in his mind vast. He remembered, now, how easily he'd fallen to Boneshard in the facility on Earth. But he would not do so again; all he need do was detonate the grenade. And he could do it now, he could bypass the timer.

Tearing his gaze from the monstrosity before him, he looked over at O'Neill.

He gave a subtle shake of his head. "Give them time."

Boneshard — or perhaps it was the parasite, Sobek — stalked closer and Sting watched in disgust as the other Wraith abased themselves before him. "My first brothers," he said, gesturing to the other hibernation pods, "await my orders. Do you see them?"

Sting tightened his grip on the grenade and stepped back. "I see them," he said. "And I will destroy them. All of them. They bring shame on us all."

Boneshard's eyes flashed and once more it was Sobek who spoke. "Your species," he said, rolling his shoulders in a languid way in which no Wraith would move, "have such literal minds. You are strong, yes, but lack a human imagination." His gaze turned to O'Neill. "I miss that."

"Right now, I'm imagining you dead," O'Neill said. "How does that work for you?"

Sobek peeled back his lips in something like a human smile. "I will not need to imagine your death, O'Neill. "

"No?"

From his position, kneeling, Adroit said, "This one, my Lord, has always been so. He thinks like a toothless blade, unable and unwilling to change."

"Unwilling to bow before another!" Sting spat. "I bow only to my queen."

"We shall see about that," Sobek said and lifted the hand bearing the parasite's device. It glowed, sending a liquid heat scorching through the air between them and drilling into Sting's skull.

"Sonofabitch!" O'Neill cursed and opened fire.

Dimly, through the pain, Sting saw the bolt hit Boneshard. It had no effect.

"You will kneel!" Sobek hissed. "You will kneel before your

god!"

Sting hissed air through his teeth. The pain was enormous, a breathing, beating thing. He'd felt nothing like it before. It was as if his brain burned. And yet, through it, he saw Earthborn's face and felt the cool weight of the stunner in his hand, and knew that he could not let go. He could not succumb to this.

"I said let him go!" O'Neill's words were misty through the pain, as ineffectual as the power of his stolen weapon.

"You are stubborn," Sobek said, drawing closer. He lifted his hand, the jewel at the center of the device glowing deeper and the pain surged forward.

Helpless, he cried out. The sound was a wordless scream; he was glad Earthborn was not there to witness it.

"Sting!"

That was O'Neill. Sting was aware of him in the periphery of his vision. And, even through the pain, he knew what he was asking. The explosive… If he lost consciousness, he'd lose the explosive. It would all be for nothing.

Stiff, on uncooperative legs, he eased himself down, one knee at a time. He could feel sweat on his skin, bile in his throat. Hunger pulsed through the pain. He was weakened, but worse than all of that was the shame of kneeling before this abomination.

Sobek smiled, a baring of Wraith teeth, and his feeding hand gaped in pleasure. "Good," he said. "Good. You know your place, Sting."

The pain stopped and he slumped forward, barely keeping himself upright amid the wave of humiliated relief.

"Aptly named," Boneshard said, taking control from the parasite. "You always were little more than a pinprick of irritation."

Sting's hair fell lank over his face, but he made himself lift his head. "I will kill you," he said.

"Why do you resist?" Boneshard looked down at the grenade

in Sting's hand. "Do you not see the glory around you?"

"I see nothing but corruption."

He growled his disgust. "Then you are blind. And you will die for it." He lifted the device again

But before he could ignite it, Sting said, "O'Neill!"

He threw the explosive and O'Neill caught it, backing up against the bank of hibernation pods. "Okay, Bonehead, you ready to die?"

Boneshard hissed and suddenly it was Sobek talking. His hand lowered as he turned to O'Neill. "Your plan has failed, Colonel O'Neill of SG-1. You cannot escape."

"Who said anything about escaping?"

And, despite the way his mind was churning, Sting could hear a chill in O'Neill's voice that he did not recognize. He glanced over and saw the same bleakness in the man's eyes. They were the eyes of a warrior prepared for death.

Perhaps Sobek saw it too, because he stopped. "You would not…"

"The hell I wouldn't," O'Neill said.

Woozy, Sting pushed himself to his feet. He knew that Sobek saw something in O'Neill that he had not seen in Sting; a readiness to die that, for all his protestations, Sting had lacked.

*Because of Earthborn…*

He knew it was true and was afraid of what it meant. How could he serve her if he could not bear to be parted from her in death?

Sobek lifted his hand and Adroit rose to his feet. Though Sting was not privy to their conversation, he sensed the dark pleasure in Adroit's clever mind. They were preparing to attack.

There was a chance that O'Neill could detonate the explosive in time — there was a chance the timer would run down anyway — but O'Neill was unfamiliar with the device and there were too many Wraith.

With a roar, Sting launched himself at Boneshard's turned back, knocking them both to the floor. His limbs were uncoordinated, the effect of the alien device on his mind still debilitating, but the distraction was enough.

Stunner fire blazed overhead and O'Neill yelled "See you all in hell!"

# CHAPTER NINE

"SIR, wait!"

Carter's yell came out of nowhere, accompanied by a burst of gunfire. Jack's finger jerked away from the grenade's detonator because, behind him, the sickly green of the Wraith force shield had dissolved.

He spared Carter a single glance. She was alone; O'Kane wasn't with her.

Sting was still wrestling Boneshard, the timer on the grenade could run down at any moment, and they still needed a hybrid.

There wasn't time for anything but a Hail Mary pass.

"Carter," he barked, pitching the grenade as far as he could across the lab. "Cover me!"

Jack turned his stunner on Boneshard and opened fire. Carter opened up on the Wraith science-geeks, keeping them pinned down and unable to retrieve the grenade. None of them tried to fight back. Perhaps they weren't armed? It was a small mercy, but he'd take it.

The hybrid bucked under the impact of the stunner fire, so did Sting; some of the charge was transferring between them. It didn't matter. Jack fired again, and again. He had no idea how much was needed to take the bastard down.

And, by now, reinforcements had to be on the way. There was no time for subtlety.

He fired again, the hybrid arched its back and Sting, by some feat of desperation, heaved the thing over and onto its back. Jack was on him in an instant, jamming his foot against the arm that wore the Goa'uld hand-device and firing again, at close range, into the thing's head.

It jerked. Sharp teeth bared, then its mouth went slack. Blood, black blood, trickled between its lips. Maybe the thing had bitten its tongue. If it had a tongue.

Breathing hard, Sting sat back on his heels. He looked like crap, but there was no time to stop.

"Move it!" Jack growled, ducking down to grab the hybrid under its arms. The thing was *heavy*.

Growling something unintelligible, Sting pushed to his feet and seized the hybrid's other arm. Together they started dragging it out of the lab, keeping low to avoid Carter's covering fire.

"Where's O'Kane?" Jack shouted as they retreated into the corridor outside the lab. Jack ducked right, taking Sting and the hybrid with him.

"On his way," Carter said, pulling back around the corner. "Sir, how long — ?"

She never finished the question.

The detonation seemed to suck all the air out of Jack's lungs, all the sound out of his head. There was a weightless moment of nothing, of screwed shut eyes and bracing for impact, and then it all rushed back in: shoulder crunching against the wall, the floor racing up to meet him. Something heavy punching into his face.

Then, the acrid burn of fire and smoke.

Shaking it off, Jack tried to push up to his knees. But there was something heavy on his legs and he kicked out, blinking through the smoke. The hybrid lay across him, Sting struggling to his feet next to it.

"Get it off," Jack growled, squirming out from under the thing's dead weight.

Distantly, he could hear the blare of an alarm. His ears were ringing, though, so the damn thing could be right overhead. Either way, it meant they should expect company.

"Carter!" he barked, as Sting hauled the hybrid back and off Jack's pinned legs. "Major!" He coughed, the smoke catching in his lungs. "Sam!"

A hand on his shoulder. "Sir." There was a gash on her forehead, her face ashen, but she was on her feet even if she looked shaken. "Are you okay?"

He nodded, dug his fingers into her arm; there was a bloody tear on her shirt, right over her heart. "You?"

"Nothing I couldn't handle, sir." She gave him a quick smile. "We should go."

He held her gaze for a beat longer, but he didn't think she was hiding anything so let go of her arm. "We should," he said. "Lead the way, Major."

Sting was struggling to drag the hybrid and Jack moved to help. But even between them there was no way they were going to get out of there and back to the dart without being caught. They were just too damn slow

Sting was moving stiffly, his limbs twitchy. Jack knew why; he'd danced with that Goa'uld hand device himself and knew the aftereffects intimately. It wasn't just a giant headache. It dug into your mind and fried the circuits, made everything misfire and disconnect. He imagined it was what a lobotomy might feel like.

"We should hide," Sting said, hissing the words through his teeth.

"Hide where?" He was open to suggestions, but hiding sounded like a recipe for disaster. He'd rather get out of this freaky city than risk being cornered — especially with a pissed-off Goa'uld-Wraith hybrid on their hands.

"I need time to heal," Sting said. "We cannot reach the dart without —"

"Sir, there may be an alternative."

"What alternative?"

"Those short stange ships James mentioned? The gate-ships? He found the docking bay, sir. And we're close."

Sting lifted his head. He didn't look like he liked the idea, but frankly he wasn't in a position to argue.

"Plan B it is," Jack said. "How far is close?"

"Five minutes." She hesitated, pressed her sleeve to the cut on her forehead, swiping away the blood before it ran into her eyes. "O'Kane is on the way. I figured —"

Jack grunted, but didn't comment on her preemptive decision. "Good call, Major. Now, let's move it."

It took, perhaps, ten minutes at their slow pace to reach the docking bay.

"From what I can tell," Carter said, bumping shoulders with Jack as they hauled the comatose hybrid along the final corridor, "this part of the city is barely used. I mean, the place is enormous. The Wraith don't even nearly fill it."

"Lucky for us."

"Yeah… Yeah, lucky." And then she stopped talking in that way she had that always made Jack nervous, the way that told him there was something she was holding back.

"Carter?"

A little shake of her head, a quick glance at Sting. "Later, sir."

He cocked an eyebrow. "Later?"

"It's —" And then her eyes were on his, intent like she was trying to impart a hidden meaning. "It's another option," she said. "Maybe."

He held her gaze as long as he could, then turned away. "Are we talking solar flares, Major?"

"Possibly more like HG Wells, sir."

He jerked his head around to look her, aware of Sting listening intently to their coded conversation. "You're kidding."

But she didn't look like she was joking. "I don't know, sir. It's possible. I'd need to look."

And holy crap… A *time machine*? "Isn't that a little sci-fi?"

Carter snorted, but didn't deign to reply. Given their current circumstances, he guessed she had a fair point. He blew out a breath and kept hauling on the half-dead alien.

Not long after that, he heard footsteps behind him and turned, stunner raised, to find O'Kane skidding to a halt, arms raised. "A little warning next time, Jim," Jack said, lowering his weapon.

"Sorry." O'Kane's attention darted to Carter. "Sam, I found it. The *navis temporis* is there."

She gave him a curt nod and Jack a meaningful look. "Show me," she said.

The docking bay looked more like a silo. It was cavernous and empty, dusty with the air of long-abandonment. It took Jack a moment to identify the 'gate-ships', because they looked nothing like anything he'd ever flown — or seen fly.

"Carter, they're boxes," he said as he dropped the hybrid on the floor and stretched his back to ease the knots. "Are you sure they even fly?"

Boneshard stirred at Jack's feet and he exchanged a wary glance with Sting. "We need to restrain him."

Sting nodded, his long hair ratty with all the fighting and sweat. "With what?" he said, glancing around.

Rummaging in his vest, Jack pulled out a couple sets of plastic cuffs — they might not hold a Wraith powered up with snake-juice, but it was all he had. He threw a pair to Sting. "Get his feet."

Together they rolled the hybrid onto his front and Jack cuffed his wrists behind him — barely getting the human-sized loops over the Wraith-sized hands. And claws. On the palm of one hand, the little mouth thing gaped like the gills of a landed fish. Jack shuddered and looked away, right at Sting.

He closed his own hand as if he'd noticed Jack's reaction, or, perhaps, was hiding something. His hunger, Jack guessed. Sting was wounded; he probably needed to feed so he could heal.

Swallowing his disquiet, Jack pushed to his feet.

Carter and O'Kane were poking about at one of the blocky gate-ships, but didn't seem to be having much luck getting in. "Hey," Jack called. "You need my magic fingers?"

He couldn't exactly see Carter raise her eyebrows, but he could certainly feel it. "Your help would be appreciated, sir," she said. "They obviously need the Ancient gene to activate."

"Keep your eyes on him," Jack said to Sting, stepping over the hybrid and heading toward Carter. Boneshard's fingers were starting to flex — the sooner they got out of here, the better.

Approaching the gate-ship cautiously, Jack let his eyes run along its unattractive lines. It was almost utterly non-aerodynamic. "Carter, tell me how this damn thing can even get off the ground."

She offered a tight smile. "I might be able to once I take a look inside, sir," she said. "But I imagine it's primarily designed for use in space."

He cocked his head. "Well, we're not in space."

"Yes sir. I'm assuming the Ancients thought of that when they designed a flying city capable landing on a planet."

Smiling on the inside — it never hurt to keep a poker face — he said, "Well, let's hope you're right, Major. Otherwise it's gonna be a very short ride."

"The doors seem to be at the stern, sir," Carter said by way of reply, and led him around to the blunt end of the ship.

Jack let out a sigh. "It's a hatchback, Carter."

"Think of it more like a landing craft, sir."

He threw her a sideways look. "There's a reason I didn't join the navy, Carter." Then he reached out, put his hand on the slick metal of the ship. "Hocus pocus."

Like actual magic, the damn thing hummed into life. The back door slowly descended, becoming a ramp, and Jack took a step back to avoid it.

"Wow," Carter said, peering inside. "It looks brand new in there."

He followed her gaze, took in the sleek design — like everything else on this city that hadn't been messed with by the Wraith. "Let's go see if we can get her in the air," he said, and headed up the ramp.

There was a large lozenge-shaped something in the back, with wires trailing up from either side to the ceiling. He stepped around that and headed into the cockpit — cockpit/hotel lounge, going by the décor. Lights sprang to life as, cautiously, he took a seat in the pilot's chair. No straps, no joystick, just lots of incomprehensible buttons in weird designs. "I feel like I'm sitting in an armchair," he grumbled. "How do I even know what the controls — Whoa." Right in front of his eyes, a Heads-Up Display floated in midair. "Carter, you seeing this?"

"Yes sir," she said from behind him. "It must have responded to your thoughts. That's…"

"Creepy?"

"I was going to say incredible, sir."

"Of course you were." He licked his lips; this whole mind-reading thing was unsettling. "Weapons status," he said, and another display appeared. Unsettling, but convenient. He peered more closely. "Looks like we have some kind of targeted missiles," he said, trying to make sense of what he was seeing. "No laser guns, though."

"Laser guns aren't a real thing, sir," Carter said, sounding distracted.

Glancing over his shoulder, he saw that she was walking slowly around the large device in back. "You found something?"

She nodded. "Yes sir, I think this might be it."

"It?"

"The, uh — From what I can gather, this is a prototype."

He turned around in the chair, glanced out the window and saw Sting crouched near the hybrid. O'Kane was making notes, gazing around the docking bay like a kid at a museum.

Lowering his voice, Jack said, "Just so I know we're on the same page, Carter. Are we talking about a…" He felt ridiculous even saying it. "A 'time machine'?"

"Yes sir. What are the odds?"

He spread his hands. "You tell me."

"I can't." She shook her head. "I mean, I can't even begin to understand the physics behind this. It should be impossible. Everything we know about physics — which, evidently, is limited — tells us that time travel is impossible."

"And yet here we are."

"Right."

"And you think this thing can take us home?"

She looked up, held his gaze. "Maybe. Sir, it would be a huge risk. It's not like we can test it or anything. But if we don't try…?" She left it hanging, but he knew what she meant.

"Janet."

"And Rya'c, and the SGC. And *Earth*, sir."

He nodded. "This is what you've wanted all along. A way to fix it."

"Haven't you?"

And that was a question. One there was no time to answer now. So he asked her something else instead. "Can we just fly this thing normally too? We need to get everyone outa here."

"Yes, sir." She rested a hand on the device. "From what I can tell, this is a separate drive. So, unless you specifically engage it, the ship should function like a normal gate-ship."

"Whatever that is," Jack said. "Okay, get the others on board. First thing we do is get Sting and O'Kane back to the dart."

She didn't answer and she didn't leave. He could almost hear her unasked question before she said it. "And then?"

"Then we have a conversation."

The isolation, Daniel had come to understand long ago, was the worst part of being imprisoned. It was somehow easier to bear captivity when the team was together, to bolster each other's spirits and stay resilient. Now all he had for company was four bare walls, a glaring yellow strip light, and his own awful theories about what might have happened to Teal'c. His solitary confinement didn't fool him into thinking that Agent Yuma was done with him, though; he knew it was only a matter of time before she came back.

So far, though, no one had come near his cell except to leave him food — and that's where things had gotten interesting. When he'd drained his cup of what tasted like powdered milk, he saw something white at the bottom, wrapped in plastic. Taking care to avoid the camera that watched him from the ceiling, he retrieved what turned out to be a tightly folded note.

*1810. Be ready.*

Ready for what, he wasn't sure, but he surmised that if it was some plan of Yuma's, there wouldn't have been any need for subterfuge. Or for any sort of warning in the first place. Though the obvious answer was that Bailey had somehow found out they were being held here and had sent help, he doubted that she would risk her position to spring them from jail.

He also worried about what Bailey might think of them now, given the discovery they had made in the datacenter about Sam's research. It would feel like betrayal and Daniel couldn't claim immunity simply because he'd voiced reservations about the plan to rectify the timeline. Whatever choice had been made, all four of them must accept responsibility. He only hoped they would have a chance to explain to Bailey in person, rather than hear a secondhand account from Yuma.

Regardless of the note's origin, it was the best hope he'd had in hours. He would just need to make sure they didn't leave without Teal'c.

He checked his watch. The last time they'd been on Arbella, Sam had pointed out that it seemed to follow a twenty-seven hour day, and though he'd tried to make adjustments in his head for the difference, he was sure he must have lost track somewhere along the way. The only thing he could do was be ready to act at any time.

Eventually, he heard a muffled disturbance in the hallway and he sprang to his feet, wishing he had a weapon. Seconds later the door burst open, slamming against the wall. A young woman stood on the threshold, her gun pointed at the guard who lay prone on the floor. There was no blood and he hadn't heard a gunshot, so Daniel assumed he'd only been knocked out.

"Who are — ?"

"No time to explain, Dr. Jackson. Come with me. We're getting you out of here."

"Not without Teal'c."

"We have him," said the woman, impatiently. "Now come on. We've knocked out the surveillance, but it'll only last a few minutes. Can you shoot a weapon?"

"Unfortunately yes," he said, taking the handgun she held out to him.

Without waiting for further instructions, Daniel followed the young officer. On the back of her shirt was the familiar square-rigger of the security force. "You're not CMF," he whispered. "Didn't Bailey send you?"

"The less General Bailey knows, the more we can protect her. It's not just the CMF who are loyal to SG-1's legacy." She stopped as if mentally checking herself. "To *your* legacy. We've been preparing ourselves for this since before you even arrived on Arbella, Dr. Jackson."

It still baffled Daniel, the status SG-1 had been granted, both good and bad, by the Arbellan people. He wasn't sure what to make of it and he certainly didn't think it was deserved. But now wasn't the time to debate philosophical differences with the woman who had been sent to rescue him.

They reached a narrow staircase that led further down into the Stargate facility. Just as Daniel was wondering how big this place actually was, they reached the bottom and found two others waiting for them. Two of them were base personnel, obviously working with the woman who had freed him. The other...

"Teal'c!" Daniel darted forward to where Teal'c was leaning against the wall. Even in the dim light, Daniel could see the bruises down one side of his face. "Hey, what happened? Are you okay?"

"I am fine, Daniel Jackson," said Teal'c, though he accepted Daniel's proffered arm and leaned his weight on his shoulder. "I will heal in time. For now, we must leave this base." He turned to the woman who stood conferring with the two men. "Hanna, have you located Lana Jones?"

Daniel looked between them in confusion. "What do you mean? Isn't Lana with her husband?"

Hanna frowned. "As far as we know, she wasn't taken to the president. We're not even sure if he knows you brought her back."

"I believe Agent Yuma has her imprisoned somewhere on this base," said Teal'c.

"Why the hell would she do something like that?"

"She perhaps intends to use her as collateral to achieve her own ends."

"Yuma is part of what's wrong with this society," said Hanna. "She's why we're doing what we're doing. She has influence with the president, but she wants to make sure that he doesn't listen to anyone else. Especially not General Bailey."

"And us bringing back his wife might just tip the scales in her favor," said Daniel, grimly. It galled him that they were discussing this woman's life as if it were a political asset; he guessed that humanity hadn't learned much at all since the end of the world. Whatever the reason, they couldn't just leave her in the hands of Yuma and her people. She deserved to be safe. "So how do we get her back?"

"It's not as simple as that," said Hanna. "I've just found out she's being held under complete lockdown. More guards than we can easily take out, and we've already more than outstayed our welcome. We have to get out of here."

"And go where?" asked Daniel. "Don't tell me you can get us back through the Stargate, because we both know that's not going to happen. So what, we hide on Arbella? And what about Sam and Jack? They'll come looking for us and walk straight into Yuma's net. No. If we're going to fix this, then we fix it now." He looked at Teal'c, unsure if he'd get back-up. He knew Teal'c's feelings about this world and how it went against the natural order as he saw it, but the Jaffa was still his friend and he hoped he could count on him in this.

Teal'c held his eyes for a moment and then finally said, "Daniel Jackson is correct. We must do what is right. Our duty was to keep Lana Jones safe and we will see it done."

Daniel gave him a tight smile of thanks and Teal'c inclined his head.

"Alright," said Hanna, shaking her head. "But we have to move out now. Chances are they're already looking for us."

"Chances are they've already found you," said a voice from the stairwell. They spun towards it to find Agent Yuma standing there with her gun trained on them. From behind her filed a half dozen soldiers, all with weapons poised. They took up positions along the hallway, cutting off the only means of retreat. Yuma descended the stairs, dragging with her a whimpering figure who she threw on to the floor. "I believe this is what you're looking for," she said and, pressing her gun against the side of Lana Jones' head, pulled the trigger.

# CHAPTER TEN

"LOOK," Jack said, "we'll be back in a day. Maybe sooner."

"Maybe much sooner," Sam added. Theoretically, with a time machine, they could be back before they'd left. The colonel gave her a look that said 'not helpful' and she offered an apologetic shrug in return.

"And where is it you're going?" Sting was sitting in the co-pilot's chair. He looked too big for the human-scale seat.

O'Kane perched on the chair behind him, the hybrid lying still in the back. He'd roused while they hauled him into the gate-ship and Sting had shot him twice more with the stunner. Sam hoped any neurological damage the stunner might cause wouldn't impede Hecate's experiment; she doubted Hecate needed brain function, just basic physiology. If it even came to that. With luck — a lot of luck — the whole plan would be rendered unnecessary and Sam would find herself...

Well, gone. At least, this version of her would be gone. It was a strange thought and one she didn't want to dwell on. There were more important things at stake.

"I can't tell you that," the colonel was saying. "Sting — you're just going to have to trust me." He gestured back toward the hybrid. "Take that, and yourself and O'Kane home. Carter and I will meet you there. If we don't —" He scratched his head, clearly trying to pick his way through the paradoxes of time travel. "Look, if everything is the same tomorrow and we're not back, then contact Dix in the Shacks. Get him to take you and the hybrid to Hecate."

Sting growled his displeasure. "That would be suicide."

"Not if you have the hybrid with you. That's what she wants. And Daniel — He'll be there. He'll speak for you. She'll listen to Daniel." He glanced at Sam and she saw all the uncertainty he was trying to hide from Sting, all the impossible unknowns.

"With luck," Sam said to the Wraith, "it won't come to that. Either we'll be back or —" She smiled. "We will be back," she said and gave it a weight of certainty she didn't feel. Or want. With luck, they wouldn't be back and Sting would be living his life in the far-off Pegasus galaxy and would never have heard of Earth or SG-1. Not that she could tell him that without raising too many unanswerable questions.

"Again," Sting said, "I find myself in a position with little choice but to trust you."

"That's worked out so far, hasn't it?" the colonel said.

Sting didn't reply; simply turned his head to the window that looked out over the empty docking bay. "Let us see if you are able to pilot this…thing…first."

Sam caught Jack's slight smile and it surprised her. The colonel wasn't always the first to warm to alien species, but he and Sting seemed to share a certain macho bond. Just like he did with Teal'c, she supposed.

"No problem," the colonel was saying, "I just need to think — 'exit'."

The back of the gate-ship began to slide open.

"Not that!" he yelped. "Damnit. Show me how to get out of the city, you piece of —"

A set of schematics appeared on the colonel's HUD as the gate-ship's doors slid shut again. Sam peered closer from where she sat behind him. It looked like two options: down to the gate room, or up through the ceiling.

"We don't want to use the gate," she said.

"Thanks, Major, I figured."

"As soon as they see the ship they will send darts to intercept," Sting warned. "I hope it has adequate shielding."

"I don't think so," the colonel said. "It — Oh, wait. Now *that's* sweet."

"Sir?"

He threw a quick smile over his shoulder. "Cloak," he said. "Nice."

Turning back around, the colonel settled. After a moment's silent concentration the ship lifted more-or-less smoothly into the air. There was little sense of movement; clearly there was some kind of compensation for inertia. It moved into the center of the docking bay and then lifted vertically. Out the window, Sam watched as they rose past another floor housing its own gate-ships, and then higher into something not dissimilar to the silo at the SGC that housed the Stargate. It brought home to her the scale of this place. In its heyday, Atlantis must have been something to behold.

Abruptly, the quality of light changed, brightening into gray and watery daylight. She craned her head to peer up and saw the ceiling opening as they approached.

"Cool," she said, earning a huff of amused agreement from the colonel.

The ship kept rising until, around and below her, Sam could see the immense city spreading out. There were disfiguring clumps of hive-flesh all over it, but, despite that, Sam could imagine what it might have looked like in the hands of the Ancients. And it was beautiful.

O'Kane was staring too, his eyes wide. Only Sting looked unimpressed. But, of course, he'd seen this place before and it was the home of his enemy.

"Okay," the colonel said, his shoulders relaxing once they were beyond the confines of the city. "So far so cool. Cloak is engaged and we are invisible." He glanced over at Sting. "You know, I could give you guys a ride home in this thing? My rates are pretty reasonable."

Sting's chin lifted. "I would rather reclaim my own ship, if it has not yet been discovered. Earthborn's darts have served me well for many years and I would be sorry to lose one. We have few left."

"I get that," the colonel nodded. "So, anyone remember where we parked?"

"The East Pier," O'Kane said, opening his notebook to the

schematic of the city. "*Pila Orientalis...* " He looked up and pointed to the right. "That way."

It took a little finding, but eventually Sam recognized the pier where Sting had landed. His sharp-nosed dart sat where they'd left it and the colonel took a couple of passes to make sure the area was clear before he set down.

"Remember," he said as the back door opened. "If we're not back by tomorrow…"

Sting nodded where he stood, with O'Kane, at the exit. "I will watch for you. Do not disappoint me."

"I'll try not to," the colonel said. Then he glanced at O'Kane. "Nice work, Jim."

O'Kane narrowed his eyes, but just said, "Thank you. It was — interesting." Then his gaze slipped to Sam and she saw rather more understanding that she'd like in his intelligent expression. But all he said was, "Good luck, Sam."

Whether or not he'd guessed the purpose of the ship, or what Sam was intending to do with it, she didn't know. But she figured it was a good bet that O'Kane knew what she was planning. "Thanks," she said. "You too."

Some things were best left unsaid.

Time crystallized, leaving Daniel aware of every excruciating second. The gunshot echoed off the metal walls of the stairwell and corridor and no one moved.

Then a voice said "What the hell have you done? What have you *done*?" and Daniel realized it was one of Yuma's men.

But Daniel couldn't take his eyes off of the prone body of Lana Jones, discarded on the floor, blood pooling around her head. They had brought her back, thinking they were saving her, only for this to be her fate. He swallowed against the bile sting in the back of his throat.

"Stand down, Officer Hayden," said Yuma, and he saw that the man who'd just spoken now had his gun trained on her. The other guards seemed at a loss to know what to do, raising their weapons but not pointing them in any particular direction.

"Are you crazy? You killed the president's wife, for God's sake!" It sounded like he was on the verge of tears.

At Daniel's side, Hanna and her colleagues seemed stricken and immobilized. This wasn't part of their plan. It wasn't part of anyone's plan but Yuma's.

"What is it you hope to achieve here, Yuma?" he said quietly.

She turned to face him, as if aghast that he would have the nerve to speak. "I don't wish to achieve anything, Jackson. I had already achieved it. Arbella was peaceful. It *worked*. And all of that in spite of the mess you and your team had left in your wake. Do you think it was people like Jones, or Bailey, who made that happen? It was people like me who saw the finer details, who made those small adjustments that kept things running. I will not have some fallacy bring down what I have built."

He saw her then for what she was; despite her calm rationality, she was another Maybourne, grasping at opportunity, trying to steal what she didn't deserve, not caring who paid the price. The dead woman at her feet was proof enough of that. But, then again, Maybourne himself was proof that even the most carefully constructed castles could crumble with the smallest shifting of sand.

Officer Hayden, it would appear, was not so willing to submit to Yuma's orders. He brought his weapon around to bear and Daniel could see that his hands were shaking. "Drop the gun, ma'am."

Daniel didn't think he was imagining it when he saw Yuma roll her eyes. "Don't be foolish, Jed. We have a goal here. Don't screw it up for yourself."

"You've gone too far. There's no way can we keep this from the president."

"I said, don't be foolish." She swung her own gun towards Hayden, but the momentary distraction was enough. Teal'c leapt forward, grabbing her arm and wrapping an arm around her neck. Daniel took his cue and swung a punch at the nearest guard. Surprise worked in his favor and the man dropped like a stone. Hanna and her men didn't waste time in joining the fray, succeeding in disarming the others quickly. Yuma still had her weapon, though Teal'c held her fast.

"Get out of here," shouted Hayden, clearing the way for them to run for the stairs, his weapon still trained on Yuma. "Get to the president."

Pushing Yuma to the floor, Teal'c made a break for it along with the others, but Daniel hesitated on the bottom step. "Lana!" he shouted up to Teal'c, dropping down next to the still body. Her eyes were staring and there was nothing that could be done. Yuma was already getting to her feet and Teal'c shook his head. There was no time even to take Lana's body with them.

With a final glance at the woman they'd failed to save, Daniel sped after them up the stairs.

After several minutes skimming over the rolling waves of the Pacific, away from Atlantis, Jack made a decision. "Okay, time to talk." He let the ship fly herself and turned around in his seat to look at Carter. "We really gonna try this?"

She gave a tight nod. "I think we have to, sir. If there's a chance we can put things right, we have to take it."

It's what he knew she'd say, and part of him agreed; they were here, they'd been given a shot. They'd be fools not to take it, wouldn't they? There were a lot of answers to that question — he knew what Daniel would say — but now wasn't the time. "Okay," he said, setting his doubts to one side for now. "So, let's say we get this thing working — where do we go? How do we change all this?"

"I've thought about that, sir. I think we go back to P5X-104. Before we — they, I guess — go through the gate."

"And do what? Warn them?"

"No sir." Carter paused, obviously choosing her words with care. "Time travel into the past is theoretically extremely problematic. One tiny change could have enormous, unpredictable consequences."

"Isn't that kinda the point?"

"Yes sir, but we only want to change one thing. We want you to get back home so you can uncover Maybourne's plot and save the Protected Planet Treaty. We don't want to give our past selves any kind of heads-up about the future."

Jack scratched a hand through his hair; this whole thing was already giving him a headache. "We have no idea if that's enough. Maybe I get home but don't save it? Maybe I do but the Wraith show up anyway? I mean, how could the Protected Planet Treaty have *any* effect on what happens in another galaxy?"

"Sir, the fact is that we can't begin to predict how an alternate future might unfold. And, really, that isn't our job. All we know is that everything went wrong for Earth when you didn't get home to stop Maybourne screwing up the Protected Planets Treaty. So that's what we need to change."

"Right. And how hard can that be?" He saw Carter's jaw tighten at his sarcasm and so took a breath, letting it out in one long, controlled sigh. "You know, Carter, the odds of this even working are —"

"Incalculable, sir. I know. It's a long shot. But I think it's worth it."

He wasn't one hundred percent convinced of that yet and glanced over his shoulder at the giant doohickey sitting in the back of the ship. "You even figured out how this time gizmo works?"

"I think so, sir. Once we engage the 'time-drive' you should just be able to think the right date and we'll be there. But that's actually not the most difficult part."

Of course not. "Go on, surprise me."

"Well, we need to get to P5X-104. And that means flying this through a Stargate." She glanced down at the DHD between them. "And this one is calibrated for the Pegasus Galaxy."

"Which means?"

"We need to go back to the gate in Scotland, sir, and hope Hecate's portable DHD is still rigged up and in one piece… And that there are no Wraith there."

"Oh," he said, returning his attention to the HUD. "Is that all?"

Carter gave a slight smile. "Fingers crossed, sir."

As it turned out, their luck held. Jack landed the ship in front of the Stargate, the valley appeared as deserted as during their first trip. The cloak helped, he figured, and he kept it and the engines running as Carter darted down the ramp and sprinted for the Stargate. Maybe it was his imagination, but he could have sworn he felt eyes on him from the hills surrounding the valley. Possibly it was Aedan Trask's people keeping watch on the gate; possibly it was Wraith. Either way, he wasn't taking any chances.

Skidding to a halt, Carter crouched down next to the Stargate and after a moment turned and gave him the thumbs up.

Whadda you know? So far so good.

After a moment, he saw the gate start dialing and Carter backing up, watching it spin. It was still at its cockeyed angle, which meant the gate-ship would enter into the wormhole off-kilter. What effect that might have on their exit vector he wasn't entirely sure; he doubted it would be good.

Once the fifth chevron had locked, he toggled his radio. "C'mon, Carter, buckle up."

With a nod, she jogged back around and into the ship as he started closing the hatch and preparing to leave.

"We're going through the Stargate," he told the ship. "So, you know, do what you need to do to make it work."

He saw Carter's raised eyebrows as she dropped into the co-pilots chair.

"What?" he said. "I figure it's best that I warn her."

"Yes sir," she said, with a smile in her voice, just as the seventh chevron locked and the wormhole erupted up toward the gray morning sky. She winced. "That'll draw some attention." She peered up at the clouds. "It's a good bet Shadow will send her people down to guard the gate."

"Then let's make sure we're gone." Jack concentrated — it really was intuitive when you just rolled with it — and the gate-ship rose into the air. "Slowly," he warned as he lined her up with the Stargate and edged forward.

"You should be careful of the exit vector, sir."

"I'm on it," he assured her. Ahead of them, the wormhole grew closer as the nose of the ship breached the event horizon. He took a breath. "Here goes nothing, Carter," he said and let the gate swallow them.

Despite the slow entry, the ride was fast and they came out nose down, the ground rushing up to meet them. "Pull up!" Jack barked and the ship responded instantly, but still not fast enough to avoid dragging its butt along the ground before it was shooting up and over the sparse woodland of P5X-104.

An alarm bleeped and was silenced. "Damage?" Jack asked and a whole slew of data cascaded down the screen. He couldn't understand any of it. "Show it diagrammatically," he snapped and the image changed to show a schematic of the ship with something flashing red beneath the tailgate.

"We took some damage," Carter said and glanced over her shoulder. "It doesn't look bad."

"Okay." He took a breath, dismissed the HUD and glanced down at the world streaming beneath them. P5X-104 had been empty of a human population when they'd been here nearly a century ago and little had changed since. The trees were now taller, maybe. "Look familiar?" he said to Carter.

"At least it's not raining this time."

He smiled. "There's that." Banking around, he took the ship back toward the barren hilltop that housed the Stargate. "Okay, so now what?"

Pushing herself from the seat, Carter made her way to the aft compartment and stood for a moment gazing at the device

MacGyvered into the ship. "Now we see if this works."

It took a good hour for Carter to pronounce herself happy with the device, and another half hour to figure out exactly when they wanted to arrive in the past. It was complicated by the fact that neither of them knew how, exactly, the 'time machine' worked.

"It's not like it's going to use the Julian calendar," Sam said, frowning at the machine. "But perhaps the computer is sophisticated enough to translate?"

"We gotta get close to the mark, Carter. We can't hang out here for twenty-years waiting for our future selves to show up."

"We *literally* can't," she said. "Entropic cascade failure means that we can't remain within what has essentially become an alternate timeline for more than a day or so."

In the end, they decided that the only thing Jack could do was think the date as they knew it and hope the Ancients' technology would be able to figure it out. "So that would be February 7th 2000, then," Jack said. He pressed his palms down onto his knees, wiped the sweat off on his BDUs. "You know, as far as Hail Mary passes go, Carter, this is a doozy."

She was silent and he glanced over at her, saw the taut line of her shoulders, the tension in her eyes. But all she said was, "Yes sir."

He let his eyes linger for a beat, then another. Then he said, "If we do this… What happens to us?"

Her mouth pressed into a thin line and she frowned down at the deck. "To you and me, sir? 'Now' us?"

"Yeah. You and me."

He could see she had an answer, but it took a couple moments for her to put it into words. "We would just — If we do it right and end this future, then we won't exist."

Which, of course, he'd known. "I mean it's just… pop. We're gone?"

A nod. "Yes sir. It's not like dying; we'd never have existed at all."

"Yeah, I get that. It's just — It kinda feels like dying."

Her eyes lifted to his and for a moment neither said anything. "Thing is, sir," Carter said eventually, "as I've been saying all along, none of this is real. Nothing that's happened here since we came through the gate all those weeks ago, matters. Not if we go back and fix it."

He rubbed a hand along the back of his neck and turned to stare out at the tree line encroaching on the clearing around the Stargate. The gate itself, just visible out the corner of his eye, swept up and out of sight to their right. "I —" He blew out a breath. "Carter, I can't tell if this is right or wrong," he said. "All the people we've met here..."

"It can't be wrong to try and save Earth, sir. You heard General Hammond's last message. We owe it to him to try — to him and to Janet. To Cassie. To everyone we knew at Stargate Command."

He understood; he did. He could feel every one of those lives weighing on his shoulders, but still... Did it give him the right? "If we went back further," he said, keeping his eyes on the forest, "we could save your mom. Charlie. Daniel's parents... The list goes on, Carter. Where do we stop?"

Carter sucked in a sharp breath, but her answer was steady. "We stop here, sir. This is the one thing we change because this is where it went wrong. We weren't meant to be sent into the future. It was just some freak accident —"

"So was what happened to Charlie. And to your mom."

"Sir —"

"I know." He took a breath, cut her off. "I know, Carter. I get it. But... There's no right and wrong here."

After a moment's silence, she said, "This machine, sir... If it works, it's incredibly dangerous. I know that. And I'd never suggest using it if the future wasn't so devastating. I'd never use it to save my mom. That would be reckless and selfish. But what we're trying, sir? It's neither of those things. We're trying to save Earth — and who knows how many other planets the Wraith have attacked? Or will attack if they're not stopped. Sir, we have to try."

He looked over at her. "Whatever the consequences?"

"Truth is, sir, we won't know what the consequences are…"

"Doesn't that make it worse?"

She was silent for a beat, looked out the window. "Like you said, sir, it's a Hail Mary pass. The alternative is doing nothing."

The alternative, he thought, was to try and help the world in which they found themselves. But as much as he felt that they had a duty here, he couldn't deny that their first duty — the one they'd sworn to when they joined the SGC — was to keep their home safe from her enemies. They'd failed in that the first time around, and maybe this machine gave them a second chance.

It wasn't perfect, but he knew that he couldn't walk away from the chance to save the Earth he knew and loved. Taking a breath, he turned back to face the window. "Okay," he said. "Yeah, okay."

"So we're doing this?"

He gave a nod. "Let's go change history, Carter."

The time travel, it turned out, was easy. He thought *February 7th 2000, Monday*, very loudly. There was a shimmer, a kind of molecular shiver down deep in his bones as reality shifted, and then he was staring out at a different set of trees with the arc of the gate in his peripheral vision and a larger clearing around the Stargate.

"Did it work?" he said.

Carter was on her feet, peering out the window. "Sir, there. Look." She pointed at the muddy ground leading away from the three stone steps at the foot of the gate. "MALP tracks."

He leaned in to see and, yeah, she was right. He remembered shoving the darn thing back up those steps when they'd sent it home after checking in with the SGC. The last time he'd ever spoken to Hammond. "So we're here then."

It was a strange feeling, to be back. Home, almost. Back

at a time before any of the crap they'd witness had occurred. And it was tempting—it was so tempting—to just head over to that DHD standing there in the rain and dial home. They could do it, they could step through the gate and back to the SGC as it had been: strong, secure, inviolate. Hammond and Fraiser would be there, going about their business. The whole world they knew would be right there for the taking.

"Sir?"

Shaking himself, he pulled his eyes from the Stargate. That wasn't his world to take; it belonged to the other O'Neill, the one slogging his guts out, trekking through the rain and mud on this pissant planet. "Yeah," he said. "So now what?"

"Now we get SG-1 home so they can stop Maybourne, sir."

"And how do we do that?"

She sat back down, fixed him with one of those steady looks of hers. "By helping them get to the Stargate faster."

"If I recall, things were kinda hairy, Carter. How are we gonna help them without giving ourselves away?"

She gave him a confident smile. "What if Daniel never got shot?"

"That would speed things along," he conceded. Not to mention, he didn't relish the idea of watching Daniel go through that again.

Carter looked at her watch. "If we assume we arrived at the same time of day we left the future, which we did, going by the position of the sun." She glanced up at the dirty gray sky. "The estimated position of the sun, anyway. Then SG-1 arrived here about five hours ago, sir." She looked at him, expression tense. "The Jaffa attacked overnight, so if we take the gate-ship and follow the path we took we should be able to locate them before the assault."

It sounded like a reasonable plan. "I'll find someplace to set down and we can recon the campsite, try to come in behind the Jaffa."

"Yes sir. We can't risk letting SG-1 see us—and definitely

not the gate-ship. That would raise far too many questions."

Jack slid her an amused glance. "Yeah, past-you wouldn't let it go until you found the answer and who knows what kinda trouble that would get them into?"

She smiled. "Yes, I think it's best for everyone if we keep ourselves hidden, sir."

It wasn't difficult to find their campsite — it was right next to the old stones Daniel had brought them here to look at in the first place — and Jack flew over it low, getting a good look. There was no sign of any Jaffa. SG-1 hadn't arrived yet, either; they'd passed them en route, keeping high enough that their cloaked ship went unnoticed. But it was weird — freaky — to look down and watch his team, himself, tramping through the scattered forest.

He remembered it well, how they'd been strung out and tense, how he'd been working to alienate them ahead of his mission to bust Maybourne. And part of him hated that, for these guys, that hostility wouldn't end. For this team, if Hammond's plan worked, it would reach the point where Jack was dismissed from the Air Force and his people wouldn't understand why he'd betrayed their trust.

They'd think he'd let them down, abandoned them.

Messed up future notwithstanding, Jack found he was glad that he'd never had to go through that in the end. But this guy slogging through the mud would have to face it; if they were successful here today, this other O'Neill would have to betray his team's trust. Despite everything they'd been through since leaving this planet, Jack found himself pitying the guy.

He looked around, scanning ahead for a suitable landing site. The trees were sparse enough that he could set down half a klick from the camp, and he was pleased to discover that the cloak stayed engaged even after he left the ship. "Let's hope the battery doesn't go flat," he said as they headed out through the rain.

Carter gave him a sad kind of look and then fixed her eyes

on the muddy terrain ahead. "With luck, sir, we won't need the ship again."

"Right," he said with a sigh. "With luck."

As it went, this was a surreal kind of suicide mission.

# CHAPTER ELEVEN

**P5X-104 — 2000**: It was a slow and steady rain, just like last time they'd been on this world. Sam remembered it well, and without one iota of fondness. The only difference was that, then, she'd had the right foul weather gear with her. This time, she only had her BDUs and tac vest.

"I prefer the future version of this planet," the colonel groused as he walked alongside her. "It's drier."

Up ahead, Sam caught sight of the ancient stones Daniel had brought them here to investigate. They were visible now through the trees, giant monoliths erected by some lost civilization in worship of indifferent gods, glistening dark and heavy in the rain.

Despite the noise of the rain on the sparse leaf canopy, she could make out the sound of voices coming from close to the stones. The UAV survey of the planet had shown it to be uninhabited, so the team hadn't taken any pains to mask their presence during the mission. That's why she could hear Daniel's voice, the pitch and roll of it rather than actual words, drifting out through the trees. From the banked excitement in his tone, she imagined he was telling them about the writing he'd found on the stones.

At her side, the colonel stopped. His expression was unreadable, eyes slightly narrowed beneath the bill of his cap. Then he nodded to their right, leading her off around in a loop away from the camp. When they were further back, he stopped and in a low voice said, "What do you remember about the Jaffa attack?"

Sam had been on watch. Even on uninhabited worlds they set a watch; there were plenty of indigenous species on most planets that could do the unwary traveler harm.

"Think back," the colonel prompted. "Direction of attack, angle…"

In her memory, it was something of a blur: the solid blast of a staff weapon detonating at the edge of their camp, the scramble for cover. She closed her eyes to visualize it better. They'd made camp with the stones to their left — she remembered their blocky shapes in the dark — and the attack had come from the tree line. "About two o'clock," she said, opening her eyes and gesturing to the right. "The first attack came from that position, relative to the camp, sir."

He nodded, squinted through the rain back toward the stones, then up at the dripping sky. "You think the Jaffa came through the gate or from a ha'tak in orbit?"

It wasn't a question Sam had considered; the disastrous fallout of their escape had pretty much wiped the attack from Sam's mind, overwriting it with more pressing concerns. She thought back. "They had air support, but the gliders could have come through the gate. On the other hand, if ground forces had come through the gate we'd have seen tracks when we arrived. It was muddy enough."

"Yeah."

"So they must have ringed down from orbit."

The colonel snatched off his cap, squeezed rainwater out of it, and settled it back on his head. "Kind of begs the question, why?"

"Why?"

"Why's a snake-head in orbit, waiting to send its Jaffa down to stop us from looking at a bunch of old rocks? If they weren't already here for their own reasons, why were they here at all?"

"You think it was a deliberate ambush?"

"I'm not a big believer in coincidence, Carter."

She stared at him for a moment. "Sir, if you're right, that means someone at the SGC must have leaked the mission rota."

"Yeah." His expressing was tight, mouth a thin line of banked anger. "Well, Hammond was looking for a mole…"

Sam took a breath, blew it out. She felt cold all of a sudden, pieces dropping together in her mind. "So this mole — whoever they were — leaked the mission to a Goa'uld? Why?"

"To get me out of the way, stop me from uncovering the mole and taking down Maybourne's operation."

But something about that wasn't making sense. "If that's the case, sir, why didn't they just bomb the site from orbit? I mean, we almost escaped. Why risk a ground assault when they could easily have killed us?"

"You know the Goa'uld, Carter," he said. "They're always over-confident."

He had a point, but she couldn't shake the feeling they were missing something.

"C'mon," the colonel said, "let's dig in and wait for the bad guys to show up."

There was a rise of land behind them, and the colonel led them up to the military crest and dropped down onto his belly to peer over the top. Sam joined him, wincing as the damp sunk into her pants.

"If I was a Jaffa," the colonel said, "this is where I'd zap in." He squinted at the sky. "How long until sundown, do you reckon?"

The light was already failing. "Less than an hour," she guessed. "You think we should take them out as they arrive, sir?"

"If we had our MP5s, maybe," he said, pulling out his Wraith stunner. "But not with these popguns. We'll have to take a more strategic approach. Harry them from behind."

"We were less than a klick from the gate when Daniel was shot," Sam reminded him. "And it was dawn by that point. I remember it was light."

"They'll move faster with us running interference," the colonel said. "We got pinned down a couple times, remember?"

She did, but now she came to think about it that felt off. "Sir, why did they even let us run? They could have encircled us to start with; they knew exactly where we were and they had air support. We wouldn't have stood a chance against those gliders if they'd kept us corralled by the stones."

The colonel rubbed a hand over his jaw. It was a little stubbly; he needed a shave. "You think they were driving us back to the gate."

"Yes sir. I think that's exactly what they were doing."

"Question is, why?"

Sam didn't have a ready answer and she didn't have time to consider it further. A bolt of golden light shot down behind the shallow rise and Sam dropped, pressing herself into the dirt.

"They're early," O'Neill grumbled, working his way backward and behind the crest of the hill as two more ring transporters deposited Jaffa behind the slope. Sam didn't wait to watch.

"Daylight makes sense," she said, squirming back down the hill. "Explains why we didn't notice the ring transporters last time."

The colonel was on his feet now, jogging toward cover in a low swathe of brush. His stunner was drawn, held loose in his hand. "This is good. Gives us time to find a position. We know they won't attack until dark."

He wormed his way through the brush, and then settled. Carter followed, crouching at his side. "Yes, sir, but why not? There's four of us. They don't need to wait until dark to attack."

"Does it matter?" the colonel said. "We already know what happens — and what we have to stop happening."

Sam shifted, easing the pressure on her legs. "I don't know, sir. I guess I've just got a feeling that there's more to it than we're seeing."

"A feeling?" He breathed out a sigh.

"Sir —"

"No," he said. "I trust your 'feelings', Carter. What do you want to do?"

She shrugged, pleased by his faith in her but keeping that pleasure to herself. She wasn't even sure why she did that anymore, especially not here and now; it had simply become a necessary habit, over the years, to lock everything down when it came to the colonel. And she couldn't seem to break it. "I want to take a closer look," she said. "See if we can figure out anything more than we already know."

"Okay," he said. "We'll do a little recon, see if we can't figure out what's going on first. What else would we do with our last night on Earth?"

Sam lifted an eyebrow. "We're not actually on Earth, sir."

With an exasperated shake of his head, he moved out, keeping low. "Pedant."

It took a half hour and they were starting to lose the light by the time they'd circled around and behind the Jaffa position. Moving silently, they crept through the trees, making use of the poor visibility and the endless rain to hide their approach. The tree cover was a little thicker here, and the colonel dropped into a crouch about thirty meters out behind a knotty tree trunk where two spreading pines butted together. He signaled for Carter to stop and she crowded in next to him behind the trees.

The Jaffa were waiting where they'd arrived. There were twelve men in total, well armored and apparently indifferent to the steady rain. Some sat on the incline of the hill, others stood and talked quietly. Sam couldn't make out anything they were saying, heard nothing more than the rise and fall of their voices. Whatever they were doing here, it was obvious they were waiting for something.

Pulling out his monocular, the colonel edged forward and took a closer look.

She noticed the moment he stopped stock still, felt the tension spreading from his shoulders to hers where they touched. After a beat, he handed her the monocular and tapped his forehead. Taking the glass from him, she looked. A couple of the Jaffa had their backs to her and it took a moment for her to see what the colonel had noticed.

The sigil these Jaffa wore was devastatingly familiar: a horned circle with a cross beneath it.

And, suddenly, everything made horrible sense. She lowered the monocular, caught the colonel's grim gaze. "Hecate," she whispered. "They're Hecate's Jaffa. Maybourne was working with *Hecate*?"

The colonel passed his hand over his mouth, leaned in close to murmur. "To kill us?"

"No." That couldn't be right; that's not what they were doing here. "To drive us into the wormhole at a specific time." She sat back a little, so she could see his face when she said, "To send us into the future."

"She's been playing us this whole damn time. Maybourne, that son-of-lousy—" He broke off as his voice rose, clamped his jaw shut. After a silent moment he leaned in again and whispered, "Does it change anything?"

Sam shook her head. "No. We can still end it here. In fact—" She smiled and wished it didn't feel so shaky. "In fact it makes the decision easier. Hecate's already meddled with the past. We're just correcting what she already changed, putting it right."

"Yeah," he said, and for a moment there was something else in his expression. "So everything that's happened here, everything since we stepped through the wormhole that night, is…a mistake. A dead end."

"Not entirely," she said. "I mean, we're here and we're going to change it, so I guess that has meaning. In a convoluted, circular kind of way."

He nodded and looked away. "So the one consequential thing we do is set the past right, everything else is meaningless."

Thinking of Sting and Earthborn, of Elspeth and Aedan—of the hundred years of struggle and life and death that had happened as a consequence of Hecate's meddling—she said, "Not meaningless, sir. Just… short lived, I guess."

"Short lived." He glanced down at the scant space between them, and said, "Sounds about right."

"Sir—"

A bark of command echoed through the trees. The Jaffa jumped to their feet, moving into formation. She put her hand on the colonel's arm to draw his attention and nodded toward the Jaffa position.

His focus lingered on her for a moment, then he nodded and said, "Let's go change history, Major."

**Arbella — 2098:** They didn't head for the upper level. Instead, Hanna led them away from the cells where they'd been held, down a narrow corridor along which ran large pipes. The noise was deafening and the heat was stifling. Teal'c felt the sweat collect on the back of his neck and soak into the collar of his shirt. Though he knew it was futile, his mind kept returning to the image of Lana Jones' twisted body lying on the floor, the ugly red wound gaping on the side of her head. There was a time when he would have accepted such a death as the unavoidable outcome of battle; he had witnessed the lifeblood bleeding from countless innocents before.

But he had lived too long among the Tau'ri — too long as part of SG-1 — to allow such mindless killing to take place, and only stand by and do nothing. He had made his choice on Chulak when O'Neill had given him the chance to rebel against the false god Apophis. Despite his opinion of this world, of the abomination of the timeline, he must see that Lana Jones' did not die in vain. Teal'c knew that he would encounter no opposition from Daniel Jackson. The pressing matter of the moment, though, was getting to safety away from the threat that lay within the walls of the Stargate base. Officer Hayden had held Yuma at gunpoint, but Teal'c had witnessed how his hand shook; the young man was inexperienced and could not be relied on to hold Yuma and those who would follow her at bay for much longer.

"Where are you taking us, Hanna?" he asked.

"The pipes run the heat and air conditioning system for the

complex," yelled Hanna above the din. "It's too dangerous to try and get out through the base, but there are vents down here that'll take us out on to the cliff side."

"Uh… the cliff side? As in, the side of the cliff?" asked Daniel, with a worried glance back at Teal'c.

"It's perfectly safe," replied Hanna. "We use them all the time to get into the base under the radar."

"We?"

"The CMF. Or, rather, those of us who are part of the movement."

It was from the way she said 'movement' that Teal'c inferred something grander than a sudden reactionary measure. "To what movement do you refer?"

Hanna grinned back at him. "We've been planning this for a long time, Teal'c. With or without SG-1's arrival, we would have made our move sooner or later."

"You plan to rise up against those who seek to rule you," he said, unsure whether he thought them foolish or admired their valor. Perhaps both.

"Wait, what?" Daniel called after Hanna as she moved quickly through the tunnel. But his words were lost as the noise from the pipes was overlaid by another sound, uncontained and wild. As they turned a corner, they were struck by a ferocious blast of air that almost blew them back against the wall. Teal'c squinted into the wind, while Daniel shielded his face in the crook of both elbows. Up ahead, Teal'c saw that a large grate was leaning against the tunnel's wall, leaving a gaping hole around six feet wide by four tall beyond which stretched the dark expanse of Arbella. Night had fallen while they had been held, a bright moon painting the landscape in colorless shades of silver.

"Through here," shouted Hanna, ducking out of the opening, followed by her two men. Teal'c crouched down and stepped through, reaching back to grasp Daniel by the arm and help him out.

"Whoa!" cried Daniel, teetering backward against the rock wall, as they found themselves on a broad ledge that fell away steeply to the shadowy plains below. Out here, the noise was not so loud, but the wind still whipped at them, as if threatening to pluck them from their ledge and fling them down to their deaths.

"Dr. Jackson, Teal'c — well met," said a familiar voice.

Teal'c turned to see a woman much changed since they had left the planet through the Stargate just weeks before. "General Bailey," he said, with a nod. "Please accept our thanks for your aid in freeing us."

The general smiled through thin lips. She looked pale in the stark moonlight, her unruly hair escaping from the beanie hat she wore to be whipped about her face by the wind. "I just pushed the button. If it hadn't been for these guys, you'd still be in there."

Teal'c did not miss the chill in her voice, nor the banked anger in her tight expression.

"General, what's going on?" said Daniel, pushing forward. "I thought we were friends when we left."

"No one knew what you were looking for in the data center when you left, Daniel," she said, with a look that proved her anger was a barely controlled thing. "Even *I* didn't know."

Teal'c felt no shame in their actions. They had been searching for a way to save more than those people who lived on Arbella — they had been searching for a way to save *everything*. But that did not stop him from regretting the secret they had kept from the woman who had been their only ally on this planet. Daniel Jackson, it seemed, felt the same.

"General, I —"

"Save it, Jackson. We don't have time for recriminations. You can explain it to Jones when you see him and hope that bringing Lana —" At that she cut off and looked over both their shoulders and then around at Hanna and her colleagues. "Where is Lana?"

Daniel frowned and squeezed his eyes closed, but Teal'c knew the truth had to be faced. "She is dead, General Bailey. Agent Yuma killed her."

The general's face barely moved bar a tightening of her jaw. "Hanna?" she said, not taking her eyes from Teal'c.

"It's true, ma'am," said Hanna, without intonation. "I'm sorry. The mission didn't go as planned."

General Bailey took a moment before speaking. "This…" She looked away across the Arbellan plains and rubbed her hands over her face, cursing under her breath. "How am I supposed to tell him?"

"You aren't," said Daniel. "We'll tell him."

Bailey shook her head. "You can't. We need to get you through the gate. If he finds out what's happened from you, then it's you he'll blame. Hell, thanks to Yuma, he already thinks you're the Four Horsemen of the Apocalypse."

Daniel shrugged. "Well, we're about a hundred years too late for that. And if he needs someone to blame, then let it be Yuma. But he at least…" He cleared his throat and Teal'c heard raw pain there still. It was pain to which he himself could not grant a foothold; in his heart, Drey'auc would always be on Chulak, awaiting his return. "Jones needs to know the truth from us, General," finished Daniel. "Regardless of what he thinks of SG-1, he has the right to know what happened to his wife."

Bailey cocked her head as if taking stock of Daniel and Teal'c, before saying, "Alright, have it your way. But if you end up back in the cells upstairs, there's nothing more I can do for you." She turned and led the way down the cliff side and, as Teal'c followed, he hoped O'Neill's plan was not reliant on their return.

**P5X-104 — 2000:** Three hours after sundown, the attack began. Jack and Carter were ready for it.

The Jaffa advanced in three squads of four, one down each flank and one down the middle. He and Carter took a flank each, following them through the drenched forest. It was lucky he wasn't getting out of this alive, Jack thought, because didn't think he'd ever be dry again. Everything he was wearing was wet and cold.

But his discomfort was forgotten when the first shot was fired, sizzling through the drizzly air to impact at the edge of SG-1's camp.

"Sir! Incoming!" he heard Carter — past-Carter — yell.

There was a scrabble, the golden flicker of their campfire disappeared and he could hear himself barking orders as his team dived for cover behind the stone monoliths.

Meanwhile, Jack moved silently through the trees toward the Jaffa squad. They were moving in poor formation, a strung out line in order to cover as much territory as possible and to keep SG-1 from breaking in the wrong direction, away from the Stargate. It probably made sense to risk being so far from their unit when they thought SG-1 was the only threat on the planet.

But of course things were different this time around, and, besides, any good soldier should know to expect the unexpected.

The Jaffa at the head of their rambling line moved further ahead, circling around the side of the camp while his comrades hung back. All were shadows amid the trees and the guy in the lead had left himself vulnerable.

Jack made himself a shadow too, moving slow enough to be silent, keeping his quarry in sight.

"I thought you said this rock was uninhabited, Carter," he heard the other version of himself hiss.

"Well the UAV survey—"

"Was wrong. Again." And, yeah, that was him playing the jerk.

Ahead of him, the Jaffa had settled behind a tree and was taking aim. It was point blank. He could have taken any of SG-1 out at that range. But he hadn't. Jack moved closer, lifted his stunner as the Jaffa raised his staff weapon.

Jack fired, the blue bolt lighting up the forest and sending the Jaffa face down and twitching into the dirt.

"What was that?" Daniel barked, as Jack ran forward and snatched the staff weapon from the Jaffa's hands.

"That wasn't a Goa'uld weapon," Carter said, nervous.

"Okay, we're pulling back to the gate *now*. Teal'c, take point. I'll cover our six. Let's move. Double time."

To his right, Jack heard movement and melted deeper into the forest before the rest of the Jaffa could catch up. He knew the route back to the gate, so doubled back around and came in closer to where SG-1 was retreating. He'd bought them a little breathing space — and gotten himself a staff weapon. Now he just had to keep his eye on them and hope that Carter had been equally successful.

Sam remembered their midnight flight to the gate in a series of stark images, and it was strange to be watching it as an outsider, jogging through the forest to the right of her team.

The Jaffa were harrying them, but it was clear from her new perspective that they were simply chasing them back to the gate. Her head was still full of the fact that these were Hecate's Jaffa, that they had a purpose here she'd never imagined that dark night so many months (decades) earlier. Why and how Hecate had engineered this, however, was impossible to understand. And maybe she'd never know — if they succeeded in getting this team home, then the hows and wherefores were all moot.

Still, it niggled at her, not understanding.

They'd been making good progress and been moving for a couple hours when things began to look starkly familiar. The trees gave way to a scrubby clearing — there was little cover for SG-1, who found themselves backing out into the open. The Jaffa, meanwhile, slowed and stayed in the trees.

Her heart rate kicked up. This was where it happened; this

was where Daniel got shot. And this was where they could change everything.

"Stay low," she heard the colonel say. Then, "Crap, we're sitting ducks here."

A staff blast shot out from the other side of the clearing, detonating against a fallen tree and sending rotting wood flying up into the air.

Her team dived for cover. "Down!" The colonel barked. "Daniel, get down."

He dropped. Sam remembered that too. He'd dropped to the ground, they'd edged back. She remembered wondering if the Jaffa were going to slaughter them there, just encircle them and take them out one by one.

"Keep moving," her own voice yelled out. "We can't let them surround us."

But a couple more staff blasts kept the team pinned down.

Sam could see Jaffa in the trees ahead of her. Secure in the false knowledge that they were alone on the planet, their attention was fixed on SG-1 and they hadn't noticed her presence yet. She was pretty light on her feet, but knew she lacked the colonel's special ops experience. Still, so far so good — she crept closer.

Their voices were urgent and they were debating something intensely, but the only word Sam understood was *chappa'ai*. No help there. But then one of them gestured to the sky in the pretty universal signal for aerial backup and she got the picture. SG-1 were moving too fast, they were slowing them down here and calling for backup to do it — which confirmed her suspicion that they needed the team to go through the gate at a specific moment. Perhaps to interact with a solar flare? Although the data she'd gleaned from the Earth gate, back when they'd first returned from Hecate's ha'tak, suggested something different had caused their jump through time.

Either way, it meant that she had to get SG-1 home before whatever Hecate had planned came to pass.

Through the trees she could see the shadowy shapes of her team start moving again, creeping backward through the clearing, keeping low. She let her mind go back to the first time this had happened, picturing the moment Daniel was hit. The staff blast had come from the opposite side of the clearing—the colonel's side. It had happened when he'd stood up to scramble backward over a fallen tree trunk, looking for cover.

Anytime now… Mouth dry she watched, keeping slow pace with her team, as they made their way back through the silent clearing.

The blast of a staff weapon scorched through the trees. Sam's heart leaped into her throat, but the blast was going the wrong way, sideways across the clearing. It didn't hit Daniel; it hit something—someone—in the tree line.

The colonel had made his play.

There was a cry, and then more shots fired within the forest. The Jaffa ahead of her turned toward the ruckus with a guttural mutter of confusion. Sam added to it by opening fire with her stunner, putting two Jaffa down in quick succession. From the clearing she heard the familiar rattle of an MP5 and the colonel yelling orders to his team, "Fall back, fall back!"

SG-1 were on their feet, vaulting the log behind which, in her memory, they'd sought shelter while the colonel patched Daniel up, and disappeared back into the trees. Sam moved too, loping along through the woods, out of sight in the dark but keeping pace.

They'd done it. They'd saved Daniel and history was unfolding along a new path. But Sam was still there—which meant there was still a chance, a probability, that Hecate would succeed.

She remembered the Death Gliders that had strafed them at the gate and ran on, getting ahead of SG-1 to secure the Stargate. The ball was still very much in play.

Whoever had the dumb idea of planting a Stargate on the top of a hill should be forced to run up the damn thing with a platoon of Jaffa on their ass.

So said Colonel Jack O'Neill.

His team — as was — wasn't far behind him. Daniel wasn't wounded and this time they were outstripping the Jaffa, which meant they should have a straight shot at the gate.

Except for the gliders.

He'd considered ignoring Carter's advice and going back for the gate-ship, but on balance she was probably right about the danger of exposing their past selves to alien technology from a galaxy far, far away.

Still, the muscles in his legs were regretting the decision.

There was no sign of Carter yet, either. He tried not to be concerned; the plan had been to rendezvous at the gate and make sure the team got through without any last minute hitches. There was no reason to suppose she wouldn't make it, and even if she didn't, he could handle it alone and then they'd both be gone anyway.

Lights out, game over.

But if, or rather *when*, that happened he'd rather not face it alone. He'd rather have Carter at his side at the end.

The crest of the hill was in sight and above it the arc of the Stargate ghosted against the black sky. Unlike last time they were here, dawn hadn't broken yet. He could barely see the DHD where it crouched next to the stone steps. Slowing, Jack dropped to a crouch and caught his breath. Listening. Mostly what he could hear was rain hammering through the leaves and their wet windblown rustle, occasionally the rattle of MP5 fire and hiss of a zat or the solid blast of a staff weapon.

And footsteps.

Swiveling, still crouched, he got his weapon up just in time to see Carter lift her hands.

"It's me."

"Carter." He couldn't keep the relieved smile from spoiling his frown. "A little more notice next time."

She rolled her eyes and dropped down next to him, breathing hard. He was pleased to see that he wasn't the only one catching his breath. "They're just a couple minutes out, sir. I think the Jaffa called for backup — gliders."

Picking up the staff weapon from where it lay next to him, he said, "I'll see what I can do about that if you keep the Jaffa busy."

"You won't be able to risk getting out in the open to take the shot, sir."

"I know. I don't need to take it down, just need to give it something else to think about while our guys get the gate open."

She glanced up through the rainy canopy. "SG-1 made good time. The Jaffa are going to need to delay them for a while — it was daylight when we went through the gate."

"And back to the future." Jack sighed. "Carter, you got any idea *why*?"

"The only…" She shook her head. "I can't explain it, sir. Unless Hecate needed us in the future for some reason?"

"And how would she possibly know that?"

Again, Carter just shook her head. "I think there are some questions we're just never going to be able to answer, sir."

He supposed she was right, given that time was running out real fast. "So when they go through the gate, that's it? That's when…" He wiggled his fingers to encompass the end of an entire timeline, an alternate universe of life. "Boom?"

"Yes sir, although there won't be an actual boom. At least, I don't think so." She gave a rueful smile. "It's not like I've ever done this before."

"And, ironically, you'll never know that you did." A world without consequences, Teal'c had called it. Jack thought that had a certain apocalyptic appeal. "C'mon, Sundance," he said, "let's go find our blaze of glory."

# CHAPTER TWELVE

WHEN DANIEL had first arrived on Arbella, he'd balked at the precarious main route they'd taken down the cliff side. Compared to the narrow, crumbling ledge they now found themselves on, that path seemed like a four-lane highway. He clung to the side of the rock face and kept his eyes on Hanna as she made her sure-footed way ahead of him, the wind dragging at them all with needy claws. He wondered how Teal'c was getting on behind him, with his huge Jaffa frame and wounded as he was, but didn't dare turn his head to look.

Their descent seemed endless, and Daniel had begun to wonder what the ancient civilization who built this place had against elevators when they rounded an outcrop and he saw that the path finally broadened out to take them a couple hundred feet to the bottom.

"Where to now?" he asked Bailey, wiping the red dust from his hands. They were grazed and sore from clinging to the shallow handholds offered by the rock face and he hissed at the sting.

She gestured them into a crouch and pointed out across the lights of Laketown to a low building that sat on a bluff on one of the hills in the distance. Daniel had noticed it before, set as it was above the rest of the town and looking slightly grander than the small stucco houses. "That's the president's residence. It'd be quicker if we could cut straight through the town to get there, but I daresay your presence would be noted. Yuma will have her people on the lookout."

"I guess the 'wookiee' tactic wouldn't work?" said Daniel.

Bailey squinted at him.

"Never mind," he muttered. He had definitely been hanging with Jack O'Neill for too long.

Led by Bailey, they set off on a route skirting the edges of the town and sticking to the rocky plains. In the gaps between the buildings, he caught glimpses of figures walking with the familiar slow gait of guards on patrol. Though they were shielded by darkness, Daniel still felt stark in the moonlight, sure that they'd be spotted. Bailey knew what she was doing, though, and their path was circuitous, their progress in staggered bursts. By the time they were within the vicinity of the presidential residence, he was winded and even Teal'c was sweating.

"You okay, big guy?" he asked, glancing down at his friend's side. Hanna had apparently dressed the wound, but Daniel was pretty sure that, no matter the healing capabilities of a Goa'uld symbiote, this exertion couldn't be good for Teal'c.

"I am fine," replied Teal'c. Daniel guessed he shouldn't have expected any other reply.

They waited, sheltered in darkness, as Hanna darted on ahead on the orders of Bailey to check out the area. "Yuma has security details everywhere," she said. "I don't expect this to be easy."

Sure enough, when Hanna returned, it wasn't encouraging. "Two on the front door ma'am, and another two patrolling the building. I'd say our best bet is going in through the terrace windows to the rear, but we have to time it well."

Bailey nodded. "Alright, then we make it as easy as possible for ourselves and keep risks to a minimum. Sergeant, you and your men are dismissed. My thanks for all you've done here."

For a second, it looked as if Hanna might protest, but then, perhaps seeing her commanding officer's expression, she came to attention and saluted. "For Arbella, ma'am. It's our honour." And then they were gone, leaving Daniel, Teal'c and Bailey to go on alone.

On Bailey's guidance, they avoided the front of the building altogether, hiding behind the property's low perimeter wall in a crouch that was almost a crawl. Though the current security measures were apparently much tighter than the Arbellan

Commander in Chief was used to, and still posed a problem, Daniel acknowledged that it could have been much more difficult for them; he wondered what President Jones would have made of the White House Secret Service and the agents who'd served at the pleasure of the president. He also wondered if any of these officers would be willing to take a bullet for their leader and hoped, fervently, that it would not come to that.

"Okay, here they come," said Bailey, as the patrol appeared round the corner of the residence. "Those terrace doors they're walking past? That's where we're headed. Hanna says we have around a minute thirty from the time they round the opposite corner to when they reappear, so we move as soon as they're out of sight."

"Daniel Jackson," said Teal'c, "my wound is slowing me down. I believe I will hinder your speed."

"I'm not leaving you, Teal'c."

"I am concealed here. I can await your return."

In truth, the thought of making his case to the president without his teammate by his side unnerved Daniel. Though his role as the diplomat of SG-1 and the Stargate program was one that he now accepted, the fact was that it had fallen to him almost by accident, purely by virtue of his academic knowledge of languages rather than any formal skills at negotiation. He would never feel entirely at ease with the task, but having Sam, Jack and Teal'c by his side always gave him the courage he needed.

But it was unusual to hear Teal'c acknowledge a weakness and Daniel knew he must be struggling. He'd have to go this one alone, and hope that Bailey would have his back — despite the betrayal she must feel because of their actions in the data center and all that it implied about their loyalty to Arbella. He had to assume that Jones knew about that too…

At last, the two guards disappeared around the other side of the building, and Daniel moved, Bailey at his shoulder. Gravel crunched beneath his feet, no matter how light-footed he tried to be. His heart beat fast as his eyes darted between the terrace door and either side of the house, expecting the guards to come running back at any second. But no one appeared and then they were on the level surface of the terrace.

The double doors were locked, of course, but Bailey produced a wide bladed knife from a pocket in her pants, and wedged it into the gap. With a swift twist of her wrist, she'd jimmied the door and it sprang open with a barely audible crack. Once inside, she moved through what looked like a library with the speed and grace of one familiar with their surroundings. As the leader of the Arbellan military, Daniel guessed that she would have been a close acquaintance of President Jones and wondered if, in fact, a real friendship had been put to the test by current tensions.

He knew what it was to butt heads over ideals with someone whom you respected more than anyone in the world. He could only hope that Jones was still willing to listen to Bailey, just like he knew Jack would have listened to him in a similar situation. All they needed was to find him in the house before the guards found them.

They were just approaching the library door when it flew open and the light came on. Daniel blinked against the glare and saw, in the doorway, the man they'd come to see. He also saw the gun in his hand.

"What the hell do you think you're doing, General?" demanded Gunnison Jones through gritted teeth. His hand was steady and from the furious look on his face Daniel didn't doubt he that he'd shoot if he didn't like her answer.

Bailey held out her hands, placating. "Mr. President, we just need you to hear us out."

"Hear you out? You break into my home in the middle of the night, and bring a dangerous traitor with you, and you want me to hear you out?"

So Jones had known that he and Teal'c had returned to the planet. He wondered how much of the truth Yuma had spoon-fed him along with her lies. He certainly couldn't have known about Lana. "Mr. President," he said, "I mean no harm to Arbella."

Jones trained his weapon on Daniel. "You were trying to take control of the gate room. After we'd extended you our trust, you chose to betray us. Why did you — ?" He broke off as if the words pained him. When he spoke again, his voice was harsh with feeling. "Why did you use my wife as an excuse to leave Arbella? Why did you give me false hope?"

"It wasn't false hope. At least, that wasn't our intention." This wasn't how Daniel had wanted to break the news to the man. He was torn between defending SG-1 and trying to soften the blow of what he had to impart.

"So she's here then?" said Jones, his tone mocking but with something raw beneath.

Daniel took a breath. "No, she's —"

"I'm sorry, Gun," said Bailey. "Lana's dead."

Jones' jaw tightened. "I know that, Roz," he said. "I had accepted it until you convinced me that these people could bring her back. You convinced me to believe them, but they were liars all along."

"No," said Bailey. "It's Karin Yuma who's the liar. She's manipulated this situation all along, since before SG-1 even arrived."

Daniel stepped forward and then halted when Jones tightened his grip on the gun. "Mr. President, we did bring Lana back." The look of guarded hope on the man's face tightened like a vice around Daniel's heart, but the truth couldn't be put off any longer. "We brought her back, sir, but Yuma... she killed her." The words tasted like ash in his mouth and, for a moment, he could feel the burn of a Goa'uld hand device on his forehead and smell the acrid stench of a staff blast.

Jones shook his head. "You're a liar." He turned to Bailey. "Roz, how could you — ?"

"It's true, Gun. I saw it with my own eyes."

"No…" Jones took a step back, as if he could back away from the horrible truth. "No, it's not possible."

Quietly, Daniel said, "I'm so sorry. If it's —" He swallowed. "I know it's no consolation. I know that nothing can ever console you for the loss of someone you love, but you should know that Lana wasn't herself when we found her. I'm not sure how much she knew about where she was or what was going on. She —" It was something of a white lie, but perhaps it would help. "She didn't suffer when she died."

Jones face was desolate, the hand holding the gun starting to tremble. "What do you mean she wasn't herself?"

Daniel glanced at Bailey and she gave him a slight nod, agreement to carry on. "Her mind had been damaged by the Wraith," he said. "But… But she knew you, Mr. President. I carried her back to the Stargate myself and she knew your name — she remembered you."

Jones pressed his eyes shut, his throat working as he tried to swallow. "I don't understand," he said in a thin, exposed voice. "Why did —? Why would Yuma kill her? Out of pity?"

"No," Bailey said. "Out of desperation."

A long moment of silence passed, then Jones opened his eyes and they were clear and hard. "What do you mean, desperation?"

"She was afraid that you'd open the Stargate, sir," Daniel said. "She was afraid that people here would trust us again — and that you'd decide to help us fight for Earth."

Jones said nothing, licked at his dry lips. Daniel couldn't get a read on his expression.

"Yuma is dangerous, Gun," Bailey said. "And she's foolish too. She thinks we can just hide behind our gate shield, live inside a bubble here on Arbella, but there's a threat out there and it's only a matter of time before it lands on our doorstep."

His eyes narrowed. "You brought it to our doorstep!"

"You know that's not true. The Goa'uld, the Wraith… They don't need the Stargate to reach us, Gun. They have ships and —"

"And now they know where we are! You've opened us up to attack."

"No, that's not —"

But their argument was cut short as the terrace door burst open and two guards surged in — holding Teal'c at gunpoint. "We found these two just outside the wall, Mr. President," said one of the guards and, as Teal'c stood immobile and expressionless, the guard shoved a second man into the middle of the room.

"Hayden?" said Jones.

Yuma's second-in-command was bleeding from a cut above his eye, his face grimy and bruised. Daniel had last seen him with his gun trained on Yuma, but if he was here…

"Where's Yuma?" demanded Bailey.

"I don't know. She overpowered me and got away. I don't know where she is now." He turned to Jones. "But I had to come here, Mr. President. I had to make sure you knew the truth. She's been lying to you for so long, but she always said it was for the good of Arbella, and I believed her. Until now."

Jones lowered his weapon now that his security detail was here, though he still gripped it so tight his knuckles were white. "Now?"

"Sir, I'm so sorry. I didn't know. I didn't know how far she'd go…" Hayden's voice cracked and tears spilled over on to his cheeks. In that moment, Daniel saw a young man completely unprepared for the depths to which greed could drive those ambitious for power.

And when he looked at Jones, he saw, finally, a man facing the stark truth of his wife's fate.

**P5X-104 — 2000:** SG-1 was coming in hot, the Jaffa close behind and apparently getting desperate. Hecate's plan — whatever it was — was about to go horribly wrong.

Sam was only sorry she wouldn't get to see Hecate's face when she realized she'd failed. And then she remembered that she didn't even know what Hecate's face looked like at this point in time. But it wasn't Janet and that thought sang like joy inside her. It would never be Janet, not now.

She had taken cover to the right of the Stargate, giving herself a clear shot past the DHD that would allow her to lay down covering fire if necessary. She didn't want to draw attention to herself, especially from her past-self or Daniel, but if needs must she'd be able to protect them from where she hid as they dialed out. The colonel was on the other side of the gate, waiting for the glider's strafing runs that they both knew were coming — just like they had the first time they'd run this scenario.

And from the tree line she could hear the other colonel barking orders, the rattle of MP5 fire and the scorching blast of staff weapons lighting up the rain-sodden night as he slid to a halt at the edge of the forest. Ducking behind a tree, he lay down covering fire and barked, "Carter. Dial us up!"

"Yes sir!"

It was strange to watch herself, bedraggled and exhausted, bolting from the tree line, head down and legs pumping. Sam kept her eyes fixed on the forest, watching for movement — there had been Jaffa covering the gate, last time — while her former-self zig-zagged across the clearing toward the gate.

Then, to her right, Sam saw movement — the dull glint of armor. She opened fire and saw the Jaffa go down, flung back against a tree.

The other Sam ducked at the sound, but kept running. She didn't even glance at the tree line, just flung herself behind the DHD and started dialing. Sam remembered having to reach across from behind the DHD to dial upside down, and she remembered how she'd thought that was the reason she'd misdialed. She'd blamed herself for not getting them home, for Daniel not getting the medical treatment he'd needed, when all along…

Hecate.

Tightening her jaw in anger, she glanced up at the gate as it began to spin. Faint, over the weapons fire, she heard shouting in the Goa'uld language and then the deadly sound of a glider on approach.

SG-1 heard it too. The colonel glanced up at the sky — still empty — and yelled, "Get to the gate!"

Daniel and Teal'c broke cover. Teal'c ran with one eye on the sky while Daniel sprinted for the DHD where past-Sam was covering him as the fourth chevron engaged.

And then the glider was on them, strafing the ground and sending Daniel tumbling forward.

Sam's heart caught in her throat. The moment seemed to last forever as he fell, rolled over and over. And then he was back on his feet, staggering to find his balance but running. He looked unhurt.

The glider banked up and hard left, coming in from a new angle.

And that's when the staff blast erupted from the trees on the other side of the clearing. The colonel. *Her* colonel. He got two solid hits, right on the nose. It wasn't enough to bring the glider down, but it was enough to send it veering left and up over the gate, clearing the egress for Teal'c and the other O'Neill.

The sixth chevron engaged and Sam pulled back, moving around closer to the colonel's position. The sand was running through the hourglass. Once SG-1 went through the gate, it was over. Her life — this iteration of her life — would be over.

She didn't relish the idea of facing oblivion alone, so she sought out the colonel.

"Nice shooting, sir," she said as she moved in closer to him. He still had his eye on the sky, but the glider hadn't yet come around for another pass. His only reply was a tense nod; it was typical of the colonel that he'd find it easier not to acknowledge what was about to happen. And then, at last, the gate opened with its usual eruption of incandescent power and the event horizon burst out into the rainy night.

"Carter, Daniel — now!"

Sam didn't watch. She kept her eyes on the shadows moving through the forest, her weapon firing at the tree line, covering SG-1's escape. The colonel did the same, moving back to stand shoulder-to-shoulder with her.

"Teal'c, with me!" the other O'Neill barked.

She could imagine them backing up together, up the three stone steps and into the gate. Her heart started to hammer, her gut twisting queasily. This was it, this was the end. It wasn't like it was going to hurt; it wasn't like she would feel *anything*. But everything would just stop. Oblivion.

The end of her staff weapon began to shake and she felt the colonel's hand on hers, pushing the weapon down.

"They've gone," he said, with a glance at the open Stargate. Its light still flooded the clearing, a few Jaffa running cursing from the trees.

She and the colonel were safe, hidden by the rain and the night and the forest. And what did it matter anyway? Once the wormhole collapsed, once SG-1 was home, it would all disappear. Nonetheless, the colonel kept his hand on her arm and tugged her back further into the darkness of the rain-sodden trees.

"So this is it, huh?" he said, drawing her attention away from the gate. Any moment now, it would close…

Swallowing, she looked at him and nodded. "Yes sir."

She thought he might say something about it being an honor, about having no regrets: the usual valiant heroism. But instead he said, "We never did find that silver lining."

Sam gave half a smile. "No, I guess not."

He nodded, his gaze drifting away for a moment, toward the gate, and then back to her. "I think," he said, "it might have looked something like this." And he leaned down and kissed her through the rain.

Sam closed her eyes, a hand on his shoulder, and waited for the gate to close, for everything to drift away.

The wormhole died and…

…there was still the steady hammering of rain through the trees, the bark of Jaffa curses.

The colonel pulled away, looking back toward the Stargate. "Um," he said, "everything was supposed to fade to black."

Sam shifted, uncomfortably. "Yes, sir."

"Well that's… awkward." He cleared his throat. "Didn't it work?"

"I —" It was difficult to think quite straight because his hand was still on her arm, but of course there was a notional explanation for the fact that they'd changed history and yet were somehow still around to witness it. "There's a — It's not a scientific theory, sir, but some people have postulated the existence of points of divergence within the timeline."

He took his hand from her arm, fingers flexing. "Meaning what, exactly?"

"Meaning that there are certain events in history that can unfold in multiple ways, each one giving rise to an alternate timeline." She paused for a moment, feeling sick and heavy as the reality began to sink in. "I guess the quantum mirror should have clued me in. I mean, we know that multiple realities exist, I just didn't imagine that we could create one…" Her throat closed as the magnitude of her failure hit home. "Sir," she said, feeling her eyes fill, "I don't think there was ever a way to unmake this timeline. We can't save Janet; we never could. We can't save any of them…"

He was silent for a long beat, the rain pattering around them. "But the other team?" he said, nodding toward the gate. "They started a different timeline, right?"

"I guess," she said, swiping at her eyes. Not that it made much difference in the rain; her face was already wet.

"One where we uncovered Maybourne's mole in time to keep the whole shebang together." He smiled, a bare glimpse of his teeth in the dark. "One where Fraiser lives to a hundred-and-five and has an army of grandkids to order around."

Sam nodded because she couldn't quite find her voice; all

of that was true, but it wasn't *her* reality — that wasn't this life. Overhead the glider made another pass, higher this time, as the Jaffa began a disconsolate retreat from the Stargate. Mission failure. She knew how they felt.

"Question is," the colonel said, "what do we do now?"

There was a weight to the question and when she looked back at him she could see he was more doubtful than he sounded. He didn't quite meet her eyes and she knew he was thinking of that *other thing* that had just happened between them. She shifted, awkward, and said, "I guess, we're stuck in this reality, sir. So we should make the best of it."

"Okay," he said, still regarding her warily. "Which means we *really* have to make the best of it, Carter. And I mean, fight for it — for Earth."

Doubtful, Sam shook her head. Ever since she'd stood in the wreckage of the SGC and figured out the dreadful truth about where they were and what had happened to Earth, she'd felt that the only way to fix the problem was to reboot. Without that option, it meant that the only home they had was the devastated ash-covered ball of rock she'd seen from the window of Hecate's mother ship. A world where civilization had been reduced to rubble, where the last of its people cowered, hopeless, in filthy camps waiting to die at the hands of the Wraith. "Do you really think it's possible?" she said. "Even if we could get rid of the Wraith and the Goa'uld, Earth has no way to defend itself — it has nothing."

"That's not true," the colonel said. "It's got one thing going for it."

She cocked her head. "Which is?"

"Us," he said. "And it's got people, Carter. Thousands of them. People like Aedan Trask and Elspeth Burne, like Hunter and the resistance. Maybe all they need is someone to lead them."

"And that's us?"

"If there's no one else." He shrugged. "Besides, I'd vote for Daniel as president of the world."

Sam laughed at that, a thin sound in the cold forest. "I guess we have to try, sir."

"Yeah," he said, squaring his shoulders as if to take the load. "That's all we can do, Carter. 'Try' is all we've ever done."

It was true enough, and mostly it worked out, but this was a whole new magnitude of saving the world. To distract from the enormity of the task ahead, Sam looked past it toward the unknowable future. "And what then, sir? Once we've saved Earth, what then?"

There was a pause before the colonel answered. "Then," he said, clapping her on the shoulder and urging her gently into motion, back toward the gate-ship, "maybe you'll stop calling me 'sir.'"

Huffing out another shaky laugh, Sam nodded. "Yes sir. Maybe."

**Arbella — 2098:** The atmosphere in the gate room was much changed from the last time Teal'c and Daniel Jackson had stood there. It was solemn — the news of Lana Jones's death had spread rapidly, as had the truth of Karin Yuma's part in it — but beneath the solemnity lay a thread of tension, a powder keg waiting for a match.

Bailey could sense it too. Teal'c had noted as much from the way she had surveyed the streets when they left the president's residence less than an hour before. Too much antagonism had been building over recent weeks and the general was waiting for it to come to a head. Teal'c admired her intuition while experiencing a certain level of guilt at the part SG-1 may have unwittingly played in fermenting unrest, a guilt only heightened by the fact that they must now leave.

"I'm sorry he refused to listen," General Bailey was saying to Daniel.

But Daniel only shook his head. "He's just lost his wife in horrendous circumstances. I don't think he's in any frame of mind to listen to anyone."

From a compassionate perspective, Teal'c silently agreed; he couldn't imagine what it must be like for Jones to have found out that his wife had been so close, only to be cruelly snatched away by someone he thought was his most trusted advisor. Officer Hayden's account of events, at odds with his previous loyalty to Yuma, had been enough to convince the president that General Bailey's version of events was true.

The man hadn't wept, but instead he had whispered to his guards, "Let them go," before walking from the library without looking back.

General Bailey had appeared distressed at leaving him, but there was nothing she could have done to spare him the pain; Teal'c knew that human grief could manifest itself in myriad ways.

The military tactician in him, however, regretted the failure of their mission and could not help but wish that the death of his wife had spurred President Jones into action. Without the Arbellan forces to secure the Stargate on Earth, the Tau'ri's chance of freeing Earth from the Wraith, and then defending it, was significantly weaker. Earth had no organized military force, nothing but the rag-tag human colonies fighting for their freedom. And, committed though they might be, Teal'c knew that they would not be enough.

He also felt a great sense of foreboding whenever he remembered that it was to Hecate's ship to which they must now return. Rya'c could give them all the reassurances he wanted, but Hecate was still a Goa'uld even if she did speak with Janet Fraiser's voice.

At the top of the steps, the wormhole erupted into life and they had already started towards it when Daniel Jackson stopped and faced General Bailey once more. "I know we have no right to ask this of you, but… keep the door open. Can you? If we need to return?"

Bailey shrugged, a defeated gesture. "What else can we do to help you, Jackson? Nothing's gone as we hoped. Yuma's out there somewhere and we're holding on to order by a very thin thread. I don't know what'll become of Arbella now."

"You'll survive," said Daniel, a calm certainty in his words. "It's what we do. But we can't do it without each other. So just… keep the door open?"

With a grim smile Bailey nodded her silent promise. It was all that Teal'c and Daniel could take back with them.

# CHAPTER THIRTEEN

**Earth — 2098:** Dawn broke the next morning just as it always had. Nothing had changed.

Sting hadn't understood why O'Neill had thought anything might be different, how the mission he had embarked upon could have wrought a change so fast, so he was not surprised to find the dawn unremarkable.

However, it left him with a problem.

Boneshard was contained, for now, in one of the few functioning cells upon Brightstar's ailing hive. His strength was formidable and Sting had set two blades, plus Stormfire, to watch him; he did not trust the bars alone to hold him.

Now, he must decide what to do with the abomination. O'Neill's insistence that he should take it to Hecate, the parasite, was almost too ridiculous to consider. But if he had been right about her plan to destroy all Shadow's Wraith, then perhaps…

*You are troubled.* Earthborn spoke mind-to-mind as she approached him where he stood beyond the hive.

Below, in the sprawl of the encampment, the humans continued their small struggles to live beneath Shadow's fist. Never before had Sting felt anything beyond contempt for those who cowered here, but his perspective had changed — as his queen well knew. *There is much to question.*

*This place makes it so,* she said. *But we are what we are. That cannot change.*

*But what we are — *

The air around them shifted suddenly, an uplift of dust and grit as if a dart was landing. No dart appeared, but there was noise, the definite hum of engines.

Putting Earthborn behind him, Sting ducked his head away from the gritty air. "Go inside!" he ordered. "Send Hearten to —"

Her hand tightened on his arm. "Look."

He turned, taking a step back in surprise as the Lantean ship appeared as if out of thin air before them. Its hull was damaged, as if it had seen battle, and through its window he could see O'Neill and Carter. O'Neill gave a wave, apparently pleased with his dramatic entrance.

*So — they have returned,* Earthborn said, her hand still firm on his arm.

The back of the gate-ship opened, spilling out light along with its human passengers. O'Neill came first, Carter on his heels. Their clothing was damp, as if they'd spent long hours in heavy rain. It gave Sting no real clue as to the nature of their mission.

"Did your mission succeed?" he said, walking around to meet them at the foot of the ramp.

"Depends on what you mean by succeed," O'Neill said with an enigmatic smile. "But we took a little heat on the way back through the gate." He glanced past Sting, toward Earthborn. "Courtesy of your sister's people camped out at the Stargate." It was inappropriate to address a queen so, but Sting had learned to expect such things from O'Neill — and to overlook them.

Earthborn said, "Shadow holds the Stargate?"

"For now." O'Neill turned his quicksilver gaze on Sting. "You and O'Kane get the hybrid back okay?"

"We did. Boneshard is being held within the hive." He allowed himself a moment of amusement. "Stormfire is entertaining himself with him."

"I'm not sure who I feel most sorry for," O'Neill said. Then he took a breath, as if steeling himself for some unpleasant task. "So I guess we need to decide what to do next."

Sting inclined his head. "Was not the plan to take the hybrid to the parasite-god?"

"Yes," he said. "That's part of it…" His attention roved to Earthborn and then returned to Sting. "We, uh, we picked up a little intel," he said. "That is, we've got good reason to think that Hecate is playing us."

"If you mean that she is deceiving you," Sting said, "then that is hardly unexpected information. Her kind are nothing but deceptive."

O'Neill tipped his head, conceding the point. "Well, Carter and I were thinking we could do a little deceiving ourselves."

In his mind, Sting felt Earthborn urging him to caution. He did not need to be told. "In what manner?"

"Hecate wants the hybrid. And maybe she wants it for the reason she told us, maybe she doesn't. But I think we need to hedge our bets."

Sting blinked, waited for O'Neill to explain the vernacular.

"I mean," he said, "we cover our bases."

Another slow wait.

Carter cleared her throat. "What he means," she said, "is that we take matters into our own hands regarding Atlantis." Her gaze travelled to O'Neill, her expression unhappy, and then returned to Sting. "Colonel O'Neill wants to go back there, with Earthborn, to take the city while you and I take the hybrid to Hecate. If we play along, maybe we can convince her to let Earthborn lead your people home — the ones who aren't hybrids. It's what we all want. Meanwhile, we'll have an ace up our sleeve." She pulled a face. "I mean, we have—"

"—another string to our bow?" O'Neill suggested.

She shot him a dry look. "We have Atlantis," she said, returning her attention to Sting. "And if the colonel can fly it, then he can take on Hecate's hive. And we'll have the upper hand."

Sting's instinctive rejection of the plan was silenced by Earthborn's command made mind-to-mind. *Be still, my consort.* Out loud, she said, "Do you think it would be possible, O'Neill, for the two of us to take Atlantis?"

He spread his hands in a gesture of bravado. "Sure, why not?"

"It is filled with Shadow's Wraith."

"Well, get me to the command center and the ship is mine."

He tapped his head. "I'll leave winning hearts and minds to you."

*I will not let you go without me,* Sting said, before Earthborn could say more. And he cared not for the niceties of protocol. *It is too dangerous.*

He felt her affront immediately, though it was softened by understanding. *I am still your queen,* she reminded him. *I do not require your permission.* Her hand touched his arm once more, too intimate for such a public place. *It is worth the risk to win everything that we desire, to take our people away from this place — to go home to the ancestral feeding grounds of Brightstar. Is it not?*

Lifting his eyes to hers, Sting said, *No. Nothing is worth risking you.*

Her mind radiated warmth, but when she spoke it was aloud. "That," she said, "is not true." Then, to O'Neill, "I will go with you." Her arm tightened on Sting's arm, forestalling his protest. "We will take two of my blades, Hearten and Flint, with us."

To this, Carter exchanged a look with O'Neill who, after a pause, said. "Fine — and I'll take Daniel."

*They do not trust us,* Sting said.

"That is reasonable," Earthborn said aloud, in answer to both Sting and O'Neill. "When do we depart?"

O'Neill made a show of stretching his back, opening his mouth in a yawn. "Carter and I need a couple hours shut-eye," he said. "And then we're good. Carter can send Daniel down when she reaches the Ha'tak and then we can go."

"Assuming he and Teal'c made it back from Arbella," Carter said with a look of concern Sting noted.

O'Neill's expression remained closed. "They'll be there."

Earthborn inclined her head. "Sunset, then," she decided. "I will prepare."

Sting watched her leave, the imperious sway of her back, her chin held high. It pained him, this plan, and he turned to O'Neill with no small amount of irritation. "I do not like this."

"I know," he said, and put his hand on Sting's arm as he moved past and into the hive. "But we've just got to keep our eyes on the prize, buddy."

Carter offered Sting a rueful smile as she followed O'Neill. "He means —"

"I understand his meaning," Sting said with a pulse of disquiet. "But I still do not like this plan."

**Hecate's ha'tak — 2098:** Daniel was resting, but not sleeping, when Rya'c arrived in their quarters. His gaze roved across Teal'c, who sat cross-legged in kelno'reem — an attempt to heal the wound in his side faster — and then came to rest on Daniel.

"Your friends have returned to the Shacks," he said in a low voice, so as not to disturb his father. "They will be here soon."

"That's good news," Daniel said, pushing himself to his feet and trying not to look as weary as he felt. "Were they successful?"

Rya'c gave a slight nod. "I understand that they were. However, Hunter tells me that the Wraith they bring has caused much disquiet among the people of the Shacks. They do not understand why we would bring it here." He gestured toward the door. "Come, you will wish to see them when they arrive."

"Yeah, thanks," Daniel said, wondering whether to disturb Teal'c, but when he looked over at his friend, Teal'c's eyes were already open.

"I will accompany you," he said and rose, stiffly and still in obvious pain, to his feet.

"You sure you're okay?" Daniel said. "You could —"

"I am well," Teal'c said, chin lifting in that familiar gesture of Jaffa mulishness.

Daniel knew better than to argue. Rya'c, however…

"Father, if you are wounded beyond your symbiote's power to heal, the Lady Hecate will aid you."

Teal'c narrowed his eyes. "I would rather endure the pain than be healed by a Goa'uld."

"Then that would be your loss," Rya'c said, and turned away. "But only a fool would go into battle weakened because they are too stubborn to be healed."

"Only a—"

"Teal'c?" Daniel interrupted. "Jack and Sam are back, with the Wraith." In other words, *stow your crap.*

After a beat, Teal'c bowed his head and said no more. Rya'c got the hint too, and led them in silence from their quarters to the ring transporter room.

There were a dozen Jaffa in there, encircling the transporter, staff weapons at the ready. It was a wise precaution; the hybrid they'd encountered in Shadow's lab had been dangerously powerful.

Daniel took his place behind the Jaffa, Teal'c at his side flexing his fingers as if in search of his own weapon.

"You may begin," Rya'c said, in Goa'uld, to the Jaffa manning the controls. A moment later the room filled with golden light and the violent thrum of rings slamming down onto the transporter platform. When they lifted, Sam stood there, alone with two Wraith. One was on its knees, bound, the other was Sting. And he had his weapon drawn.

"Don't shoot," Sam said, holding up her hands. "He's with me."

"Where is O'Neill?" Rya'c said.

Sam kept her hands up. "He's, uh — I need to talk to Hecate," she said, and then turned to gesture at the Wraith kneeling behind her. "This is Sobek-Boneshard, the prototype hybrid. Hecate will want to see him."

"And the other one?" Rya'c's disdain was thick as he looked Sting up and down.

"He needs to talk with Hecate too," Sam said. "We have a proposition to make."

There was a low murmur at that, the Jaffa glancing uneasily between each other.

"The Lady Hecate," Rya'c said, "does not negotiate with Wraith."

"Well, she's going to have to start," Sam said. "If she really wants to see this planet free of them." Then her expression softened, and Daniel didn't miss the shadows under her eyes, the weariness in her face. *Something's changed*, he realized. "Rya'c, please. We all want the same thing; we all want to save Earth. We have to work together."

He hesitated for another beat, and then said, "Very well. But you will leave your weapons here." His gaze, as he spoke, fell on Sting. "All of you."

Sam turned around too, facing the Wraith. "Trust me," she told him. "You won't be harmed."

His lip curled up over his sharp teeth, a look of distrust even as he allowed the Jaffa to take his weapon. "You appear to be in no position to offer that assurance, Major Carter."

"But *I* am," Rya'c said. "If you do not play us false, Wraith, you will come to no harm here."

Sting turned to face Rya'c, bowed his head in a gesture similar to Rya'c's own — a strange similarity between two such alien and dangerous races. It seemed to be enough, however.

Rya'c gave orders and the Jaffa moved in, two taking hold of the hybrid and hauling it to its feet. It snarled but didn't struggle, allowed itself to be pushed into motion, armed guards all around it as Rya'c led the way out of the transporter room. Sting was scarcely less well guarded, although the Jaffa didn't dare touch him and he stalked along behind the hybrid in silence.

"Hey," Daniel said, and crossed the room toward Sam. He squeezed her shoulder in lieu of a hug. "What happened? Where's Jack?"

"He's okay." She smiled at him, then Teal'c. "You're hurt?"

"It is minor," Teal'c said, although Daniel suspected it was less minor than their friend was letting on.

"There was trouble?" Sam said, looking between them.

"You could say that," Daniel said. "How about you? Was Atlantis…?" He didn't even know how to finish the question. *Was it amazing?*

Sam smiled, but it was a watery expression. "You'd have loved it," she said. "Aside from the Wraith and the fighting." She touched his arm, squeezing through his sleeve. "You might get to see it." She lowered her voice as they began to walk, falling in at his side. "The colonel wants to go back, and he wants you with him."

"What? Now?"

Sam nodded. "Daniel, something happened." She pushed out a breath, glanced over her shoulder at the Jaffa following behind. "Things aren't what they seem."

Which, generally speaking, could have described any given day since they'd arrived in this messed up future. He looked ahead to Rya'c, then back to Sam. "You mean with regard to our, uh, host?"

"We can't trust her."

He had to fight not to snort a laugh. "Well, no. Obviously."

"I mean — Look, just follow my lead. But if things start going south, get yourself down to the surface and find Jack."

He lifted an eyebrow. "Jack?"

"The colonel." She frowned. "I meant the colonel."

Resisting the urge to comment further, Daniel just said, "Okay."

"And Teal'c?" Sam went on, "I need you to speak with the Arbellans; we'll want the CMF to come through and hold the Earth gate."

Daniel exchanged a look with Teal'c, neither of them wanting to confess their failure.

"What?" Sam glanced between them. "Daniel, what's wrong?"

"I, uh…" He pulled off his glasses, pinched the bridge of his nose. "Sam, I'm sorry. Things didn't go well on Arbella — the CMF aren't coming."

Her jaw dropped. "Why not? What happened?"

"Long story short, the security forces are staging a coup. Sam, they killed Lana Jones."

She closed her eyes. "No…"

"And President Jones is… Well, he's not thinking straight. General Bailey wants to help but us but" — Daniel spread his hands — "Jones won't listen."

"No, Daniel, you don't understand." Sam lowered her voice to an urgent whisper, casting a quick glance at Rya'c. "We *need* the CMF. We can't rely on *anything* from Hecate, and Shadow's forces are already holding the Stargate on Earth." She scrubbed a hand through her hair. "Damn it. The colonel wants you on Atlantis, but I think you're gonna have to go back to Arbella. We can't do this without them, Daniel."

"Sam, they arrested us. We barely got out of there alive. If I go back, I don't know what —"

"I will go," said Teal'c. "I will return to Arbella while you travel to Atlantis with O'Neill."

"But you're injured," Daniel protested. "And you're not exactly flavor of the month on Arbella."

"My wound is healing. And did General Bailey not offer to leave a door open for our return?"

"General Bailey might not be in charge of the door anymore, Teal'c, as you well know."

He lifted an eyebrow. "Fear of failure is no reason not to make the attempt, Daniel Jackson. It is simply a reason to try harder."

"Right." Jack would have called the homily 'fortune cookie logic' but Daniel had always appreciated Teal'c's stoicism. He blew out a breath and turned to Sam with a helpless shrug. "I guess it's the best we've got."

"Yeah," she said, without much confidence. "Teal'c, if you can persuade the CMF to help, they're gonna have to come through hard. Shadow's got a lot of personnel at the Stargate. The colonel and I only made it past them because our ship was cloaked."

Daniel bit his tongue to keep from asking questions. It sounded like Sam had a long story of her own, but now wasn't the time to hear it so he just said, "What about Hecate? If we can't rely on her support, where do we go from here?"

"We still have the same end goal," said Sam. "The colonel has a few… suggestions he wants me to put to her."

Daniel raised his eyebrows. "And if she doesn't like his suggestions?"

With a glance around the ship, Sam said, "Then we do what we always do when we come across an unfriendly System Lord."

The three of them shared an uneasy glance; they all knew what that meant. Only, this time, destroying the System Lord also meant killing their friend. The thought sat like a rock in the pit of Daniel's gut.

The party slowed as they reached Hecate's laboratory, its nondescript doors opening as Rya'c approached. In front of him, a head taller than the Jaffa that guarded it, the hybrid bristled as it stepped into the laboratory. Daniel could see muscles standing out along its shoulders, down its back. Its arms flexed against its bonds.

He exchanged a wary look with Sam. He would have expected more resistance from a creature so powerful.

"My Lady," Rya'c said, and as Daniel filed into the lab he saw Hecate standing behind one of the work benches. His heart constricted painfully; had she been wearing a white coat it could have been Janet.

At his side Sam sucked in a breath and averted her gaze, as if she couldn't bear to see her friend like this. Daniel knew exactly how she felt.

"Sam," Hecate said in Janet's voice. "I'm pleased to see you return successful, and unharmed."

"Yeah," Sam said, nothing soft in her voice at all. "So now you have what you need."

"And more," Hecate said, walking around the bench to regard

Sting. "What is this one?"

Moving closer to Sting, Sam said, "He's an ally. A potential ally."

This close, Daniel could see that Hecate's eyes were hard, very unlike Janet. Somehow, that made it easier. "I need no allies among the Wraith."

"Sting's different," Sam said, "he —"

"I *need* no allies among the Wraith." Hecate's eyes travelled the length of Sting's body. "They will all die."

"Actually, he won't," Sam said. "Neither will his queen, or those in his hive."

Hecate tilted her head. "How so?"

"Because they haven't taken Shadow's immunosuppressant. Your poison won't work on them, Hecate. But they do want to leave this galaxy — and they can help you bring down Shadow if you'll listen to them."

"Yes," Hecate said. "I know of Earthborn and her desire to leave this galaxy. To take with her the most powerful weapon ever created."

Wrong-footed, Sam had nothing to say. She exchanged a confused look with Daniel, but he couldn't help her; he had no idea what was going on either.

"And how do you know of Earthborn?" Sting hissed. "What spy is there who has betrayed my queen?"

A smile crossed Hecate's face, something dark and malevolent. "Oh, don't be concerned. It is not only you who have been betrayed. It is all your kind."

Turning, she moved toward Boneshard and, standing on tiptoe, she pressed a hand to his cheek. The Wraith snarled at her, straining forward against the Jaffa who held his arms. "Bring me the suppressant," she said, one hand lifted as she waited for someone to place a syringe in her hand. "Boneshard," she said, and her voice carried the deep resonance of the Goa'uld, "you have served your god well."

"You are not my god," Boneshard hissed. "*I* am the god and

you will bow before me!"

Hecate smiled and with one swift motion jammed the needle into the Wraith's neck. Boneshard convulsed, head arching back, lips peeled away from its teeth. And then its head fell forward, shoulders rising and falling. After a moment it rose, slowly, eyes flaring gold. "Lady Hecate," Sobek said, inclining its head slightly. "Well met."

"The suppressant works?" Hecate said, studying the Wraith's face.

"It is most effective," Sobek said. "Nothing of the host remains. This body is now mine."

"Unbind him," Hecate ordered, and then turned with a slow smile to Daniel and Sam. "You understand?"

And, yeah, he did. Daniel understood all too well. "You're not trying to kill them at all," he said, aghast. "You want to *use* them."

"The Wraith mind is… powerful," Hecate said watching as Sobek's arms were unbound, as he flexed his fingers. "We needed a way to ensure that the Goa'uld would always be supreme in the body of the host. And now, we have it."

At his side, Sam said, "So you never had any intention of ridding Earth of the Wraith?"

"On the contrary," Hecate said, smiling. "The poison is very real. And it will be released just as I promised. Then all the Wraith who do not host a Goa'uld will die." Her gaze travelled to Sting. "Including your friend and his little queen."

"And including Queen Shadow," Sobek said, baring his teeth in a smile. "Atlantis will be ours and no System Lord will dare stand against us."

"But you can't use Atlantis," Daniel said. "You can't fly it any more than Shadow could…"

"Daniel," Hecate said, putting her hand to his face. He recoiled from the touch, even though it felt warm and familiar. "Why do you think I went to so much trouble to bring you here in the first place?"

Sam sucked in a breath. "Colonel O'Neill…" she said. "You want him to pilot the city."

But Daniel was still a step behind. "What do you mean you brought us here?"

"She —" Sam said. "Daniel, the attack on P5X-104? It was Hecate, she drove us into the wormhole at a specific time, to interact with a solar flare or —"

"I don't understand," Rya'c said from the other side of the room. His voice was taut to the point of snapping. "Major Carter, what do you mean?"

"I mean we've all been played," Sam said. "Hecate engineered all of this. She's to blame for everything."

"Wait," Daniel said, his mind spinning. "All of this? The Goa'uld invasion, the *Wraith*? How's that even possible?"

Hecate tipped her head, preening in a way that was all Goa'uld arrogance. "The first time," she said, prowling toward Daniel, "I simply had you killed. It was sufficient to allow Maybourne to break your little treaty and facilitate Apophis's invasion, but then the Wraith came…" She put her hand on Sobek's arm. "So strong, so vicious — so completely unexpected. Apophis, the fool, insisted on fighting. He didn't stand a chance. I, on the other hand, recognized an opportunity when I saw it. And I realized I needed assistance if I was to take Queen Shadow's city from beneath her claws. So, the *second* time, I brought you here instead of killing you." Her attention shifted to Sam. "I used the gravitational lensing effect of a drifting black hole," she said, drawing her finger in a loop. "The wormhole was caught in its accretion disk for ninety-eight years. Very precise. Very elegant, don't you think?"

Sam opened her mouth, closed it again. "You're wrong," she said at last, making a good show of bravado although Daniel could tell her mind was spinning as fast as his own. "You're wrong if you think Colonel O'Neill will help you."

"Oh he will," Hecate said with a smile. "He will because I have his precious team." She tapped her head. "Janet knows *exactly* how much you mean to him." Her gaze swept them all, lips curled into a cruel smile. "And with the city of the Ancients and my hybrid army at my back no one will stand in my way: no human, no Wraith, no System Lord." Her expression turned speculative. "Where will I go first, I wonder? Oh! Arbella, of course. I will enjoy watching their final defeat, the terrible moment when they realize that the fabled SG-1 has failed them once more. I will enjoy making those *shol'va* kneel before their god at last."

There was a long beat of horrified silence. Then, from behind him, Daniel heard a sharp growl.

"Then you must be stopped," Sting snarled as he launched himself at Hecate.

# CHAPTER FOURTEEN

NOT KNOWING was the worst of it.

One of Earthborn's darts had deposited Carter, Sting, and the hybrid in the middle of the Shacks and the rest had been up to them. There was nothing Jack could do but wait for them to make contact. There was no reason for it all to go FUBAR except for the fact that, in his experience, FUBAR was the usual state of the universe.

So he kept himself busy. He conducted a depressing inventory of his kit — no C4, no grenades, no ammunition for his MP5 — and then went in search of O'Kane. Their objective had to be Atlantis's bridge — the one place in the city where he could control everything. And O'Kane was the only person who might have a clue where to find it.

Jack found him alone in Crazy's lab, poring over one of the Wraith computer screens. He looked up when he noticed Jack hovering in the doorway and offered a wary smile. "Colonel."

"Jimmy," Jack said, just to be difficult.

O'Kane looked at him for a long beat, and then returned his attention to the screen. "I understand you're planning on returning to Atlantis?"

"Seems like the smart thing to do," Jack said walking further into the lab. He remembered being there before, as Crazy's prisoner. It felt like a long time ago, back before he knew where and what this place was — when he still thought they were headed home.

"The *navis temporis* didn't work?" O'Kane said, still not looking up.

Jack paused before answering. He supposed Carter must have told him about the time ship — or, more likely — vice versa. "It worked," Jack said, because there was no reason to lie. "We just couldn't change anything."

To his surprise, O'Kane's head drooped. "You were — you sought to change the past?" he said in a low voice. There was a tremor in it that Jack thought he understood.

"We're not meant to be here," he said by way of explanation. "Looks like Hecate brought us forward from our own time just to screw things up. No idea if the Wraith were part of her plan, but they were definitely a consequence." He took a step closer, let his fingers trail idly over the gizmos on the work bench. "We had to try fixing it, James."

O'Kane nodded. After a pause, and in a tight voice, he said, "Why didn't it work?"

"You're talking to the wrong person," Jack said. "But Carter thinks — Something about creating two different realities."

"Could you try again?"

It wasn't the question Jack was expecting. "Try again?"

O'Kane looked up and his face was stricken. "Could you go back and try something different to change all this?"

"You do realize," Jack said carefully, "that if we did that — not that Carter thinks we can — but if we did, if it worked, the odds are that you'd never have been born?"

O'Kane gave a bitter smile. "Yes, that would be the objective." His eyes roamed around the lab. "None of this would be here."

"Look," Jack said, moving closer, lowering his voice. "We'll get you out of this — away from the Wraith. We won't leave you behind, James. When Earthborn takes Atlantis back to Pegasus, you'll stay here. And things will get better, Earth will be safe and —"

"Earth isn't my home," O'Kane said. "I'm from Arbella, remember? Everything I —" He cut himself off. "I can never go home. Do you have any idea how it feels to…?" He trailed off, ducked his head. "I'm sorry, of course you do."

Jack huffed out a bleak laugh. "Yeah. But why can't you go home?"

"The Arbellan gate is closed," he said. "And even if it wasn't, they'd never trust me now. I've been gone too long and

Caroline…" He shook his head, turned back to the screen. "It's been too long."

"No it hasn't," Jack said. "Listen, the gate isn't closed and there are people there who want to keep it open. My team's been there, and Daniel and Teal'c have —" Of course, he didn't know for sure; this was just hoping, but there was nothing wrong with a little of hope. "They've gone back to Arbella to convince the president to help us fight for Earth — to come back to Earth and fight."

O'Kane stared. "Impossible."

"It's true, I swear. And if anyone can persuade him, it's Daniel."

"You mean the CMF are coming here? To Earth?"

"Right through the Stargate. That's the plan."

"It'll never happen."

There wasn't much Jack could do about that assertion, given the fact that he didn't know whether Daniel and Teal'c had been successful. So he changed tack and said, "Who's Caroline?"

O'Kane blinked, and then looked away. "She's — she's my wife. Or she was. She must think me dead by now, of course."

He waited a beat, taking in O'Kane's pained expression. "Listen to me," he said then, lowering his voice, "we'll get you home, okay? However this ends, we'll get you back to Arbella. Even if the gate's closed, there are other ways — the gate-ship, Atlantis itself. You've just gotta keep hoping."

"Do you really think it's possible?"

Jack put a hand on his shoulder, drawing his eyes back to him. "Yeah, I do," he said. "We'll make it happen. You have my word."

"So all we have to do first is steal Atlantis from Queen Shadow and drive the parasite-god, Hecate, from Earth?" O'Kane delivered it dead-pan, but Jack detected a vein of humor beneath the words.

"Sure," he said letting go of the man's shoulder. "Piece of cake."

O'Kane gave a thin smile.

"Speaking of which," Jack said, "we're going to need to know how to take control of the city. Full control. And I don't mean the operations center we found last time. I mean somewhere that will let me get the thing airborne."

O'Kane nodded. "That's exactly what I've been looking for." He tapped his finger against the screen. "And I think I've found it. They call it the 'control chair' — it's what powers the city's weapons and its star drive."

"Star drive? Cool."

"The chair appears to be a very powerful piece of technology," O'Kane conceded.

"And where is it?" Jack said, getting down to what mattered. "Somewhere easily accessible, close to a landing platform, and far away from Shadow's soldiers I expect?"

O'Kane made a face. "It's at the top of the eastern most tower in the inner city. And well-guarded."

"Yeah," Jack said with a sigh. "Of course it is."

Once Sting had made his move on Hecate, the lab was thrown into chaos and Sam found herself pinned down behind one of the benches. Teal'c was on the far side of the room, with Rya'c, and Daniel was taking cover somewhere behind her. None of them were armed.

Daniel had a good shot at making it to the door and she was determined he was going to take it. Getting Daniel to the surface so he could tell the colonel what was going on, and help him secure Atlantis, was a top priority. At this point, the Ancient city might be their only chance of rescuing the situation.

Sting's play had thrown everything out the window and the only option now was to retreat and find backup.

After the initial flurry of Sting's attack, Hecate — Sam refused to see Janet — was crouched at the far side of the lab, protected by the hybrid, Sobek-Boneshard, while Sting circled them both.

His teeth were bared, he looked feral with rage. If he had a plan, she didn't know what it was; taking on Boneshard unarmed would be suicide. Then again, it wouldn't be the first example of macho posturing she'd seen get people killed. She guessed Wraith were no different.

While Sting circled, Rya'c's Jaffa stood by uncertainly. Hecate was their goddess and they were sworn to protect her, but to open fire on Sting risked harming her.

More to the point, Rya'c wasn't giving any orders. She could see him crouched with Teal'c behind the slim shelter of a lab bench. Teal'c had his hand on his son's shoulder.

Shifting around, Sam caught Daniel's eye. She nodded toward the doorway, but he looked stubborn. He wouldn't want to leave without the rest of them. Teal'c must have caught the exchange, because he glanced over and then spoke in Rya'c's ear. Rya'c looked up, over at Sam and Daniel, then back to the stand-off in the center of the room.

Boneshard bristled, his eyes flaring gold as Sobek spoke. The only saving grace was that he was no longer wearing the hand device. "It is past time that you died, Wraith," he said.

Behind them, Hecate pushed to her feet. She moved awkwardly, as though injured, and Sam looked away. Despite everything, it was difficult to watch.

"Kill him," Hecate said in a voice that was all Goa'uld resonance and nothing like Janet's. "Kill him now."

Sting braced himself. "I will not let you destroy us," he hissed at Sobek. "You are an abomination and you will die."

But it was a vain gesture. Sting didn't have a chance against the hybrid and he knew it.

Cursing, Sam pushed to her feet. She couldn't let him do this alone. "Hecate," she said. "You can't win. The lab on Atlantis breeding your hybrids? We destroyed it."

A flicker of anger crossed her face. "You lie."

"No. The lab, the symbiotes, the Wraith hosts — they're all gone. And…" A little bravado never hurt anyone, right? "And we've already got control of Atlantis. Surrender now and we'll spare you."

Behind her she heard movement; Daniel was moving toward the door, taking advantage of the distraction.

Hecate laughed, a nasty sound. "Do you think me a fool?" she said. "Do you think I don't know who controls Atlantis? Do you think I would leave *any* of this to chance? Your Colonel Maybourne keeps me well informed, I assure you." Her gaze swept to her Jaffa. "Kill them," she said. "Kill them all and release the poison into Earth's atmosphere."

A dozen staff weapons rose. It was a killing ground, if the Jaffa opened fire it would all be over.

And then Rya'c got to his feet. "Jaffa!" he said, striding out amid his men, one hand raised. "Jaffa — hold."

Hecate hissed. "What are you doing?"

There was a tremor in Rya'c's shoulders when he turned to face Hecate, but his chin was held high even if his face was drawn. "You have deceived us," he said, and then, to his men, "the goddess... She has deceived us all. She seeks to place these *creatures* above us. Brothers, would you bow before this *thing*?" He flung his arm toward Sobek. "Is this to be your god?" He turned back to Hecate. "I served you because I believed your lies; I believed you would destroy the creatures who murdered my mother, that you would free the galaxy from their threat."

He took a step back. "I believed you because you wore the face of a friend, because Colonel Dixon had also been deceived. And, perhaps, because I wanted to believe that there was a way to fight back against the devastation of the Wraith." His gaze moved to Sobek. "But you are a deceiver, as are all your kind. And I should have known it, because my father —" His voice cracked and he stopped, took a breath, nostrils flaring with the effort of retaining control. "My father raised me to know better, but in anger I turned my back on him and on the truth. This is where that anger has brought me. But I will not be deceived anymore."

Sam darted her gaze to Teal'c. His face was bright, alive

with pride and a kind of joy she'd not seen in him since the first moment he saw Rya'c in the ruins of the SGC.

He caught her eye and, with an imperceptible movement, she gestured to the door; Daniel would need help getting down to the planet's surface. Teal'c nodded and retreated, with one final glance back at his son.

"Brothers," Rya'c was saying, facing his men. Some watched him with astonishment, others with suspicion. "Hecate is a false god. And we do not need to serve her. We can serve a more glorious cause."

"And what cause is that?" Hecate said, her eyes glowing bright. "What cause is more glorious than that of your god?"

Rya'c paused, and when he spoke again, it was his men, not Hecate, that he addressed. "The answer, my brothers, is simple: that cause is freedom."

The gate-ship was loaded and ready to go.

Earthborn stood some distance from it, her two blades staying close to her. Their attention was divided between Jack and the camp that sprawled below them, as if unsure which presented the greater threat to their queen. Jack watched them from the shadow of the hive where he sat resting. Waiting.

It was an old habit, this anxious resting before a mission. No point in wearing yourself out with pacing, or endlessly going over the mission details. The trick was to relax your body and your mind, even while the adrenaline was starting to pump and all you wanted to do was get the hell on with the job. It wasn't easy, but he'd mastered the trick over the years.

Nevertheless, when his radio squawked to life he was grateful that the wait was over.

"Jack, this is Daniel. I could use a ride."

With a smile, Jack pushed to his feet. Earthborn turned to look at him as Jack toggled his radio. "Daniel, what's your situation?"

"I'm in the Shacks, close to the tunnel exit."

"On my way," he said, striding toward the gate-ship's ramp. "How did it go?"

There was a silence, then the radio hissed static and Daniel said, "Depends what you mean by 'it'."

Which, while typical of Daniel, wasn't exactly helpful. "Sit tight," Jack said — it would be better to have this conversation elsewhere anyway. "I'll be there in a couple minutes."

While he ran through the last of the pre-flight checks, Earthborn came to sit in the co-pilot's seat. She looked around with her customary imperious calm, although he thought he detected tension in the set of her shoulders. Behind her, the two Wraith took position in the rear of the ship.

In the doorway of the hive, he saw O'Kane watching, one hand lifted in farewell. The Wraith, Stormfire, lurked in the darkness behind him. Jack didn't like to imagine what would happen to the pair of them if the mission was a bust, if no one came back. Just another reason they couldn't fail.

"We're collecting Daniel from the Shacks," he said, as he mentally summoned the HUD and started lifting the ship. "You guys probably need to stay out of sight." He glanced at Earthborn to make sure she understood. "Wraith aren't exactly flavor of the month around there."

She just inclined her head and kept her eyes on the view as the ship rose up over the damaged remains of her hive. He engaged the cloak and banked left, out over the Shacks, flying high enough not to draw any attention from the people below but giving him enough visual clues to navigate towards the subterranean entrance to the SGC. What had once been the SGC.

It took a couple passes — the camp was vast and there were few landmarks — but eventually, as he brought the ship in low, he saw a flash of light on Daniel's glasses where he stood amid the flapping canvas of the shanty town.

There wasn't a lot of space to land. "Don't squash anything," he told the ship as he initiated the landing protocol. Out the window he could see the backdraft whipping up the dirt, Daniel covering his eyes and turning away. Hunter was there too, he realized, and a couple of other resistance fighters. "Stay in the cockpit," he told Earthborn. "They'll see you."

She bristled at the direct order, but Jack didn't have time to cater to her ego. Perhaps she'd figured that out, because she beckoned her men into the cockpit as the tail ramp descended.

Swinging out of his seat, Jack headed down the ramp into the dirt.

"Jack," Daniel said, coming around the side of the ship. He looked tense but relived, his gaze roving across the cloaked ship. "Wow," he said. "This is interesting."

He wasn't the only one gaping. Jack could see faces peering out from the hovels these people called home and then Hunter rounded the ship, his eyes like saucers. "I ain't never seen nothing like it before."

"Clever toy, huh?" Jack said, and then frowned as he glanced between Hunter and Daniel. There was some kind of tension between the two that he didn't understand. "Everything okay?"

After a moment of silence Daniel said, "Sure. We should get going."

Which was definitely code for, *I'll tell you later.*

Uncertain, exactly, what was going on Jack just said, "Then let's go. Hunter — keep your eyes open and your head down. Things might get interesting around here."

Hunter touched his forehead in the gesture Jack remembered, half deference and half rebellion. "By the grace of the Lady Hecate," he said, "we'll be ready."

Jack decided not to comment on Hecate's role, instead nudging Daniel toward the tail of the ship. "Good luck," he said to Hunter. "Be careful."

"You too, O'Neill."

He waited until they were inside, Daniel casting a wary

look at Earthborn's blades as he followed Jack into the cockpit, before he asked, "So what's going on?"

Blowing out a breath, Daniel dropped into the seat behind Jack as the ship lifted. Out the window, Jack could see Hunter shielding his eyes against the swirl of dust the ship left in its wake.

"It's started," Daniel said, his voice heavy.

"Hecate didn't go for the deal with Sting?" It had been a long shot anyway.

"No. Jack, she double-crossed us all."

"Yeah, I figured. You know how she did it?"

"In every way!" He rubbed a hand over his mouth. "She was never going to destroy the hybrids; she wants them for herself. She's building an army. But she *is* going to kill all the other Wraith — poison them. And she wants Atlantis. Jack she said she brought us into the future to make you pilot it for her."

"Like *that's* gonna happen."

Behind them, Earthborn said, "What of Sting?" She was standing in the doorway to the cockpit, her chin lifted and teeth bared.

There was a beat of silence, and then Daniel said, "It's chaos up there. Rya'c has half the Jaffa in rebellion. The hybrid — Sobek? — he's allied with Hecate, and Sting... Last thing I saw, Sting was taking them both on. I'm sorry, I don't know more than that." He sat forward in his seat, pulled off his glasses. "But, Jack? I think I made it worse."

"Made what worse?"

He sighed. "Everything."

"What?" Jack said. "Daniel..."

"I told Hunter what was going on. I told him Rya'c had turned on Hecate. I thought —" He shook his head. "Stupid," he said. "I don't know what I thought; I wasn't thinking."

"I take it he wasn't over the moon?"

"You saw him," Daniel said. "'By the grace of the Lady Hecate...'"

"Hunter's just one man," Jack said, although he didn't like it; he didn't like leaving loose threads behind. He cleared his throat. "Carter and Teal'c?"

"Teal'c's holding the ring transporter so I could get down here. If he and Rya'c can reach the gate room, they're headed for Arbella ."

"And Carter?"

He paused for a beat. "I think she's going to destroy the ha'tak. I just hope she can do it before Hecate releases the poison into the atmosphere."

"Right." And, tactically, that was the right thing to do. Absolutely. "Damnit."

"It's Sam," Daniel said, his confidence unconvincing. "She'll be fine. She'll get out."

Jack didn't answer that; he knew the odds, they both did. But Carter would have to take care of herself — and she damn well better — because Jack had his own job to do. "Buckle up, kids," he said, growling the words past his tension. "We're going to steal ourselves a city."

# CHAPTER FIFTEEN

BY THE time Teal'c emerged from the transporter room, Sam was pinned down in a nearby corridor along with Rya'c and a handful of Jaffa who'd taken up his challenge to fight for their freedom. Teal'c nodded at her, a reassuring gesture; Daniel, at least, was on his way.

The rest of Rya'c's supporters had been sent to proselytize to their brother Jaffa; a literal battle for hearts and minds. A volley of staff blasts prevented either faction from gaining the upper hand and it was a stand-off, for now.

"Where is Hecate?" he said, surveying the scene with a soldier's eye as he came to crouch by her.

"We think she's headed for the bridge with Sobek, but we haven't been able to pursue with her Jaffa laying down fire."

"Whatever she is planning, she must be stopped."

That much went without saying, but they were fighting a battle here on more than one front. She and Sting could handle Hecate; Teal'c's purpose was better served on Arbella. "We need to get you to the gate room. Can you use the ring transporter to reach it?"

"I can, but I do not wish to leave you here alone, Major Carter. You are greatly outnumbered." His gaze darted to Rya'c and back to her, and although he didn't say it out loud, she understood; he didn't want to leave his son either.

Her heart ached for him, but they just didn't have any choice. "Teal'c, you need to bring the Arbellans through the Earth gate. If we're going to win this, we have to secure the Stargate."

"My men will protect Major Carter," Rya'c said. "We can —"

"No," Sam said. "No, you need to get your men off the ship, Rya'c. As many as you can, before —" She exchanged a glance with Teal'c, wondering how much she should say. He gave a slight nod: *tell him everything.* "Rya'c," she said, "I'm going to destroy it before she can release the poison. I'm going to destroy Hecate's ship."

*And Hecate,* she thought bitterly. *And Janet...*

Rya'c's shock was evident, but short-lived. "Yes," he said. "Yes, of course you must."

"So you need to get your men out of—"

Suddenly, a familiar sound echoed down the hallway towards them; the rings were activating again. Heart thumping, Sam turned. Teal'c had armed himself with a staff weapon and held it ready. Sam had only managed to scavenge a zat.

"Watch the corridor," Rya'c ordered his men as he, too, turned toward the transporter room entrance, his weapon raised.

But as the doors slid open, Sam let out a breath of relief; they weren't Jaffa reinforcements. Instead, Hunter stood on the threshold, his weapon leveled, along with Rya'c's friend, Zuri, and a couple of other Resistance fighters from the Shacks. Sam smiled and turned to Rya'c, but he wasn't smiling. And he hadn't lowered his weapon.

"Zuri," he said. "Why are you here?"

She met his words with a cool stare. "Why do you think I'm here, Dix?"

"Zuri—"

Her weapon lifted. "I'm here to fight for the Lady Hecate. The question is, what are *you* doing, *shol'va*?"

Teal'c bristled but Sam put a hand on his arm to restrain him. "Zuri," she said, trying to sound conciliatory.

"You will be silent!" Zuri stepped forward, out of the room, Hunter matching her step for step. He looked uncomfortable, lacking the zeal Sam saw in Zuri's sharp face, but there was anger in his expression too. And hurt. He looked like a man betrayed.

"Dix," Zuri said to Rya'c, "you were our leader, our... our *friend*. We *trusted* you. "

"I am still your friend, Zuri, and would be your leader if you will listen."

"You betrayed our god!"

"No!" He took a step forward, but came up short against Zuri's staff weapon. "It is Hecate who has betrayed us," he said. "She has betrayed everyone."

"An' how's that?" Hunter said. "Because she wants to kill all the Snatchers? That ain't betrayal, Dix, that's good sense."

"Not all of them," Rya'c said. "Not the worst of them, Hunter. She's using the Snatchers to build a terrible army."

"*Our* army," Zuri hissed. "To protect Earth from the Snatchers, from other gods —"

"They are no gods," Teal'c said, shaking off Sam's restraining hand to step forward. "They are *parasites*, and they will enslave you."

"I am no slave," Zuri spat, looking Teal'c up and down in disdain.

"Then fight for yourself," he said, "and not for your false-god. Fight for Earth."

Zuri snorted. "And who are you to preach?" Stalking closer, she glared up into his face. "I have fought for Earth my whole life. I will die fighting for Earth. What have *you* done, Teal'c of Chulak, but abandon your son?"

"Zuri!" Rya'c snapped. "Enough. Join us. We'll fight together, you and I, as we've always done."

She spun to face him. "You are a *traitor!*"

And that was her mistake; at such close range she didn't stand a chance against Teal'c. In one fluid motion, he had her flipped and flat on her back, his staff weapon pressed to her throat and the breath knocked from her lungs. "My son," Teal'c growled, "is no traitor."

"He is. As was his father."

Teal'c's lip curled, his staff weapon activating. "You —"

"No!" Hunter lunged forward. But Sam got him between the shoulders with her zat and he fell, back arching as he twitched. The other two resistance fighters opened fire as Rya'c's Jaffa turned from the doorway. One of Zuri's men went down to a zat, while the other hit the deck looking for cover.

"Get to the rings!" Sam barked. "Rya'c, Teal'c — get to the rings!"

She sprinted along the corridor into the transporter room and headed for the controls, programming the transporter for the gate room. Rya'c was already on the platform, Teal'c backing away from Zuri with his weapon leveled as she twisted to her feet.

Sam hit the control, activating the transporter. "Teal'c, now!"

The rings slammed down around Teal'c and Rya'c, taking them away an instant before the electric shock of a zat sent Sam sprawling to the floor.

Despite the end-of-the-world consequences of their mission, Daniel couldn't help but feel awed as they swept over the spires of the Ancient city.

The Lost City of Atlantis. He spared a wry smile for the stuffed shirts at the Society for American Archaeology — *if they could see me now!* The idea that this astonishing piece of technology — of architecture — had once been on Earth, back in pre-history, and that it had left its mark so deeply in the human psyche that stories about it had continued to be told right up until the twenty-first century, was mind-blowing. He was hard pressed to explain how it could have happened and yet it was evidently true.

If they made it out of this alive, if he was ever in a place of peace again, Daniel thought he could easily devote the rest of his life to investigating the truth of Atlantis and its role in Earth's distant past. And, ironically, her distant future.

"So, the eastern most tower," Jack said, from the gate-ship's pilot seat. "Any ideas?"

"Given that they won't have oriented it north to south," Daniel said, "not really." There were a lot of towers.

On the other side of the cockpit, Earthborn shifted in her

seat. Her gaze was ostensibly on the city below but there was an abstracted expression on her face and Daniel wasn't surprised when, a moment later, she said, "There is confusion here; something has happened."

Jack snorted. "Yeah," he said. "*We* happened."

"No," Earthborn said. "More than that. Shadow is… She is very angry."

"Perhaps she's found out about Hecate's plan?" Daniel suggested. "And Sobek's betrayal."

Earthborn sat up straighter, lips pulled back. Although she was young, and slight compared to the male Wraith, there was something deadly in her posture. Something frightening. "Perhaps she senses the presence of her rival and the imminence of her death."

"Or maybe she just ate a bad taco," Jack said. "Let's dial back the melodrama, shall we? Especially if she can hear you thinking."

Daniel smiled, but Jack wasn't wrong. "The first thing has to be taking control of the city's systems," he said. "We can deal with Shadow later, if we have to."

"If? It is not if, Daniel Jackson. While Shadow lives, the city will never be ours." Earthborn straightened her back. "And I must kill her and take her place, or her blades will not bend the knee to me."

Daniel didn't have much to say to that, so kept quiet. He could practically hear Jack's eye roll, however, even if he could only see the back of his friend's head as he said, "Here we go," and banked the ship around. "This is where we parked last time," he said as he brought the ship in to land on one of the piers that stretched out around the beautiful city.

Beautiful except for all the gnarled bits of Wraith hive-flesh that clung to its spires, of course. Like termites, Daniel thought, and hoped Earthborn couldn't hear him thinking.

Jack left the ship cloaked once they landed, and then led the little group along the pier and into one of the massive towers.

"There's an elevator," he said, voice low as they made their way through a corridor thick with the dank scent of hive-flesh. "It should take us right there. Right to the control chair."

"And then —" Daniel stopped abruptly as, in front of him, several figures emerged from the shadows. Wraith, five of them.

"Damnit." Jack had his weapon raised, so did the two blades that moved to cover Earthborn.

From behind them came another sound, and Daniel glanced over his shoulder to see their exit cut off. This was no accident; someone knew they were coming.

"Hello, Jack," came a familiar and unwelcome voice.

Another figure wound his way through the Wraith blocking the way in front of him. Human, ragged, he was half hidden in the shadows, but Daniel knew his voice all too well.

"Hecate mentioned you'd be dropping by."

"Maybourne," Jack said, grinding the word between his teeth.

If he'd looked emaciated when they'd seen him in Shadow's lab, Maybourne looked positively skeletal now. His eyes were too large for his gaunt face, his scant hair stuck up in greasy tufts, and he bared his teeth in a gappy parody of a smile. "Queen Shadow would like a word," he said. "She's very keen to meet you and she's very…hungry."

"Well I'm flattered," Jack said. "But I don't have time for a dinner date. Especially when I'm the dinner."

Maybourne laughed, a high-pitched giggle that spoke of a life extended too long, of suffering Daniel didn't want to imagine. As much as he loathed this treacherous man, he made a pitiable sight nonetheless. "I didn't say you had a choice," Maybourne said. "We must go; she awaits."

"Wait," Daniel said. "You're working for Shadow? Hecate said you were working for her."

Maybourne spread his arms. "I work for whoever is winning. And at the moment that is Queen Shadow." He bared his teeth again, looking hungry and desperate. "And she will reward me. She will reward me for my loyalty."

Daniel shuddered a little at the thought of what form that reward might take. "Why don't you come with us?" he said, eyeing the faceless drones behind Maybourne. "We can help you."

"Daniel…" Jack said, a warning.

He ignored him. "We can free you, Maybourne. If you help us."

Maybourne laughed again, a mad laugh. "Free me?" He sobered abruptly. "I don't want to be *free*, Daniel. I want to win."

"Win?" Daniel said, looking at the wreckage of the man. "I think you lost the moment you betrayed your friends and your planet, Maybourne."

His face twitched, a flare of something lucid and raw, quickly replaced by fury. "We'll see," he snarled. "When Shadow has you in her embrace," he reached out his hand, fingers curled into a claw, "then we'll see who's *won*, Daniel Jackson."

With that, he gestured to the drones and two stepped forward.

"Come no closer!" That was Hearten, one of Earthborn's blades. He stood before her, his weapon raised. "You are in the presence of Queen Earthborn, drone. Know your place!"

The drone stopped, hesitated like a worker ant that had lost its trail home. Remarkable, Daniel thought.

Maybourne looked confused, peered past Jack to where Earthborn stood with her back straight and chin lifted. Clearly, he wasn't expecting *that*.

"Hearten," Earthborn said, one hand on her blade's arm. "Stand down."

Jack turned. "Stand *down*?"

"Don't fear, Colonel O'Neill," Earthborn said. "I believe this is for the best. I must confront my mother's sister and the sooner I am victorious, the better."

Hearten looked unsure — Jack looked furious — but Earthborn was adamant. "Take me to Queen Shadow," she said to Maybourne, "for I have long desired to meet her."

"Great," Jack growled, as they were disarmed and shoved into motion along the dark corridor. "You know, for once, I'd like to actually stick to the plan?"

Daniel huffed a laugh. "That would be boring."

"I *like* boring. Boring is good. Boring keeps you alive."

Rya'c found himself in the vast room housing the ha'tak's chappa'ai, among the towering columns that lined the vast space. Through the window, he could see the dirty gray ball of dust that was now the Earth and, as the transporter deactivated, he could hear nothing but the sound of his harsh breathing in the silent chamber.

"Zuri…" She had been his friend, his ally over many years.

His father's face was set hard. "We cannot spare time for sorrow," he said. "They will know where we are." He eyed the chappa'ai. "We must leave while we can."

"But my men…"

"They must make their own choice, now, son. Come with me to Arbella; the people there are unskilled in battle. Your leadership will be of great use — as will your friendship with General Bailey. She…" There was a hesitation. "Her trust in SG-1 has been weakened, your presence will reassure her."

"Weakened because of your attempt to erase this timeline and exterminate all who live here? Yes, I know what General Bailey discovered in their data center."

His father inclined his head, but did not apologize.

And Rya'c found he had no appetite for argument; his own judgment, he now knew, had been profoundly lacking. How could he challenge his father on his? Instead he said, "Will we be welcomed on Arbella? Their chappa'ai has been shielded for many years."

"I believe General Bailey will have kept the door open to us, Rya'c." There was a pause before his father added, "Whether or not we will be welcomed there, we must return and rally the Arbellan forces to Earth's cause. There is now no other option if we are to win this battle."

"Do you believe it possible?" Rya'c found that he lacked his father's faith; he had long believed that the peace enjoyed by the planet's residents was a fragile one, built as it was over a foundation of two philosophies, diametrically opposed.

"Yes," his father said with conviction. "Matters on Arbella were in a state of tension when we left, but I believe honor and generosity will overcome fear in the end. Arbella will open its doors; it will come to the aid of its ancestral home."

"I pray that you are right," Rya'c said as he moved to the dialing device and set the chappa'ai spinning. There was no time to contact General Bailey, no time to ask permission. He must trust only in his father's words and the character of the people of Arbella.

By the time the wormhole was active, Rya'c could hear weapons fire coming closer. The battle for Hecate's ship would be brutal and it felt wrong to leave his men here to die or flee as they chose. His father's hand landed on his shoulder. "It is time," he said. "You will do more good for more people on Arbella, leading her people back to reclaim Earth, than you will dying here."

"That does not make the choice easier."

"It does not. But we are Jaffa, we were not born to make easy choices, son. We were born to make right choices."

Rya'c held his gaze, seeing, perhaps for the first time as a grown man, the conflict in his father's heart. "As you did when you betrayed Apophis to fight with the Tau'ri."

A slight nod. "As you did in rejecting Hecate's lies."

A detonation shook the doors to the room, bucked the deck beneath their feet.

"Now," his father said, fingers gripping his shoulder tight. "Now, son."

And he was right. With a scant nod, not looking back, Rya'c walked to the open chappa'ai with his father at his side and stepped into the wormhole with no idea what would face him on the other side.

As it turned out, the gate room in which they emerged was entirely silent. Not a soul was present. "This does not bode well," he muttered.

"I agree," said his father. "Be vigilant."

They advanced down the ramp and through the empty room, staff weapons at the ready. Rya'c's senses were, indeed, alert for danger, but there was another reason for the tension that thrummed through his veins.

He had been such a fool.

He had trusted Hecate entirely and bowed to her supposed wisdom and compassion, believing it to be genuine, the influence of Janet Fraiser who had been so kind to him as a child. Only now could he see how foolish it had been to disavow all that he knew of the Goa'uld, forgetting the deceptions of which they were capable. Hadn't his mother taught him of Apophis' lies? How could he have believed that any System Lord was capable of benevolence?

It was not the time for such a conversation, but he could not continue with this mission knowing that his father thought him a traitor to the cause of freedom. "I am sorry, father."

Teal'c paused and glanced back at him over his shoulder. With a final glance around the room, he came back to stand next to Rya'c. "Your apology is unnecessary, my son. You have done nothing wrong."

"You did not think so when you first saw me again."

His father reached out and gripped his shoulder. "My anger came from the impossibility of the situation. If I had taken time to consider my words, I would not have spoken so harshly. I know you would not bend the knee readily to a false god."

"And yet I did."

"You acted for the good."

Rya'c shook his head, finding it hard not to give quarter to self-censure. "I let myself be fooled. You were right. What must you think of me?" He could only imagine how difficult it was for his father, who had endured so much in the name of freedom, who had been spat upon and called *shol'va*, to see his son serve yet another Goa'uld — and to then find out that the same Goa'uld had taken his friend as host and been responsible for bringing them to this hideous future. For creating it…

"I think I am proud of the warrior my son has become. Now we have much to do. You must not allow self-doubt to cloud your judgment."

Steeling himself, Rya'c nodded; there were more urgent matters to be dealt with here. He could only hope that Major Carter was not outgunned back on the ha'tak. Many of his Jaffa would stand by her side, but too many were blindly loyal to Hecate.

They made their way through corridors that were eerily silent. As he opened his mouth to voice his concern, he heard a sound: a rustling movement behind one of the closed doors that lined the corridor.

Exchanging a glance with his father, they approached the door. On a silent count of three they burst inside, weapons raised and armed.

The room was small, crowded with several desks covered in papers, behind which cowered a single man. His face was stripped of color, eyes wide in fear.

"Wait! I'm unarmed!"

"Who are you?" demanded Teal'c. "What has happened here?"

"I'm David Frey," he said, shaking hands raised. "I work here — logistics."

His father repeated his question. "What has happened here? Where are the base personnel?"

"Everyone's gone," the man said, shaking his head as if struggling to believe his own words. "I don't know what's going on; it's crazy down there. This seemed like the safest place right now."

"Down there?" asked Rya'c.

"In Laketown. Yuma's gone rogue and the place has gone

to hell. I think they're getting ready to storm the president's house. Go see for yourself."

His father lifted his gaze to Rya'c, gave a subtle nod, then said to the man, "You are wise to remain here, David Frey. Keep silent and await further instructions."

With that he and Rya'c left him in his refuge and made their way to the main entrance of the base.

They ran out into a breaking dawn over a wide, russet desert of rocky spires and plateaus — atop one of which they stood. For a moment Rya'c's breath was stolen by the vista but, as they made their way through crumbling ruins and across the narrow bridge to the next plateau, he saw that the man had indeed spoken the truth. For the streets of the settlement clinging to the shores of the lake below — Laketown — were crowded with a throng of bodies. Even at this distance, they could hear the chants and the shouting, though it was impossible to make out the meaning of their words.

"That does not look good," said his father and Rya'c thought he could hear inflections of Jack O'Neill in his voice.

"What can we do?"

"Nothing from up here," Teal'c said. "We must find General Bailey."

"You're making a mistake," Sam said as Zuri shoved her forward, one hand on her shoulder and her fingers digging in hard.

"It is you who are mistaken," Zuri hissed. "About everything."

Sam's hands were tied behind her back and she walked with Zuri behind her, Hunter stalking along in front and a handful of Resistance fighters around them.

The ha'tak was descending into chaos as news of Rya'c's defection spread — along with news of Sobek, and what he represented. She could hear firefights in the distance, the echoing yells of men, and the air was filling with the unmistakable stench of battle. "Listen," she said. "Hecate isn't what you think she is, she's not a —"

"Be silent," Zuri hissed. "I'll hear no more of your lies. They've done enough harm."

"They're not lies." She tried to shrug out from under Zuri's grip, but couldn't get free; the woman was strong. And she was angry. "They're not —"

"I knew, as soon as I saw you, that you were trouble. As soon as Dix first saw him — the one who claims to be his father — he was lost."

"No —"

"He betrayed his people, his planet — and his god! And he did it, all of it, for you: for SG-1." She shoved Sam forward, hard enough that she stumbled. "For a *lie*."

In front of her, Hunter half turned. He still had a troubled look on his face, brow drawn low as he chewed at his bottom lip.

"It's not a lie," Sam said, turning her appeal on him. "Hunter, Hecate did this. She brought us here because she *wanted* this — enslaving Earth is her endgame."

"She is a god!" Zuri hissed. "And better to be ruled by the Lady Hecate than feed the Snatchers."

"She speaks true," Hunter said. "Hecate wants rid of the Snatchers —"

"But she doesn't!" Sam said. "Please, you have to believe me. She's going to enslave us all and use the Snatchers to —"

Zuri slapped her hard across the face, jarring her jaw. "I said enough," she hissed. "Your words are poison; I'll hear no more of them. We will leave it to the Lady Hecate to decide your fate." With that, she shoved her forward again.

Sam worked her jaw from side to side, easing the sting of the blow as she side-eyed Hunter. He wasn't looking at her but his expression was still clouded. Sam hoped he might still prove to be an ally.

The sound of fighting intensified the further they walked and Zuri sent Hunter ahead to investigate. He reported back, looking shaken. "There's Snatchers ahead," he said. "And the Lady Hecate, she's…"

"What about her?" Zuri snapped.

"One of 'em's got her."

"*Got* her?" Sam said. He must mean Sobek.

"Then we must help her!" Zuri shoved past Sam. "We must protect the Lady Hecate!" She started to move forward, her men close behind.

Sam shrank back against the wall, hoping to be forgotten, but Hunter said, "Zuri, what about Major Carter?"

Zuri looked back over her shoulder, gaze running down to Sam's feet and up again. Her expression was cold. "Kill her," she said, and then turned to run toward the battle.

Backed to the wall, her hands tied behind her back, Sam stared at Hunter. "Don't," she said. "Don't do this."

He licked his lips, glanced at Zuri's retreating back, then at Sam again. "You brought Snatchers here," he said, raising his weapon. "You're *working* with them."

"I know it's difficult to understand —"

"It ain't difficult! And I ain't stupid. You're working with Snatchers."

"But they're not all the same, they don't all want —"

He shoved the weapon forward, jabbed it against her chest. "I seen them feed on my friends in them pens," he hissed. "And you seen it too. Hell, they even tried to feed on you."

Sam nodded, tried to swallow and focus on Hunter and not the head of the staff weapon heavy on her chest. "Yes," she said. "I know. But it's more complicated than we thought, Hunter. They want to go home — to leave this galaxy — and we can help them do it."

"I don't care what they want!" he hissed. "*I* want the bastards *dead*. And so does Hecate."

"But she doesn't!" Sam protested. "Hecate is using them — she's turning them into her soldiers, into gods!"

"You're lying!"

The weapon sprang to life. She could feel the electronic hum of it dig under her skin. Sweat broke out on her forehead, her mouth and throat dry. "I'm not lying," she said. "Hunter, please. If we don't stop her, Hecate will create an army of Snatchers and she'll use them to destroy you. To enslave you. And not just you — whole other planets will fall if she gains control of Atlantis. Hunter, no one could stand against her. She'd become *worse* than the Snatchers."

"My whole life," he said, through gritted teeth, "I served her. An' I prayed to her, I prayed for her blessing. It ain't possible that — Dix *fought* for us! He helped us when there weren't no one else."

"But Dix was deceived too, Hunter. You saw him — he told you that."

"Zuri said you poisoned his mind."

Sam took a breath, attempted to ease the cramping in her shoulders, and tried a different tack. Assertion wasn't working. "Did you see it?" she said. "Just now, did you see the Snatcher who she made a god?"

From the troubled look in his eye, she knew that he had. "That ain't — I don't know what I saw."

"You saw the future, Hunter," she said. "That thing — that hybrid? It's what your Lady Hecate will use to crush you."

But he was still shaking his head, the staff still pressed to her chest. "You don't understand. The Snatchers took everything, they took —"

Suddenly there was a roar from the end of the corridor, a wild and desperate sound. Sam jerked her head, felt the weapon shift against her chest as Hunter did the same.

A melee erupted around the corner: Rya'c's Jaffa were backing up, firing as they went, and behind them strode Sobek. Sting hung limp in his grasp, held off the ground with one hand.

"You dare to challenge your gods?" Sobek hissed. "This is the fate of those who try!" He flung Sting's body into the retreating Jaffa, knocking several of them flying. The others scrambled back to their feet and continued to retreat.

Behind Sobek, walked Hecate. She favored her left leg, but kept her head high and haughty. Sam glimpsed Zuri at her side.

"Hunter!" Sam hissed. "Please — help me stop him."

Behind them, Sobek snatched up one of the fallen Jaffa and slammed it against the wall with his feeding hand. Within moments, there was nothing but a husk remaining and Sobek bared his teeth in ecstasy. Hecate made no attempt to stop him.

Hunter stared; the weapon dipped.

"She won't help them," Sam said as Sobek grabbed another Jaffa, plunging his feeding hand against its chest. "She won't stop him." And, after a beat, she realized, "She *can't*. He's stronger than her." Sam's gaze moved back to Hecate, to the lifted chin and imperious gaze, and she saw fear behind her eyes.

*Frankenstein's monster* — and everyone knew how that story ended.

With a curse, Hunter spun Sam around, pushed her hard against the wall. Her heart stuttered, she squeezed shut her eyes as she waited for the kill-shot, and then there was the slide of a blade next to the skin of her wrist and her hands were free.

"Go," Hunter said behind her. "Do what you gotta do."

She turned, flexing feeling back into her hands. Sobek was advancing toward them, Rya'c's Jaffa helpless to resist. "Help me," she said. "Help me destroy the ship and take him with it."

But Hunter shook his head. "I can't," he said. "I'm sworn to Hecate, an' I'll die for her before I turn my back."

"She's not worth your life," Sam said, grabbing his arm. "Hunter —"

"I said no!" He pushed her off. "Now go, 'fore I change my mind."

Sam hesitated, but Hunter was already walking toward Sobek with his arms lifted. She cursed, furious with him — at herself for failing to convince him — yet she had no choice but to move. There was a door to her right, standing open, and inside it was dark. Slipping inside, she pressed herself against the wall and waited.

It seemed to take forever, but at last Sobek, trailed by Hecate, moved past the open doorway. She saw Zuri and Hunter walking behind, and with them those Jaffa remaining loyal to Hecate. There was no sign of Rya'c's rebel Jaffa; they were all dead.

Gritting her teeth against a wave of sorrow, of anger, Sam made herself give a slow count of one hundred before she peered out onto the silent corridor again. It was a grim scene that confronted her, bodies everywhere.

Most were dead from staff weapon injuries, but she counted at least three desiccated corpses. And among the dead, she saw Sting.

Glancing each way along the corridor she crept out of her hiding place. Sting was a friend, of sorts — an ally at least — and Sam knew she couldn't just abandon him. Besides, Earthborn would want to know how he died.

Keeping low, Sam made her way through the dead and the dying until she reached Sting. He lay slumped on his front and she had to use both hands to roll him onto his back. His long hair straggled over his face and there were wounds on his throat that looked like claw marks. Scorches on his leather armor suggested he'd been hit, and when Sam put her hand there it came away sticky with his black blood. Grimacing, she wiped it on his sleeve and sat back on her heels, leaving her hand resting on his arm.

"I'm sorry," she said, for want of anything better. "I hope you're in a better place, I guess. And I'll tell Earthborn —"

Beneath her fingers, his hand twitched.

"Sting?" She felt a sick kind of sinking feeling; he wasn't dead yet, but it seemed inevitable. "Sting, can you hear me?"

There was nothing. She thought, perhaps, the movement was just the shifting of his body, the way it happened with the dead. But then his eyes opened and they were lucid and fixed on her. His hand twitched again, his feeding hand, she realized, and his lips bared his teeth. "Help me…" It was nothing more than a hint of a whisper.

Cold with horror, she knew what he was asking. "I… I can't," she said, but closed her eyes as she said it. Could she?

Again his hand twitched. "Please…"

Sam felt dizzy with the choice in front of her: leave Sting to die, or help him live by killing another?

"Earth…" Sting whispered. "Earthborn…"

She nodded, understanding—knowing what he meant, how he felt, how she would feel if the situation were reversed. She turned away and cast her eyes over the bodies in the corridor. There were men—Jaffa—dying here. Would it be so bad to hasten their deaths to save another?

In truth, she didn't know. She wasn't sure what was right here; there didn't seem to be a right choice. She just had to choose—do something, or do nothing.

And Sam had never been one for doing nothing.

Gritting her teeth against her distaste, Sam pushed herself to her feet and made her way toward the first Jaffa she saw who was still breathing. Gripping his shoulders, she dragged him closer to Sting. He groaned in pain as he moved, but he didn't seem to be conscious; she couldn't do this if he were.

When she picked up Sting's hand and placed it on the Jaffa's bare chest her own hand was shaking, her stomach turning. And when he started to feed she had to turn away, breathe hard through her nose in slow, regulated breaths, to keep from emptying her stomach.

She'd killed hundreds of Jaffa in battle—there was no reason that this should feel worse. And yet it did. It was.

Sam wasn't sure how she'd ever look herself in the eye again.

# CHAPTER SIXTEEN

THE THRONE room — if that was the right word — of Queen Shadow was like nothing Jack had ever imagined.

Not that he spent much time imagining throne rooms, but he'd had the misfortune to be in a couple over the last few years and this was something very different to the glitz and glitter preferred by the Goa'uld.

Despite the sweeping architecture of Atlantis, Shadow's throne room was dark and humid. Hive-flesh covered the walls and ceiling, sagging low and claustrophobic. There was a dais in the center of the chamber, and around it stood Wraith who could only be described as courtiers. At least, they strutted and preened and eyed each other warily. Jack had the distinct impression of banked violence, of plotting and daggers in the dark.

At his side, Daniel murmured, "Fascinating."

Jack resisted the urge to roll his eyes. "You know she's going to kill us, right?"

Daniel gave an equivocal hum in the back of the throat, his eyes fixed on Earthborn who walked ahead of them with her head high. The two blades at her side, however, looked almost as freaked out as Jack felt. He couldn't blame them. Shadow's people were looking at them the way a shark considers breakfast.

They drew to a halt before the empty throne, a bony construction that glistened like beetle shells or oil slicks. Maybourne was already abasing himself in front of it. In the gloom, he looked more cadaverous than ever. More pathetic.

Jack gritted his teeth against feeling pity; everything that had befallen this man, he had brought down on himself. And on the whole damn world. He didn't deserve any pity, and yet seeing him pressing his face to the floor, no more than a bundle of ragged bones, Jack found he didn't have the heart to feel anything *but* pity for him.

"Obviously an extremely matriarchal society," Daniel whispered. "The *only* female Wraith appears to be the queen. Like bees or ants — I mean, literally. Not to dehumanize them in any way, but —"

"*Dehumanize* them?"

"So to speak," Daniel conceded. "You take my point. They're —"

He broke off when a sudden hush rippled through the room, a whisper of fabric and creaking leather as Shadow's Wraith sank to one knee, heads bowed.

Maybourne whimpered, "She's coming," and pressed himself flat to the floor.

Jack glanced at Daniel, who just gave a little shrug. They stayed standing. So did Earthborn and her nervous escort.

And into the room swept Queen Shadow, living up to every inch of her name. Her hair was black and long, falling down her back and stark against her pallid, alien face. If Earthborn was imperious, Shadow was downright intimidating as she stalked in with deadly grace, the embroidered black of her dress casting shadows in her wake. When she stopped before her throne, casting her eyes about her assembled courtiers, she looked terrifying in her power.

Jack swallowed, found a lump in his throat. He had no doubt that this creature could kill him as easily as he would step on a bug.

Shadow bared her teeth. "Earthborn," she hissed, "daughter of my sister. Have you come to bend your knee to me at last?"

"A queen bows to no one," Earthborn said.

"A queen does not," Shadow said, taking her seat on her throne. Her taloned fingers gripped its arms, tapping against the chitinous substance. *Click, click, click.* "But of what are you queen? A dying hive and a few old warriors who cling to what Brightstar once was?" Her gaze traveled back toward Jack and

Daniel. "And your human pets, of course. This is the force with which you challenge me, Earthborn?"

"You are right," Earthborn said, "I don't come to challenge you by force. I cannot. But I come to challenge what you are, Shadow. Truly, you were named well for you have cast such a shadow over our people — you have corrupted them, made them weak. Too weak to hunt, they are fit only to feed. And now you corrupt them with the parasites!" She turned her gaze on Shadow's blades, all watching her with sharp-eyed suspicion. "How can you bear to witness what she is doing to you, to your brothers? Blades of Shadow, how can you permit it?"

"Enough." With a slashing gesture, Shadow called for silence. "You have a small mind, Earthborn. You see only the past, only a dream of the past. But you did not know the barren feeding grounds of Pegasus. You did not know the great *hunger*." At that, her blades shifted, murmuring agreement. "Had we stayed in Pegasus, we would have died — died fighting over the humans, died of hunger in our wretched long sleeps. But here…? Here there is no hunger. Here, my people thrive. And with the army I am building, we will return to Pegasus in triumph — we will exterminate our enemies and retake our feeding grounds for ourselves alone." She leaned forward, her eyes devoid of anything human. "And we will take this galaxy too. The parasites carry in their minds all the knowledge of their kind — and now it is *ours*. Now, we know the secrets of this place and we will *take* it. All of it."

A silence fell, Earthborn apparently taken aback.

Of course, it was Daniel who spoke first. "Yeah," he said, "about that? Not so much, as it turns out."

Shadow's head swung toward him, as disdainful as if a bug had just deigned to voice an opinion. "Who speaks?"

"Ah, that'll be me," Daniel said, taking a step forward and raising his hand.

*Raising his hand?*

Shadow rose to her feet. "Earthborn, your pets have no discipline."

"Well, you might want to listen to this," Daniel said. "Because I've just come from Hecate's ship and I have news for you."

Among the courtiers there was a stir. "My Queen, allow me to silence this insolence!" came a voice.

"Hold, Consort." Shadow lifted a hand. "I would hear what it says."

"Daniel…" Jack warned.

"Jack…" came the reply — the *butt-out-I-know-what-I'm-doing* reply. To Shadow, Daniel said, "Hecate's outwitted you. The hybrids? She's going to take them. And this city too."

Shadow threw back her head, mouth wide and teeth like daggers. The sound she made was something between a growl and a shriek — or maybe it was just a freaky-assed Wraith laugh? "That wriggling larva has outwitted *me*? You waste your breath, human."

"She's going to poison you," Daniel said. "It's what Hecate *does*. Medicines, poisons: it's all the same to her. The only Wraith who will survive are the ones carrying symbiotes, and them she can control."

"No one can control a Wraith," Shadow hissed. "We are too strong. It is your lies that are poison, vermin."

Daniel shrugged, hands spread. "Well, you can't say I didn't warn you." And then, with a look at Maybourne, he added, "But ask him, he knows."

*Crap*, Jack thought. *Crap…*

Shadow's gaze dipped to where Maybourne was making like a carpet on the floor. "Steadfast," she said, using his Wraith name. "Of what does he speak?"

"Nothing, my queen." He shook his head. "I know nothing. I'm loyal. Always loyal."

"Rise," she said, the word oily through her teeth. "Look upon me."

Hesitant, Maybourne pressed up onto his knees, head bowed. "My queen…"

"Speak, if you know any truth in this," she said. "I will reward you."

At that, his head shot up and, even in the dim light, Jack could see the gleam of hunger in his eyes. "Yes, I am loyal."

Shadow bared her teeth. "Speak."

"Hecate…" He glanced back toward Daniel and Jack, and for a moment Jack thought he saw regret in his ravaged face, some notion of paths not taken, but then it was gone and he shuffled forward toward Shadow. "She has planned this for years, my queen. For decades. She wants this city, but you can stop her from taking it. You are powerful. Strike now, before she has released the poison. Then it will all be yours!"

Shadow rotated her head, breathing out in a low angry snarl. Like lightening, her hand reached down and snatched Maybourne up, lifting him off his feet. "You swear this is true?"

He nodded, struggling limply in her grasp. "I swear, my queen."

"And you have heard this from the parasite yourself? From her human lips?"

Another nod. "My queen, I swear it."

Shadow bared her teeth. "Then you will have your reward, Steadfast."

"Thank you," he gasped, fingers scrabbling against Shadow's wrists. "Thank—"

The word choked off as Shadow plunged her feeding hand into Maybourne's chest. "The Gift of Life," Shadow breathed, bringing him close to her face, "is a precious gift for our loyal subjects."

Maybourne nodded, even though he grimaced in pain as her claws closed on his chest. "My queen…"

"Here, then, is your reward. *Traitor.*"

And then Maybourne was screaming, his legs kicking as his

body arched back and desiccated before Jack's eyes.

He had to look away, stomach turning at the sight.

"Oh God," Daniel whispered and for a moment their eyes met.

"Not your fault," Jack said.

"But I shouldn't have —"

"Daniel. He's the reason for *all of this*." He glanced over in time to see Shadow throw Maybourne's body to the floor, sending it tumbling over the edge of the dais. Jack looked away from his gaping mouth, his blank eyes. Stupid sonofabitch. "It was always gonna end this way for him, Daniel. Always."

But he could see Daniel hunch his shoulders, turning in on himself, and knew he wouldn't view it that way; too much compassion had always been Daniel's problem.

"Consort, send blades to hold the *Astria Porta* on the planet," Shadow hissed, turning to her courtiers with a swirl of her skirts. "And then go to the cruiser, take command yourself. I would see the parasite's ship burn; there will be no quarter."

One of her courtiers stepped forward, his long coat sweeping the deck as he bowed low. "As you command, my queen."

Daniel gripped Jack's arm. "Sam," he said. "Sam's still on the ha'tak."

So was Sting.

Perhaps Earthborn's mind had turned the same way, because she said, "It seems we have common cause against this parasite-god."

"Now hold on," Jack said, but then Earthborn turned and met his eye — not for long, but long enough to understand that she considered this a ruse. But what her endgame was, Jack couldn't tell. His fingers itched; he wished he still had his weapon.

"Hecate must be stopped," Earthborn said aloud, turning back to Shadow. "We must do all that we can to ensure that happens — even if that means working together, sister-of-my-mother."

Shadow's head twisted in a profoundly alien gesture. "I have no reason to trust you, Earthborn."

"Nor I you," Earthborn said. "Your human pet has betrayed you and now Hecate threatens the lives of us all." Her gaze swept over Shadow's courtiers. "You have led our people wrong, Shadow, but I am willing to overlook your folly because we are blood. We are Wraith. And we must stand together against the parasite that now has the means to destroy us."

There was an unsettled murmur from the Wraith, a shifting of feet, of glances. If Jack was Shadow, he'd be worried; he'd seen crowds turn like this before. "You speak true, of blood," Shadow said. "Your mother was my sister, and the hives of Brightstar and Shadow were ever close." She swept an imperious hand toward her, as if she was doing Earthborn a favor when it was obvious the tables were turning. "Come, sister-daughter, we will face this enemy together. Our hives united once more."

It was a politician's answer, Jack thought, a blatant attempt to mend fences before they gave way.

"I accept your offer," Earthborn said. "You will find—"

"Your blades may attend," Shadow said, speaking over her. "The humans will be taken to the feeding pens."

Crap.

"The humans are not—"

Shadow whirled around. "Do not press your luck, child."

Earthborn fell silent.

Jack swallowed, felt the tension radiating from Daniel. Shadow had no reason not to use them as a snack on the road, but he knew there was a play to be made here that might just keep them alive. Might just turn the tables again.

Earthborn fixed her eyes on him. Her alien features were difficult to read, but Jack thought he was getting better at interpreting their expressions—for all their bloodsucking weirdness, the Wraith were more human than they liked to believe. Earthborn blinked her reptilian eyes and said nothing, leaving the ball in Jack's court.

And, really, there was only one thing to do. "Uh, your majesty?" he said to Shadow, bracing himself for the fallout. "As much as I'd love to be turned into tomorrow's cheesesteak, that's probably not the best use of my talents."

Peeling back her teeth, head crooked, Shadow said, "You are insolent."

"Yes," Jack agreed, "insolent, impertinent — even downright impudent. But the thing is, I can do something no one else here can do. Something you want very, very much."

Daniel murmured, "Jack…"

He ignored the warning.

Nostrils flaring, Shadow hissed, "And what is that, human?"

Jack just looked at her and said, "I can pilot the city."

On the ground, it was not as bad as Teal'c had anticipated, but he knew that it was only a matter of time before the tension boiled over. He had seen restive crowds such as this before, when he had enforced the will of Apophis upon unwilling populations. Already, a few scuffles had broken out but they had been quickly dealt with by those who were still keen to retain order. Common sense still prevailed — for now.

He and Rya'c pushed their way through the crowd towards the president's residence, drawing more than a few glances, some of them in open hostility. But no one acted, and there were enough people shouting their support of SG-1 that Teal'c felt no immediate threat.

Still, though, the atmosphere thrummed with an unspent friction; if they did not act, it would spill over into violence. And he would rather that violence was focused in the right direction — against the Wraith and the forces of Hecate.

"Teal'c!" A voice echoed over the shouts of the crowd and Teal'c turned to find a familiar figure making his way towards them.

"Lieutenant Jefferson."

The soldier came to join them. "Isn't this something?" he said and Teal'c saw that the man was eager for combat. Perhaps that might be a good thing — but not here. "We owe it all to SG-1, man! Hey, you're Dix, right?" he added, turning to Rya'c who was surveying the crowd with concern.

"If it ends in bloodshed here on Arbella, it is not 'something'," Teal'c said. "If you owe SG-1 anything, then help us use this anger in a way that can save both Arbella and Earth."

Jefferson nodded readily. "Anything."

"Where is General Bailey?"

"She's with the president. To be honest, I don't think they know how to handle this."

"Then perhaps we can offer some clarity. Will you take us there?"

With Jefferson's aid, they approached the president's residence, from the front this time. When they reached the door, the two nervous-looking guards stationed there glanced at each other before motioning the three of them through. Teal'c surmised that they were more concerned with a potentially riotous mob than three men who may or may not have been allies. Teal'c hoped they could all be allies yet.

"Dix, Teal'c," said Bailey in surprise, when they entered the library. Jones was seated behind his desk, looking worn-down but in control. Teal'c thought it likely that General Bailey's calming influence had much to do with that. She turned to the president and said, "Sir, this is Dix. He's… he's a friend of Arbella."

There was a pause as Jones watched Rya'c with careful eyes, before nodding and saying, "You've picked a poor time to visit, Dix."

"President Jones, I prefer to go by Rya'c now. It is the name my father gave me. And I believe I have come at a fortuitous time for both of us."

"Oh?" The president's raised eyebrows looked skeptical.

"There is indeed a battle to be fought," Rya'c said. "But your task is to ensure that it is not between your own people."

"Don't you dare tell me what my job is," replied Jones, his voice fraught with emotion.

Teal'c knew they must tread lightly and reached out to put a stilling hand on his son's arm. He wished for Daniel Jackson's calm counsel at times like this. He himself was not a statesman, but he could speak from the heart. "President Jones, when I was dispossessed and anathema to my own people, I found a home among the people of Earth. *Your* people. I have seen first-hand the great deeds of which the Tau'ri are capable. I believe you can achieve greatness once again. I believe you must."

"You've seen what's happening outside," said Jones. "Is that what you wanted to achieve by coming here?"

Teal'c bowed his head. "SG-1 did not seek to bring strife to your planet."

"Maybe not, but you did."

"Come on, Gun." Bailey leaned forward, resting her hands on the desk. "You know this has been coming for years. If we don't handle it right we could have an insurrection on our hands. Surely it's better to focus our efforts on something decent and good. Otherwise we'll have bloodshed in our streets. "

"General Bailey speaks true," Teal'c said. "Your people face a greater threat than this disorder. The Goa'uld, Hecate, has turned her eyes on your world."

"Our gate shield —"

"It will not protect you," Teal'c said. "Hecate seeks to gain a ship of vast power, a ship constructed by the Ancients. If she is successful, she will use that ship to impose her will on the entire galaxy. None, not even the System Lords, could stand against her. And she intends to begin her campaign of domination with Arbella."

Jones eyes flashed and he thumped a fist on the desk. "Because *you* betrayed us to her, because *you* —"

"No!" Teal'c allowed his own anger to show. "You are a fool if you believe Hecate has not been planning this for decades.

The Goa'uld are a cruel and vengeful species who rule by terror. Your ancestors escaped them, they *defied* them. Do you believe Hecate will allow that defiance to go unpunished?"

"My father speaks the truth," Rya'c said, his voice thick with remorse. "I too heard the Lady Hecate speak of her intention to crush Arbella. It is… It is still difficult for me to believe, but it is the truth and cannot be avoided. Hecate was never a friend to Arbella; she has planned this day for many years."

Teal'c's heart went out to his son and yet swelled with pride at the same time; he understood the pain of facing harsh truths, and the courage it took to do so.

Returning his attention to President Jones, Teal'c took the anger out of his voice. This man, too, must face a painful truth and must face it now. "Nothing can stop Hecate from reaching for your world," he said. "Nothing can stop her from crushing it. Nothing but your decision to fight." He leaned closer, pressed his hands on the desk and loomed over the president. "Hecate must be stopped. Will you lead your people against her, President Jones? Or will you hide with your arms over your head and hope to be spared? I warn you, your hope will be in vain."

The president rubbed his chin, brow furrowed as he considered the situation. He looked resigned, the anger having left his expression. After a taut moment he raised shrewd eyes to Teal'c and said, "It seems I have no choice."

"Not if you wish your people to survive."

He made a curt gesture to the dark and riotous streets beyond. "Then tell me how we handle this."

Sting felt the life flowing back into his body slowly, sluggish. He fed thrice more, for the dying Jaffa provided scant sustenance. It was enough to heal him, but not enough to make him whole. Yet it would have to suffice for now.

Major Carter stood with her back turned. She had appropriated one of the Jaffa staff weapons and held it at the ready as she watched the empty corridor. Perhaps responding to his footsteps she said, without turning around, "Are you done?"

He allowed a moment to pass before answering, aware of the disgust — even horror — emanating from the woman. "I thank you for your assistance," he said stiffly. "I am recovered enough."

With a nod, she turned her head slightly, not enough to really look behind her, and said, "I need to get to the engine room — our best chance to destroy Hecate and the hybrid is to take out the whole ship."

"I would rather that Boneshard — what was once Boneshard — die at my own hands."

"He almost killed you," Major Carter said, moving away from him and stooping to retrieve a second staff weapon. "You'd be dead now if—" She cleared her throat. "Anyway, there's no way you can take that thing down. You've tried twice." This time she did turn to him, her expression tight. "Help me," she said, holding out one of the weapons. "Take this — take as many as you can carry."

Sting eyed the weapon with some doubt. "I'm unfamiliar with these weapons…"

"I'm not asking you to fire it," she said, and threw the staff toward him. He caught it in one hand, turned it over to feel the balance. "I'm going to use the liquid naquadah in the power cells to build a bomb."

Sting was no cleverman and unfamiliar with naquadah, however Major Carter's certainty was compelling. "You are ingenious," he said and bent to collect another of the weapons. He thought again of Stormfire's assistant, the human called O'Kane. "Your species is more inventive than I had realized." It was an increasingly difficult insight.

"Really?" She collected a third weapon, hefting them in her arms. "Six should be enough," she said. "And we should get out of here."

Sting slung his three weapons over one shoulder and

said, "I will take the lead, Major Carter." He owed her his life — again — and it was incumbent on him to protect her. "But you must show me the way, if you know it."

"Well, this isn't the first ha'tak I've blown up," she said, and he thought he saw a hint of a smile on her face. "Fastest way would be to find a ring transporter, but they're gonna be too heavily guarded — especially with the Jaffa still scrapping."

He assumed she referred to the distant sounds of fighting, to the faction of Jaffa who remained loyal to the parasite and those others loyal to their commander. It was not unlike the internecine squabbling in a hive when the succession of a new queen was in doubt. And, again, the parallel disturbed him.

"Sting?" Major Carter touched his arm. "This way."

Leaving the corridor that had been the site of the battle, they made their way deeper into the parasite's ship. It was a cold place, dead — a thing only of moving parts, without soul, without flesh. Like the technology of the Ancestors, it was just a *thing*. It made him grateful for the biological technology of his own people. To live aboard such a thing as this, protected from the void of space by nothing more than sheets of metal, was a terrifying prospect which he dared not consider too closely.

To distract himself from the thought, he said, "How long will it take you to construct your weapon?"

Carter gave a small noise of consideration from where she walked at his shoulder. "It depends," she said. "I need a detonator. That's going to be the biggest challenge. Possibly, I can engineer one of the cells to overload. It'll be a couple hours."

Much could happen in such an amount of time — both here and elsewhere. His thoughts, of course, went to Earthborn. Major Carter's, too, apparently, because she said, "I hope the others are doing okay. I hope Teal'c got Rya'c off the ship."

"They must fend for themselves," Sting reminded her. As must Earthborn, he reminded himself. "We can only complete our element of the plan."

"Yeah," she said shortly. "I just hope —"

The ship jarred suddenly, knocking Sting to his knees. Carter dropped into a crouch at his side. Another jolt jarred them further and Carter lost her grip on the staff weapons. They clattered to the deck, rolling away. "That was weapons fire," she said, her gaze fixed on the ceiling.

He agreed, but the question was: "From within, or without?"

A third detonation followed and the air began to fill with the acrid stench of burning. Major Carter said, "Outside. We're under attack."

"Shadow's cruiser," Sting guessed. "There is no one else it could be."

"If you're right," Carter said, "then it means she knows Hecate's planning to move against her."

Her words made him stiffen with disquiet. "Which means..."

"Not necessarily," Carter said. "She could have a spy here — an informant. It doesn't mean the colonel and Earthborn have failed." But from her face, Sting could see that she spoke more bravely than she felt.

"Earthborn would not order the cruiser to fire upon this ship, knowing that we are aboard," he said. "This means Shadow has not been defeated."

"Yet," Carter insisted. "C'mon, let's keep a little optimism here, okay?"

Another shudder rippled through the deck and then there was another sensation — one familiar to Sting. The ship was moving.

Startled, Carter said, "She's breaking orbit."

"No doubt to engage with the cruiser more effectively."

"Or she's just gonna run." Pushing herself to her feet, Carter grabbed hold of her fallen weapons, bracing herself against the hull with one shoulder as the ship lurched under another assault. "If we leave Earth, we're in trouble. The only way off the ship would be through the Stargate and there's zero chance of reaching it before the bomb detonates." She paused. "There's zero chance of reaching the gate, period."

Sting bared his teeth, part in anger and part in pride. "I am willing to give my life to see this creature dead."

"Yeah," Carter agreed. "But I'd rather not. So we need to keep Hecate from going anywhere until I can rig the bomb and get to one of the ring transporters." She looked at the staff weapons he carried and said, "Give them to me. I'll get to the engine room and start working on the bomb, you head to the bridge. Do what you can to keep us close enough to Earth so that I can ring down to the surface — and then get the hell off the ship."

"And you?"

There was a slight hesitation before she said, "I'll be right behind you."

She said no more and he pressed no further. Major Carter was a warrior, as were all of O'Neill's people — she would do what was necessary to fulfill her mission.

As would he.

Jack found himself bracketed by Wraith as he and Daniel were led to the tower where the captain's chair was located.

Unlike Sting, and Earthborn's other ragged followers, Shadow's people were slick and well groomed. Some of them looked like they spent hours braiding their fancy long hair and polishing their boots. Courtiers was definitely the word for them, and Jack recalled the disdain Sting had expressed for them — the way he'd talked about Earth and it's plentiful food supply corrupting his people.

They walked swiftly along the corridor, Daniel pale but stoic at his side. He'd convinced the Wraith that he needed Daniel to translate the Ancient language, but they both knew that things could change at any moment; they were swimming in a shark tank and all it would take was a drop of blood for the feeding frenzy to begin.

"So," he said, as much to keep up the pretense of Daniel's

expertise as anything else, "what should I expect when I get there?"

"Um…" Daniel pinched the bridge of his nose because, for once, he knew as little as Jack about any of this. "I guess it'll be similar to the systems on the gate-ship only — maybe more immersive?"

"Immersive?" He didn't like the idea of that; he needed to be fully aware of his surroundings in case the Wraith decided he wasn't playing ball. Which he, most definitely, wouldn't be.

"The Ancient device we found on P3R-272 certainly interfaced directly with your mind," Daniel reminded him. "And given all the systems a city this size would need in order to run, I doubt there's a way for one person to control them that *isn't* immersive…"

Jack let that idea filter deeper. They were in an area of the city unoccupied by the Wraith — the corridor blank, cool gray lines defining doors and windows. Sunlight streamed in, reminding him that they were still on Earth. And that this was a city, not just a weapon. The climb to the top of the tower, up a sweeping spiral staircase, offered startling glimpses of Atlantis through tall, narrow windows. It reminded him of a cathedral, or some other sacred place, and the fact that it had been despoiled by the Wraith only made their presence here more obscene.

It didn't help that Jack's knees were beginning to seriously protest the number of stairs. But the Wraith barely broke a sweat — if they ever sweated — marching on until, at last, they turned away from the stairs and led Jack and Daniel through a doorway.

The room beyond was dark, although a few lights flickered on as Jack stepped inside — responding, he supposed, to his genetic on-switch. But there were no windows, no natural light.

"This is it," Daniel said, somewhat redundantly. It's not like you could miss the enormous chair that sat elevated on a hexagonal platform in the center of the room.

Two Wraith took position outside the door, and the third

followed Jack and Daniel into the room. Jack felt a hand grip his shoulder, talons curling into his muscle. "If you can do what you claim, human," the Wraith hissed, "do it now. Or I will feed; it has been some time since I ate anything as *vigorous* as you."

And if that wasn't the creepiest thing he'd ever heard....

Ducking his shoulder out from under the Wraith's grip, Jack took a step toward the chair. "Daniel," he said, "you , uh, wanna help me out here?"

Slowly, they circled the platform. Jack could feel the eyes of the Wraith on him, but he wasn't going to let them rush him. He needed to do this right; he couldn't fumble the ball on this one. There was too much at stake.

But at last Daniel said, "I think you'll just have to sit down and see what happens."

"No instruction manual, huh?"

"When did you ever read the instruction manual?"

It was a fair point.

Taking a breath, Jack nodded. Daniel was right, of course, there was only one way to do this and that was head first. He stepped up onto the platform, then stopped and turned to the Wraith at his shoulder. "Just out of curiosity," he said, "what happened to the last guy who did this job?"

The Wraith's only answer was a snarl.

"Right," Jack said. "I figured." He took a final moment to ready himself, and then sat down carefully. Immediately the chair moved, reclining and tilting his feet up. "Hey, you didn't tell me it was a La-Z-Boy..."

Nobody laughed.

"Jack," Daniel said tensely, coming to stand next to the chair. "You need to put your hands on these pads."

Jack glanced down to see that the arms ended two glowing circular pads. He touched one with a tentative finger — it was cool, gel-like. A little gross. Making a face, he put his whole hand on the pad, then his other hand on the other one. At first nothing happened, and then… *everything.*

It was like his mind had expanded to encompass the entire city, as if he could see and hear it all — the vastness of it, the emptiness, the wrongness of the Wraith incursion. Every beating heart in the city was his to hear: Wraith and human. And, yes, there were humans here, cocooned and waiting to be fed upon. His mind recoiled from them, from the sense of their suffering, from the damage the Wraith had done. System upon system he saw truncated, rerouted, and the city trying to heal itself like a wound scabbing over an infection. And questions, a thousand questions bombarded him from all directions, peppering his mind: alerts, warnings, rerouting suggestions, and aborted protocols. It was like the whole city, left leaderless for years, was asking for help, for instructions.

And Jack realized Daniel was right — he'd felt something like this mental overload before, when his brain had been overwritten by the Ancient database on P3R-272. Atlantis might not be biological, but there was no doubt in Jack's mind that it was somehow alive and that it recognized him as its master. It's savior, even. And what it was asking to do was get rid of the Wraith, to clean itself of the violent incursion. Because the Wraith hadn't just come in and set up house, they'd dug deep into the city's systems to circumvent whatever protocols the Ancients had left behind to defend it from the Wraith. And the city was hurting.

"Is it working, human?"

Although Jack's eyes were closed he could sense the looming presence of the Wraith close to his shoulder. He smiled and opened his eyes. To his surprise, the space above his head was swimming with light, a graphic representation of the images with which the city had filled his mind. "Yes," he said, watching the surround-sound HUD with fascination. "It's working real well."

"Then launch," the Wraith said. "Make the city fly."

"Just give me a minute. It's complex."

And then he looked up at Daniel and caught his eye. He tried to convey, *Get ready.* Daniel's subtle nod, the way he backed away from the chair, told him he understood.

Sinking down to embrace the city, he closed his eyes and began to reroute containment and purification systems toward the room in which he sat. He knew he was clumsy, still finding his way, but there was no time for subtlety; in some peripheral corner of his mind, he could already see the Wraith cruiser engaging Hecate's ship. He had to take control of Atlantis and he had to do it now.

*Seal the door,* he said and felt something shiver under his skin. As if from far away he heard a static hum, a startled exclamation as the force shield closed over the doorway into the room.

"What have you done?" the Wraith snarled.

Jack's eyes flew open and his fist jammed up as the Wraith lunged for him. His blow caught it in the eye and the Wraith reeled back, hand to its face and its stunner skittering across the floor.

Daniel dived for it, rolled to his feet and fired. The Wraith staggered and Daniel fired again, and again, until it folded to its knees and went down. He fired, once more, into its back as the thing lay still.

Through the force shield, the other Wraith stared at them, impotent and full of rage. Reinforcements were probably already on the way and Jack didn't know how long that force shield would hold against a concerted Wraith assault.

Breathless, Daniel turned to him. His eyes were wide behind his glasses. "Now what?"

Sinking back into the chair, Jack closed his eyes and said, "Now we see what this thing can do."

# CHAPTER SEVENTEEN

AS A CALL to arms, it was not the rousing speech that Teal'c had seen in the movies of the Tau'ri. It was not met with rapturous applause or unanimous support. Some of the crowd catcalled and heckled as the president addressed them from the steps that led down from his residence, but all of them listened. And it was with his closing statement that Gunnison Jones secured the loyalty of his people.

"We must rally and, yes, we must fight. Because too much has been taken from us. Too much has already been lost, and we cannot stand by and watch as the blood of our people is spilled indiscriminately. This is a fight, not for Arbella, not for Earth. But for *humanity*. And if it is to survive, humanity *must* reclaim its home."

In the end, they were pledged five-hundred troops made up mainly of CMF personnel, though it was heartening to see the members of the security force step up to volunteer. But they were too green and untrained. Even with General Bailey's robust training of her CMF forces, their lack of battle experience was concerning. But it was what they had and it would be enough to achieve their goal — securing the Earth's Stargate.

With a sense of trepidation, in the early morning light, Teal'c and Rya'c led their warriors up to the Stargate complex, ready to join the battle for Earth. Teal'c knew that his hurried briefing in Laketown could not possibly prepare these people for the awful reality of the Wraith — nor the awful reality of war. They would learn in the heat of battle and he knew that many of those who followed him to this world that was foreign to them would bleed their life blood into its soil.

But as it turned out, it was not the Wraith who posed the most immediate threat.

It was Rya'c who spotted the body first, sprawled on the

red-dirt in front of the narrow bridge that led to the plateau on which the Stargate complex stood. He turned. "Father?"

"I see it." Teal'c gestured for the others to halt behind him. The body had not there when they left the complex less than two hours ago. Bailey, looking over his shoulder, drew her weapon and stepped in front of President Jones. Teal'c approached the body, taking note of the bullet wounds in its back — this man had been shot while running away. Two fingers to the neck confirmed what was already obvious and, gently, Teal'c set down his staff weapon to roll the corpse over. It was the man they'd encountered earlier — David Frey — who had thought he was safer hiding in the empty base.

"Step back, Jaffa," came a voice from the darkness of the complex's doorway.

"You have no hope of escaping here, Agent Yuma," he replied, without looking up. As slowly as he could, he began inching his hand toward his staff weapon.

"Karin, what are you doing?" Jones pushed forward, ignoring Bailey's protests and shrugging off her attempts to pull him back.

Yuma swung to face him, taking in the troops who stood at his back. There were more than enough people to overpower her, but the narrow walkway meant a bottleneck, and she could easily do much damage before she was restrained. "I see you've lost your mind, Mr. President. Pandering to the whim of a vocal minority."

"You killed my wife," he ground out.

"Your wife was already gone, sir. She was mindless. God knows what they did to her on Earth, but I knew how they'd try to use her to control you. I couldn't afford for you to be emotionally compromised."

"What is it you want, Yuma?" Bailey came to stand by the president, her own gun trained on the agent. "I won't allow you to escape through the gate."

Yuma gave an incredulous laugh. "Escape? You think, after

all I've done for this planet, that I would run? Consider this a coup, General. Our Commander-in-Chief has been compromised and I'm taking control." She turned her weapon back on Jones, just as Teal'c grabbed his staff weapon. But he was a fraction too slow and a gunshot rang out through the night, a cry of shock going up through the assembled troops.

Jones was on the ground, Bailey crouched over him, but it was Yuma who staggered back, a bright bloom of red across her button-down shirt. She looked down at the gunshot wound in her chest with an expression that was almost angry, as if enraged that a bullet would dare to pierce her. She staggered back. Teal'c darted forward, across the bridge, as her foot went over the edge of the cliff in a shower of red rubble. He landed on his belly as she fell, his hand closing on thin air. He could only watch as she grew smaller, until the red Arbellan earth stopped her descent. She hadn't even screamed.

Two feet appeared next to him and he looked up into the furious face of President Jones. For a moment, Teal'c thought that the man might spit over the edge. But instead he just said, "Let's go. We have a battle to win."

Though outwardly Shadow turned the face of friendship toward her, Earthborn knew it was mere pretense.

And she was glad of it; killing her mother's sister would not be easy, but to do so in the face of an offer of peace would be harder still. Shadow's seething mistrust, her envy that Earthborn had brought the Lantean to the Ancestor's city, made everything easier. As did the fact that Shadow continued to underestimate her — a thought Shadow did little to hide.

In the secret part of her mind, the space not even Shadow could reach, Earthborn thought her mother's sister foolish. Shadow could not conceive of defeat.

That would be her undoing.

Shadow led the way into her inner court, the zenana where only her most trusted blades and clevermen held audience. They watched Earthborn with closed minds and narrowed eyes, but she recognized some of their faces from her mother's hive. It surprised her that Shadow trusted them enough to admit them to this sanctum, but perhaps her pride was such that she did not believe their former ties could be rekindled.

Into each mind she recognized, Earthborn projected a sensation of forgiveness, of hope. *Serve me, and I will love you.* She saw three blades shift with discomfort, turn away, their minds unsettled.

That was enough. Unease was all she would need — the ruin Shadow had brought to her people, the corruption, would undo the rest. If she was lucky.

At her side she felt the nervous presence of Hearten and Edge and reached out to calm them. *All will be well, my brave ones.*

Once at the heart of her zenana, Shadow turned. Her dress, elaborate and rich in a style Earthborn had long ago eschewed in favor of practicality, rustled across the floor. She was magnificent to behold, but within she was as dark and cold as her name. This close, Earthborn could feel the corruption at her very core.

Shadow turned her head and spoke, mind-to-mind, with one of her blades. He bowed, and a moment later the wall of her zenana lit up. It was a device of the Ancestor's, a screen which showed the battle taking place above the planet as if they stood upon the cruiser's bridge. The cruiser was firing on the parasite's ship — Earthborn was surprised at how large it was — but so far, she could see no damage. Its shielding appeared impressive.

Earthborn stepped closer, careful to conceal her concern for Sting. That he was aboard the parasite's ship — that his life may be forfeit — was like a needle beneath her skin that she could not ignore. Neither could she let it keep her from doing what must be done to protect, not just her own people, but all Wraith.

"The ship's trajectory is changing," said a voice from the

screen, speaking from the cruiser. "It's maneuvering for attack."

Another voice added, "Its launching fighters."

Shadow hissed, teeth bared in triumph. "Launch darts. Fire all weapons — target their shielding. And witness the fate of any who challenge the might of Shadow."

And just like that, Earthborn could wait no longer; she could not permit Shadow this victory if she ever hoped to take her place. With a savage cry, her feeding hand outstretched, Earthborn plunged it into the chest of her mother's sister.

"Child!" Shadow snarled, ripping Earthborn's hand away, fingers curling around her wrist and not letting go. "Dare you lift your hand against me?"

Earthborn hissed, undaunted even as Shadow drove her to her knees. "I dare because I must! You have brought ruin to all Wraith — and you will spread it further if you are not stopped."

"Ruin? I bring glory!" Her head swung toward one of the blades standing by the view screen. "Why have they not fired?"

He looked down at Earthborn then back to Shadow, but did not answer. Earthborn felt a flare of hope; he had not answered his queen.

"Your blades see what you are!" Earthborn said. Shadow still had her arm in her grip, bent at a painful angle, but she would not be cowed. And she would speak the truth.

Teeth bared, Shadow twisted hard on Earthborn's arm. "You will die for your treason, sister-daughter, though you are a queen."

Feeding hand raised, she slammed it down hard but Earthborn caught it before she could reach her chest. Shadow was strong; her mind was powerful, drilling into Earthborn's thoughts.

*You will fail and I will feed on you and all your kind!*

Earthborn's hand began to cramp where she gripped

Shadow's wrist. Her arm shook with the strain.

No blade of Shadow's moved to intervene; all knew that whoever triumphed in this death match would become queen. And anyone who had opposed the victor would soon be dead.

No blade of Shadow's moved, but not all blades within the zenana were Shadow's…

The sensation was intense.

The power Jack was channeling was almost incomprehensible: the scale of the city, the brilliance of the star drive as he brought it to life with a thought, the complexity of the display filling the air above his head.

He didn't need the HUD because he could see it all inside his head. Which was freaky on a whole different level, but this wasn't the first time he'd had Ancient technology crawling around inside his skull and he figured it wouldn't do any permanent damage. Not much, anyway.

He could see — it felt like seeing — the outside of the city: all the piers and towers soaring above the water, the deep struts and tanks that sank below to provide ballast, and the shield that hummed almost as if it were under his skin, impenetrable as it wrapped itself around the city.

Through the chair, he could feel the reverberation of the star drive as it warmed up, ticking through a thousand self-diagnostic checks in the back of his awareness. All good so far.

And he could sense something else too, something the Wraith couldn't — he could sense the way the city was starting to cleanse itself under his orders, starting to the repair the systems the Wraith had bypassed in order to make their incursion. Starting with the holding cells, he could feel it attacking the hive-flesh. It wouldn't be long, he knew, before the Wraith in other parts of the city realized there was something wrong. But by then, he hoped, it would be too late.

"Are we moving?" Daniel said.

Jack sank deeper into the city, let his consciousness spread out and down into the star drive. Taking a deep breath, he sent out the command, *Lift*.

The city responded immediately, the drive firing with a slow but accelerating thrust. He felt systems shut down, shift into flight mode, life support and gravity starting to compensate as the city rose. And he could see it too. Somehow both outside and within Atlantis at once, he could see the water cascading from the underside of the city as it rose up and out of the ocean. Impossibly graceful for something so enormous, it pushed through the cloud layer, making a fool of even the deepest air turbulence until the atmosphere began to thin.

And then they were beyond Earth's pull, with nothing but the black of space above and the once-blue planet turning slowly below.

Perhaps it was the strange beauty of Earth below him that distracted him, that kept him oblivious to the Wraith stirring where it lay on the floor. Perhaps that's why the next thing he knew was that Daniel was flying across the room, dropping boneless to the floor, and the Wraith had its taloned hand curled into Jack's shirt.

"Now," it said, hissed the words into Jack's face, "you will destroy the parasite's ship."

"For Brightstar!" Hearten launched himself at Shadow, grabbing hold of her and barreling them both to the deck. Shadow kicked free of his grasp, pushing him onto his back with her hand raised to feed.

That was when Earthborn drew the knife from her boot. A lifetime on Earth had taught her to fight like a blade, not a queen, and she slashed it across Shadow's throat.

Hearten flung up his hands against the spray of black blood as Shadow twisted away from him, one hand clutching her neck. Her hiss gurgled as she lurched toward Earthborn.

"Your time is over, Shadow!" she said, the bloody knife held loose and ready in her hand.

*I will peel the skin from your bones*, Shadow howled into her mind, her ruined throat making it impossible to talk. *I will burn your flesh, all your issue! Your consort, your people...*

"You are weak!" Earthborn hissed. "You are—"

Her words cut off as, beneath her feet, she felt the city of the Ancestors come to life. It shook enough that she stumbled a fraction. And then she bared her teeth in victory. "Atlantis rises!"

On the view screen, from the cruiser's perspective, she could see it lift from Earth, clouds spilling from its shield as it left the atmosphere behind and rose into the cool of space.

Shadow hissed, or tried to, the air sucking wetly through the slash in her throat as she fell to her knees. She reached a hand toward the view screen.

Earthborn shook her head, chin lifting. "O'Neill will not do your bidding," she said. "This is not your victory, Shadow. It is mine." With that, she stepped forward, grasping hold of Shadow's hair, tipping back her head to expose her neck. Shadow's eyes flared, her hands grasping at Earthborn's arm, but she was weakening. She was dying.

All around them, her blades stood still.

Earthborn knew what she must do, though now it came to the moment there was regret as she brought her blade beneath Shadow's chin, her hand almost tender in her hair. "I never knew my mother," she said. "She died in the battle with the parasite-gods. Sting says you were night to her day, shadow to her light. But we were kin, mother-sister, and we could have been allies, served our people together, if you had walked a different path. "

"Your mother," Shadow hissed, the words hard to make out through her wrecked throat, "was...weak...foolish... As are you."

"Foolish, perhaps," Earthborn said. "But I am not weak." And with that, she jammed her blade up under Shadow's chin and watched as she jerked, fell back and lay still.

Earthborn lifted her hand and the bloody knife it held.

"Blades of Shadow," she said, looking around at the Wraith of Shadow's zenana who watched her with narrowed, suspicious eyes. "Your queen has deceived you, unmanned you, and led you along a dark path. But her reign is over and, though I may be earth born, I intend to lead us home to Pegasus. There we can once more live as Wraith: hunt our prey and hone our skills against each other and against nature. Here, we have become weak but in the place of our origin we will become great." She looked around at them all. "Atlantis has risen once more and, under my command, the city of the Ancestors will take us home."

For a long, slow moment nothing happened. Then Hearten stepped forward and went to his knee. "My Queen," he said, head bowed.

Edge, at his side, followed. "Queen Earthborn."

She felt her heart give five slow beats before the next blade bowed, stiff kneed. Earthborn knew him — Eldritch, a cleverman of Brightstar's hive . "My Queen," he said.

And then the others followed, some of them reluctant, but all of them eventually bending their knee to their new queen. Earthborn felt their fear, their uncertainty, and their fragile hope as if it were her own.

"Do not be afraid," she said, throwing the knife aside. "Today, we free ourselves of this debasing world. Today, we start our journey home."

Her eyes moved to the view screen, to the parasite's ship — to Sting.

"But first, we must destroy the parasite before she destroys us. No matter the cost."

Sam had the bomb mostly assembled when Sting found her.

He looked terrible, holding one arm cradled against his chest, with a gash across his forehead. The dried blood smeared across his face gave him a more ghoulish appearance than usual as he made his way into the engine room on unsteady legs.

"I told you to get off the ship," Sam said, glancing up but not stopping work on the explosive. "We haven't left orbit so I guess you succeeded?"

"I did." Breathing hard, Sting sank down to the deck next to her. "But I did not wish to leave without you," he said, voice tight as though his teeth were gritted.

"I told you—"

"You do not give me orders, human."

She looked up at him again, caught the grim humor in his expression. "Guess not," she said. It occurred to her then that it was quite something for a Wraith to care about the life of any human enough to risk his own. "Thanks," she said, more generously. "I appreciate it, Sting."

He made an equivocal noise, somewhere between a grunt of pain and a grunt of irritation. "I do not think O'Neill would have been forgiving had I left you behind."

"The colonel," she said, returning to the final adjustments on her makeshift bomb, "knows I can take care of myself."

"I have no doubt of that, however he would still be concerned for your safety. As I am concerned for that of my queen, though I know her to be formidable. The two feelings do not exclude each other."

"Yeah," she said, shortly, because she knew it was true. But it didn't negate her whole career in the Air Force, having to prove over and over that she didn't need protecting or rescuing. Not that Sting would have any idea about that, of course. He came from a society that venerated all females as queens. It was hardly comparable.

After a silence, Sting said, "How long will we have to escape the ship before this device detonates?"

Not long was the real answer. "Long enough, if we're quick," she said.

Sting hissed, shifted where he sat. He didn't sound like he'd bought her lie. "I will not slow you down."

"I know," she said, and flung him a quick smile. It didn't last long. "Listen," she said, because she had to know even if she didn't want to. "What happened to you? Was it — ?" She cleared her throat and asked the question she really wanted to ask. "What happened to Hecate?"

Hecate, not Janet. It wasn't Janet.

Sting's gaze left hers, focused somewhere on the far wall of the engine room. "Boneshard — But, no, it is no longer him. The parasite that controls him, Sobek, was already challenging Hecate for control of the ship when I reached the bridge. The..." He paused over the alien word, "the 'Jaffa' did not take his usurpation well. To their credit, they fought well for their queen but her death — and theirs — was inevitable."

Sam's heart thumped hard in unexpected grief. "Hecate's dead?"

"Yes, but Sobek's victory was dearly bought. It allowed me the opportunity to sabotage the controls to the hyperdrive. Sobek was angered, but wounded, and I managed to escape with my life, though I would have laid it down to see that thing dead by my hand."

Sam nodded, but all she could think about was Janet. "But Hecate," she said. "You're sure she's dead?"

Sting turned his eyes on her, his expression one of disgust. "I saw it die with my own eyes, Major Carter. I saw the parasite leave its host. I saw Sobek crush it beneath his boot. Such is the loyalty of their kind."

Sam froze, her hands stilling on the weapon. "The Goa'uld left the host?"

"Yes. The body was wounded."

"Fatally?"

His eyes narrowed. "I do not know."

Sam squeezed shut her eyes, took a breath. It was impossible that Janet could still be alive, that anything of her could have survived a hundred years of possession by a Goa'uld. She knew that. She *knew* it. And yet it was equally impossible not to find out for sure; she couldn't leave Janet behind. Even if it was just her body, she couldn't leave her here alone.

When she opened her eyes again, she turned them on Sting and said, "Get off the ship. I'm gonna — The woman who Hecate took as a host was my friend. I can't leave her here."

"It is likely that she is dead," Sting said. "Or soon will be. I am sorry, but —"

"It doesn't matter," Sam said. "No one gets left behind. That's just how we do things." She set her hands on her makeshift bomb, settling the decision in her mind. It was the right one, she knew it was. "I'm gonna find Janet, get her to the surface, and then detonate the bomb."

"But what of you?" Sting said. "Will you have time to make your escape?"

"You betcha." And she would. It would be tight, but she could make it. She'd have a few minutes, so long as nothing went wrong. She cleared her throat. "Listen, uh, if I don't… Tell Colonel O'Neill why I stayed, okay? He'll understand."

With some effort, Sting pushed himself to his feet, still cradling his injured arm. "Your loyalty and honor is worthy of a blade, Major Carter." He took a breath. "I wish I found that less disturbing."

Sam didn't have an answer to that; they were each what they were and there was nothing to be done about it. Strange bedfellows indeed.

Climbing to her feet, she offered him her hand. "Good luck, Sting," she said. "As we say on Earth, God speed."

After a pause he took her hand in his own, huge clawed fingers wrapping around hers. "Then 'God speed' to you too, Major Carter."

She had a feeling she was going to need it.

"I said, destroy the parasite's ship," the Wraith hissed.

Jack could feel the tips of its claws digging through the fabric of his shirt.

"Just wait a minute," he snapped, pulling up a better visual on the inside of his eyelids but keeping it off the HUD so the Wraith couldn't see it.

Something had happened on the ha'tak — it had gone from trying to make a break for it to turning and attacking. He didn't know how to interpret that, didn't dare make assumptions.

But the fact that Shadow's cruiser wasn't responding, was just sitting there taking the assault, implied that things had gone wrong for the Wraith. It was no surprise; the ship was seriously outgunned by the ha'tak.

A sharp pain in his chest made him gasp, eyes flashing open. The Wraith's face was very close to his own now, its breath feculent as it snarled, "Destroy the parasite's ship."

Carter was on that ship, trying to destroy it.

Jack licked his lips. "I'm working on it," he said. "Can't rush these things…"

Abruptly, the Wraith jerked its head up as if hearing something Jack couldn't. Its feeding hand lifted from Jack's chest and he breathed out in relief. Small mercies.

Cocking its head, the Wraith closed its eyes. And then it slumped forward and reached out a hand to brace itself against the chair. "No... My queen."

Jack felt a shiver of unease. Had Earthborn done her job? He tried to breathe quiet, to draw as little attention as possible.

"We must go to the aid of the cruiser," the Wraith decided. Its head swiveled to Jack, its expression hard with anger and repressed fear. "You will open fire on the parasite's ship."

Jack swallowed, firmed his fingers into the gel pads on the chair. He had to give Carter more time. "Not gonna happen."

With a sudden flare of rage, the Wraith swung back toward him and plunged its fingers into Jack's chest. He gasped, arched his back at the horrific pain. "Do it!" the Wraith hissed. "Destroy it or be destroyed."

"Can't," Jack hissed through the pain. *Won't.*

"You *will*," the Wraith hissed.

Jack shook his head. "Not yet."

The Wraith bared its teeth. "Then I will make you."

And suddenly he felt a dreadful ebbing of energy, like he was in freefall, his head spinning light away from the rest of his body. When it stopped, leaving him breathless and disoriented, he peered at the Wraith through blurry eyes. He shook his head, tried to clear it, but it was no good. And when he lifted his hands from the gel pads he saw them gnarled and leathery through his dim vision. "Sonofa…" His voice whispered like dead leaves.

The Wraith hissed at him, its braided hair falling forward to brush across Jack's face. "Do as you are instructed, human," he said. "The child-queen is not here to speak for you now. You are mine to command."

"If you kill me," Jack said, in his reedy old-man's voice, "we'll all die. There'll be no one to fly the damn ship."

Lips peeled back from its needle-like teeth, the Wraith said, "That is of no import; without Queen Shadow, there is no life for any of us. All that is left is vengeance."

# CHAPTER EIGHTEEN

TEAL'C, Rya'c and Bailey led the vanguard, darting through the gate as soon as it opened so as to retain the element of surprise. They took out four Wraith drones by the gate as soon as the wormhole spat them out. Bailey's face was a picture of schooled impassivity, though Teal'c guessed she was just as horrified as he and SG-1 had been when they'd first set eyes on these creatures.

Behind them, more troops came barreling out of the wormhole, the dizzying effects of gate travel exacerbated by the skewed angle at which it sat. But they recovered admirably, rolling into a crouch to fire at the oncoming enemy. The plan was for them to clear the area, before the others joined them. Bailey had been happy to defer to Teal'c in a temporary chain of command, given his knowledge of both the terrain and their adversary.

The energy blasts from Wraith stunners pounded into the soil next to them and Teal'c recalled the warnings from Major Carter about the level of radiation here. Not only that, but they had no cover. They needed to get to higher ground. With a called command, he gestured for Bailey and Rya'c to head for the skeletal trees on the hillside on which they'd made camp so long ago. As a cover, it was woefully inadequate, but they would have to make do and hope that they did not get pinned down.

As more troops made it through the gate, Teal'c couldn't help but be impressed by the tight formation of the CMF troops; Bailey had trained them well. But there were many Wraith and they did not fall easily to either Goa'uld or Arbellan weapons. If O'Neill and Earthborn were unable to call off the attack from Atlantis, the people of Arbella would not survive long and the Wraith would escape through the Stargate.

So far, at least, the sky had remained clear of darts and Teal'c hoped that was a sign that O'Neill and Daniel Jackson's mission had been successful. He cast a glance upward, wishing he could see through this unremitting cloud cover to where Major Carter was waging her own battle in orbit. Much was at stake on all battlefronts, but mostly Teal'c worried about his friends.

On the ground around the gate, gunfire rattled and Wraith stunners took down too many of the Arbellan troops before they could make it to safer ground. And Teal'c heard screams that told him some were not so fortunate to be only on the receiving end of a stunner; the Wraith drones fed as they fought. He fired at the oncoming onslaught, his and Rya'c's staff weapons finding their mark more often than not. But the Wraith were many and strong and he could see the CMF troops tire under the relentless onslaught. He was sure that the horror in which they'd found themselves was causing as much damage as the Wraith and their feeding hands.

"We're outnumbered," yelled Bailey. "We have to get back through the gate!"

"We cannot," he called back. "We must hold it!"

"This is killing my people, Teal'c."

Frustration beat at him as he cast his eye around, looking for a means of retreat. And then, from over the brow of the opposite hill, came a sight that gave him hope.

"Who the hell is that?" said Bailey.

"They are the people of Earth, General Bailey," he said and he watched as Aedan Trask commanded his people down the slope to engage their enemy.

With a yelled command, Teal'c charged forward and began the fight back in earnest.

The closer Sam got to the pel'tak, the more eerily quiet it became. It was the opposite of what Sam was expecting, especially with the ship in battle.

Or, formerly, in battle. Although the distant hoots of alarms were still sounding she hadn't heard or felt any weapons fire for quite some time. And the ha'tak was starting to look reminiscent of the *Mary Celeste*. Sam hoped it meant that Rya'c's Jaffa were winning the argument, but didn't want to take it for granted. There were a dozen worse possibilities.

The pel'tak itself looked like a war zone as Sam peered around the doorway, her staff weapon held at the ready. There were bodies everywhere, and evident signs of damage to the control systems. Deliberately, she didn't look for Janet, made herself assess the situation fully first. On the view screen she could see Earth, but, between it and the ha'tak, she saw the crippled remains of Shadow's cruiser. It looked like it was in a bad way, spinning in a lazy pivot that spoke of a total loss of engines and thrusters. The odds weren't good for any of the Wraith stranded there, but Sam couldn't bring herself to care. A few darts wove around it like bees returning to a poisoned hive.

But, more interestingly, at the bottom of the screen she could see the tips of Atlantis's spires and that gave her a jolt of relief. The colonel had done it — he was flying an Ancient city-ship. She just hoped he wasn't doing it under duress...

From the view screen she turned her attention to the room. There were bodies — she counted six Jaffa, two of whom were dried out corpses — and more, she thought, at the back of the bridge, hidden behind the command chair and the flickering braziers that stood to each side.

Keeping low, Sam crept into the room. She stepped over one of the desiccated Jaffa, moving to the back of the room, but then stopped and looked more closely at the corpse. Her heart sank, stomach turning sickly; she recognized the body. It belonged to Rya'c's friend, Zuri. "Damn it," Sam murmured. This was where loyalty to Hecate had gotten her.

A sudden movement startled her, and she brought up her weapon, dropping into a defensive crouch. Someone was alive behind the command chair. "Who's there?" Sam called.

"Major Carter?"

She knew that voice. "Hunter?"

He peered out from behind the throne, looking ruined. His face was blood streaked from a nasty gash on his forehead, and Sam could easily see tear tracks running through the gore. "Didn't think to see you again," he said. "Told you to go. Ain't nothing here but death."

"You're hurt," Sam said.

"Don't matter." He sniffed and limped out from behind the chair, his right arm hanging bloody and useless at his side. "It's all gone now. That thing killed the goddess and we ain't got no more hope."

"I'm sorry," Sam said. "I saw Zuri's body."

Hunter nodded, licked at his lips like he was thirsty. Sam didn't even have water to offer. "She died trying to protect the Lady Hecate. I should'a done the same." He touched the wound on his head. "But I just got smacked down and when I woke up they was all gone." He turned and looked behind him. "So I figured I'd just stay with her. 'Til the end."

Sam's gaze darted past him to the shadows beyond. "With Hecate?"

"I seen what come outa her," Hunter said, nodding to a dark smear on the deck. "But that ain't my goddess."

Sam couldn't get the next words out of her mouth, past the knot that was thickening there. "Is she — ?" She cleared her throat. "Is she still alive?"

Hunter shrugged. "She's still breathing but —"

That was enough. Sam moved past him, shoving the staff weapon into Hunter's good hand. Janet — it was Janet again, now — lay on her back in the shadow of the command chair, eyes closed and her hands folded over the bloody wound in her chest. Hunter must have arranged her that way. She looked corpse-like and Sam hated it. So she took one of Janet's hands in her own, squeezed. Her fingers were cool, but not cold. "Janet?"

She leaned down, put her cheek close to Janet's lips and — like a miracle — felt breath there. Weak, but breath nonetheless. There was blood around her lips and Sam knew why; that's how the symbiote would have left the body of its dying host.

"Janet?" she said again, tapping her cheek. "Janet, it's Sam. Can you hear me?"

There was no response. Tears tightened the back of Sam's throat, welled up in her eyes. She blinked them away; this wasn't the time. She looked over her shoulder to Hunter. "We have to get her out of here."

"There's no time."

"What do you mean?"

Hunter nodded to the view screen. The image had changed — the ha'tak was moving fast, Sam realized, orbiting Earth. It was a pretty low orbit too, certainly inside the lunar orbit. "Her ship will be her chariot to the heavens," Hunter said. "It'll kill the Snatchers too. So I figure, least Faith an' my little'un might live free."

For a beat, Sam just stared. Then she understood with an uncoiling sense of dread. "The ship's going to crash? Hecate deliberately chose to crash her ship into the planet?"

"Weren't her," Hunter said, his eyes going back to Janet. "Lady Hecate loved her people. The other one done it."

"Sobek." And of course that made sense. "He's going to crash the ship to release the poison."

"Kill the Snatchers," Hunter said. "All except him and his kind."

"But he'll have lost his ship…"

Hunter shook his head. "This ain't his and he don't want it." He gestured to the view screen again. "He wants that."

"Atlantis, of course." That had been Hecate's plan all along, and now Sobek had double-crossed Hecate to take it for himself. Kill the Wraith, take Atlantis, rule the galaxy. "We have to stop it," she said, scrambling to her feet and heading to one of the control consoles.

"Why?" Hunter said. "It'll kill the Snatchers. I been fighting for that my whole life."

"Because there's a better way," Sam said, studying the alien screen. "Because those Snatchers... Look, if they die there'll be no one left to fight Sobek. And what he wants for Earth is a whole lot worse, believe me.'"

"Ain't nothing worse'n Snatchers."

"That hybrid is," she said, but she was too distracted to say more. The console wasn't responding to her commands; the helm had been disabled, the ship locked into its decaying orbit. Like an hourglass, each orbit ticked down to the ship's destruction and there wasn't a damn thing Sam could do to stop it.

Except that there was. "We have to destroy the ship before it reaches Earth," she said. "If we destroy the poison before we enter the atmosphere, it can't hurt the Wraith."

Hunter gave a grim snort. "And how do we do that?"

"Ha'taks come with a failsafe self-destruct. If I can —" But, no, that was locked too. Sobek wasn't taking any chances. "Damn it." There was still her makeshift bomb in the engineering room, but...

She looked again at Janet, at the subtle rise and fall of her chest. By her calculation, at their current rate of descent, they had no more than thirty minutes before the ship entered Earth's atmosphere. That meant there was no time to get Janet off the ship and then go back to the engine room to detonate the bomb before it was too late. And carrying Janet would slow her down — Hunter was in no shape to help — so even if they hit the engine room first they'd never be able to escape the ship before the bomb detonated. It was hopeless and she slammed her fist down hard on the console, staring out bitterly at the planet below, at the crippled Wraith cruiser, at Atlantis and —

She stopped dead, her fist half raised for another frustrated blow. Maybe there was a way? A dangerous one, but wasn't that how they always did things? Sam licked her lips, wiped suddenly sweaty palms on the legs of her pants. "Okay," she said, "I've got an idea."

"We are under attack."

Jack didn't need the Wraith to tell him, or even the subtle shiver from the bones of the city. He could see it in glorious technicolor. The ha'tak had crippled the Wraith cruiser all too easily, and now Hecate's ship had turned its weapons on Atlantis. There was only one reason Jack could think of for that — Carter and Sting had failed in their attempt to depose Hecate and the snake was getting her revenge on her treacherous ally. Which probably meant Carter was dead. Or soon would be.

And that — Sitting there in his old-man's body, plugged into this enormously powerful piece of technology, and yet powerless to help her, Jack felt despair. Carter had failed. Daniel was down. And Teal'c and Rya'c were in the wind... Who knew if they'd even made it back from Arbella?

There was only him, alone at the end of the world.

He supposed he might as well take Hecate out too — a small vengeance for the loss of his friends, his family, his *world*. But even as he powered up the weapons, felt the Wraith's fingers lighten on his chest, he knew that this vengeance would taste of nothing but ashes. Just like the world revolving below them.

At his request, Atlantis summoned its weapons — the same little missiles he'd used on the gate-ship. It seemed to think four would suffice to take out the ha'tak. Jack had no reason to doubt it.

He sent them into their launch tubes, each one glowing bright with more power than a nuke. And then, just as he was about to let his mind release them, he saw a small alert blink in his peripheral vision. When he looked closely, it showed him that the ha'tak was in a decaying orbit with twenty-three minutes left until it entered Earth's atmosphere.

That, he thought, was strange. The ship wasn't damaged, which meant someone had deliberately aimed it at Earth. They wanted it to crash. So why open fire and invite Atlantis to destroy it before it hit the ground?

Unless...

His heart gave a little jump, hope finding its way to the surface despite the odds. It was just the kind of crazy plan Carter might come up with if she was desperate — if she knew he was flying Atlantis and wanted him to destroy the ha'tak before it entered Earth's orbit.

Question was, why?

"Jack?" The voice, taut with pain, was Daniel's. Jack spared him a glance, his newly blurred vision turning Daniel into a shadowy shape. He was climbing to his feet, took a couple of unsteady steps toward the chair and then froze, failing to hide his horror at the sight Jack presented. "Oh my God," he said. "What...?"

"Yeah, I know. I've looked better."

"You —" Daniel broke off, and despite his poor eyesight Jack could see the way Daniel's eyebrows rose over the tops of his glasses. He was looking past Jack now, toward the door. "Uh," he said, taking a step closer to the command chair, "Jack? You might want to lower the force shield."

Jack turned his head at the same moment the Wraith at his side sucked in a stuttering breath. "No..." Its hand clamped down hard onto Jack's chest. He grunted in pain, but refused to scream. Through the blue shimmer of the force shield, he could see Earthborn standing with a dozen Wraith at her back. Her hand was lifted toward them — he wondered if she was projecting her thoughts into the Wraith's mind, because it was shaking its head, a low growl in its throat. "Fire the weapon," it hissed, opened its hand and started to suck on Jack's life force. "Fire the weapon!"

Despite the agony, he ignored it and sent a different command to the ship.

*Drop the force shield.*

It disappeared, falling away like water, and Earthborn and her people swept into the room. The Wraith jerked away from Jack and he sucked in a breath of relief as the pain stopped, but he wasn't kidding himself that he had much longer to go — he could already feel his body failing, pain wracking his ruined organs.

"Help him!" Daniel called out. "Earthborn, help him!"

Jack couldn't see much of anything now beyond the images Atlantis projected into his mind, but he felt Earthborn approach, felt her hand on his chest.

Instinctively he flinched away from her touch, but then he felt something new — a cool flood of energy, of life. He felt his broken body begin to mend. Just a little. Just enough. He opened his eyes — his vision was still blurred — and looked up into Earthborn's face.

"What are you doing?" Daniel said from somewhere behind him. "Don't stop there, you have to —"

He cut off abruptly, and Jack was peripherally aware of a struggle behind him.

Earthborn leaned closer, her alien features and sharp teeth a breath away from his face. "The parasite ship will crash to Earth," she said, "and in so doing release the poison that will destroy my people."

Jack struggled to swallow, tried to wet his dry lips. "Okay..."

"Destroy it. Destroy it now, and I will grant you the Gift of Life."

He looked up at the display and said, "Nineteen minutes."

Her eyes narrowed. "I don't understand."

"Carter..." His voice sounded cracked and reedy. "Sting... We can give them nineteen more minutes."

She shook her head. "It is too great a risk. Destroy the ship now."

Blinking up at her, he said, "But Sting —"

"He would understand, as would Major Carter."

And maybe they would, but that wasn't something Jack was prepared to live with — not unless he had no other option. "Eighteen minutes," he said, bracing for the pain she could inflict. "We owe them that much. And I'm damn well gonna give it to them."

Sam's arms were burning with the effort of carrying Janet, her deadweight cumbersome as she ran through the deserted corridors of the ha'tak. Part of her — the sensible, soldier part — told her it was a dangerous waste of her energy to take Janet with them. She was risking their escape for what was little more than sentiment; it was clear that Janet was close to death, the wound in her chest fatal. But the other, larger part of her answered that with one simple fact: it was Janet. And Sam wasn't leaving her behind.

Hunter was slightly ahead, nursing his injured arm. His face had a sheen of sweat, and not just from the heat inside the ha'tak — he was in pain and trying to hide it.

"Almost there," Sam said, grunting the words out as she shifted Janet in her arms. "Around the next corner and —"

Janet moved. Sam almost stumbled with the shock, looking down at where Janet had turned her head toward Sam's shoulder. "Janet?"

There was no answer, but that didn't matter; Janet had moved — something of her remained.

"Hang in there," Sam said, readjusting her grip so she could glimpse her watch. They had eight minutes until the ha'tak entered Earth's orbit.

"Which way?" Hunter said as he slowed at the junction with a cross corridor.

"Left," Sam said. She could see the open door to the al'kesh hanger bay. With luck, they'd make it out before the colonel started firing on them, although she'd kinda expected him to have already opened fire. If he left it too late and the ship entered Earth's atmosphere… But she had to trust he knew what he was doing; it was very possible that Atlantis possessed enough fire power to blast the ha'tak out of the sky with a single shot.

Either way, there was nothing she could do about it now. Her only concern was getting herself, Janet and Hunter off the ship. "In there," she told Hunter and he slipped into the hanger ahead of her.

In Sam's arms, Janet shifted again. "Easy," Sam said, following Hunter inside. "We're —"

Janet made a noise, a harsh rasping sound.

With a start, Sam looked down and saw that her friend's eyes were open and staring at her. "Janet!" Everything else flew out of her mind. She was dimly aware of Hunter racing toward the single ship left in the bay, but all Sam could see were Janet's brown eyes, fogged with confusion, gazing up at her. "Hey," she said, easing Janet to the ground. "Hey, it's okay…"

Janet's mouth moved, mouthing words. Bloody spittle bubbled on her lips as she tried to speak.

"Shh," Sam said, laying her gently onto the ground, resting Janet's head in her lap. "It's okay." There was a deathly pallor to her friend's face, a rattle when she breathed, and her eyes were distant. Sam swallowed the sharp lump in her throat; she'd seen this before, this face. She knew what it meant. Gently, she stroked Janet's forehead. "I'm taking you home," she said. "Back to Earth."

Janet blinked at her, lips moving again. "Sam…" Her throat, torn when Hecate's symbiote had fled, made the word little more than a rasp.

"Yeah," Sam said, blinking through suddenly blurry eyes.

Something like a smile touched Janet's face and she lifted a feeble hand toward Sam's wrist. Sam took it in her own, squeezing her fingers around Janet's. "Knew…" Janet rasped again, so quiet Sam had to bend to hear the words. "Knew you'd come back…"

Sam pressed her lips together and nodded. "Yeah," she said, almost too full to speak. "Sorry it took so long."

Janet's fingers moved, squeezing weakly. It was admonition, forgiveness, friendship. And then her eyes went wide, drifted past Sam's shoulder. "Sam..." she rasped, and for a moment Sam thought this was it, her last moment. "Sam..."

But then she saw the shadow fall across Janet, turned with a start to find Sobek looming over her.

"This one, it seems, will not die."

He raised his feeding hand, ready to attack, and Sam lunged forward over Janet, shielding her with her body. It was a futile gesture, born of instinct, of everything she was.

And then a staff blast shrieked across the hanger, catching Sobek in the side of the head and spinning him back and away. He landed with a heavy thud on the deck and didn't move.

Sam looked up. Sting stood at the entrance to the hanger, a staff weapon held in one hand and his injured arm hanging loose at his side. He stalked toward her, lips pulled back into a feral grimace. "Did you really think I would leave without seeing this abomination dead?"

"Come on!" Hunter shouted from the open doors of the last al'kesh, his wild gaze darting from Sam to Sting and back again.

In her lap, Janet was very still. Her hand was limp in Sam's and when she looked down, Sam saw Janet's sightless eyes gazing up at the ceiling. A sob caught in her throat and she bent over, hauling Janet into her arms. "I'm sorry," she whispered into her hair. "Janet, I'm so sorry."

"Carter!" Hunter yelled again, his voice piercing her grief. "We gotta go!"

"I will help you carry her," Sting offered.

Shuddering in a breath, Sam shook her head. Her heart felt like lead, her chest too tight to breathe, but it didn't matter; she still had a job to do. Obstinate as O'Neill, she got her feet under her and pulled Janet back into her arms and stood up. She was taking her friend home.

But one look at her watch told her it may already be too late. They had less than a minute before the ha'tak entered the atmosphere — before Atlantis had to open fire or see all the Wraith poisoned.

# CHAPTER NINETEEN

JACK FELT his withered heart stutter as the clock ticked down past one minute.

Earthborn made a sound, somewhere between a hiss and a growl. "Do it," she said. "Do it now or my people will die — and so will you, Jack O'Neill. And your friend."

On the other side of the chair, Daniel cleared his throat. "They, uh — If they could have gotten off the ship in time…"

Jack didn't need to hear that; he knew it himself, felt it in his weakened heart. If Carter could have escaped, she'd have already done so. But there was no way to know whether she had — she'd made no contact — and he had no more time to give her.

Closing his eyes, he reached for the weapons, felt the missiles bright in their launch tubes. Atlantis calculated the distance, knew when to fire in order to hit the ha'tak and keep its debris — its poison — from falling to Earth.

He felt Earthborn's hand on his chest, her talons deepening the wounds in his flesh. He didn't care; heal him or kill him, if Carter went down with Hecate's ship — and at his hand — he was indifferent about what came next.

But then he felt Daniel's hand on his other shoulder, fingers warm through Jack's shirt. An anchor, a route back to the light — a testimonial of the friendship SG-1 shared. Whatever happened, he would always have that.

Taking a breath, Jack gave the silent command to fire.

In his mind's eye, he saw the bright missiles burst free of Atlantis, wend their way with deadly precision to the ha'tak in its low, skimming orbit.

One, two, three, four simultaneous hits.

And the ship detonated like the Fourth of July. No hesitation, no slow death, the damn thing was vaporized. And with it, anything and anyone aboard.

Under Earthborn's talons, his chest constricted. *Sam*, he let himself think. *Sam…*

And then he felt the cool, sweet, sensation of life flooding into his body and let out a sigh that was one part relief but mostly grief at what he feared he had done — and what he feared he had lost.

There had often been times when Teal'c mused that Apophis's demise had been down to one factor — his woeful underestimation of the will of the Tau'ri. It was only once the battle was done that the thought struck him once more, that he realized anew how formidable this race of people could be. For they fought a foe unknown to them and more horrific than any they could have imagined. Some fought with clubs and knives and bows, some with guns that had never been fired in combat, but they fought all the same.

The Wraith were powerful, but the Tau'ri were ferocious and gave no quarter.

But then Teal'c heard the sound that he had dreaded since they had first come through the Stargate — the whine of darts. Panic gripped Aedan's people, sending them sprinting for the trees, while those of the CMF simply squinted at the sky in weary concern — unsure what new horror approached.

Yet it was no horror and it soon became apparent that the darts had come to rescue the scattered remnants of the Wraith on the ground, scooping them up in their snatching beams.

Whether it signaled surrender or a simple regrouping, Teal'c would not know until he learned who now controlled Shadow's Ancient city.

Nonetheless, there was a moment of silence as the last of the Wraith disappeared into the blinding beams and then a cheer erupted through the valley. Teal'c watched, exhausted and aching, as Arbellans and Earth's people embraced one another, jubilant in their small victory. He hoped it was not premature.

Across the battlefield, General Bailey scrubbed a hand across her blood-streaked face, tears cutting their way through the black grime. As Teal'c watched, a young woman approached her and extended an arm of friendship; Elspeth Burne welcoming her people home. She looked behind her and made a gesture of summons. Aedan Trask came to join her, throwing his arm around her shoulder and kissing the top of her head with eyes closed tight.

"Father." Rya'c stood by his side, leaning heavily on his staff weapon.

"You are injured," said Teal'c. Halfway through the battle, he'd lost sight of his son and had dreaded searching the faces of those who lay still on the ground.

Rya'c waved him down. "It is nothing serious. It was a hard battle and I am getting old."

That was a thought he couldn't spare room for right now. "It was a well fought battle," he said.

Rya'c nodded and then said, "But not the only battle today."

Teal'c said nothing, but cast a glance to the skies and wondered whether his friends would also celebrate victory tonight.

The journey from Atlantis, back to the cock-eyed Stargate in Scotland, had been made in silence.

Jack might have been restored to full health by Earthborn — the 'gift of life' as she'd called it — but he was wound as tight as a trip wire. Daniel had known better than to offer any platitudes. Jack wouldn't take them at the best of times, and this definitely wasn't the best of times. Anyway what was the point? Until they knew for sure that Sam had still been aboard the ha'tak when it blew there was nothing either of them could do but hope.

And that was best done privately, and in silence.

Jack had brought the gate-ship in high over the site of the battle, a quick reconnaissance of the situation before dropping down lower. Whatever the HUD had told Jack, Daniel had seen the devastation with his own eyes as they'd flown over more bodies than he wanted to count.

"I hope Teal'c and Rya'c are okay," he'd ventured.

Jack had just grunted.

But as the gate-ship had landed, Daniel had seen Teal'c, standing close to the gate with Rya'c and General Bailey, lift his hand in greeting. Teal'c hadn't exactly smiled, but his pleasure in seeing his friends alive had been evident.

Jack had breathed out a slow breath. Neither of them had mentioned that there was no sign of Sam.

That had been an hour ago.

And there was still no sign of Sam.

Jack sat with his back resting against the gate-ship, letting the world move on around him. He had his head bent forward, his arms resting on his knees. And Daniel didn't know whether to go to him or let him brood alone.

"It is probable," Teal'c said at Daniel's shoulder, "that Major Carter left the ha'tak using the transportation rings. In which case, she would now be in the Shacks."

Daniel nodded. "Rya'c hasn't heard?"

"He is attempting to contact his people. There has been…" His face darkened. "Some among his people did not support his defection, and continued to fight for Hecate."

"And I'm guessing they wouldn't be too pleased to see Sam…"

"Nor Sting."

"Ah—" Daniel grimaced; he well remembered the hatred men like Hunter felt for the Wraith. He couldn't blame them for it; they had good reason. He'd felt the same about the Jaffa, once, until he'd met Teal'c.

"Daniel?"

He turned to find General Bailey standing behind him, dirtied and bloodied by the battle, but alight with victory and—he had to imagine—the wonder of standing on Earth, the world her grandparents had fled. "General." He found a smile for her despite his nascent grief for Sam. "Welcome to Earth."

She made a face somewhere between wry and wondrous. "It's so green," she said, which took him aback because, to him, it felt so gray, such a shadow of what it had once been. "And damp," she added with a broader smile, turning her hand over. "Even the air feels moist on my skin. It's very strange."

And he supposed, compared with the arid heat of the settlement on Arbella, Earth would seem all of those things: green, damp, strange.

"Do you think you'll like it here?" he said.

She glanced around the hills and scrappy woodland, took in the rag-tag group of Aedan's people camped on the other side of the gate from the Arbellans. "We must," she said. "This is our true home and we have a duty to return. President Jones is already organizing a relief effort so that we can help to rebuild."

"He has our gratitude," Daniel said. "And remember, you're not alone here. I mean, aside from us, there are other people who can help — in the Shacks, probably all over the world, and we can—"

A commotion broke out on the other side of the makeshift encampment. At first he thought it was trouble between the Arbellans and the Aedan's people, but then he noticed that the people were actually pointing to the cloudy sky. "What now?" he muttered, and turned to Teal'c.

His eyes were already fixed on the sky, one hand raised to shield his eyes from the defused brightness. "A ship," he said.

"Whose?"

Teal'c didn't move, just said, "Hecate's."

Daniel felt his stomach pitch, half in hope and half in dread. "Sobek?"

"Or fleeing Jaffa."

Daniel didn't give voice to the third option, he didn't dare. Neither did Teal'c. Jack, he noticed was pushing himself to his feet, his gaze also fixed on the sky.

A moment later, Daniel saw it too, a dark shape approaching through the low cloud. "It's an al'kesh."

Teal'c lifted his staff weapon, primed it and held it at the ready. Jack glanced at him over his shoulder, and then turned back to the sky. The al'kesh were short range bombers—if it was hostile, none of them would stand a chance out in the open like this.

But the ship didn't seem to be lining up for a bombing run. In fact, it was flying erratically as it dropped out of the clouds and into the far end of the valley. Daniel squinted through the plume of smoke billowing from one side. "Looks kinda beat up."

"Indeed."

The ship dropped lower and Jack said, "It's coming in to land." Then, in a yell, "Get back! It's trying to land!"

There was a scuffling as the Arbellan's drew back, Aedan's people darting up toward the tree line, stopping halfway to watch as the engine noise reached them and the al'kesh scorched down the length of the valley toward the Stargate.

"I hope the brakes are working," Daniel said, taking a nervous—useless—step back. "It's going down!"

And a couple seconds later it hit the ground, bounced, hit again, spun around, kicking up dirt—radioactive dirt, Daniel remembered with a wince—and skidded a couple hundred yards until it stopped amid a cloud of smoke at the far end of the battlefield.

For a long beat, everyone stared.

General Bailey shot Daniel a look as if to say, *Now what*?

He could only shrug in reply.

Then something on the ship moved, a door opening to reveal a figure standing amid the smoke. And Jack was moving, walking steadily through the milling crowd toward the ship.

Daniel felt his pulse kick as he followed, Teal'c at his shoulder. Jack started to run as the person stumbled down the ramp on unsteady legs, smoke and dirt clogging the air. And Jack was still running and he didn't stop until he collided with the figure, spun her around and just held on.

Daniel laughed, half choked by the smoke and his own relief because, yes, it was her. It was Sam.

For the longest time she and Jack just stood there together, foreheads touching, and Daniel thought, *Yep — new world, new rules.*

He glanced at Teal'c who merely lifted an eyebrow.

Clapping him on the shoulder, Daniel grinned and headed over to join the rest of his team. Against all the odds, SG-1 had survived, they were together and they were safe.

That was something worth celebrating.

Breaking away from Jack, Sam said, "Daniel," and put her arms around him, holding him close. "I tried to save her." There was only one person she could be talking about. "I tried, Daniel… But all I could do was bring her home."

"That's all she'd have wanted, Sam." Daniel looked around at his team, the four of them united in grief and hope, and right then he realized that Sam had got it right. It didn't matter that they couldn't go back, because this team, SG-1, was his family, and this Earth, broken and bleeding, was his Earth. And these people, the Arbellans, Aedan's folk in the hills, Hunter's people in the Shacks, they were his people.

So, no, SG-1 couldn't go back. But they didn't have to; they were already home.

# CHAPTER TWENTY

**Stargate Command, Earth — one year later:** The transformation was incredible.

What had once been a rubble- filled silo now looked something like the gate room Jack remembered. The control room was gone, but that didn't matter because they had an actual DHD hooked up to the Stargate for now. Carter was talking about integrating Ancient technology she'd persuaded Earthborn to allow her to 'borrow' from Atlantis in order to create a better dialing program, but as far as Jack was concerned, the DHD did the job.

The Stargate itself sat in its old position at the center of the room. It even had a ramp instead of steps. Jack had insisted on that, for old time's sake.

Standing at the foot of that ramp now, with Daniel at one shoulder, Carter at the other, he felt a heavy beat of nostalgia. The long year since they'd defeated Hecate and buried Janet hadn't been easy, but the truth was, given the choice between going back to his old life and living his new one, he wasn't sure which he'd choose.

There was something about living on the edge, in a place with no rules, no real government, a place where everything was being made anew that gave Jack a sense of purpose he'd not felt since he was a young cadet going out in search of adventure.

Well, that adventure had brought him here and he couldn't say he was sorry. To reshape a world, to see it begin to thrive once more? He wasn't sure anything in his old life could have topped that. And then there was Carter...

He threw her a look and she returned a tight smile. "Any time now," she said.

On cue, the gate began to turn. It wasn't the very first time they'd gotten it working, but it was close enough that the sound sent a thrill down the length of Jack's spine.

"I wish Janet could have seen this," Daniel said with a sigh. "And General Hammond."

"They never lost faith," Carter said. "They always knew we'd come back."

Jack took a breath as the chevrons locked, one after the other, the air filling with that static ozone smell that brought back vivid memories of the SGC, of Hammond and Fraiser. All of them. "I think they'd be proud," he decided.

"I concur," said Teal'c.

As the final chevron locked and the gate engaged, Jack found himself holding his breath in anticipation. And then it happened: the wild blue eruption of light surging out into the gate room. Just like always. He couldn't help but smile, and when he looked at his team he saw them smiling too. "Yeah," he said. "The SGC is back in business."

A moment later, General Bailey and President Jones stepped through the gate. Bailey offered a formal salute, which Jack returned even though he didn't consider himself military now. But the Arbellan's liked their protocols and he was still USAF enough to understand.

"Colonel O'Neill," Jones said, formally, "permission to bring my people through?"

"Have at it, Mr. President," he said. "And welcome to Earth — we need all the help we can get."

And so Jack stood back and watched as the people of Arbella — Earth's refugees a century before — came home. Led by James O'Kane and his wife, Caroline, they brought with them medicine, technology, agricultural know-how, military discipline — everything the impoverished people of Earth needed to recover from the violence that had been done to them.

"This is good," Daniel said as he watched the wondering faces of Earth's new settlers. "This feels right."

"Yeah," Jack agreed. "Yeah, it does."

Daniel cast him a sideways look. "Talking of people coming home," he said and lifted an enquiring eyebrow.

At his other side, he heard Carter let out a quiet breath. It was more resignation than anything else; she wasn't one hundred percent onboard with the whole plan, but a deal was a deal. To Daniel, Jack said, "I'll take a gate-ship up tonight. We'll leave for Pegasus in the morning."

"I am willing to accompany you," Teal'c offered — not for the first time.

"We all are," said Daniel.

But they'd had this discussion already and Jack was resolved. "I know you guys want a vacation," he said, "but no deal. Someone has to keep an eye on things around here while I'm gone. I want a planet to come home to, okay?"

Daniel smiled, nodded. It wasn't really an argument. "Don't worry," he said, "we'll keep the lights on."

"You'd better."

"Couple weeks there," Carter said, doing a good job of sounding positive. "And Sting says you can gate right back to the SGC from Atlantis."

*Hopefully.*

"See?" Jack shared his smile between them all. "You'll hardly know I'm gone."

"It will be quieter," Teal'c observed.

Carter nodded. "Actually, I'm hoping to catch up on my reading. We've downloaded so much from Atlantis and I just haven't had time to look at half of it yet."

"Right," Daniel agreed. "Hey, actually, there was something I wanted to ask you…"

Jack let them carry on — his team, his family — and watched the continuing flow of people arriving from Arbella.

All in all, life was pretty good. There was just one more thing he needed to do before he left for Pegasus, but that couldn't be done from here — for that, he needed Atlantis.

Under the careful scrutiny of Earthborn and Sting, Jack sank into the command chair of the Ancient city. It was familiar now, after a year of preparation, although the thrill hadn't abated. To govern so much raw power with just a thought was quite something — he'd probably miss it when this mission was over. Assuming he hadn't been used as trail mix *en route*.

But, no, he wasn't afraid. Not much.

The Wraith were what they were, but he trusted Earthborn to keep her word and Sting to protect him if necessary. He looked down at the brown planet that was Earth and thought that, perhaps, he could see a hint of blue in its swirling, dirty atmosphere. Wishful thinking, maybe. Or maybe he was just optimistic about its future. But one day, he knew, it would be that beautiful blue globe he remembered. He hoped he'd live long enough to see it, but if not then he hoped his children would — or his grandchildren.

And that was a thought with which to conjure.

In that spirit of optimism, he closed his eyes and went about his last task before taking Earthborn and the Wraith back home where they belonged. Sinking down into the city's systems, he found the comms channel and told it to broadcast as far and wide as possible. It was only then, when it came to it, that he realized he hadn't figured out exactly what to say. He thought for a moment — short and sweet usually worked best when it came to speeches — and said, aloud:

"This is Colonel Jack O'Neill from the planet Earth. If you can hear this, then know that Earth is back and open for business — we want your trade, we want your friendship, and we want your support. We know that we can stand alone if we must, but we would rather stand together as friends and allies. Stand with us now, help us now, and we won't turn our backs on you again."

He didn't know whether anyone was listening — whether anyone *friendly* was listening — but that didn't matter. Maybourne had thought the future lay in turning in on themselves, in abusing their allies and standing in isolation, but he'd been so very wrong. For good or ill, Earth was part of the wild and crazy galaxy and their only option was to greet it with arms open.

Jack was looking forward to what came next.